MI 5/14

OS MAY 2016
GO AUG 2016

D0760411

Soul Identity

Dennis Batchelder

NetLeaves

Soul Identity

Copyright © 2007 by Dennis Batchelder

All rights reserved. No part of this publication may be reproduced, stored in, or introduced into a retrieval system, or transmitted, in any form, without the prior permission of the copyright owner, except by a reviewer who may quote brief passages in a review.

This is a work of fiction. Names, characters, places, and incidents are either the product of the author's imagination or are used fictitiously, and any resemblance to actual persons, living or dead, events, or locales is entirely coincidental.

The scanning, uploading, and distribution of this book via the Internet or via any other means without the permission of the copyright owner is illegal and punishable by law.

First edition July 2007
Second edition April 2009

Library of Congress Control Number: 2007932540
ISBN 978-0-9798056-0-8

Printed in the United States of America

For Irina

prologue

THE YOUNGER AND CUTER of the airport security ladies glanced down at my license. "Nice smile," she said.

I put on an identical one as she looked up at me.

Her eyes narrowed and she swiped another look. "Just a second," she said. She thumbed the microphone on her left shoulder. "I've got Waverly here at the head of the line."

I put away the smile and tried a look of exasperation. "Is there a problem? My flight leaves in thirty minutes."

"Just a minute, sir. They're getting ready for you."

I raised my eyebrows. "Ready for me?"

She frowned. "Nice try." She thumbed the mike again. "Tell me when."

Her radio beeped, and a man's voice came on. "We need another minute," it said.

"Let me know." She put a little pout on her lips. "You almost snuck by me with that smile."

I sighed. "At least I have no carry-on."

She checked me out and raised her eyebrows. "You have almost nothing on."

"It saves time, with all the special treatment I get."

Her radio squawked. "Send Mr. Waverly to the left line."

She pointed. "Over there. You know the drill."

I nodded. "Can I have my papers back?"

She held them out. "You won't make it through. Not this time." This with a stern expression.

"We'll see." I tugged the papers free of her grasp and headed to the left, toward the big man in the black and white uniform. I handed him my papers. "Hey, Fred, good to see you again," I said.

He frowned at me. "I wish I could say the same. Where are we going, Mr. Waverly?" He looked at my ticket. "Chicago? Dressed like that?"

"I hear there's a heat wave."

He scratched his head. "Nobody flies on Sunday morning from Baltimore to Chicago wearing flip flops, a muscle shirt, and a bathing suit."

"Just trying to make your job easier," I said. "Can we get started? My flight's leaving soon."

He leaned toward me and dropped his voice to a whisper. "We're gonna get you today, Mr. Waverly."

"We'll see." I took my cell phone and wallet out of my pockets and handed them over. "This is all I'm carrying."

He put my items in a tray and handed me my ticket. He pointed to the detector. "Keep them shoes on and walk on through. I'm right behind."

I headed through the detector. No beeps.

Fred grabbed a portable wand. "Hold out your arms, please."

I held them out. No beeps.

Fred aimed the wand at his watch and got a big beep. He pointed at a chair. "Sit down, Mr. Waverly."

I sat. Fred wanded my feet. He took my flip flops and bent them in half. "You hiding anything in these?"

"They're flip flops."

"All the same, I gotta be sure. Sit tight." He stood up, took them to the machine, and ran them through.

The two x-ray attendants huddled by their monitor and whispered to each other. They straightened up when Fred came over. "Nothing, sir."

"Would you bet your jobs on it?"

They both gulped, rechecked the screen, then nodded.

Fred picked up my phone, wallet, and shoes. "Lemme hand-check these. Mr. Waverly, come and watch."

I watched. Fred swabbed everything and ran the gauze through the spectrometer. "Clear."

I smiled. "Nice to know I'm clean. You done?"

"I'm gonna tear everything apart."

"Knock yourself out."

He popped the back off the phone and pulled out the battery. Then he opened my wallet. "You don't have much in here, Mr. Waverly. No pictures, no credit cards. Just a twenty dollar bill."

"I told you. I'm making your job easy."

"Easy would be if you gave up the goods."

I shrugged. "You think that just maybe I'm flying to Chicago?"

"And maybe I'm Superman, moonlighting as a TSA employee. Don't worry. We'll get you."

"So you keep telling me."

Fred reassembled the phone. He handed it to me. "Call somebody."

I dialed, held it to my ear, and then handed it back. "It's for you."

Fred took the phone. "Hello?" He glared at me. "Yes, ma'am, it's Scott Waverly's phone…no, he's clean…I'm sure." He nodded. "Of course you can." He hung up.

"Now can I go?" I asked.

He laughed. "You had to be a smart ass and call my boss. Now she's gonna check you out herself. Have a seat."

"Hope she hurries."

Two minutes later, the door behind Fred opened, and Jane Watson, a tall and shapely forty-something brunette, wearing a uniform identical to Fred's but filled out so much better, walked out, looked around, and came over to me. "Mr. Waverly," she said, "how nice to see you again."

I smiled. "Now say it like you mean it, Jane."

"I do mean it. I've been wondering all week if you'd be dropping by." Then she frowned. "You're not getting anything by me, Scott. Not on my watch."

"We'll see." I stood up and held out my arms. "Come and get me."

Fred held out the wand, but she waved him away. "I'm doing him manually."

"Lucky me," I said. "Can we go behind the screen? I don't want to get your other passengers jealous of my free massage."

Jane shook her head. "Fred needs to watch and learn."

"Your call." I turned around. "Start with the back first—I have a couple knots that need working out."

"Very funny." Her hands squeezed me up and under each arm, across my shoulders, and then down my back.

"Easy, Jane," I said. "People are watching."

"It's for their protection." She ran her hands over my butt, lingered for a minute, and then squeezed her way down each leg. She lifted each foot and checked between my toes. Then she patted me on the shoulder. "Turn around, please."

"I didn't know you were allowed to check my bare skin," I said.

"I do what's necessary to protect my country." She felt my neck, chest, and abdomen. Then she looked down at my bathing suit.

I stepped back. "Don't ask me to take it off, I've got nothing on underneath."

"My lucky day." She patted my waist, then stepped up close against me and shoved her hands inside while she looked me in the eye.

I cleared my throat. "I wish we could have cuddled first."

"In your dreams, mister." She withdrew her hands and looked at Fred. "You were right—he's clean."

Fred nodded. "Now what?"

She frowned. "It seems Mr. Waverly really is just taking a trip to Chicago. Let him go."

Fred handed me my belongings. "You have fifteen minutes. You can make it if you hurry."

"Thanks." I looked at Jane. "Next time I'll bring flowers."

"Next time drop by on somebody else's shift," she said.

"And let you miss all the fun?" I slipped on the flip flops, walked into the terminal, pulled out my phone, and dialed. "I'm through, Dad," I said when he answered.

"Took you long enough."

"Full body search. You guys ready?"

"Your mother is wandering around. I'll send her over. Keep an eye out."

"Cool." I hung up the phone and headed toward the exit. I stood right before the "Warning: any passengers crossing this line must re-enter through security" sign.

A security guard sat behind the wooden podium. "Busy day?" I asked.

The guard glanced at me and then back toward the exit. "Not too busy yet," he said. "Sunday mornings are slow until after ten. You going out?"

"No, just waiting." I stepped back, out of his line of sight. I watched my mom walk around the corner on the other side of the exit and head down the hall toward the guard. She wore a white wig and a slightly askew cardigan. She carried a green leather old-style suitcase and a large pink purse.

I pulled out my phone, held it down by my waist, turned on the camera, and started recording. I had to step back to get both the guard and my mother in the screen.

Mom tottered toward the guard, and he waved her back. She took another step and looked at him. "Is this the way to the airplanes?" she shouted.

"No, ma'am."

She brought her purse hand up to her ear. "Excuse me?"

"You have to go through security." The guard pointed behind her.

Mom nodded. "Thank you." But as she turned around, she slipped and fell to the floor with a clatter.

Her pink purse went skidding to the far wall, and her green suitcase hit the ground and burst open. A large number of small items spilled out. I saw handkerchiefs, loose papers, and two prescription bottles of medicine. One of the bottles dumped out a handful of pills as it rolled along the floor. Mom lay on her back and let out loud moans.

She had put on quite a show.

The guard ran over. And as he helped her sit up and then repack her suitcase, I focused the camera on her pink purse.

A box the size of a thick book, colored the same gray speckled shade as the floor, slid out of the purse. I raised the camera up toward the exit and caught my dad fiddling with a black plastic remote control. I pointed the camera back at the box.

It slid along the floor toward me. When the guard turned around to retrieve the pink purse, the box stopped, and when the guard turned back to my mom, it came shooting my way. I stepped in front of it.

The guard turned and held up his palm toward me. "Stay back, sir."

I nodded. When he handed the purse to my mom, I bent down, picked up the box, and walked to the security gate.

I caught Fred's eye. "Where's Jane?" I asked.

He used his thumb to point over his shoulder. "In her office," he said. "Why aren't you on your plane?"

I rapped on Jane's door. "Come on in and I'll show you."

"Oh, man," he said as he followed me.

Jane opened the door and smiled. "Why Scott, did you come back to congratulate me?" She looked down at the box in my hand, and her smile evaporated.

I pointed into her office, and Jane stepped aside to let us in. She closed the door and crossed her arms. "Tell me."

I held out the box. "You're not gonna like it."

"Might as well get it over with." She took it, turned it over, and spun the wheels that stuck through its underside. "A rolling box?"

I nodded. "It's got a remote control car inside. Open it up. There's Velcro along the edges."

She ripped the side open and pulled out a large and shiny chrome plated pistol. "Dammit." She looked up. "Now tell me how."

I held up my phone. "I filmed it for you."

Fred and Jane watched the replay. I tried not to look too pleased, but still ended up with a big smile on my face.

"You snuck it in the exit." Fred said.

I nodded. "You've focused all your security on the entrance. That exit's your weakest spot, even during the slow times."

"Who's the old lady?" Jane asked.

"My mom. She's wearing a wig."

"And your dad guided the car?"

"They said I've been having all the fun, and they wanted in this time."

She sat down behind the desk and held her head in her hands. "Okay, Mr. Security Consultant, I guess congratulations are in order again." After a minute of rubbing her temples with her fingertips, she said, "I'll work on the exit. Send me the report."

"You'll have it next week."

She nodded. "Hey, some guy asked me about you this morning. I told him you were the best."

"You get a card?"

"He wouldn't give it. Twenty-something, dark hair. A little freaky looking."

"Thanks." I paused. "You guys are getting better, you know."

"But not fast enough," she said. "Eleven months now and you're still getting through." She dropped the pistol in her drawer.

"You'll get there." I opened the door. "Oh, and Jane?"

She raised her eyebrows.

I winked. "Your massages are getting better too." I stepped outside, but not before I heard Fred burst out laughing.

one

A DELIVERY MAN IN a green van carried a package down my dock later that afternoon. He should have delivered it to the house, but we were out back fishing, and he needed a signature.

I watched him as he walked out the dock. He wore a green long-sleeved uniform and a small pair of silver sunglasses. When he got close, he pulled a green pen out of his pocket and held out a clipboard. "Delivery for Mr. Waverly," he said. "Can I get a signature?"

I took the pen and clipboard and wrote John Doe in the signature box. The loops on the J invaded the neighboring boxes. "Here you go." I handed him the clipboard and glanced at the embroidery on his shirt pocket. "I didn't think delivery companies worked Sundays, Robert."

"Ours does," he said. "And my name's Bob. Not Robert."

"Did you change your name after you ordered your shirts?"

"Another Bob started before me." He shook his head. "They told me I could add an initial at the end, but then it would say Bob O. That sounds like a clown." He looked at my signature. "Mr. Waverly, can I see some identification?"

I was still wearing the bathing suit from the airport work. "It's in the house," I said. "You got the right address. What's the problem?"

"You signed John Doe in the box."

"You claim your name is Bob, but you're wearing Robert's shirt."

His frown made his forehead crinkle between his eyebrows. "I need to be sure that I deliver this package to Scott Waverly."

"You have. That's me."

He sighed and pulled a small handheld computer out of his pocket, flipped open its cover, and typed on its miniature keyboard. "Just a second while I verify, sir."

"Verify what?"

"You." He tapped the screen. "Here we are. Five foot eleven, medium build, brown hair, hazel eyes." He tilted the screen my way. "It's you, all right."

A photo of me standing in the airport this morning graced his screen, along with my address and information about our company. "So it was you talking to Jane this morning," I said. Jane was right; he was a little freaky looking.

Bob flipped the handheld's cover shut and shoved it in his pocket. "Yes sir." He handed me the package and headed up the dock.

"Hey, you forgot your pen!" I called.

"You'll need it, sir." He climbed into his green van and drove away.

Dad examined the package. "It's from Soul Identity—do you know them?"

"Nope," I said. "Wait, I do. Somebody from Soul Identity called on Friday. I gave him the spiel about our security auditing services." I handed him the bait knife.

He slit the package open and pulled out two yellow envelopes. He pointed at a READ ME FIRST label. "We should start with this."

"I'll get the other." I tore the end off my envelope and pulled out a yellow plastic device, oblong in shape and flat on its sides. It looked like a bright yellow slice from the middle of a hard boiled egg. Instead of the yolk it had a button labeled "Soul Identity reader." A lens the size of a pea glinted from the small end, and a key ring dangled from the other.

Mom plucked it from my hand. "It looks like a keychain flashlight."

"It's not a flashlight," Dad said. "Listen to this. Dear Mr. Waverly, blah blah blah, we wish to engage your services, but in order to commence the engagement—" He looked up. "Commence the engagement? Who writes like that anymore?"

"Old people. Old companies. Old lawyers." I said. "What do they want?"

"In order to commence the engagement, you must signify your acceptance by providing us your soul identity. Kindly use the enclosed reader, blah blah blah, return the reader by the same delivery company, blah blah blah, instructions for using the reader are attached." He read to himself. "The rest is just legal stuff, and then it's signed by Archibald Morgan, executive overseer of Soul Identity."

"Scott, what kind of wackos are you involving us with?" Mom asked.

"Beats me," I said. "We're not involved. Yet. Let's see the instructions." I took the sheet from Dad and read:

Using the Soul Identity Reader:
1. Press and hold button for five seconds, until lens flashes red.
2. Place lens two inches directly in front of right eye. Do not blink.

3. Press and hold button for one second. Lens will flash green if successful. If lens does not flash green, start over.
4. Place lens two inches directly in front of left eye. Do not blink.
5. Press and hold button for one second. Lens will flash yellow if successful. If lens does not flash yellow, start over.

Just then the tip of my fishing rod jerked down. I handed the paper to Mom and grabbed the rod. I adjusted the tension and fought the fish in close. It was a bluefish, the only kind in the middle bay that puts up a decent fight.

Dad snagged him with the long handled net, and together we lifted him onto the dock. "Careful with his teeth," he said as I grabbed the fish under his gills.

Bluefish love to bite, and they have razor sharp teeth. Many bluefish fishermen have lost a finger or two by not paying attention.

I got the hook out with my digits intact. "You're one lucky fish," I said. House rules: the first fish caught is returned to the bay to appease the fishing gods. I was about to toss him back, but then I stopped. "This guy can help us out," I said. "We'll read his soul identity."

"From the fish?" Mom asked.

"They want an identity, so we'll give them one. Dad, bring that reader over here. I'll hold him steady."

Mom looked at the instructions. "They say press the button for five seconds. Did it flash red?"

"It's too bright out here." Dad cupped his hands around the reader. "Let me try again. Yes, it's flashing red."

"Two inches from the right eye," Mom read. "No, the fish's right eye—that's his left one. Press the button for one second. Did it flash green?"

"It's flashing red," Dad said.

"You must have held the button too long," Mom said. "Do it again."

Dad did the fish's right eye, and the lens flashed green. He shifted to the left eye, and the lens flashed yellow. Mission accomplished.

I tossed the bluefish back into the bay and watched him swim off. I wiped my hands on my towel. "Now what?" I asked.

"We're done," Dad said.

The tricky part was figuring out where to send the reader. We could not find Soul Identity's address in the documents. Bob was right about the pen: written on it in white was "Delivery," followed by a toll free phone number. I used Dad's phone to call.

A cheerful man's voice answered on the first ring. "Dispatch."

"May I speak with Bob?" I asked.

"Which Bob?"

"Sorry, it's not Bob. His shirt says Robert. He's a delivery guy."

"Please hold while connecting to Robert." I heard a click, and then another ring.

"This is Bob." I recognized the voice of our delivery man.

"Uh oh. I was holding for Robert."

Silence on the other end. Then, "Is this Mr. Waverly?"

I must have made an impression. "Yes, Bob, it's me. I want to send the package back to Soul Identity. What do I have to do?" I slipped the key ring onto my finger and twirled the reader.

"Sir, I can be there in five minutes."

"You left here a half hour ago," I said. "Do you have turbo in that green van?"

"No, sir. I am waiting at the end of your street. I was instructed to stay close and wait for you to call back."

"Am I your company's only customer?" I spun the reader faster. It made a pretty yellow whirl.

"No, sir. Soul Identity is our only customer."

The reader flew off my finger and landed inside the bait cooler. "You're kidding," I said.

"No sir, I do not kid. We are Soul Identity's delivery service."

I examined the green pen. The word Delivery and the phone number stood out in white lettering. But then in dark green I saw the initials SI. And after the phone number, again in dark green, I read "est. 1732."

"Okay, Bob," I said. "You've got me interested. But give me a half hour to clean up before you return." I hung up and fished the reader out of the bait cooler. I flipped it over and brushed the seaweed off the back. A strand clung in a crack near the key ring, and I wiggled it out and saw small dark yellow lettering underneath. Holding the reader up to the sun, I read "Access Port."

"Where's that bait knife?" I asked. Dad passed it to me, and I wiggled the blade into the crack and twisted. The key ring end flipped open like the cover on a Zippo lighter and exposed a Universal Serial Bus, or USB connector. I could use it to see what was on the reader. "We'll have to check it out before Bob gets here," I said.

We packed up the fishing gear, grabbed the package and envelopes, and walked up the dock to my house.

I live on Kent Island, smack dab in the middle of the Chesapeake Bay, on the western edge of Maryland's Eastern Shore. My parents and I must cross the four mile Bay Bridge to visit each other. This gets tedious on the summer weekends when the highways are stuffed with cars bound for Ocean City, but my house faces west and gets gorgeous sunsets, so usually my parents come my way instead of me going theirs. The fishing also helps bring them over, and since we run our company out of my house, they commute here to work a couple days each week anyway. This morning they had come early for our trip to the airport.

Dad put away the fishing gear and Mom got a mailing package ready. I fired up my laptop, plugged the reader into the USB port, and watched as the system grabbed and installed the driver software.

The reader had a mini file system, which meant I could read its data from a regular folder window, much like an MP3 player's music files or a digital camera's pictures. My laptop popped the reader's folder onto my screen, and I saw one file named "1608-233052.SIR."

Dad looked over my shoulder. "What's a SIR extension?" he asked.

"I'm guessing Soul Identity Reader. The sixteen-oh-eight looks like the day and month, and the rest is probably the time."

"It wasn't eleven thirty when we did the bluefish," Dad pointed out.

"Universal Time," I said. "That would be seven thirty for us." I pointed at the screen. "Sixteen minutes ago, and that matches the time on the file."

I pulled up the file's contents. It contained two sets of date, time, map coordinates, altitude, and spatial axis data. I scrolled down and saw a reader serial number and a large binary chunk.

"Can you figure out what it says?" Mom asked.

"We sure can." Dad pointed at the screen. "Male bluefish, age six years, puncture wound on the lower lip and jaw."

Mom crossed her arms. "How can they know all that?"

"He's kidding, Mom," I said. "Bob's on his way, so I kept a copy to decode after he's gone."

She slipped the reader into the package and taped it shut. "I still think these guys are wackos," she said. "Do you really want to send this?"

"We could use the work." I walked out of the office and into the living room. "I'm going to wash off that bluefish smell. Say hi to Bob for me."

While I was in the shower I wondered what had triggered Soul Identity to contact us. We do more than airport security work; we provide computer security consulting. Most of our business comes right after our clients discover somebody has stolen their customers, money, ideas, or intellectual property. They call us to protect them from further losses; they are proof that people really do love to fix barn doors after their horses are gone.

Soul Identity hadn't yet told us what had been taken, but that was typical for our clients. Nobody wants to advertise their losses.

I walked back to the office and saw Bob sitting in my chair and drinking a cup of tea with my parents.

"Bob's waiting for your signature," Mom said.

"You look good in that chair, Bob," I said. "You want to join our business? We could get you out of that green uniform and into a nice pair of shorts."

Bob shook his head. "No thank you, sir. I have been with Soul Identity for many years, and they have always treated me well."

Bob didn't look old enough to have worked anywhere for more than a few years. "What does Soul Identity do, Bob?" I asked. "Why scan people's eyes?"

He looked uncomfortable. "Sir, I am not authorized to talk to you about our organization."

I grabbed the clipboard and scribbled another John Doe, this time with my left hand. The loops stayed inside their borders. I stuck the pen in my pocket and handed him the package.

"Well, sir, maybe I will see you again." Bob opened the door and stepped outside.

"If I'm lucky and you're not." I waved goodbye and used the green pen to write down his license plate number as he drove away.

I went back to my laptop and opened the reader file again. Time to figure out what Soul Identity was up to.

Dad came over. "I looked on the Web," he said, "and these guys have published nothing. There are a few sites out there referring to Soul Identity, but I don't think they're related, because they don't mention anything about readers. No news articles, either. I'm going back to the public records."

"I grabbed Bob's license plate, if you want to try that." I handed him the number.

"Did that already. Those plates are registered to SI Holding Corporation. And the only thing on them is a post office box in Baltimore."

"If they wish to hide, why are we looking for them?" Mom asked.

We both looked at her as if she was crazy. "Because we can," Dad said. "Besides, we have an hour before the bridge traffic lets up."

Mom shook her head. "You boys keep playing detective. I'm going to download my pictures and read my email."

"Pictures…that reader must be encoding pictures," Dad said.

I nodded. "That would be the binary chunks—pictures of each eye." I extracted the data and saved it as a file on my desktop. Then I opened a photo editor and dragged the file into it. "Let's see what it contains."

A window reading "Enter password to view images" popped up on my screen.

Dad looked over my shoulder. "What's the password?"

I thought about this. If the reader collected eye images, either each reader had a built-in password, or the information in the attached file generated the password. Maybe it was both: the file contained the reader information. "I'm guessing it's the reader serial number," I said.

"Wouldn't that be too primitive?"

"Many primitive people walk among us. We call them customers. Let's try." I typed the reader serial number into the password box and pressed OK.

Two bluefish eyes filled the screen. "That was it," I said.

"But we still don't know why," Dad said.

After my parents left, I thought about how big and diverse our world must be to include people who make devices that capture eye images.

A person's irises are as unique as his fingerprints. From a distance the iris looks brown or black or blue, but up close it contains many distinct shapes and colors. These change as you grow, but once you become an adult, they settle down and remain the same.

A couple of companies made iris scanners, but few security systems relied on them. It used to be that anybody could fool their scanners by wearing contact lenses with iris images printed on them. To counter this, the scanners grew in sophistication; they now shine a light into the eye to verify that the iris moves as the pupil contracts. This takes time to check, and as that time increases, the usefulness of the scanners decreases.

I figured that Soul Identity was collecting lots of eye images; otherwise they wouldn't have their own reader. And if they were using the system because they needed my identity, Bob would have hung around to ensure I used my own eyes. He didn't stay, so they were assuming it was in my interest to be accurate. They also read both eyes, even though a single iris image provides more than enough unique data points for identification.

I looked at the letter: Use the enclosed reader to obtain your soul identity. These guys were assuming that people wanted to have their eyes photographed, but I couldn't figure out why. The whole thing was a bit creepy, and I decided I didn't want them as a client.

Maybe it was tied to the airport. Bob did have a picture of me from this morning on his handheld. I wondered how Soul Identity had access to that kind of data. And the pen saying the firm was established in 1732: what was that all about?

I filed away the images. I'd worry about this only if Soul Identity called back.

two

EIGHT DAYS LATER I sat on my dock with my coffee and enjoyed a Monday morning on the bay. The rising sun lit up the western shore in yellows and pinks. An osprey searched for his breakfast; he plummeted into the water and took off with a large fish gripped in his claws. The fish wiggled and struggled and eventually broke free, but the osprey dove down and snagged him in midair.

Maybe the osprey had caught the same bluefish we photographed with the Soul Identity reader. Probably not, but I get a kick out of searching for surprise connections. It's part of my job, I guess.

I had better chances of winning the lottery every day for one week straight than I did of seeing an osprey scoop up the same bluefish. Still, I strained my eyes and hoped to spot a connection between me and the fish in the osprey's claws. Maybe I could coax the osprey to drop the fish onto my dock, where I could verify its identity.

I shook my head. Soul Identity, although they had not called back, had wiggled their way into my morning coffee philosophy. Just like they had been doing all last week.

I walked back to the house, ready to begin work. I still owed Jane Watson her airport security report.

I waved to my neighbor as I opened my door. I secretly called him Santa because of his white beard and round belly.

Santa looked up from his plants and waved back. "Morning, Scott."

"Morning." Two years since he moved in, and I didn't remember his name. I thought for the hundredth time that I should find it out before I embarrassed myself.

I sat behind my desk and pulled out the unfinished airport security report. I glanced out the window and watched a green van pull into Santa's driveway. It looked like the SI Delivery van, but the bushes in Santa's front yard obscured my view. Then I saw Bob the delivery guy walk over and speak to Santa. They both went into Santa's house.

Interesting. Was Soul Identity running reference checks on me? Was Santa telling them if I was naughty or nice? The connection-seeking portion of my brain shifted into overdrive.

I wanted to head over and ask, but first I needed Santa's real name. Maybe public records could help. The Maryland State Department of

Assessments and Taxation had an online form. I entered the county, street number, and street name. Bingo: Santa bought his house two years ago, was up to date on his taxes, and did his official business under the name Arthur Berringer.

I saw nothing about a Mrs. Claus or any little elves. The name Arthur didn't ring any bells. I probably had forgotten it, but just to double check, I searched for Arthur Berringer images on the Web. I located an unflattering, but a bit better groomed, photo of Santa boozing it up with his buddies at the Atlantic City Electric Wheelchair Manufacturers convention a few years before. I had found Santa.

I gave up on the airport report. Figuring out what Santa and Bob were cooking up was more interesting than documenting the security holes at the airport. I walked across the lawn and over to my neighbor's house.

Before I could knock on the door, it flew open, and Bob burst out. He ran full tilt toward his van. My neighbor chased after him and waved a shotgun in the air. Santa had been replaced by an old man with a wild fire in his eyes.

"You're a cheat!" Santa fired a blast into the air. Bits of leaves and branches showered us.

Bob backed out of the driveway. He knocked over my mailbox, swerved at the last minute to avoid the drainage ditch, and scuffed up the corner of my lawn. A cloud of dust and junk mail drifted in his wake.

"You all right?" I asked. If Santa wanted to shoot at me, I'd have to start running before he reloaded. Once I read that when you're fleeing from somebody with a gun, you're supposed to zigzag. I could get in maybe three zigs before reaching my door.

I watched the wild look fade from his eyes. "Come on inside, Scott," he said. "Have some coffee with me."

Why not? I followed my neighbor into his house for my very first visit and looked around. Two dusty electric wheelchairs sat parked along the living room walls where a couch and chair normally would have been.

Santa put the shotgun on the dining room table and wiped his sleeve over the wheelchair seats. "Have a seat—I'll be right back."

I noticed the pictures framed on the wall. One of them was the same Atlantic City photo I had seen on the Web. The other pictures showed more wheelchair conventions. I saw a red-haired Santa, a salt-and-pepper Santa, and an all-white Santa that looked pretty recent.

He returned in a minute holding two steaming mugs. "I added cream and sugar. That all right?"

I took a sip. "Thanks, Arthur. It's perfect."

He froze and stared at me. The wild look crept back into his eyes, and I realized I had made a mistake. He set his mug down on the seat of a wheelchair and took a step closer to me. "What did you just call me?" His eyes flickered to the shotgun.

Uh oh. Santa must not like being called Arthur. Or his name wasn't Arthur. Maybe he went by Art, or Artie. I calculated the odds; there was no way I could guess this one right.

"I called you Arthur. Isn't your name Arthur Berringer?" I held my breath.

Santa took another step closer. He stood less than a foot away. He breathed hard and clenched and unclenched his fists. "Yes, it's Arthur, but nobody except my mother ever called me that." He looked out the window and then back at me. "You're with them, aren't you?"

I got up and wondered if I would be able to defend myself with the coffee mug. We stood eye to eye with our noses almost touching. "No, I'm not with Soul Identity." I bit my tongue. Damn, now why did I have to say the name of the company? Santa's eyes flicked back to the dining room table. "Just give me a second to explain—that guy Bob stopped by to see me last week, and I thought he had come to ask you about me."

"And why would he be asking me about you?" His voice came out in a growl.

"They wanted me to do some security work for them, and I thought they were running a reference check. I wanted to find out what they were asking you, but I had forgotten your name."

Santa stared at me.

"So I searched the Web, and found you in the tax records. That's where I saw your name was Arthur Berringer."

We stood there, face to face, for what seemed like forever. Probably it felt a lot longer to me than it did to him. I listened to a jet ski go by outside, and wondered if anybody had heard the earlier shot blast and called the police.

Finally Santa spoke. "You forgot my name? Jeez, Scott, I've been your neighbor for two years now."

"I know," I said. "I'm so stupid sometimes. I wanted to ask you, but the longer I waited, the harder it became."

The wild look receded. "Hell, we're neighbors." He smiled and stuck out his hand. "Let's start over. Everybody calls me Berry."

I shook his hand and looked him in the eye. I figured I might as well confess all. "And I've been calling you Santa behind your back."

Berry laughed and slapped me on the shoulder. "You and the rest of the world." He picked up his mug and sat down on the other wheelchair. "Sit down and tell Santa what you want."

Whew. I told him about Bob's visit the previous Sunday. "They sent me a reader in the mail, but I sent them the eyes of a bluefish."

Berry raised his eyebrows. "You're just gonna give it all away?"

I smiled, not sure what he meant. "I'm giving nothing away, Berry. They asked me for my soul identity, and I didn't want them to have it. Why would they want my eyes, anyway?"

"You really don't know, do you?"

I shook my head. "I thought they were crackpots."

Berry shook his head. "They're not crackpots. They're for real. I believe it." His eyes filled with tears, and his voice cracked. "And that bastard told me no."

I separate how I handle people's tears into four buckets. The first contains tears from those caught doing something bad or stupid. I wait until the histrionics end and offer them a tissue as they sort out what their next step will be. The second bucket's tears come after I say something insensitive and hurtful. I apologize to these people for being such a blockhead. The third's tears come on their own from those who cry at weddings and at the end of mushy movies. It works best when I act like I don't notice these tears. Of course, joining in by dabbing my eyes and making sympathetic sounds can lead to happy endings on dates.

Berry's were filling up the fourth bucket—the one that holds tears from deep, heart-rending losses. Usually I just say, "I am so sorry," and I sit with them and reflect on the good times before the loss. But I had no clue of what Berry might have lost.

I leaned forward on the wheelchair. "What happened?" I asked.

He wiped his eyes on the back of his hand and sat silent for a minute. "Do you believe in past lives?"

"Reincarnation?" I shook my head.

"Me neither, until a few weeks ago." He blew his nose on a handkerchief. "In fact, for the last couple of years, I've wanted nothing except to hurry up and die and get it over with. Living out here has become so lonely for me."

I had watched Berry putter around his yard many times from my office window. Until this morning, I couldn't recall seeing anybody visit him.

"I moved here when I retired," he said. He patted his armrest. "For forty-two years I sold these wheelchairs. I lived alone, but I was busy with work and my buddies. We did six conventions a year—see the pictures?" he asked as he pointed at the wall. "It was a good gig. But once I landed here I lost my way."

I thought about how little I knew my neighbor. And how crappy that made me feel. "Do you have any family?" I asked.

"Nobody I talk to. My brother's kids, but I haven't seen them for more than a decade." He sighed. "It wasn't supposed to end like this. I planned to work until I keeled over, but then some bozo at the office cooked up a mandatory retirement age. And my buddy from work got married to our teenage receptionist and bolted to Puerto Rico. He died two months later. Too much stress on his heart, I guess. Lucky bastard."

"So how does Soul Identity enter the picture?" I asked.

"They showed up right after I visited that palm reading place out on route fifty." He counted on his fingers. "A little over three weeks ago."

"That tiny cottage with the big hand outside?" I asked. It was just a few miles north and west of us, on the main route to Ocean City. "Why'd you go there?"

"I know it sounds crazy, but I wanted to know how long before I kicked the bucket," he said. "My life insurance agent claimed their actuarial tables showed nine years, but he didn't know how much I'd been drinking. My doctor guessed four. I was looking for a third opinion."

"Why'd you want to know?"

Berry shrugged. "The shortest path, I guess. I have no kids, no friends, and busy neighbors. Just me and the bottle keeping each other company. I wanted out."

I thought how lousy a neighbor I must be, how I had been unable to see through the Santa façade and into the agony that made up Berry's lonely days. "Did the palm reader help?" I asked.

He nodded. "I spilled my guts to this little old lady. And she predicted that somebody would soon give my life a purpose." He stared at me. "She was right, you know. The very next day a Soul Identity member came by the house and gave me a reason to live."

So it seemed Soul Identity preyed on lonely people, selling false hopes of reincarnation and taking their money. I felt better about ignoring them—they weren't the kind of customer I wanted.

I thought both of us could use some fresh air. "Can we take a walk as we talk?"

"Sure." Berry carried our mugs into the kitchen and set them in the sink. He nodded at a box in the corner. "I started recycling three weeks ago. Everything's different now." He pointed to a folder on the countertop. "Those are their forms. Bob had come to pick them up, but then we had a little problem."

I glanced at the shotgun on the dining room table. The problem seemed more than little.

Berry helped me right my mailbox, and we collected the scattered junk mail. Then we headed north and walked along the road next to the shore. We could see the Annapolis capitol building and a swarm of sailboats over on the western side. Two container ships headed north toward the Port of Baltimore. The breeze filled our noses with the salty smell of the bay.

Berry pointed to the Chesapeake Bay Bridge four miles in front of us. The twin spans soared majestically over the bay and glittered in the morning light. "Have you ever thought about the changes that first bridge caused?" he asked.

I enjoyed having the bridge on the northern edge of my horizon, but I had given no thought to its impact. "No, not really."

"Sixty years ago most people on this island were farmers and crabbers. The bridge replaced the ferry, and the islanders became commuters. People live here and work in Baltimore or Washington. You can reach the beach from the cities after work in time for sunset."

I thought about the traffic. "Not on Fridays you can't. Where are you going with this?"

"The bridge united two different worlds," he said. "When that first Soul Identity member came to my house, he showed me the bridge that connects me to my own future world."

"Aren't we all connected to our future?"

Berry stopped walking. "Scott, my future was over in four to nine years. Soul Identity showed me how I could extend it forever, by building a bridge between my present life and my future lives."

First past and now future lives. What was this organization up to, anyway? I resumed our walk, this time back toward our houses. "I thought that the common thread tying all the beliefs in past and future lives was that you could never really be sure where your soul had been, or where it was going next."

"These guys at Soul Identity are different," he said. "Don't ask me how, but they can identify and track your soul. They read it, and after you die and come back in a new body, they find it again."

Right. I stopped in the middle of the road. "You said that these guys can find you again in a future life? That's tough to swallow."

"They're not looking for you," he said. "They're looking for your soul. It's a big difference."

That was interesting. We reached the front of Berry's house. "But why would I want to keep track of my soul?" I asked.

"Think about it from my side," he said. "I saved some money, and the school of hard knocks taught me some tricks on making it in this world. I have no kids to pass the money and tricks to. But what if I could give it all back to me? I could jumpstart my next life by using this bridge, Scott. That's what is so exiting."

I thought about it. The belief that people have a soul is common. But the idea that some group could track your soul, find it again in the future, and pass along the information and money you banked seemed pretty novel. And if they could really do that without cheating you in the process, it also sounded compelling. I could see why Berry was interested.

We went inside. I sat down at the dining room table this time. I moved the shotgun to the side and opened the folder.

Berry's questionnaire mostly dealt with geography and dates: where, when, and for how long he had lived or visited different places. "Why so many questions on location?" I asked.

"They said it has to do with their recovery formula."

"It sounds pretty complicated. If you missed a place on your questionnaire, are they saying that your soul can't be found?"

Berry smiled. "No, but they did say it helps if they know where to look."

Why wasn't Berry seeing these guys as a pyramid scheme? Or a freaky cult? "Let's say that I buy into Soul Identity's bridges," I said. "What's in it for them? They can't just be doing this because they love to help people."

Berry shrugged. "Maybe they charge a commission for delivering your money back to you."

This organization promised to deliver to a future person only if he turned up and asked to be identified. They could operate with virtually no oversight, because their clients were mostly dead. Whoever cooked up this scheme was a genius. "Do you really trust these guys to turn over your lessons and your money, and not to keep it, or give it to their buddies?" I asked.

"Dammit, of course I do! Even more so, now that they won't let me play." He sighed. "It doesn't really matter if I trust them or not, does it?"

Back to the little problem. "So why didn't they let you in?" Maybe Berry didn't have enough money to make it worth their while.

"Bob didn't want to tell me. He just said that I wasn't suitable." He patted his shotgun. "But when I got a little persuasive, he coughed out the real reason."

"Which was?"

"This." He tapped his left eye. "It's glass. Had it for eight years now. I lost the original in a freak accident. I wore a patch for a year or two, until I got tired of looking like a pirate."

I looked closer. I had never seen a glass eye before. It looked real enough to me, except now that I knew, I saw that its pupil was smaller than the right eye. "They told you they needed to read both your eyes?" I asked. "They told me that too."

Berry nodded and started sniffling again.

I noticed that the glass eye cried just as much as the real eye.

Berry wiped his eyes. "So now I'm screwed. How could I have been so stupid to get my hopes up?"

Berry believed that Soul Identity was for real, more so now they wouldn't let him in. They were the fish, or the girl, that got away.

I never took on clients that I felt stretched the law or exploited people. In fact, I regularly turned down working with groups I suspected had criminal or religious ties.

Soul Identity was creepy from the start, and Berry's story only made it worse. My gut told me I should walk away. But these guys were still in my thoughts over a week later, and I was feeling guilty about being such a lousy neighbor for Berry.

I looked at him. "You really want in with these guys, don't you?"

He sighed, then nodded. "I do."

I took a deep breath and stood up. "Berry, I'll take Soul Identity on as a client. And I'll do my best to find a way to get you in."

three

I PUT MY FEET up on my desk. Jane's unfinished report glared at me until I flipped it over.

I thought about Berry and what might have driven him to Soul Identity. He was lonely and looking for something to live for, but he could have joined any number of clubs and charities that would have been happy to fill up his time and give him a purpose in life. He could have used his Internet connection to enter the wild world of online dating. He even could have joined a church; most of them offered some sort of eternal life.

With all those options, why did he latch on to something so far out of the mainstream?

We all have a strong urge to obtain or achieve something special. Maybe we build the largest collection of coins or stamps or beanie babies. Maybe we become experts in trivia or geography or famous movie stars. Maybe we join a church which teaches that only the select few who learn God's real secrets will be saved. Whatever path we take, we want to be seduced into thinking that we are special and different and maybe even better than everybody else.

Churches employ this seduction to attract and retain members. Successful love relationships thrive on it too: both partners feel they're the luckiest people to have found each other. Until one of the partners finds somebody else who makes them feel even luckier. Like my ex-wife did.

Soul Identity seduced Berry by offering him immortality and a purpose for living. When it dashed Berry's hopes, I seduced myself by thinking that only I could help him. I guess we weren't that different after all.

I had made a promise to Berry. Jane's report could wait. Time for me to make nice with Soul Identity.

Archibald Morgan, executive overseer. How could I reach him directly? Our cursory search had turned up neither phone numbers nor email addresses. I would ask Bob the delivery guy.

I called the number on the green pen, and the dispatcher put me through. "Bob, this is Scott Waverly," I said. "You delivered me a package last Sunday."

"Hello, Mr. Waverly."

I wondered if Bob had recovered from his scare with Berry. "Didn't I see you tearing out of my neighbor's house this morning?"

Silence on the line for a minute. Then, "yes, sir, you did."

"You know you knocked over my mailbox? I had junk mail flying all around the neighborhood."

Another long pause. "I am sorry, sir. If you fill out a damage form, my company can reimburse you."

Yeah, he had recovered. "I need a favor from you," I said. "I'd like to speak with Archibald Morgan. Can you give me his number?"

"Sir, the only way you can reach Mr. Morgan is through me. I'll be happy to deliver a letter for you."

"Maybe I can email him?"

"Sir, it really is a very fast service I offer. When should I pick up your letter?"

"When can you get here?"

Bob said he'd come by in forty-five minutes, so I cranked out a letter to Archibald Morgan and asked him to call me on my cell phone. Then I walked next door and told Berry to put away his shotgun. He promised to stay inside until Bob was gone. I spent the next fifteen minutes racing through the airport report. I emailed Jane my analysis, my concerns, my suggestions, and my invoice.

Bob reached my house on the forty-fourth minute. He looked at his watch. "I need to get moving to deliver this today."

"Today?"

Bob smiled. "This is what we do, sir. We've gotten pretty efficient over the years." He took the envelope and handed me his clipboard.

Just like last time, I signed my left-handed John Doe signature on his form, kept his green pen, and watched as he drove away. But this time I followed.

I'm a bad follower. I am reminded of this each time my relatives come down to visit DC; we pile into our cars and head to the mall. I get frustrated when I can't telegraph to the leader to pass the slow guy, switch lanes, or watch out for the cop ahead. So I end up trying to lead from behind, which doesn't work if the guy in front still thinks he's in charge. Leader-follower situations work best when I lead.

But I couldn't tell Bob to let me lead. Fortunately he drove a big green van, which is not that common on the Eastern Shore. The cars out here are SUVs and Beamers for the coastal dwellers, and pickup trucks and Mustangs for everybody else.

I stayed a quarter mile or so behind the van. This wasn't difficult, as the road north runs straight. I expected him to make a left onto Route Fifty and cross the Bay Bridge toward Annapolis, but he surprised me and continued north. I sped up to keep him in sight.

Bob took the next right and drove parallel to the highway. This road had more turns, and for a few seconds I thought I had lost him. But then I saw his van parked on the right, next to the same palm reading outfit which Berry had mentioned earlier. There was a sign out front that read "Madame Flora's."

I doubted Bob was getting his palm read. And I hoped that the palm reading place wasn't the headquarters of Soul Identity, because there would be no work for me, and I would have to break some bad news to Berry. Was this another pickup for Bob? I drove past him, parked on the left in front of a gas station, and kept an eye on his van.

Staking out a joint looks a lot more fun in the movies than it really is. I scanned the radio stations, fiddled with the AC controls, and played with the seat buttons. I wondered if I could take a chance and run into the gas station to buy some snacks. In about fifteen minutes, just as I was about to give up, Bob walked out of Madame Flora's. I followed as he drove back toward my house.

My phone rang as we neared my neighborhood.

"Mr. Waverly, this is Archibald Morgan."

"Hi." I took a stab at being friendly. "Archie, where are you calling from?"

"Please call me Mr. Morgan."

My stab missed; he wanted to be formal.

"I am calling from our Massachusetts headquarters," he said.

Or maybe he was hanging out at Madame Flora's place. I could at least check his area code if he'd give me his number. "I'm about to drive through a dead zone. Can I call you back?"

"I will call you again, Mr. Waverly. Would that suit you?"

No number for me. "Give me two minutes." I hung up.

Bob's van pulled into my driveway. I parked next to him and got out. "All delivered?" I asked.

"Yes sir. Mr. Morgan said he'd be calling you within the hour."

I held up my phone. "He just called. Bob, where is he located?"

He looked uneasy.

"Is he in Maryland?" I asked.

He shook his head. "No, sir. He's rarely in Maryland."

"Then how did you deliver my message?"

"Perhaps you can ask Mr. Morgan that question."

"I did. He said he was in Massachusetts."

Bob looked relieved. "Yes sir. That's where he usually stays. At our headquarters."

"I followed you when you left here. You only went to Madame Flora's. No other stops. Are you sure Mr. Morgan isn't at the palm reading place?"

"Sir, I delivered your message to Mr. Morgan by using equipment at Madame Flora's."

"What kind of equipment?" I waited for an answer, but then my phone rang, and Bob slipped away.

"Is this Scott Waverly?"

"Hi Archie." I just couldn't resist.

"Please call me Mr. Morgan."

"Okay. Mr. Morgan, why does your delivery guy communicate to you from a palm reading joint?"

Silence on the line.

"You still there?" I asked.

"Yes, Mr. Waverly. Did Bob give you a reason to follow him?"

I didn't want to get Bob in trouble. "No. It's a sample of my work, free of charge."

"Ah yes, charges. We need to discuss your rates."

They were going to be high. Especially since these guys transformed my happy Santa neighbor into a shotgun-firing, crying old man. "Let's talk about what you need me to do," I said.

"We offer financial services to members wishing to eternally preserve and multiply their accumulated wealth. We also offer an escrow service, providing a place for members to deposit articles for future withdrawals."

"You sound like a bank," I said. "Where do I come in?"

"Our organization wants to offer these services over the Internet. However, there are some of us inside the organization who are apprehensive about the risks inherent in this untested medium. We wish to apply some risk management to the process."

Archibald Morgan sounded like one of the apprehensive types. "So you want me to make sure your computer security doesn't catch you with your pants down?"

"I would have chosen different words, but that is essentially correct. There will be other tasks, but making sure we are safe is my top priority."

I thought about it for a minute. "Usually my reviews take a few weeks to perform and a few weeks to write up the report and recommendations. When do you need this done?"

"Right away."

I gave him our standard rates.

Morgan answered without a pause. "Very good. When can we start?"

That surprised me; my rates are high, and most clients try to talk me down. Better make sure he was committed. "If you want me to start right away, you'll have to pay a month's retainer in advance."

"Bob can deliver a certified check tomorrow morning. Can we start Wednesday?"

I stared at the phone. These guys must have a huge emergency on their hands. What wasn't Morgan telling me?

"Mr. Waverly?" Morgan's voice was faint.

I brought the phone back to my ear. "One more thing. I don't like formality. I call you Archie, and you call me Scott."

He laughed. "If that is what it takes to engage you, I can certainly call you Scott." He paused. "Most of our operations are run from Massachusetts. I suggest that we start here and see where else you need to go."

"Okay, send me your address and a recommended hotel and I'll see you in time for your morning coffee."

Archie cleared his throat. "I will send somebody to pick you up at your house in Maryland at six o'clock Wednesday morning. We will provide all transportation and accommodations."

Now he was getting too weird. "I'm not sure I'm comfortable with that, Archie."

"I assure you that you will be well taken care of. Soul Identity will pay for your services around the clock, starting Wednesday at six o'clock in the morning, and continuing until your work is completed."

I almost dropped the phone. "Around the clock pay?"

"Yes."

"Why would you do that?"

"This work is extremely important and critical to us. We would like your complete and undivided attention for the duration."

It sounded good enough for me. "Archie, you have a deal. Send the round-the-clock month's pay tomorrow so we're ready." I disconnected, and then stared at the phone. Mom was right; these guys were nut cases.

That night I dreamed I saw an osprey dive down and scoop a bluefish out of the bay, but then I realized it was me and not the bluefish wriggling in its claws. I broke free and started falling down to the water. Good, I thought, now I get to wake up, right before I hit. But the osprey caught me and carried me high up in the air. I was shivering from the cold as we broke through the clouds, only it was no longer an osprey, but an airplane that held me buckled into my seat. I looked into the cockpit and saw Bob was piloting.

The airplane transformed into Bob's green delivery van. Bob swerved to avoid ramming a silver gray car, and he drove off a cliff. I woke up, right before we hit the ground, and sat straight up in bed.

These Soul Identity guys were getting inside my head. I wanted to see how the dream ended—not the cliff part, but where Bob was taking me. I lay back down and tried to rewind, but I couldn't keep the dream alive.

I walked into the bathroom. An image had repeated in the dream. It was on the osprey's breast, the back of the airline seat, and the side of Bob's van. I closed my eyes to see it again, but the image swirled away from me like mist on the bay breaking up at sunrise.

I sat on the bed and tried to squeeze out the image, but I ended up falling asleep and tumbling to the floor. I grabbed a pencil and a piece of paper and put them next to the bed, just in case.

In the morning I discovered that I had written the following: "Soul Identity =", a triangle, "Is," and a comma. Underneath this I had written "(that's how)." Apparently I had woken up with a bright idea. I stared at it and tried to decipher it, but got nowhere.

I had the coffee ready by the time my parents arrived for work. I poured out three cups. "Starting tomorrow we have a new customer," I said.

"You finished the airport report?" Dad asked.

"All done, billed, emailed, and filed." I smiled at their reactions. I rarely do the paperwork.

"Who's the new customer?" Mom asked.

I pointed out the window at Berry weeding his flowers. "Santa dragged me into this. Did you know that his real name is Arthur Berringer?"

"He goes by Berry," Dad said.

"I wish I had your memory for names, Dad. Not knowing it almost got me killed." I told them about Berry shooting in the air and Bob peeling away.

"The same delivery guy from last week?" Mom stared at me. "Don't tell me we're doing business with those Soul Identity wackos."

"We're doing business with those wackos. And they're paying us a month in advance for round-the-clock work."

Dad almost choked on his coffee. "We charge so much for your time because you only bill ten hours a week." He punched some numbers on a solar calculator. "The advance will be more than we made last year. Is this for real?"

"I guess we'll find out if the check shows up today," I said. I relayed what Berry told me about Soul Identity's bridges between lives, and how I promised that I would help him out, even though I didn't like what I had heard.

"Tough call on taking them as a client," Dad said. "Though it's a nice thing for Berry, and maybe they won't be as bad as they sound."

"Maybe," I said. "Hey, I need a favor from you two. Can you come and get your palms read with me this afternoon? There's a place we need to check out."

They smiled when I told them how I followed Bob to the palm reader's. "With money like this, why not?" Mom said.

I remembered my dream, and I showed them the paper. "What do you guys make of this?"

"Looks like you were programming in your sleep," Mom said.

"With lousy English, too," Dad said. "What language ends its sentences with is?"

"Maybe it's not programming. Maybe it's math," Mom said. "Soul Identity equals delta is comma."

Dad said, "Maybe it's not a comma, but just Scott's lousy handwriting for an apostrophe. Try this—Soul Identity equals delta eyes."

I thought for a minute. "Maybe I meant delta of the eye images. Maybe these guys compute the soul's identity by figuring out the difference between the eyes."

Dad shrugged. "I guess you'll find out tomorrow."

"Let's find out now." I fired up my laptop and opened the bluefish eye images. "The spatial data can help to line up the eyes on the same axis," I said. I rotated the left eye image until the numbers matched. "Now let's get them the same size." I zoomed up the right eye image until it matched the left.

Mom looked over my shoulder. "How do you get a delta from that?"

"They probably have a more sophisticated program than my photo editor. One that overlays the images and shows the differences."

"You're not going to write all that now, are you?" Dad asked.

"Of course I am." I opened a new window and started coding. I grabbed a graphics library to manipulate the images and borrowed some old code to display the data nicely. An hour later I looked around, but my parents were outside on the dock. I went to work on the compile bugs.

After another half hour I was close. I stared at my code. It loaded two images, calculated the delta, and then displayed it. Where was the bug? There: I was trying to display an empty buffer.

I fixed and recompiled my code, loaded the images, and clicked the delta button. This time a new pattern came up on the screen. I added a slider that let me control the delta threshold.

I re-ran the program and tried out the slider. My parents came in and saw me moving it around.

"All done?" Dad asked.

"Yeah, the slider controls how strong the deltas have to be to get displayed." I tapped the screen. "This window shows the differences."

"Let me try," Mom grabbed the mouse and fiddled with the slider. "That's as clear as it's going to get."

"So that's what a bluefish's soul identity looks like," Dad said. "Now I've seen everything."

I looked at the screen. Four small yellow triangles sat placed around the pupil. "It doesn't look like much to me," I said. "But then again, neither does a fingerprint. Maybe human eyes are different."

We decided we would combine our palm reading trip with a celebratory lunch at a local restaurant. While my parents wrapped up the office work, I visited Berry. I told him I had gotten the contract and would be gone for a while.

"You think there's any hope to get me in?" he asked.

"Tell me again when you lost your eye."

"About ten years ago."

I walked over to the living room wall where the pictures hung and studied each one. "Do any of these show your real eye?"

Berry pointed. "That convention in Philly was just one week before the accident. And this one too." He tapped another frame. "From a couple years earlier."

I looked at the images. The Philly picture had Berry's hair obscuring part of his left eye. The second picture looked much cleaner and focused. "Can I borrow it?" I asked. "I might be able to grab an image of your missing eye and calculate your soul identity."

He helped me take the picture down.

"I'll call you as soon as I know something." I looked at him. "Can you keep it together for the next few weeks?"

He nodded. "I'll keep it together. But bring me back some good news."

four

DAD DROVE WHILE I navigated us to Madame Flora's tiny parking lot. I checked my watch; we were two minutes early. Did palm readers keep a tight schedule?

We went in and stood in a tiny foyer. A large diagram of a hand graced the door in front of us. Its palm showed three horizontal lines labeled Life, Head, and Heart, and three vertical lines marked Fate, Sun, and Hepatica.

I rapped my knuckles on the intersection of Life and Fate. The lights dimmed, and the door swung open.

Madame Flora sat on a couch behind a low glass coffee table. She wore a long maroon robe. I could not gauge her age in the dim light. My parents sat down on the couch facing her, and I sat on a chair to her right.

Madame Flora stared intently at a crystal chandelier hanging above the table. She waved her left hand in the air. I leaned forward and noticed she was holding a remote control in her right hand. She pressed one of the buttons with her thumb.

A woman's sultry voice crept up the walls of the room. "Welcome to Madame Flora's. Together you and Madame Flora will discover the answers you have been seeking. Madame Flora will use your astral projection to help you find your direction in life. Madame Flora is the only palm reader in the Mid-Atlantic region who has been certified by both the New Eastern Astrological Society and the Unified Palmists of North America."

Some kind of squeaky Eastern instrument played quietly over the sound system.

Madame Flora thumbed another button, and the voice continued. "Please use the paper and pencil provided to write down your heart's most burning questions. When you are finished, drop it in the slot in the middle of the table. This will allow Madame Flora to concentrate and release your astral energy so the answers to your questions may be revealed." A spotlight brightened and illuminated the coffee table between us.

I saw a pad of paper, a can filled with pencils, and a small slot in the center of the table. Under the slot sat a narrow clay vase.

I took pencil and paper and wrote my question: "Will you help me speak with Archibald Morgan at Soul Identity?" I slid the paper down the slot in the table.

Madame Flora pressed another button. The spotlight dimmed and the voice continued. "Please hold your hands palm-side-up in your lap. Madame Flora will gather the projected astral energy." The music's volume increased to the point where I could hear a drum getting whacked and somebody wailing almost in tune with the squeaky instrument.

We held up our palms, but only a minute later the music stopped abruptly and the lights came on. A little old lady stood in front of me, hands on her hips, shooting daggers with her eyes.

Madame Flora sat on the couch with a look of astonishment on her face. "Grandma, I was handling this just fine." She pulled off a wig and shook out her long brown hair.

The old lady frowned. "They're not here for palm reading, sweetie. They're here for Soul Identity."

I looked at the young girl on the couch. She was slim and cute, no older than nineteen or twenty. "What's your real name?" I asked her.

"Rose," she said. "I'm Madame Flora's granddaughter, and I'm helping her out with her summer workload before I go back to college." She pointed at the old lady. "She's the real Madame Flora."

"What do you want?" the real Madame Flora asked.

"I'd like to see how you talk to Archie," I said. "Bob told me that this is the way he does it."

She crossed her arms. "Bob who?"

I shrugged. "His last name begins with an O. He said you have the equipment."

Madame Flora nodded. "Do you know how to work the machine?"

"No."

"Neither do I. But I've watched others do it many times over the last few years. We could probably figure it out together." She walked to the far wall, pulled aside a black curtain, and went through an opening. "This way," she said.

My parents followed. Rose motioned for me to pass through the curtain. I waited a second for my parents to get out of earshot. "So there's a hole in the bottom of the vase?" I asked.

She giggled. "Gypsies never tell, you know?" She looked at me and cocked an eyebrow. "But what do you think?"

"I think I've really ticked off your grandma," I said.

She chewed on this for a second. "I think if she was really ticked off, she wouldn't be bringing you to the back." She slipped off her robe and tossed it onto the couch. Underneath she wore jeans and a pink t-shirt. "That robe is like so hot," she said. "Anyway, what's Soul Identity?"

"I was hoping you knew," I said. "What's this machine your grandma's talking about?"

"Let's go and see." She parted the curtain, and I followed her through.

We were in a hallway. There was a kitchen on the right and a bathroom on the left. Further down on the left was a bedroom. I peeked in and saw two single beds with pink covers.

Rose stood in front of the doorway on the right. "This is the office."

I saw my parents standing next to a beige fax machine. Rose was talking to her Grandma. How was that? I looked behind me, and Rose smiled at my reaction. "Meet my little sister, Marie. Marie, this is Scott."

"Twelve minutes and eleven seconds doesn't make me your little sister," Marie said. "Is the fax machine broken?"

"It's not a fax machine," Madame Flora said. "It's a secret contraption that Soul Identity members use when delivering messages of utmost importance."

Marie rolled her eyes. "Grandma, that's not a secret contraption. That is a fax machine. Just last week I used it to send some stuff to Mom."

Madame Flora looked from Marie to Rose. "You kids think you have answers for everything. Somebody came here from Soul Identity and asked if they could keep this contraption here, because they needed a way to communicate their secret messages."

Rose giggled. "I guess it is a secret contraption to you, Grandma. But to us, it's just a plain old fax machine. We really do use it to send papers to Mom." She walked over to the machine and pointed. "We put the papers in here. This part takes a picture and sends it over the telephone to Mom's machine. She gets a copy."

Madame Flora shook her head. "Sending papers to your mother over the telephone. What will they think of next?"

"I just heard of an invention that sends movies through the airwaves. They're calling it television," Rose said. She turned and mouthed "Di-no-saur" to the rest of us.

"Are you laughing at me?" Madame Flora asked.

Rose patted her on the back. "It's fine, Grandma, that's why we're here this summer. We're easing you into the twenty-first century." She turned toward us. "Next week we're getting her a computer, broadband, and an email account. Woo-hoo, Grandma's going surfing!"

"And it's a good thing, too, because I'm dying from being offline for so long," Marie said. "All my friends must think I hate them."

I looked at Madame Flora. "Why did Soul Identity ask you in the first place? Did you know about them before?"

She looked at Rose and Marie. "Well, girls, it's time you knew anyway."

"Time we knew what?" Marie asked.

"My grandmother was a member of Soul Identity many years ago. She was also a soul reader." Madame Flora unlocked a cabinet in the corner and pulled out an old, battered traveling suitcase. "I kept her equipment somewhere. Here it is." She lifted out a wooden box from inside the suitcase and put it on the counter.

We gathered around the box. "Was your grandmother also a palmist?" Mom asked.

Madame Flora smiled. "Yes, the oldest daughter of each generation in our family always becomes a palmist." She nodded at Rose and Marie. "Or in this case, the oldest daughters."

Rose looked at us. "Grandma says we both have to do it, but neither of us really wants to."

"I'm going to be a children's rights lawyer," Marie said. "And Rose is going to be a marine biologist."

"As long as you also read palms, you can be anything you want," Madame Flora said.

"Yeah, that's the problem." Marie looked at me. "Picture a lawyer's office with a large hand stuck outside. Madame Marie—children's advocate and palmist."

"Or how about a palm on the side of a boat?" Rose asked. "Madame Rose's underwater readings."

"A good palmist is hard to find, and it pays the bills. And that's not even counting the Soul Identity commissions." Madame Flora turned the box around. "Now let's see what's in here."

"Wait a second. You get commissions from Soul Identity?" I asked.

Madame Flora's hand flew up and covered her mouth. "Did I say that? I have become such an old lady."

Right.

"But now that it's out," she said, "please tell your Soul Identity friends that I'm very upset that they rejected the Berringer fellow. They should find a way to make him a member and pay me my share. I was the one who brought him in."

"Grandma, open the box," Marie said. "You can talk money later."

Madame Flora lifted the lid and smiled. "Look, Granny's membership card." She showed us its picture of a triangle with two eyes in the middle. There was no company name on the card; just the picture and an illegible handwritten name half covered with an embossed seal.

Last night's dream flashed through my mind. "Do you know what this symbol means?" I asked.

She shook her head. "I see it on the sides of the vans when the delivery men stop by."

I tried to picture Bob's green van. I recalled an image, green on green, barely visible, on the sliding door. It could be the same.

Dad picked up the card and examined it. He looked at me. "Looks like your formula, Scott."

With the triangle and two eyes, it did resemble my delta formula. So I wasn't a genius after all. "What else is in there?" I asked.

Madame Flora rummaged through what looked like tubes of oil paint and brushes. She held up a green velvet bag. She pulled out a shiny gold instrument built around some lenses and mirrors. It looked a bit like a small pair of binoculars. "Granny called this her reader," she said.

I held out my hands. "May I?"

"Be careful with it." She handed it to me.

Other than its lenses, the reader bore little resemblance to the electronic one I used on the bluefish. I saw some hinges, and I carefully unfolded the attached gold rods.

"Those look like the temples from a pair of eyeglasses." Dad pointed. "Look at how they curve at the ends, like they could fit over your ears. And here's the nose bridge." He took the reader out of my hands and held it up. "My head's too big." He examined the reader again. "Hold on, there's another set on this end."

I looked at the twins. "Would you two try this on?"

Madame Flora nodded, and Rose and Marie stepped forward.

Dad put the temples over Rose's ears and settled the bridge on her nose. He maneuvered Marie closer and put the other temples over her ears.

Marie gasped. "Rose, you have one big eye right in the middle of your forehead."

"I can't see anything," Rose said.

"What else do you see, Marie?" Madame Flora asked.

"I'm not sure, Grandma. Just a sec."

We were silent as Marie looked again.

"Okay," she said. "Rose looks like she has only one eye, but the colors are a little off, like they're too bright in some parts and too dull in others. There's a bunch of triangles and crescents around the edge of the white part."

"Cool, let me see, Marie," Rose said.

"Wait!" Madame Flora said, but the girls were already taking off the reader, turning it around, and putting it back on.

"Wow, Marie, your eye is huge. You have some funny shapes around your iris." They took off the reader and gave it back to Madame Flora.

Madame Flora folded the reader and put it back in its velvet bag. She looked at the twins. "Maybe you can make us some tea?"

"Yes, Grandma," they said together. They left the room.

Madame Flora frowned. "You're not Soul Identity members, are you?"

"No," I said, "But we're about to work for them, and we want to know what we are getting into. Do you trust them?"

She shook her head. "Trust isn't part of the formula. It's business. I tell hopeless people their lives will improve, and Soul Identity members come along and do the rest. Then I get a commission." She paused for a minute. "Their lives do get better. They stop worrying all the time. And they become repeat customers."

One of the girls called out, "the tea's ready, Grandma."

We sat with Madame Flora at a little kitchen table. Rose poured the tea and Marie brought out cookies.

"We're not very good at house stuff. But I can make tea, and Rose can sort of bake cookies," Marie said.

"What do you mean sort of?" Rose looked at us. "Go ahead, taste them."

Mom bit into her cookie. "Interesting. What are they?"

"Chocolate chip," Rose said. "Only Marie and I ate all the chips yesterday. And I couldn't find the salt, so I substituted with extra—"

"Maybe it's better to keep your recipe a secret, sweetie." Madame Flora took a sip of tea and grimaced. "Oh dear. What flavor is that?"

"Green tea with rosehips," Marie said.

Madame Flora put down her cup and stood up. "That designer stuff is not tea." She collected our tea and cookies and placed everything in the sink.

"Grandma, it wasn't that bad," Rose said.

"Yes, it was," Madame Flora said. "Just what does your mother teach you anyway?" She sat back down and looked at us. "Is there anything else? We have a client coming in ten minutes and we must prepare the room."

"Did your grandmother tell you why she became a reader?" I asked.

Madame Flora frowned. "Our family has been involved with the organization for many generations." She stood up. "I don't want to be rude, but I must get ready for my next client. If you do speak with somebody from Soul Identity, please inquire about my commission on Arthur Berringer."

The restaurant was a few minutes from Madame Flora's. We sat on the patio and watched the boats pass under the bridge.

"Soul Identity sounds creepy," Dad said. "They're paying commissions to their recruiters—they must be bilking their members for piles of money."

"Scott, you said that your neighbor Berry has a new purpose for living," Mom said. "They sound like a cult that steals their members' possessions."

"But her grandmother was involved. What cult lasts more than a generation?" I asked. "Don't they burn out or kill themselves off? Or dissolve when the leader kicks the bucket?"

"So maybe they're not a traditional cult," Dad said. "But they sure don't seem to be a religion either. What religion doesn't advertise?"

I ordered cream of crab soup, figuring I should load up while I was still in Maryland. I asked the waitress, "Do you believe in past lives?"

She gave me a funny look. "I have only one life, and I have given it to Jesus. Past lives? That's the devil talking, son. Don't listen to him." She walked away.

Guess not. "Hey, was Madame Flora for real or was she just playing us?" I asked.

Dad shrugged. "It's hard to believe she's never used a fax machine before."

"Let's talk about her granddaughters," Mom said. "Did you think those girls were cute?"

Even though I work with my parents and we spend a lot of time mired in each others' business, I try to draw a line of separation at the edge of my love life. "They're what, nineteen years old?"

Dad laughed and grabbed Mom's hand. "I try to keep her off your back, son, but she's been wearing me down. You owe us a couple of grandchildren sooner or later."

Mom shook her head. "Scott, you're thirty-two years old. You still have most of that curly dark hair. You're in shape, intelligent, and some people think you're pretty funny."

I sighed. "You've told me all this before."

She leaned forward. "I have. Now stop fooling around and settle down before the rest of your hair falls out, your belly hangs over your pants, and you forget how to make the girls laugh."

The soup came just in time to fend off the rest of that conversation. The waitress gave me my bowl and placed a religious pamphlet next to my spoon. "I'd like you to read this," she said.

I looked at the back of the pamphlet. It was rubber stamped with the address of a local evangelical church. "Thanks, but I'm really not interested," I said.

"Read it now, son. It will save your soul." She left.

"Everybody seems to be worrying about souls these days." I opened the pamphlet. It talked about the meaning of life, hope, love, forgiveness, clean starts, and eternity. "You know, these guys are offering the same things that Berry was searching for."

"How can that be?" Mom pulled the croutons off her salad and dropped them onto her bread plate. "Christians believe that we have only one life."

"Isn't heaven just a way to stuff your same soul into a new body?" I asked. "That sounds like reincarnation to me."

"That's an interesting twist." Dad grinned. "You want to bounce that idea off the waitress?"

"I doubt she'd appreciate it," I said. "But both Soul Identity and the Christians seem to be focused on our souls' futures."

"But doesn't the Soul Identity approach seem more selfish?" Dad asked.

I shrugged. "When you strip the candy coating away, don't all religions hinge on a 'sow now and reap later' plan?"

We discussed this for the rest of the meal. Since it was a celebration, we ordered our traditional single serving of cheesecake, three forks, and three coffees. "Here's to our new wacko client." I raised my coffee cup. "May they bring us a happier neighbor and lots of money."

"And may you be safe," Mom said. "I'm worried."

five

I KEPT MY EYES closed so I could fall back asleep, but the voice on the phone penetrated through the fog of sleep and pierced into my consciousness. "Mr. Waverly," it said, "this is Bob from Soul Identity. Are you ready for your six o'clock trip to Boston?"

I opened one eye and peeked at the clock. It was a few minutes after four. "Why are you calling me now?" I asked.

"We are on a tight schedule, sir."

"And just how long does it take for you to get ready in the morning?" I demanded.

"Thirty minutes at most."

"Call me back at five thirty." I hung up the phone, but my sleep had fled. Damn these guys. I kick-started my coffee maker and glanced out the kitchen window. A stretch limo idled outside on the street; its lights illuminated the Chesapeake pre-dawn fog. If my ride was here, I might as well get going.

Twenty minutes later I filled two travel mugs with coffee and stepped outside. Before I reached the limo, the door opened and the driver stepped out. It was still dark, and I could only see his silhouette.

"Mr. Waverly? You're an hour early."

I recognized that voice. "You called me an hour early, Bob." I nodded at the limo. "Don't tell me you also moonlight as a chauffeur."

"Mr. Morgan has assigned me to be your driver for the duration of your contract with Soul Identity."

A driver would be nice. I held out the mug. "Pleased to work with you, Bob. But call me Scott from now on."

He scrunched up his face. "How about I call you Mr. Scott? Soul Identity requires our formality."

"Good enough."

He opened the back door. I hopped in the front seat instead. "I'd rather ride shotgun," I said.

Bob drove out of my neighborhood and turned north. I pointed at his dark green suit. "What is it with you guys and green?"

He smiled. "Our uniforms and vehicles are green. Our buildings and tools are gold or yellow. Always."

He turned east on Route Fifty, away from the bridge. "Whoa, Bob," I said. "BWI is that way."

"I'm driving you to Massachusetts, Mr. Scott. We'll take 50 to 301 to 95, then over to the New Jersey Turnpike, across New York, up Connecticut, and into Massachusetts. Arriving no later than," he looked at his watch, "three o'clock this afternoon. Maybe two o'clock, since you woke up early. But that depends on the traffic and the number of stops you require."

These crazy guys were paying for my time whether we flew or drove. "Driving works for me," I said.

Bob pointed over his shoulder. "Mr. Morgan sent me some materials for you to review before we arrive. I put them in the back, along with your uniform."

"Do I get to wear green suits too?"

"No, sir. Only Soul Identity employees may wear green on the campus. Contractors all wear black."

I looked in the back and saw three couches arranged around a narrow center table. A pair of black jeans, a black leather belt, and a black polo shirt lay on the couch in the rear. A manila folder, a DVD case, two pillows, and a blanket sat on the one running back to front. I stuck my head through the partition and looked down, and I saw a flat screen television monitor on the countertop just below me.

I pulled my head back. "Last week you told me that you had worked for Soul Identity for many years, but you don't look very old," I said. "How long has it been?"

"Only for five years this time."

This time?

He continued. "But if you add it all up, next Friday makes exactly one hundred years of service." Bob smiled. "They're throwing a big century party for me at headquarters."

"If you add what up?" I asked. "Overtime?"

"Overtime doesn't count." Bob glanced at me. "You really don't understand what we're about?"

I shook my head.

"Well, sir, Mr. Morgan did say to help you in any way I could." He paused. "Maybe you could ask me some questions."

"All right. Let's start with Soul Identity. How old is this organization?"

"I don't know, sir."

"You don't know?"

"No, sir. Pretty old, I would say."

"Your green pen said you were established in 1732."

"That's when we moved our operations to America. We're much older than that."

"I don't think identity is that old a word."

"It's older than you think," he said. "It comes from the Latin *idem et idem*, which means *again and again*. We've been using that name since well before we made the move to America." Bob reached into his breast pocket and pulled out a badge-sized piece of gold-colored plastic. "My membership card."

I looked at it. Again the same image: a triangle with two eyes inside, only this time I could see some detail. The eyes reminded me of Egyptian Eyes of Horus, and the triangle looked like the pyramid on the back of the US dollar bill. "What does this picture mean, Bob?"

"That, sir, sums up what I believe. It represents how the eyes are truly the portal to our souls. I wear it proudly around my neck as well." Bob stroked a bump in his shirt high up on his chest. I saw him move his lips in a silent chant.

"So it's like what a cross would mean to some Christians?"

He nodded.

"Did Soul Identity give you the necklace?"

"No, sir. I belong to a church in Baltimore, and our pastor gives out these pendants as gifts." Bob sucked in his breath and cringed. "Um, sir," he said hurriedly, "Soul Identity doesn't know I go to this church—please don't tell them."

"Would they get upset?"

"It's like this, sir. Even though Soul Identity connects souls to past and future lives, they don't say what it all means. All they do is recruit members, collect money, and identify souls. They leave the meaning to the churches."

"And why wouldn't you want them to know?"

"Because I'm an employee," he said. "To avoid conflicts of interest, we're instructed to steer clear of the churches." He looked at me with wide eyes. "But sir, many of us need more. Soul Identity is not just a job—it's our whole purpose for living."

"So you hide your church membership?"

He nodded. "It's like a 'don't ask, don't tell' policy. You won't tell, will you?"

"Of course not," I said. "But tell me, are there many churches like yours?"

"There used to be hundreds. They've been consolidating, though. Most members belong, but we employees have to be careful how active a role we take."

And although it was interesting about the churches, I wanted to know more about what Bob did for the organization we were driving toward. "What is it that you deliver?" I asked him.

"All sorts of things, sir. Redemptions, deposits, statements, and messages. I'm also certified to take readings, but only with the electronic readers."

I'm pretty good about getting people to talk about themselves. Everybody has a story to tell, and the easiest way for me to do my security consulting is to get people to tell me more—much more—than they intended.

Bob seemed eager to tell me things—almost too eager. I wondered whether he was being friendly, sharing his religious fervor, or trying to mislead me.

I scratched my head. "Back to your one hundred years of service. Did you work for Soul Identity in your past lives?"

Bob nodded. "Seven of my soul ancestors served for a total of ninety-four years."

I glanced at him, then turned back to watch the road. This was going to be a weird month up north.

After a pit stop I sat in the back. Bob showed me how to bring up the GPS map. Then he pressed a button on the same control panel. "This may interest you," he said. The back of the rear couch folded down and joined with a set of cushions behind it, producing a queen sized bed.

I could recover my missing sleep. "Just wake me up a couple hours before we arrive." I said.

"No problem, sir."

I woke up at eleven thirty. The GPS display showed us navigating through the messy split of Routes 95 and 91 in New Haven. Bob headed north on 91 toward Hartford.

He looked at me in the rearview mirror. "Did you sleep well, sir?"

I nodded. "The bed was great." I grabbed the remote and tracked our path. I noticed the Manhattan section showed a detour—our limo had circled Central Park.

"What's with the Manhattan tour?" I asked.

Bob looked at his display. "That loop you see there? I made a pickup while you were sleeping."

"What kind of pickup?"

"One of our members was returning some items to his soul line collection."

"Couldn't he use an overnight delivery service?"

"He is using one. That's my job. The items are priceless, and we cannot trust just anybody to deliver them. Only we know how to do it right."

"You take your job pretty seriously."

He nodded. "I am the number one driver in the Mid-Atlantic region."

Good for Bob. "What is he returning?" I asked. "Can I see them?"

He shook his head. "Only he and the depositary clerks will ever see them. Even I don't know what's inside the package."

At least Soul Identity seemed to take privacy seriously. That would make my job easier—once I found out what it was.

"Do you use SI Delivery for your own deposits?" I asked.

"Yes, sir."

"Does a driver come to your house in a limo?"

He laughed. "No, sir, I handle my own transactions."

"What kinds of deposits do you make?"

He seemed to hesitate before answering me. "Sir, many non-believers think what we do is strange."

He got that right.

Bob continued. "We've been persecuted, thrown out of our homes and towns, and even burned and drowned as witches and wizards. We've learned to be cautious about sharing too much with non-believers."

"Yet you're sharing all kinds of information with me."

He sighed. "I am, but Mr. Morgan says you need to understand so you can do your job. And, sir, I fully expect that you'll become a believer once you see what we're all about."

And though I thought Bob was over-optimistic about my impending conversion, that wasn't where he was heading. "You're asking me to be careful with what you tell me."

He nodded.

"I'll be careful."

Bob took a deep breath. "We collect dolls." He winced as he said this.

"Dolls?"

He nodded.

"What kind of dolls?"

"The kind that kids play with, sir."

"Who's 'we'"

"We, sir?"

"As in, 'we collect dolls.' Does all of Soul Identity collect dolls?"

He shook his head. "'We' means my previous selves and me. My soul line has collected thousands of dolls over the past thirteen hundred years. It's my turn now, and then my futures selves will be adding even more."

"You must have quite a collection."

"We do, sir. One of my predecessors had them on display at a doll museum in London back in the nineteenth century."

I had nothing to say.

After a few minutes of silence, Bob pointed at a billboard advertising a Chinese all-you-can-eat lunch buffet. "How's that look?" he asked.

"It'll do," I said.

"So why dolls?" I asked when we returned to our table, our plates heaped with noodles, egg rolls, and General Tso's chicken.

Bob sat down and pulled his chopsticks out of their wrapper. "My soul line founder was an eighth-century noblewoman living in Breton March, France. The Basques ambushed and killed her husband as Charlemagne's army returned from its Spanish campaign. She made ends meet by delivering packages between Soul Identity and the royal court. Before she died, she assigned us the task of assembling a doll collection."

It sounded like Bob had recited this story many times before. "Why is it that every time somebody talks about their past lives, nobility is involved?" I asked. "Nobody ever seems to come from horse thieves and murderers."

"That's a very common question, sir, from the skeptical family of our new members." He frowned. "Usually soul lines start with somebody who has a lot of money or status. Somebody who wants to preserve their achievements. They begin a soul line and pass down their money, lessons, and assignments to their future selves."

That sounded reasonable. The rich and powerful have the time and interest to get these lines going. "But what about you, Bob?" I asked. "How did you get involved? Were you searching?"

Bob sucked on the end of a noodle and it wiggled its way up into his mouth. "No, Mr. Scott. Soul Identity found me." Bob looked off into the distance, his eyes focused somewhere over my head. "I was an assistant physical therapist, working at a clinic and fitness club in Tampa."

I waited for him to continue.

He sucked another noodle into his mouth. "One day this man came into the club and told me that a distant relative might have left me a large inheritance, but he needed to first ask me some questions. Later I learned he was a soul seeker."

"What did he ask?"

"The usual—when and where I was born, and where I lived growing up. Then he pulled out a reader and took a picture of my eyes. He told me he would let me know about the inheritance within the week."

I put down my chopsticks and pushed my plate aside. "I would have thought somebody was trying to con me."

A waiter came by and cleared our plates. Once he was gone, Bob continued.

"I also thought he was conning me. But I figured there was no harm in giving him a picture of my eyes, especially if there was a potential inheritance out there with my name on it."

"And of course he called back, or you and I wouldn't be sitting here and talking about it."

Bob laughed. "That's right, sir. He did call back. And he introduced me to Soul Identity, and he started me down the path to finding the real purpose of my life."

Which seemed to be collecting dolls and driving delivery trucks. But I kept that thought to myself.

The bill came, and Bob paid it in cash. As we walked outside to the limo, I asked, "How did you get from Tampa to Maryland?"

"Everything changed after that day," he said. "I quit my job, packed my car, and headed to Massachusetts. I went to the depositary and looked at my soul line collection and got to know my previous selves. I joined SI Delivery once I realized we shared a common work heritage. Within a year I was assigned to the Maryland routes." Bob stopped at the limo. "Sir, my life started again almost six years ago, and I remember that joyous feeling as if it were yesterday. I can't wait until you also share that joy."

I opened the back door. "Well, Bob, it's nice to see that you've got your direction figured out. Just knowing where you're going puts you ahead of most people in this world." I climbed inside.

"Yes, sir." Bob got into the front. "We have a couple hours before we arrive at our headquarters. Maybe you can watch the DVD Mr. Morgan sent."

The video opened with the image of the Soul Identity logo emblazoned in gold on a dark green shield. The shield was hanging on the wall of an office. The camera panned left to a window, through which I could see a tree-lined pasture. It then zoomed in on a man sitting at a desk, his hands clasped together on an empty blotter.

The man smiled and said, "Good day, Scott. I am Archibald Morgan."

Archie looked like he was at least in his seventies with a full head of pure white hair. He wore a light green shirt and a dark green bowtie with white polka dots. His eyebrows were long and white, and his clean-shaven face had just a few wrinkles around his mouth and eyes.

Archie continued. "During the next few weeks, it is my intent to work closely with you as you review and improve Soul Identity's security procedures."

I pressed pause on the remote. "Bob, are you watching this?"

"No, sir, I'm driving."

"Can you pull over and watch this with me?"

"Yes, sir. There is a rest area coming up in a mile or so."

I waited as he drove into the parking lot. When he didn't move, I said, "Come on back here—I want to ask you questions about what we see."

He climbed in back and sat next to me.

I went to the beginning and paused when the camera was at the window. "Where is this?" I asked.

Bob studied the monitor. "That's the view out the back windows of our headquarters. We're going there now."

Good answer. "Let's move forward." I pressed play until Archie was smiling, then I paused. "Who's this guy?"

"That is Mr. Morgan, our executive overseer."

I pressed play. Archie introduced himself. Another pause. "Does it sound like him?" I asked.

"Yes, sir. That's definitely Mr. Morgan."

We continued watching the video together. Archie told us about my role as his security consultant. He gave a quick tour of the Soul Identity grounds. Then he showed us a guesthouse.

I paused the video again. "We're not staying at a hotel?"

"No, Mr. Scott, we don't stay in hotels when we visit headquarters. Soul Identity provides us private housing on the campus grounds."

"What if I want a hotel room?"

"Sir, I assure you that you will be very comfortable in the Soul Identity quarters. We have much better amenities than you would find in a hotel."

These guys were paying me twenty-four hours a day, so I figured they had the right to choose the place I slept. I nodded and hit play.

Archie resumed speaking. "George and Sue will take good care of you while you reside with us." The camera panned to the left, and a smiling fifties-something-looking couple waved at the camera.

The video reverted to the office. Archie stood next to his desk. "You are already learning about Soul Identity. I am sure Bob has even shared his physical-therapist-to-delivery-person story with you."

Bob sat up straight. "Mr. Morgan knows my testimony?"

Archie continued. "And I would guess that by now you have discovered some information from Madame Flora." He sighed. "But there is something that I must share for you to understand our urgency."

He walked behind his desk and sat down. He seemed to struggle to turn his thoughts into words. He closed his eyes and took a deep breath. Then he nodded twice, as if he made up his mind.

He stared into the camera. "Soul Identity is under attack from some very bad people. I do not know if we can survive. I need your help before we are destroyed."

The screen froze for a second, stuck on an image of Archie with a big frown on his face. Then it went blank.

Bob stared at the dark screen. He stroked the pendant under his shirt and chanted to himself.

"Are you all right?" I asked him.

"We have enemies, sir, but I didn't know Mr. Morgan was worried." He stared at me, and I could see he was working himself into a panic. He grabbed my arm. "Mr. Scott, Soul Identity cannot be destroyed. We need it. I need it." He squeezed hard. "You must help us."

As an outside security consultant, my job is limited to giving advice. I don't implement solutions. Furthermore, my clients are very creative at coming up with reasons for not following my suggestions. But explaining this to Bob wasn't going to help. So I said, "I'll try."

Bob nodded, and after a minute or two he seemed to calm down. "Thank you, Mr. Scott. I'd better get you to headquarters right away."

I watched the New England scenery flash by outside the window. There were more evergreens up here than on the Eastern Shore, and a lot more rocks and hills. I alternated between dozing and watching until we turned off the highway.

I flipped back to the GPS and zoomed in. We had reached the town of Sterling Massachusetts. I looked out the window, and saw a metal sculpture of a lamb.

Bob pointed at it. "That's Mary Sawyer's lamb, as in 'Mary had a Little Lamb.' The author was from Sterling."

I filed away the trivia. "How often do you come here?" I asked.

"Oh, maybe three or four times a year, sir," he said. "We will arrive in six minutes—would you like to put on your uniform?"

I didn't really want to change in the car. "Is it necessary?" I asked.

"Yes, sir. Otherwise I have to bring you to the guesthouse first, and as you can see," he held up his left arm and showed me his watch, "it's already two forty-five. You have a three o'clock appointment with Mr. Morgan."

I looked at the black jeans and polo shirt. "Will these clothes fit me?"

"Yes, sir."

"How do you know my size?"

He smiled. "Madame Flora told me. She's been pretty accurate in the past."

Definitely wackos. I finished changing just as we rolled up to the gate.

six

BOB FLASHED HIS MEMBERSHIP card at the guard, and the gate rolled open. We turned into a large and empty parking lot.

I couldn't see any buildings. "Where are we?" I asked.

He got out and opened my door. "Mr. Scott, it is my privilege to welcome you to the Soul Identity Headquarters."

"Can only true believers see it?"

He pointed behind me at two mounds covered with a carpet of lush green grass. "The main hall is right behind those hills."

I gestured at the empty parking lot. "Are we the only people here?"

"Of course not, sir. Hundreds of employees work in this office. The limo doesn't fit in our underground parking lot." He took a deep breath, brushed some fuzz off his pants, and straightened out a wrinkle in his shirt.

I watched his preparations. "It looks like you're getting ready for a date," I said.

"Something like that." He bent down and checked his hair in the limo's side mirror. "While you are meeting with Mr. Morgan, I will be with membership services, planning my century award ceremony."

"This is for the hundred years of service?"

He nodded. "I have to make a speech."

We drew closer, and an immense Georgian Architecture building loomed in front of us. It stood three stories tall and over a hundred feet wide. The occasional dormer window broke up the otherwise straight black roof line. White trim accented its pale yellow siding. I could see an underground garage entrance on the building's left side.

"I feel like we've stumbled into an Edgar Allen Poe story," I said.

"There's nothing scary about our headquarters, sir."

Bob sounded like he was trying to convince himself. He walked across the driveway and up the porch steps. "Let's go inside," he said.

I hurried to catch up. We entered through a tall wooden door and stood inside a large lobby. A young receptionist smiled from behind a massive oak desk across the room. "May I help you?" she called.

We walked closer, and I saw she wore a light green silk blouse and small emerald earrings. "Bob!" She jumped up from the desk and gave him a quick kiss on the lips. "I was wondering when you'd get here." She went back to her seat, her blonde ponytail bouncing behind her.

I looked at Bob. "So that's why you fixed your hair."

Bob's cheeks flamed red. "Elizabeth, this is Mr. Scott Waverly. He's got a meeting with Mr. Morgan."

Elizabeth stuck out her hand. "I'm very pleased to meet you, Mr. Waverly. Especially since your arrival brought Bob back up north. He's been avoiding me, I think."

Bob looked at me with a 'what can I do' expression on his face. "I'm sorry, Elizabeth. I've been—"

"Busy, I know." She held up her hands and mimed quotations. "Number one delivery person in the Mid-Atlantic region." She threw me a wry smile. "He's very proud of that, Mr. Waverly."

"I've noticed." I looked around the lobby. "Who are the people in all these portraits?"

Elizabeth pointed at the walls. "The current overseers are on your right, and past overseers are on your left." She pointed above her, and I saw a picture of a middle aged lady wearing a green scarf over a lime colored blouse. "That's Ann Blake up there, the depositary chief. She's also my mom." She picked up her yellow telephone. "Excuse me while I inform Mr. Morgan of your arrival."

I walked around and examined the portraits. Apparently there were only two current overseers: one painting was of Archie, looking forty years younger than he appeared in the video. The portrait of the other overseer was of a younger man barely out of his teens.

Elizabeth hung up the phone. "Mr. Morgan is ready. Bob, please escort Mr. Waverly upstairs."

As we walked through the door behind her, she called out, "And come back here after you drop him off."

The door closed, and we stood in what appeared to be an elevator lobby. I nudged Bob with my elbow. "Somebody's really happy you're in town, dude."

Bob leaned in close to my ear. "I'm scared of her mother," he whispered. "I'm afraid to get anywhere near her daughter at the office."

"Why, is Ann Blake an old battle axe?"

"Actually, I'm very nice, Mr. Waverly." A live version of the lady in the portrait above Elizabeth's desk stood next to me. She had a strong Texas drawl. Four men in spiffy dark green suits stood behind her and waited as she smiled and stuck out her hand. "Ann Blake."

"Call me Scott." I took her hand.

She squeezed hard and released.

"Do you know Bob?" I stepped back to get out of the line of fire.

"Of course I know him, and I like him too, whatever he may think. We wish we saw more of him around here." She slapped him on the shoulder. "How are you, Bob?"

He stammered out a "Good afternoon, Ms. Blake."

"You're coming for dinner at our place tomorrow night." She pointed at me. "Bring Scott with you. Be there at eight thirty sharp." She strode off with her retinue.

I smiled. "That went well."

Bob shook his head. "I'm going to be sick."

"Is her cooking that bad?"

"No, sir. She intimidates the heck out of me."

"She puts on her pants one leg at a time, just like you." I smiled. "But then you put on shoes, and she puts on cowboy boots. Maybe it's the boots that are scaring you."

"Maybe." He pressed the elevator call button and the doors opened. An ancient elevator attendant sat inside on a yellow stool. He was wearing green pants with suspenders, a white shirt, and a green cap.

"Third floor, James, we're going to Mr. Morgan's office," Bob said.

James sat up straight. "Next stop third floor. All aboard who's getting aboard." He closed the doors and the elevator hummed. It stopped, and the doors opened. "Third floor, and mind the gap as you disembark."

We got off, the elevator closed, and we stood on the marble floor of a grand foyer. "James used to be a train conductor," Bob said. "Old habits die hard."

"Was he a train conductor in this life, or in a previous life?" I asked.

"Of course this life, Mr. Scott. Nobody remembers anything from their previous lives. Except what you learn in there." He pointed to the left. "The depositary is just down that hall."

We walked to the right, made another right, and entered an open door on the left. Archie sat at the same desk, in the same pose, wearing the same smile he wore in the video. He sported a different bowtie, though: this one had green and white stripes. He stood up when we approached.

"Welcome to Soul Identity, Scott." Archie shook my hand. "Did you have a nice trip?"

"We had a great trip."

Archie turned. "Welcome back, Bob. Thank you for taking good care of our guest."

Bob nodded. "You're welcome, Mr. Morgan." He reached into his pocket and handed me a card. "Mr. Scott, here's my phone number. When you're ready to go, just give me a ring." He left.

I walked over to the window and gazed down at a green field bordered with evergreens and lined with stone walls. "This is quite a view."

Archie stood next to me. "It reminds me of stability. The view hasn't changed in the last thirty years."

I looked at him. "You've been here for thirty years?"

"More than that, I am afraid. I came to this organization sixty-four years ago, when I was twenty-one years old." He turned to me. "Did you watch the video?"

I nodded.

He pointed to the left corner of the room. I saw four comfortable looking leather chairs arranged around a low oak table. "We can sit there. Can I get you coffee?"

I sank into one of the chairs. "Coffee would be great. With cream and sweetener, please."

He picked up the yellow phone on the table. "Two coffees, Brian. A fatty fake for my guest." He hung up.

"Are you from Seattle?" I asked.

"My assistant spent a few years out there before coming back east. He insists I use his awkward names for the coffee." He frowned, and his bushy white eyebrows stuck straight out. "Let us discuss why you are here."

That sounded good to me. But then a short and slim young man walked in. "One skinny bitter and one fatty fake, as ordered." He put the cups and saucers on the table. "I also brought some cookies for your guest. They are not for you, Mr. Morgan." He laid a plate of two steaming chocolate chip cookies next to my coffee.

"Thank you, Brian," Archie said. "Do you have any more bran muffins?"

"You've had two this afternoon. Are you sure you should?"

Archie sighed. "I suppose not. Please close the door on your way out."

Brian smiled. "You betcha, Mr. Morgan." He left.

I slid my plate of cookies toward Archie. "Wanna share with me?"

He leaned forward and picked up one of the cookies. He took a bite and sank back in his chair with a sigh. "He tortures me with these cookies every time I have a visitor."

"So get a new assistant," I said.

Archie shook his head. "Brian has made himself indispensable. And my daily ration of bran muffins is probably good for me." He leaned forward and dropped his voice to barely above a whisper. "I told you I need our Internet applications audited, and I do. But the real reason you are here is to stop those who are destroying Soul Identity."

"That's what you said on the video." I crossed my legs. "But if you know who is destroying you, why do you need me? Call the cops and let them handle it."

"Because I cannot pin them down. Even with the signs all around us." He held up his hand and counted on his fingers. "Unrecovered overseers, unreported members, and misplaced deposits, just for a start."

"I'm lost."

"Let me show you." Archie walked over to his desk and opened a drawer. He withdrew a bulging yellow folder. Back at the coffee table, he rifled through it and pulled out a stack of papers. "This is what they are doing to us." He handed me a sheet.

I looked at a chart labeled "Overseer Recoveries." The line showed an early decline, then a steady rate until a precipitous drop-off on its far right. "If this was your stock price chart," I said, "people would be jumping out the windows."

He nodded. "As well they should. It is our overseer recovery rate. Each data point covers one century."

The first century showed forty overseers recovered. It dropped to seven for the next century, and then hovered between nine and eleven for the remainder, until the last one. That bar had only two.

"What's wrong with this?" I asked. "The twenty-first century is less than a decade old, and you've already had two, what are they?"

"Recoveries." Archie shook his head. "We do not use your calendar. In July we completed our twenty-five hundred and ninety-second year. That last bar is only eight years short of a century. Ninety-two years, and only two overseers recovered. We're being strangled." He handed me another sheet.

"New deposit value over the last century," I read. The chart showed a drastic falling off in the last three years.

"They're keeping the money away." Archie thrust another in my hands. "Look at our membership rates."

This chart was labeled "New members this century," and showed that relatively few members had joined in the last decade.

Archie gave me another sheet. "This is the last one, and it is by far the worst," he said.

The final chart said "Depositary withdrawals this decade." It showed a huge recent spike of activity in the last year.

"We are close to the point of insolvency," he said in a whisper.

I cycled through the four sheets again, trying to make sense of what they meant.

After a minute I glanced up. "I have no clue what a recovered overseer is," I said. "I don't know the impact of no new deposits or no new members. And I'm struggling to believe that you guys have been around for almost twenty-six hundred years."

He looked ready to interrupt, but I held up my hand.

"I do understand the threat of insolvency." I handed him the papers. "But if you want me to help, you've got to get me up to speed. I'll try really hard to suspend my disbelief."

Archie stared at me, and I stared back. After a minute he nodded. "I shall keep reminding myself that you are neither a member nor a believer." He drummed his fingers on his armchair, looking out the window. "But how can I explain?"

I sat waiting.

His expression brightened, and he stood up. "We shall start with the basics," he said. "I will show you my soul line collection in the depositary."

seven

ARCHIE LED ME TO the depositary and through its automatic steel doors. We stood in a waiting room. A lady receptionist sat on the far side behind a thick acrylic window. Archie walked up and leaned on the countertop.

"Good afternoon, Mr. Morgan." The receptionist smiled. "What can we do for you?"

Archie smiled back at her. "I would like to bring a guest to see my soul line collection."

"Sure, just fill out this waiver for him." She slid an index card-sized form under the window.

Archie filled it out and passed it back.

"Thank you," she said. "Now if we can verify your identity, you'll be all set."

Archie picked up the goggles and put them on. "Like this?"

"That's right. Now just a sec. Ok, Mr. Morgan, we have you verified."

Archie took off the goggles and straightened his hair.

The receptionist passed him a badge-sized card. "Here's your smart card, Mr. Morgan. Room number four is available." She pressed a button, and a door behind her opened. "Just through there—it's the second door on your left."

Archie inserted the card into the door of room number four, and it swung open. I heard a hiss as it closed behind us.

"The room is hermetically sealed to keep out dust and mold," Archie said.

"What about the dust and mold we just carried in?"

"That will be removed after I do this." He slid the card into a slot on the wall. "You may want to close your eyes."

I heard a low humming, and a bright light made me see red through my eyelids. I felt the air swirl around me, and I smelled some sort of disinfectant. The humming stopped and the bright light switched off.

I opened my eyes. "Now what?"

"Now we wait for them to deliver my collection," he said. He pulled out of his pocket a small stack of laminated cards, wrapped with a rubber band. "But take a seat and let me give you a taste of our history."

I sat down.

"I told you that we started almost twenty-six hundred years ago, correct?"

I nodded.

He slid the rubber band off the stack of cards and handed me the first one. It showed a bust of a bearded man with curly black hair. Underneath the picture I read, "Thales: Soul Identity founder, circa 580 BCE."

I flipped the card over. The back showed a map labeled "Anatolia (Asia Minor)." It appeared to cover the lands in the northeast corner of the Mediterranean Sea. A small star about two thirds down Turkey's western coast marked the city of Miletus.

I flipped back to Thales' face. "This is the man who started it all?" I asked.

Archie nodded. "Thales was a philosopher, one of the Seven Sages of Greece, and a businessman. Aristotle called him the father of modern science. He lived in Turkey, and he mastered Greek mythology, Egyptian mathematics and astronomy, and the ancient Phoenician and Jewish legends.

"We like to tell a story of how Thales made a fortune by cornering the market on olive oil. He bought all the olive presses in his city after he predicted there was going to be a bumper year for olives."

"I like this guy," I said.

Archie smiled. "I like him too," he said. "Now when Thales was studying in Egypt, he discovered a band of priests who had spent centuries painting exquisitely detailed images of people's eyes on papyrus. These priests claimed if you calculated the difference in the patterns of a person's eyes, the difference would exist at most once per generation."

Archie handed me the next card, and I saw a painting of a group of priests sitting cross-legged under a tent in front of a pyramid.

"The mainstream priests persecuted the band because they did not teach that a glorious afterlife awaited each good person," Archie said. "Thales persuaded the group to return with him to Miletus."

"So what did Thales do with them?"

He smiled. "This is where we enter the picture. Thales set up a new society which he called *Psychen Euporos*, which roughly translates from ancient Greek to *Resourceful in Soul*."

He handed me the next card, and I saw Soul Identity's logo, with "Psychen Euporos original shield" written below. So this was the original name of Soul Identity.

Archie flipped the card over, and I saw a picture of a large stone building with huge pillars holding it up. "That was our first depositary," he said. "Thales realized the business value of being able to connect people between their past and future lives, and he established Psychen Euporos as a way people could invest in their future selves."

Thales seemed to have been all about the money, much like Soul Identity acted today.

Archie smiled at me. "Our historians believe that Thales also had a personal reason to found our organization—he had no children, and he wanted to pass down his accumulated scientific wisdom to his future self." He let out a chuckle. "We would not call it wisdom today—Thales believed that everything in the world was made from water."

"It's nice to see the ancients didn't know everything." I held up my hand. "Before you continue," I said. "Thales believed his future selves would inherit his characteristics, and I've talked to Bob and others—they also expect their future selves will be like them."

"Most of our members expect that." Archie leaned forward. "What is your question?"

"Are they right?"

Archie sat back. "As you might imagine, we have performed centuries of research on soul line inheritance. And the results are inconclusive. We know for sure that one's memories and physical characteristics are not inherited, but our writings are filled with anecdotal evidence of passed-down intelligence and personality traits."

I thought about what Archie didn't say. "So you can't prove it," I said.

"We cannot. Other than the soul identity, that is. Anything beyond that, and what it means, is left to each member to work out for themselves."

Bob had also hinted that Soul Identity didn't delve into the spiritual realm. "You're telling me Soul Identity forces no special beliefs on its members?"

Archie was silent for a moment. "Not all overseers have felt like me. In fact, throughout my tenure, I have fought many battles against those trying to force their own views on the rest of us. But these days, the business of Soul Identity is business. We let the churches run the spiritual side."

I nodded. "Thanks. Let's get back to Thales."

He handed me another card, and I saw a picture of two armies on a battlefield. Instead of fighting, most of the soldiers stood pointing in the sky at a solar eclipse.

"Thales advised the Lydian general Croesus, who was embroiled in a five year war with the Medes. Thales predicted an eclipse of the sun, and he told Croesus to plan for a battle. When the eclipse darkened the day, the Medes and Lydians spontaneously put down their weapons and made peace."

"Good news for Thales," I said.

"Yes, and even better news for Psychen Euporos," Archie said. "With the war over, we flourished. Thales had a motto—*sophotaton chronos aneuriskei gar panta*—which means *time is wisest because it discovers everything*. We still live by that motto—we mark the time and aid the discoveries by keeping the soul lines intact."

If nothing else, the concept was fascinating.

Archie handed me the next card, and I saw man with shoulder-length hair, wearing a white robe and sandals. Underneath it said "Cyrus the Great, circa 550 BCE."

He continued his tale. "Over the next thirty-five years, Croesus sided with the Medes and together they fought the Persians, until they lost to Cyrus the Great. Cyrus spared Miletus and gave it favorable terms, mainly because he and most of the Mede and Persian nobles became members of Psychen Euporos."

I was getting overloaded with history. "When do we get to the overseers?" I asked.

"Only one more card," he said. "Thales died in 543, leaving behind a solid set of Greek and Persian members. The organization was wealthy, and many people had deposited riches for their future selves." He paused. "But when Thales died, Psychen Euporos floundered. The priests kept care of the images and the investments, but the organization lacked a leader."

I thought about this. "Without somebody driving a vision, no organization lasts for very long," I said.

"That is correct," he said. "We drifted while Persia grew. Cyrus captured Babylon in 539, and a generation later Darius married Cyrus's daughter and became the King of Kings." He handed me another card, this one with a man with a long beard and a gold cap on his head. It was labeled "Darius the Great, 522 BCE."

The other side of the card showed a map labeled "Persian Empire." It extended from Egypt to Romania in the west to the India-Pakistan border in the east.

"Darius and his court joined Psychen Euporos and invested heavily in their own soul lines," Archie said. "He uprooted the priests and moved us east to Babylon, and there we stayed until Alexander the Great came through two hundred years later."

"Was Darius an overseer?" I asked.

"No, although he was a great financier and organizer, he was too busy running his vast empire. However, Darius did create the institution of the overseers." Archie smiled. "The best part about having a King of Kings as a member was that we had a chance to find some matching identities."

"How's that?" I asked.

"Remember the original eye images?"

"The ones Thales brought with the Egyptian priests?"

"Correct. Darius had the priests train thousands of mystics how to read soul identities. He sent these mystics out with copies of the original images to the far reaches of his empire and charged them to search for matches."

I tried to picture how Darius had all the millions of people in his empire read. "It must have been a massive undertaking," I said.

Archie nodded. "The mystics spent nine years. Altogether they uncovered thirty-five matched identities and sent the people to Babylon." He spread the remaining cards onto the desk, and I saw pictures of farmers, fishermen, and philosophers, old men, young women, and even a baby.

"They were forcibly sent," he said. "Darius put them in school to learn Persian and Greek, then castrated the men and plucked the hair out of the women's heads."

I winced. "Why would he do that?"

"To focus them on the organization, and to keep them docile and out of the harems. They became our first overseers. Their job was to administer and guide the organization for all time."

I shuffled through the cards on the table. The women in the images had hair—maybe they wore wigs. "So the first overseers were the people whose soul identities matched the ones from the ancient Egyptian paintings," I said.

"That is correct, Scott. I am a proud member of the soul line of one of those original overseers, a young woman from Scythia." He plucked one of the cards off the desk and handed it to me.

I stared at the current head of this twenty-six hundred year old organization—a man who believed he was the reincarnation of an ancient Egyptian and a Scythian woman whose picture I held in my hand. "Bob told me he had an eight person soul line," I said. "How long is yours?"

"Not very long, I am afraid. I am only the fourth member in my line. Either we missed finding my predecessors along the way, or I have a wandering soul." He put the card back on the table. "The last member lived over two thousand years ago. I caused quite a stir when my dormant overseer line was recovered."

"Does that happen often?"

He shook his head. "The recoveries are usually well distributed. Each of the thirty-five overseer soul lines has been recovered several times."

But none recently, according to the chart he had shown me in his office.

"I think I'm following," I said. I tapped the table. "But we didn't come into this itty bitty room so you could tell me this story. We could have done that in your office. How long does it take to bring up your soul line collection?"

Archie looked at his watch. "It should only be a few more minutes. It would have been faster if I had thought to warn them of my visit." He gathered up the cards, put the rubber band back around them, and slipped them into his pocket.

"What happened to the mystics?" I asked.

"They became our recruiters and soul seekers. We pay commissions to those who bring in new members and find soul matches."

Something clicked. "Like Madame Flora," I said.

He nodded.

Madame Flora did tell me that her family had been involved with the organization for a long time. But was every mystic involved? I shook my head. "Are you telling me that all the palmists and fortune tellers in the world are Soul Identity employees?"

"Good heavens, no. We do not hire them as employees."

Not quite an answer to my question, but I let it slide.

Archie continued. "More interesting than the mystics are the numbers of priests and psychologists who send us recruits."

How could he possibly expect me to believe in the existence of this vast and secret network? "This sounds too big," I said.

"Soul Identity has millions of active members, most of whom keep very quiet about their involvement."

Now why would they keep their membership a secret? I scratched my head. "If it really is so big, somebody's gotta be talking about it."

He looked at me. "We tell our members that only harm comes from sharing with outsiders."

Good point. Whose children would understand Dad leaving his fortune to himself? And who would invite scrutiny into an inheritance they received based on something in their eyes?

A white door set flush in the back of the room slid open, and a young man dressed in a dark green uniform wheeled in a small service cart. "Your soul line collection, sir." He held out a clipboard, which Archie signed. "I'll leave you alone," the young man said. "Take your card from the wall when ready to go, and I'll come back and return your collection to the vaults."

We watched him shut the door on his way out.

"I have not rummaged through my soul line collection for a good while," Archie said. He leaned over the cart, closed his eyes, and inhaled deeply, holding it in for a few seconds before exhaling.

"Checking for mold?" I asked.

"To be completely candid, maybe I am hoping for a little extra connection with my previous selves."

I nodded. "There seems to be a bit more spirituality involved than you like to admit, isn't there?"

Archie looked away for a moment. "When you dig through the layers and reach the core of our innermost desires," he said, "we all want to connect with the supernatural. We all want what we do to matter. Being connected in a soul line, knowing that you are the current link in the chain between the past and the future, makes you part of something so significant that it feels sacred and even holy."

I was feeling uncomfortable. The idea of people believing in actual bridges between themselves and those living centuries before and after them intrigued me. And the ways that Archie and Bob expressed their faith in these bridges both fascinated and moved me. But at the same time, I was intruding on their private and deep-set convictions, encouraging them to share with me while not sharing my own thoughts.

"Archie, I want to tell you something before we go any further."

He looked at me for a minute. "You are about to tell me that you do not believe in all this silly stuff," he said.

Right on. "I was going to try to say it nicely, but yeah, that's the gist of it."

He nodded. "Your skepticism is exactly what I am counting on. A believer will never be able to find and root out the treachery in our organization."

Now I was curious. "And how were you so sure that I wouldn't believe?"

His eyes twinkled. "When you sent me the eye images of the bluefish, I knew I was dealing with the real thing—a true skeptic. Welcome aboard, Scott."

"Wait—you knew it was a bluefish?"

"Of course," he said. "We have been looking at eyes for almost twenty-six hundred years. Our researchers have conducted many studies to determine if we can spot identities in other species."

"And can you?"

"No, we cannot. Only humans have soul identities."

"If you can't spot the identity, how did you know it was a bluefish?"

"Besides humans, all animals within each species share a single identity," he said. "You sent us an identity with four small triangles, arranged at one, three, seven, and nine o'clock—a Chesapeake Bay bluefish."

That did match with what I saw with my own program.

I pointed at the cart. "What do you have in there? Let's give my non-belief a real run for its money."

He chuckled and lifted out a flat wooden box. "My soul line proof papers." He opened it up and carefully pulled out four large sheets of paper sealed inside clear and rigid plastic covers. He handed me the first sheet. "This one has my eyes and my identity."

I looked at the sheet. It was about fifteen inches square. I saw two colored photographs of Archie's irises, each six inches in diameter. There were pencil lines radiating from each photo like the points on a compass.

"This was done with a black and white photographic reader," Archie said. "Our seeker then hand colored the images. It took thirty minutes to read each of my eyes. This was a step up from the previous approach, which took an hour to draw each iris."

I held the drawing up in front of Archie. "They do look like your eyes." The vibrant blues, yellows, and grays matched perfectly. I laid the sheet onto the table and pointed at the bottom circle. "What's this?"

"My soul identity. After the images of the eyes are accurate and complete, the seeker records the differences in the shapes and colors between the two images and puts them in the circle underneath."

I examined the identity, which seemed to be calculated on only a portion of the eye. "You only use the middle band of the iris?"

He nodded. "Depending on the light, the pupil can obscure the inner third, and the eyelids sometimes hide the outer third. The middle band gives enough unique data for the calculation."

"And these fifty or so circles, diamonds, swirls, and triangles are what made you an overseer?"

"They are. Let me show you the other sheets, and it will make sense." Archie slid the next sheet in front of me.

I looked at the iris images on top. "This person had dark brown eyes, and it's a painting, though pretty faded. Who is it?"

"Liu Shing. The previous overseer in my soul line. He lived in China twenty-one hundred years ago." He pointed at the right hand image. "It is not the color that counts, but the difference. Watch." He reached under the table and flipped a switch, causing the tabletop to light up. "If I line up the bottom circles on our light table, you will see what I mean."

He lined up the plastic sheets, and I saw that the identity images matched up perfectly.

Then I got it. The chances of two people sharing fifty or more same-shape and identical-location marks were astronomically slim. These guys were really onto something here.

I looked up and nodded. "Now I'm impressed."

He laid the next sheet on top of the other two. "I am not done. This was the first overseer under Darius, the girl from Scythia whose picture I showed you."

Her soul identity matched the other two.

"And this," he put the last sheet on top, "is the original Egyptian painting, person unknown."

I looked at the composite image made by overlaying the four bottom circles. There was no question; the images and their locations on the four sheets of paper matched perfectly.

Archie stared at me. "You're not convinced, are you?"

"Not yet."

He nodded. "Let us go back to my office." He put the sheets back in the box and the box back in the cart. Then he pulled the smart card from the wall. We waited until the delivery person came and rolled away the cart.

Back in his office, Archie settled into his leather chair. "You were not convinced," he said.

I had been thinking about this as we walked back. "The technology is fine," I said, "but I have questions on the process. Let's start with the match. I don't know if the seekers did the reading blindly, or if they had a target identity and they were forcing a match."

"Our seekers learn to construct a rough identity in their minds," he said. "They may check this against our catalog of long lost matches—these have the biggest rewards—and if they think they have a hit, they perform a full reading."

I nodded. "How do you protect against fraud?"

"Our rules force every match to be validated by our match committee."

That was a good start. Now to test its limits. "What's stopping a reader from building a fake set of eyes that matches a well known identity?" I asked.

He smiled. "The match committee validation compares the eyes of the person with the iris images. No fake eyes are allowed."

I nodded. "How big is this match committee?"

"Three members. All three must be in agreement for the match to count."

I thought about this. "If I wanted to get a false match done, I'd have to make sure the seeker and all three members of the match committee were in on it. Four people would need to work together to fake a match."

"That's correct." He smiled. "We have a good system."

Not so fast, partner. I pointed at him. "But think about this—it only takes a single person to invalidate a match."

Archie seemed disturbed by that suggestion. "Do you think that has been happening?"

I shrugged. "We have lots of areas to explore before we start making conclusions. For instance, how do you know for sure that the eye images actually belong to the person you ascribe them to?"

"Because the match committee validates the images against the real eyes."

"But how do you know that the person is who he says he is?"

He paused, then shook his head. "I guess we really don't know for sure."

I had lots of work to do here.

"Archie," I said, "at first blush, it seems you have a system that works when all the players are honest and trustworthy. Like the way the Internet worked in the early days."

He frowned. "What does the Internet have to do with Soul Identity?"

"As it connected more people and organizations, the value of its data increased, and the trustworthiness of that data decreased. The result? Lots of security problems. Lots of theft. Lots of anonymous bad people wreaking havoc on an innocent system."

"Then they should shut the Internet down."

"That's one solution, I guess," I said. "It's pretty drastic, though. That same Internet enables great advances, saves money, and enriches lives. What happens is that the Internet evolves over time. It keeps up with its changing environment."

Archie shook his head. "We do not evolve. We use the same overseer rules that Darius established in Babylon. Other than updates in the way we perform readings, little has changed in the way we provide oversight."

Hadn't these guys heard the expression "evolve or die?"

"I definitely have my work cut out for me," I said.

"You do. Remember your real goal is to find and stop the bad people before they break us. Security improvements are good, but they are not the priority."

I thought about the best place for me to start. "You brought me in to audit your security policies around your new Internet launch," I said. "Why don't I start by examining the new system? Chances are the bad guys are all over it."

"Good idea," He picked up his yellow telephone. "Brian, please ask Val to come to my office." He hung up the phone. "Val runs the new system development. She is visiting us this week to make sure we have the right equipment in place. She can tell you all about it and answer any questions you may have."

"Great," I said. "It's five o'clock now. How late do you guys work?"

"Val works until the wee hours of the morning."

They were paying me around the clock, so who was I to complain?

I needed to know how much he wanted me to share with his staff. "Archie, how open can I be about what I'm doing here?"

He clasped his hands together. "I have informed my staff that you are here to audit the Internet programs. I also told them that you will be looking for potential security breaches."

"Should I be open about your fears of the organization being attacked?"

He frowned. "If they bring it up, by all means please discuss it. But they probably all think I am a paranoid, out-of-touch old man."

I could see how they'd get that impression.

"Is there anybody I should avoid in my questionings?" I asked.

He thought for a minute, then shook his head.

Brian knocked on the door and cracked it open. "Val said she's too busy to come up here," he said. "Should I escort Mr. Waverly to the dungeon?"

"Yes, thank you, Brian." Archie looked at me. "Let us meet tomorrow morning at nine."

eight

"THE DUNGEON SOUNDS OMINOUS," I said as Brian and I headed for the elevator. "You're not going to torture me, are you?"

"No, Mr. Waverly, we only torture on Fridays." Brian flashed a thin smile. "It's a windowless computer lab in the basement of a musty old building. What else would you call it?"

We reached the elevator and he pushed the button. "You don't need me to go down there with you," he said. "Tell the attendant to take you to the basement. The dungeon's on your left." He turned and walked up the hall.

The elevator door opened. James sat on his stool, and I smiled as I got in. "Does your train make a stop in the basement?" I asked.

"Of course it does," he said. "All aboard!" James threw a switch and the elevator dropped.

Where the third floor was marble and chandeliers, the basement was vinyl and fluorescents. My sneakers squeaked on the floor as I walked down the hall. I smiled at a video camera in the corner, then rang the doorbell at the end of the hallway.

A kid with greasy long hair, large glasses, more than a few pimples, and a dirty light green lab jacket poked his head out from behind the metal door. "You need something?" he asked.

"I'm here to see Val."

He pulled the door open. "Come on in."

I followed him down a hallway. He paused in front of a small office. "Some dude's here to see you, Val," he said.

"Thanks, Forty," she said without looking up.

Forty left, and I stepped into the office. "Your guys go by numbers here in the dungeon?" I asked.

"He once won the Nintendo championship in a record forty seconds." Val had a slight Eastern European accent, and she spoke as she typed on her laptop. "The name stuck, I guess." She looked up and smiled at me for the very first time.

I don't remember much about what Val and I discussed that first hour. Later she reminded me that she gave me an overview of the system and showed me its architecture and implementation plan. She said that I even asked some questions. But all I saw were her locks of auburn hair and her big blue eyes that grabbed my gaze and held it until I felt dizzy. All I heard was her soft accent and her magical laugh. And all I thought was how lucky I was to spend a few minutes in her presence.

Usually I'm fine talking with pretty girls. But usually these girls aren't geeks like me. Just thinking about the possibility of having meaningful conversations with somebody so attractive turned my mind to mush.

I stood up, right in the middle of her explanation of some item on her Gantt chart. I had to clear my head and start focusing, because for the last few minutes I had daydreamed about how nice it would be to spend a summer weekend with Val on the bay. I had no clue what she was talking about, and I desperately wanted to impress her. "I'm sorry," I said, "I need to take a quick break."

"Come back soon," she said as she swiveled her chair around to face her laptop.

Damn, the lady was all business. I found the bathroom, and I brushed my hair with my fingers and made sure my teeth were clean. I exhaled into my cupped palms and sniffed it to check my breath. I even made some faces in the mirror: eyebrows up in a questioning look, bedroom eyes while smiling. Why did I feel like a high school student out to impress the new girl?

I stopped in the pantry. Forty was sitting with some other guys at a table. He smirked and walked over. "Is this your first meeting with our goddess manager?"

I nodded.

"Don't worry," he said. "You'll survive the experience. The first time Val visited the dungeon, I fell off that chair. Spilled my Coke all over my lab coat." He nodded at my black shirt and jeans. "We don't get many contractors in the dungeon—what are you here for?"

"Mr. Morgan wants me to audit the security controls on your new system. Val's been explaining it to me, but honestly, I'm having a hard time paying attention."

He nodded. "Here's my trick. Look at the papers, the wall, the white board, the clock. Anywhere but into those big blue eyes. Once you fall in there, you can't climb out. Think Medusa, man. You'll turn to stone if she catches your eye."

"Good advice." I walked into the hallway.

"Remember, avoid the eyes or it's game over," he called.

I stood at the door of Val's office and peeked inside.

She looked up. "Ready to continue?"

"Um, Val, would you mind if we rewind fifteen minutes or so?"

She frowned. "What's wrong?"

I took a deep breath. "I've never met anybody like you," I said. "And I can't concentrate on what you're showing me. You're so gorgeous, and yet you're speaking geek language." I slumped against the door. "I can't believe I just said that."

Val walked over and stood in front of me. She was just about my height. She wore a serious, almost shocked, look on her face. I winced and closed my eyes and waited for the slap.

Then I felt her hand softly caress my cheek, and before I could react, it was gone.

I opened my eyes, and Val smiled at me. "You're so sweet," she said.

I stuck out my hand. "We need some proper introductions. Scott Waverly, software security guy."

She shook my hand. "Valentina Nikolskaya, software girl."

We shook for a while, smiling at each other. Then I reluctantly pulled my hand free. "Back to your design. But I have a few questions first."

"What about?"

"When I went to the depositary with Archie—"

Val raised her eyebrows. "You two are on a first name basis?"

I nodded. "Anyway, he showed me his soul line collection—"

She leaned forward. "You saw his collection? What does he have in there?"

I shrugged. "He only showed me his soul line proof sheets. Then we left."

She sat back.

I continued. "To get to his collection, Archie had to put on these goggles. I'm guessing that they authenticated him."

"Not him—just his soul identity."

I thought about that. "I'm trying to understand why you build your systems around soul identities instead of around people."

"Because that's how everything is tied together. Mr. Morgan, for example, shares his soul identity with three previous overseers."

"So he claims."

She rested her chin in her palms. Her fingers played with some free strands of her hair. "And now I know you're not a believer," she said.

Yikes. Anybody else, and I would have laughed and said, "Of course not." But how could I say that to this beautiful angel sitting in front of me?

I laughed and said, "Of course not." Hopefully the angel was a big girl.

"This has got to be tough for you." She frowned. "You must wonder how anybody can be crazy enough to believe their soul can be identified."

"And that it gets recycled in the future. I'm sorry, Val. I don't believe."

She shrugged. "You'll get there. We all do, sooner or later." Then she smiled, and I felt a flush spread across my shoulder blades. "Maybe I can help."

"Wow." All sorts of ways she could help flashed through my mind.

"But first I can explain why we use the soul identity to tie our applications together," she said. "Let's say Mr. Morgan wants to collect all the lessons he's learned, bundle them up into a big book, and pass them on to his next self. He checks his book into the depositary, and it goes into his soul line collection."

I nodded.

"After he dies, we find the next person matching his identity. This new person won't know anything about Mr. Morgan until he opens the collection."

"And finds the big book of lessons," I said. "Only then will he know about his soul's past lives."

"You've got it—we identify people by their soul identities so we can thread the lifetimes together." She smiled. "Make sense?"

I nodded again. "Have you ever had two people simultaneously share a soul identity?"

"Never. It's not possible."

I scrunched up my face. "'Not possible' sounds more like a faith statement than a scientific fact."

She chewed on that for a minute. "I suppose it does. But so far all the empirical evidence we've collected throughout the ages supports my faith."

It sounded a lot more plausible when she said it.

"Okay, let's talk money," I said. "I'm assuming that you keep track of each time something's checked in and out of the depositary."

She nodded. "We preserve the items and invest the money. And at the end of each year, we tally up the value of each account and keep one percent as our fee."

I decided Val could help me nail down the financial side. "Let's say I deposit one thousand dollars—what happens next?"

"First of all, your recruiter gets a one percent commission on your deposit."

"There goes ten bucks. What's next?"

"We invest the remaining nine hundred ninety. Let's say we have a good year and raise the account's value to one thousand twenty dollars by the end of the year."

"Soul Identity takes their fee of ten dollars and twenty cents, right?"

She nodded.

"Do that for a few hundred years, and my future carrier will be rich," I said.

She smiled. "That's the idea."

"Can I get my account balance from the depositary?"

Val nodded. "All members get an account transaction report each year, personally delivered to them."

That explained Bob's job. "Now let's say it's two hundred years later," I said. "I'm long gone, and some soul seeker finds my identity hanging out inside of somebody else. Does the soul seeker get a commission?"

"They get one percent of the account value."

"That could be quite a lot of money."

"I've seen commissions in the hundreds of thousands of dollars, and I've heard that they've gone into the millions."

Talk about a temptation for the overseers and whoever works in that depositary. With funds like this floating around, and the chances of getting caught so low because most of the clients were dead, how could they possibly expect to prevent fraud?

I shook my head. "This could easily turn into quite a racket, Val."

She sighed. "It can only become a racket if the systems don't work. My job is to make sure they're perfect."

"And my job is to make sure they're secure. That makes us partners."

She flashed me a huge smile, and I felt a tingle rush through my body.

"If you keep smiling like that, you're going to have to keep on repeating yourself," I said.

She cranked up her smile's volume, then glanced at her watch. "It's seven thirty—you want to get some dinner?"

Yes yes yes! "I'd love to," I said. "Do you want to ride in my limousine?" I don't know why I thought that would impress her.

Val shook her head. "I have wheels, so you can come with me. Where are you staying?"

"The guesthouse."

"Okay. I need a few minutes to wrap up. What if we meet out front of the building in a half hour?"

I walked backward out the door, keeping my eyes on her as long as I could. I backed right into Forty, knocking him over.

"Dude, watch where you're going!" He scrambled back to his feet. "Hey, Scott." He peeked into the office and dropped his voice to a whisper. "Did you avoid the eyes?"

I shook my head, smiling.

"And you're still alive?"

I shrugged, smiling even wider.

"Head over heels, huh?"

I nodded.

"Poor bastard. Let me know when you need rescuing. I have some experience in these matters."

I shook my head. "Not in a million years."

nine

BOB BROUGHT ME TO the guesthouse we saw in Archie's video. The smiling couple, George and Sue, showed me my quarters. Bob was right; it was better than a hotel. I had a bedroom, office, bathroom, and a huge flat panel TV screen in what George called the gadget room. I wanted to rush back and meet Val for dinner, and I disappointed George by not letting him show me each gadget. After I promised to go through a demonstration session in the morning, I got them to leave, and then I hurried and changed out of the black contractor uniform and into my normal blue jeans.

Bob drove me back to the main building. I would have walked, but he wanted to make sure I knew the way. "Did you have a good day?" he asked.

"I found out more history. Soul Identity's almost twenty-six hundred years old."

"That's twice as old as my own soul line." Bob shook his head. "People with lines that long must be the luckiest people in the world."

"Thirteen hundred years seems like nothing to sneeze at," I said. "Does that make you luckier than those just starting their lines?"

He seemed to ponder this. "I don't know. I sometimes feel less important around those who have longer lines." He glanced over at me. "One of the delivery people in Baltimore has a soul line dating back two thousand years. You wouldn't believe how much attention he gets at our monthly meetings."

"Everybody listens to his advice?"

Bob nodded. "Nobody dares make a decision unless he agrees with it."

"How old is this guy?"

"He's twenty-eight. He's been with us for only two years, and his line has only thirty years of total service."

"Is yours the next oldest soul line, after him?"

"No, sir. There are other delivery people with older lines than mine. Why do you ask?"

"I thought maybe you had lost your position as top dog and you weren't quite over it yet."

Bob looked at me. "Sir, I am the best delivery person in the Mid-Atlantic region. They're all pretty much jealous of me."

"Even though your soul line is shorter than theirs?"

Bob didn't answer right away. "I suppose they are jealous," he said, "even with my shorter soul line." He was silent again. "But I still wish mine was longer."

The Soul Identity headquarters was in front of us. "I've got a ride home, so I'll see you some time tomorrow," I said.

Bob drove off and left me in the dark. Twilight had ended; the half moon still shone, but it sat low on the horizon and threw long shadows off the evergreens. The air was cooler and drier than back in Maryland, and I enjoyed the pine-scented breeze as I stepped up onto the porch and sat on a wooden rocking chair.

The wind carried the faint sounds of a man's voice. I stopped rocking. The man was talking on a cell phone, and as he got closer, I could make out what he said. "Yes, he's here. Bob dropped him off this afternoon." Then, "He's currently at the guesthouse...No, he doesn't seem to know." A long pause. "Yes, sir, I'll do it just like you said...No sir, he won't know. I'll be very careful." Another pause. "Yes, sir, the same time tomorrow."

I heard gravel crunch on a pathway next to the porch, and I sat still. The man snapped his phone shut. I tried to make out any identifying features, but it was too dark. He walked around the corner toward the underground garage and out of my sight.

So the games had begun. I smiled. This contract had started off pretty interesting; throw in a potential problem from some bad guys plus a little spice from Val, and I was going to have a lot of fun.

A minute later, a motorcycle rolled up the front driveway. The driver pulled off a helmet and shook out a mane of dark red hair.

I stepped off the porch. "When you said wheels, I assumed you meant four of them."

Val unhooked a black helmet and tossed it to me. I got on behind her. I looked for some handles, and decided her hips looked more inviting. I hooked my fingers into the belt loops of her jeans. "You changed at work?" I asked.

"Yeah, it's better than driving in slacks." She patted her bag slung around her shoulder. "This is big enough for my laptop and a pair of pants."

We cleared the main gate and screamed down the back roads. I leaned forward and shouted, "Where're we headed?"

"I've been thinking about a grinder all day," she shouted back. "Is that okay?"

"Sure, but what's a grinder?"

"You'll see!" We drove past a 'thickly settled' sign and weaved down a hill and into the center of Sterling.

Val pulled up to a sub shop. We clipped our helmets to the sides of the bike. "We'll get our grinders to go," she said.

We walked into the shop. The guy behind the counter smiled. "Hey, Val."

"Hi Jerry, I've been craving one of your everything grinders." She glanced at me. "Make it two, Scott needs to experience this."

"Two everything grinders coming right up." Jerry smiled at me. "They're wicked good."

"So a grinder is a sub?" I asked.

He nodded.

"What's in it?"

He gestured at the various meats, cheeses, and veggies under his glass countertop. "Everything."

"And it's wicked good." Val winked at me.

"I can't wait." I grabbed two bottles of iced tea. "You want anything else?"

"We'll be stuffed after the grinders," she said. "Thanks, Jerry," she called as we left the shop.

"So where do we eat these everything grinders?" I asked.

She handed me the bag. "We'll drive to a magical place."

Val pulled to the side of a back road fifteen minutes later. We sat in a forest of tall pine trees.

I removed my helmet. "What's next? A magic carpet?"

Val laughed. "No, silly. We use magic shoes to climb the hill." She wheeled the bike behind a rock.

"Have you done this before?"

Val nodded and started up the path.

We avoided the tree roots that seemed to reach out and grab at our feet. The moon had almost set, and it was pretty dark. We made it to the top after ten minutes.

A large granite boulder towered over us. She walked around to the other side. "Over this way," she called.

I came around the rock, but I didn't see her.

"Up here." Val smiled down at me. "This is the magic spot. Hand me the grinders and pull yourself up."

I passed the bag and climbed up next to her. We sat on a ledge of rock above the trees overlooking a valley. The setting moon illuminated the treetops, and its reflection danced on the rippled surface of a reservoir. White steeples pointed up from churches nestled in sleepy town centers.

"It's breathtaking," I said. "You come here often?"

"Is that a pickup line?"

"No. Well, maybe."

Val hugged her knees. "I found this place last summer when I was riding by. I climbed the path and fell in love with the view. Now I come here when I'm stuck on a bug and I need to sort it out."

I chuckled. "A true geek. I also have a thinking place back at home. It's on the water."

"Where's that?"

"Maryland. On the Chesapeake Bay. The Eastern Shore, if you've heard of it."

She laughed. "Of course I've heard of it. I live in Annapolis."

I stared at her. "You've got to be kidding. That's just across the bridge from me."

She smiled. "Told you this was a magical place. Let's eat our grinders."

I pulled them out of the bag. "Everything, huh?"

"Jerry puts a tiny bit of everything in them. Don't get too attached to a mouthful, because each one is different."

"Is that the draw? Not too much of any one thing?"

"No, it's the mixes I like." Val took a bite. "See, I just had salami and cream cheese. I think." She swallowed. "That wasn't bad. It could have been horrible, but it's only one bite, and the next one may be great."

I tried my own. I tasted sweet pickle and some unrecognizable deli meat. "Interesting," I said. "I don't know what it was, but it doesn't really matter, I guess."

"You're getting it."

We ate in silence for a minute. Then I caught her eye. "So you're a member of Soul Identity?"

She nodded. "For two years now."

"How'd you get involved?"

"One of my co-workers was approached by a soul seeker, and I went to the reading with her. She wasn't a match, but the idea of starting my own soul line fascinated me. I signed up, and then they recruited me to run their development."

"I'm also intrigued," I said. Mostly because of the present company, but I wasn't going to tell her that. "Somehow you made a leap from interest to involvement."

Val was silent for a minute. "You know, I was born in the Soviet Union, in its dying years. I was nine when the wall came down. Do you remember that?"

"Vaguely. I was twelve. That makes you twenty-nine?"

"Almost thirty. Those years were tough. I remember how little food we had to eat, and how nobody was paid. Everybody in my city hated the words *glasnost* and *perestroika*. We all craved the stability we had lost."

"We were taught that you Soviets used to stand six hours in line for a sausage and a loaf of bread, and it all changed after the evil empire collapsed."

"It did change," she said. "But not for the better, not at first. My parents were history teachers, and they struggled to recover from the shock that they had spent their lives teaching a pack of lies. My father researched some Stalin-era information, only to learn that his parents were loaded onto a Volga river ferry and drowned. Just to meet some quota."

"Yuck."

"They are now happy with their new life in Mother Russia. They have joined the Orthodox Church, and with the extra money I send them, they have a comfortable life. But I want more."

"More what?"

She picked up an acorn and tossed it over the ledge, and then she turned to face me. "I want to make a difference and leave a legacy of improvement behind. By starting a soul line, I can affect lives far into the future."

"But can't you do that as a parent?"

"Maybe I can, and hopefully I will. But it only took one evil person and some stupid bureaucrats to prevent me from ever knowing my grandparents—I'd like some extra insurance. A soul line is a safe way to project my legacy."

We sat silently. I thought about how Val had some pretty deep waters running under her beautiful top layer.

She studied my face. "What's your difficulty in believing in Soul Identity?" she asked.

I took a deep breath. "Here's what I see. They claim to help me plan for my future. They use a massive army of recruiters and seekers to grow, and I would guess that many people turn over their money in exchange for simple ego stroking. They seem to have no oversight, which means the potential for corruption is huge."

She smiled. "It sounds like any organized religion, doesn't it?"

She had a point. "I guess there's not much difference," I said. "Both require believers who have faith in the message and in the system."

She nodded. "That's what I see too. Each has believers who have found a purpose in life. Each has members who are uncommitted. And each has bad guys who are only in it for selfish or sick reasons."

We sat there and looked out over the valley. "Now that you put it that way, Soul Identity doesn't seem so strange," I said.

She smiled at me. "Actually, the premise is much simpler here. Your soul identity is unique, and somebody else gets it after you die. All the rest is added in later."

"Added in?"

She nodded. "That everything grinder you just ate? Soul Identity is like that. The bun is the basic premise, but it can be filled with lots of beliefs—some that fit well, and others that are vile."

Bob did mention that various churches have formed over the years, each adding different meanings to the base message.

Simple or not, the premise was still a big stretch for me. "I wish I could sit here and tell you I'm there with you," I said. "But I'm too much of a skeptic to believe this quickly."

Val nodded.

"Though I've gotta tell you," I said, "I like what you're doing. Creating a positive legacy is a really nice thought. So much more unselfish than thinking 'I want to live forever' or 'I don't want to burn.'"

She frowned. "Don't make me into too much of a saint. I don't want to become untouchable."

God forbid that happened; I'd been fantasizing about the touching part all evening long.

She took a deep breath and looked me in the eye. "I'm twenty-nine years old," she said. "I got married at twenty-four, and it lasted three years. No kids. I have an apartment in Annapolis. No pets, no roommate, and no significant other."

I raised my eyebrows.

She patted my knee with her palm. "Your turn," she said.

So she was raising the bar. "I'm thirty-two," I said. "I got married at twenty-seven and divorced last year. No kids, but my parents tell me I owe them two grandchildren. I live on Kent Island. No pets, no roommate, and no significant other."

We stared at each other, and then we both burst out laughing.

"Is there anything else you need to know?" I asked.

"You're not gay, are you?"

"Nope."

"Do you hate children?"

"Nope."

"Do you have a psychotic ex-wife or ex-girlfriend?"

"Not as far as I know," I said. "But you must've had some crazy relationships if you're asking these kinds of questions."

"There's been some bad ones," she said. "I've got one last question—are you as good at computer security as you seem, or was that an act this afternoon?"

I smiled. "I'm better than you can possibly imagine."

Val leaned over and started a kiss that I hoped would last all night. After a few minutes, she pulled away, breathing hard. "So am I."

ten

IT TOOK ME A few seconds when I woke up to remember I was in the Soul Identity guesthouse. Val and I had climbed down the hill and returned to the office, where she wasted a few hours giving me demonstrations of her new online applications.

I laughed out loud when I remembered how disappointed I was to go back to work. But I had earned my round-the-clock pay, even if I did have a hard time staying focused on the software.

Val had called it a night at two o'clock in the morning, brought me back to the guesthouse, and agreed with my assessment that it was too late for her to head back, alone, to her place. I rolled over and again was stunned by the most gorgeous blue eyes I had ever seen.

She smiled. "What's so funny?"

I reached out and stroked her cheek. "I was remembering how sad I was when we came down the hill and went to the office."

"And you call yourself a computer geek?"

"Hey, I had some good suggestions for you, didn't I?"

She reached out and ruffled my hair. "You did. What time is it?"

"Seven thirty. Let's get up. George is coming to show me his gadgets at eight."

We got out of bed and hopped in the shower. We didn't even wait for it to warm up, figuring the cold water would wake us up faster.

"Ahhh!" I yelled. The water must have passed through a freezer on its way to the showerhead. We pressed ourselves against the walls and avoided most of the spray as we waited for the heat to kick in.

"Check the handle," Val screamed.

I reached into the spray and pointed the handle toward the other direction. We waited a bit, but the water only felt colder.

"Let me find the cutoff valve." I crossed the spray and climbed out of the tub. I turned on the sink faucet: that water was nice and hot. I ran into the next room and looked for an access panel.

"Any luck?" Val called.

"Nope. I can't find a valve."

"That's okay, I'm done now. Come finish up."

"You've got to be kidding."

"You scared of a little cold water?"

I went back in the bathroom and saw Val toweling off. I took a deep breath and got back in. Damn, it was cold.

In less than a minute I was done. "Where's my towel?" I asked. "I need to scrape off the icicles."

"Sorry, there was only one." Val tossed it to me, and I dried off as best as I could.

"That was invigorating," I said. "Don't tell me you did that all the time in Russia."

She nodded. "It brought back lots of memories." She pointed to the clock. "You have ten minutes before George comes. I have to get to my place for some fresh clothes. Will I see you in the dungeon today?"

"I think that's the plan, but it's up to Archie. I can call you when I know something."

We exchanged cell numbers and finished getting dressed. Val gave me a quick kiss.

"How far away is your place, anyway?" I asked.

She smiled. "Maybe twenty feet."

"You're in the guesthouse?"

"Right above you."

"But last night you said you were too tired to go home alone."

She arched her eyebrows. "Are you complaining?"

"We could've taken a hot shower upstairs."

She laughed and gave me a longer and lingering kiss. "That should warm you up."

I looked down. "I'm gonna have to get back in that shower."

George knocked on my door promptly at eight. We headed straight for the gadget room.

"When's the last time somebody stayed here?" I asked.

"It's been a while," he said. "Why, was it dusty?"

"It was clean. But there was a problem with the shower. No hot water."

"You're kidding me," he said. "I've never had a complaint. Did you work the handle properly?"

I walked into the bathroom. "Maybe you can show me how it's done."

"Sure." He reached out for the handle. "Just turn it like this and it will warm right up." He stuck his hand under the shower and shook his head.

"Let's give it a minute." He checked again. "Maybe I need to turn it the other way."

That didn't work either.

"Well, Mr. Waverly, you have me there." He scratched his head. "What the devil could have happened to the hot water?"

"When did you say somebody stayed here last?"

He thought for a minute. "Golly, it's been about ten years since we used this room. Mr. Feret stayed for a few weeks while they did his validation." He chuckled. "I called him Mr. Ferret when he first arrived and I thought he was going to bite my head off."

"Not the nicest guy, huh?"

"Nice enough for an overseer, I suppose. I haven't seen much of him since. Not since the troubles started."

That got my attention. "Troubles?"

"You'll have to talk to Mr. Morgan about that."

I nodded. So Feret was the other overseer. I remembered seeing the portrait of a young man in the lobby. If that was only ten years ago, he must still be pretty young.

"Maybe Feret likes cold showers," I said.

"Maybe, but he was the kind of guest who would have immediately complained, if you know what I mean," he said. "I'll call the plumber today. You can expect hot water by this evening."

"Could I have an extra towel? I'm having company tonight."

He looked at me. "Don't tell me you had a guest this morning."

I nodded.

"With just cold water in the shower?"

"Yup. And we didn't realize it until we were already under that cold spray."

He seemed to try to hold it in, but he burst out with a huge laugh.

"It wasn't that funny," I said. "It was pretty damn shocking."

But George couldn't breathe, much less say anything. He doubled over and held his belly and shook. Finally he stood up and wiped the tears from his eyes. "I'm sorry, but that is just about the funniest thing I've ever heard." He started laughing all over again. "I'll make sure it's fixed today."

George was all business when we reached the gadget room. "Okay, Mr. Waverly, in the entertainment center we have the standard toys—large

screen satellite television, sound system, DVD player, and satellite radio."
He showed me how to work the universal remote.

Then he patted the leather sofa. "This reclines, and it has built-in
massage, heat, and air cooling." He sat down and demonstrated the couch
to me. "Right here on the coffee table," he pointed to a small box, "is the
central lighting control."

"This seems more like an entertainment room. Why do you call it a
gadget room?"

"I'm glad you asked." George went to the wall next to the television.
He pressed a button on the remote, and the wall panels opened up to
reveal a small display, microphone and speakers, and a rack of yellow
electronic equipment with blinking blue lights. He smiled. "Gadgets."

"What're they for?"

"This is one of our communications centers. The radio lets me receive
Soul Identity broadcasts and talk to our members all over the world. If it
goes over the air, you can probably pick it up here."

I nodded. "Why are you showing this to me?"

"Mr. Morgan told me to show you every gadget I have." He checked
his watch. "Don't forget to come up for breakfast. Sue's an excellent
cook."

I examined the gadgets after George left. Maybe they'd be able to help
me track down that mysterious phone caller I overheard last night. After
a few minutes of playing around, I grabbed my bag and headed upstairs.

In the dining room, Val sat next to Sue and both of them laughed at
something George had said. The three tried to hide their smiles when I
walked in.

"What's so funny?" I asked.

Sue snorted and said, "George was telling us about your cold shower.
We're so sorry, Mr. Waverly." Sue looked at Val. "Ms. Nikolskaya, please
meet our guest, Mr. Waverly."

"We've already met," Val said. She flashed me a dazzling smile, and
George and Sue went to the other room.

Val pointed to a plate in the middle of the table. "Have a bagel."

I raised my eyebrows. "George just bragged about what a great cook
Sue is. What's with the bagels?"

She shrugged. "We have bagels every morning. Sue makes great juices,
though." She lifted her glass. "Carrot tangerine, with a hint of lime."

I made a face. "Does she have any simple juice?"

"How simple?"

"Coffee bean juice, served hot. Cow juice mixed in."

"Let's find out." She turned toward the door. "Sue, do you have any coffee?" she called.

Sue came out, wiping her hands on a towel. "I have organic coffee somewhere in the closet," she said. "How do you take it?"

"Cream and sweetener, thanks," I said.

Sue nodded. "Is soy milk okay? We've been reducing George's lactose intake."

"Let's skip the milk then."

She balled the towel in her hands. "And I only have real sugar. Actually, it's organic raw cane sugar. It may have a little aftertaste, but it's better for you."

I held back a grimace. "How about I just have the same juice that Val is drinking?" I asked.

Sue beamed at me. "Excellent choice. One carrot and tangerine, with a hint of lime, coming up." She went back through the door.

I looked at Val. "How do you start the day without caffeine?"

"I get coffee at work. You met Brian yesterday?"

I nodded. "Archie's assistant."

"He gets us great Seattle coffee. I drink my vitamins here and my caffeine at the office." She stood up and stretched. "I have an eight forty-five design meeting, so I guess I'll see you later on."

I remembered Ann invited me to dinner with Bob and Elizabeth that evening. "I have a dinner date this evening at Ann Blake's house," I told her.

Val smiled. "Me too. Eight thirty, right?"

I nodded. "This time you can ride with me and Bob. He's going anyway, and he's got this big limo."

"Okay, see you here by eight fifteen." She flashed me one more smile and headed out.

Sue came back and handed me the juice, then stood waiting for me to try it. It was refreshing, and I finished it off in a few quick swallows.

I put the glass down and wiped my mouth. "That was much better than I expected."

She put her hands on her hips. "What did you expect?"

I made a face. "After all that organic talk, I thought it would be full of brewer's yeast and wheat germ."

She smiled.

"Don't tell me they were in there."

She nodded.

"Anything else?"

"Parsley and wheat grass. But don't worry. It will do you good. George and I have drunk this every morning for the last fifteen years, and we feel great."

George walked in. "It's incredible. Especially if you're having the ladies over." He gave me an exaggerated wink. "It gives you extra juice. EJ, we call it."

Sue smiled. "Let's not scare Scott off with our stories, Georgie." She rubbed his arm, picked up my empty glass, and the two left the room.

I called Bob from my cell phone while walking to the headquarters. "Tonight we have that dinner date with Ann and Elizabeth," I said.

"Yes, sir, I remember. Eight thirty this evening."

"Val is also coming, so I said she could ride with us. We leave here at eight fifteen?"

"Of course, sir." Bob paused a second. "Would it be all right if Elizabeth comes along?"

"Absolutely."

I hung up as I got to the porch stairs. I went in and saw Elizabeth at her desk. After we said hello, I pointed at the portraits. "You have only two overseers?"

She nodded. "We were down to one, until Andre Feret came along almost ten years ago."

I pointed at his picture. "Feret seems pretty young. He should last a long time."

Elizabeth giggled. "I hope so. He's only thirty. Just a couple years older than me."

I looked closer at the portrait. "So he was only twenty when he started?"

Elizabeth nodded. "Awfully young, I remember Mom saying."

"Can I see him today?"

Elizabeth shook her head. "He works from Venice. He's here every couple of months, though. Just a sec and I'll tell you when." She opened a calendar on her computer. "Oh, it's soon. Mr. Feret will be in town next Thursday and Friday."

"Maybe I'll still be here." I headed toward the elevator.

eleven

JAMES BROUGHT ME UP to the third floor. Brian stepped out of Archie's office and into the hallway. "Good morning, Mr. Waverly," he said. "Would you like some coffee?"

"Coffee would be great." I held up my hind as he walked by. "Brian, how long have you been working here?"

He stopped and turned to face me. "Ten years," he said.

"You came during the dot-com boom?"

He nodded. "Seattle was getting way too busy for me. Sterling is more my speed." He smiled. "Hey, how do you know when you're addicted to coffee?"

I shook my head.

"You walk a mile on your treadmill before you notice it's not plugged in." He laughed.

I gave him a polite smile. "Did you make that up?" I asked.

He shook his head. "I get these jokes off the coffee packages in the morning."

I patted his arm. "Well, there's always tomorrow, then."

Archie looked up from his desk when I walked in.

I pointed at the door. "Is Brian for real?"

He frowned. "Did you just get a coffee joke?"

I nodded.

He sighed. "I have suffered through them every morning since I asked him to start showing a softer, less contemptuous side to his co-workers."

"Maybe he could work on his material."

"Maybe he could." Archie smiled. "Did you find our guesthouse satisfactory?"

"It was great," I said. "A beautiful place."

"And did George show you the gadgets?"

"He did. He said you make world-wide radio broadcasts."

He sighed. "I used to do it monthly. But not at all in the past decade."

Brian brought in my coffee, and I waited for him to leave the room and close the door. Then I said, "Lots of things seem to have changed in the last ten years."

"Nothing important has changed, Scott. We are the same organization that we have always been."

That couldn't be true, or he wouldn't have called me. "Did your troubles start ten years ago?" I asked.

He narrowed his eyes. "What do you mean by 'troubles'?"

"That's the word George used." I spent a minute arranging my thoughts. "Your chart yesterday showed your recruits starting dropping off ten years ago," I said. "Then Brian told me he's been here for ten years. You just said the broadcasts stopped ten years ago. And George mentioned this morning that it's been ten years since Andre Feret became an overseer."

He closed his eyes for a minute, then looked up at me. "It is true that we went through a series of changes to our systems and policies right around the turn of the century," he said. "This could be the troubles that George is referring to."

I thought I should keep pressing this point. "So you find no link between George's troubles and your own fears of an attack?" I asked.

He compressed his lips into a thin line. "Definitely not. George is focusing on appearances, not on substance. He lacks the perspective to understand what is truly happening."

I decided to let it go for now, so I nodded.

Archie stared out the window for a minute, then gave a little shudder and sat down with me around the coffee table.

"What did Val show you?" he asked.

A lot more than I was going to admit to him. "Her new online depositary system," I said. "I saw how members will be able to register, log in, check their accounts, and request withdrawals."

He leaned forward. "And what did you think?"

"It's good, but you've got a gaping hole in your member registration. She needs to fix it before you deploy."

He frowned. "What kind of hole?"

On the face of it, the system was fine. Soul Identity planned to send each member an electronic reader, just like the little yellow one they sent me. The members would upload their iris images to a Web site. Once these images matched appropriate soul lines, they'd choose a password and access their depositary accounts.

Convenient, yes. But not secure. "Yesterday I mentioned that your system seemed to be designed for honest people," I said.

Archie nodded.

"Same thing here. The new service is convenient for your members. But you don't really know if the guy at the other end of the Web browser owns the eyes that he's presenting."

I could see he was still confused, so I tried again. "How will you know if the eyes really belong to him? Maybe he sent you his mom's images. Or his neighbor's. Or a pair he lifted from a model in a magazine. You won't know—and you can't know—if you don't certify him."

Archie nodded slowly. "I see the problem—but what do we do about it?"

"Tighten up the registration process. Have your members provide proof of identity at their local offices. Or, if you trust your delivery people, send them out to do onsite certifications."

"And that will close the hole?"

I shook my head. "It'll just make it manageable. You'll still need controls to watch for fraud by the local offices and delivery people."

His shoulders slumped. "Our actions are making us appear as an incredibly naïve organization."

He was right—Soul Identity's Internet project looked to me more like it came from a startup than from an ancient organization. Either Val's team wasn't working with the existing culture, or the existing culture had gotten lost.

I looked closely at him. "I'm wondering if your naivety is the cause or the effect of your current problems."

He crossed his arms. "There is nothing to wonder. Indeed it is the effect of our problems. If it were the cause, could we have lasted for so many years?"

No need for me to answer his defensive rhetoric. I waited for him to continue.

Archie glanced at his watch. "I have another hour—do you have any other questions for me?"

Usually attackers go after my client's money, and if I was to catch them, I had to walk the money trail and search for holes. But first I needed to steer the conversation away from opinions and into facts, before Archie got too defensive.

"Yesterday you told me about Darius introducing the overseers—thirty-five castrated men and bald women," I said.

He smiled. "Fortunately for me, we no longer follow those traditions."

I had wondered about that.

"The overseers brought order and attracted many Persian noblemen," he continued. "The mystics found additional matches, and the role of the soul seeker was established."

"Val explained that both recruiters and soul seekers get paid by commission," I said.

He nodded. "Paying commissions brings in new members and finds existing soul lines, year after year."

"Are all your recruiters mystics?"

Archie shook his head. "Most members are referred by other satisfied members. Some come through the mystics, and others through doctors and priests." He frowned. "And I must admit that a few members reach us through unsavory types lurking around nursing homes and hospitals, offering immortality to those about to die."

"And how effective are your soul seekers?" I asked.

Archie pursed his lips. "How is this relevant?"

Maybe it wasn't. But I wanted to know—new members were great, but somewhere along the way Soul Identity needed to produce enough matches to keep the excitement going.

"I'm looking for holes in your money trail," I said.

Fortunately he seemed satisfied with my lame explanation. "Recovering soul lines is quite an art," he said. "Over the years we have gotten quite good at it."

"Can you project where a soul will end up in a future life?"

"Some recruiters believe they can," he said. "They claim that if they map out the exact time and location of where a soul has been in four carriers, they can plot the trajectory and speed of the soul's orbit around earth, and even predict its next appearance."

"Do you believe it?"

Archie shrugged. "I have read studies showing the successful prediction and recovery of some soul lines this way. Many of our seekers start their efforts with research into the activities of the soul line carriers."

"That's gotta be tricky, nailing down the exact location of people that lived a long time ago."

He smiled. "Especially when you realize that if your time or location is off by just the tiniest bit, the predicted soul's emergence could vary by hundreds of miles or years."

I thought about the reader I had used on the bluefish. "Is this why your electronic readers record the time and GPS coordinates?"

Archie nodded. "We will have enough data to evaluate the theory in ninety more years."

I shook my head. "You guys sure think long term."

"We only think long term." Archie steepled his fingers and rested them against his chin.

"I suppose that in twenty-six hundred years you've accumulated lots of theories and methods of soul seeking," I said.

"We have many theories on recruiting." A sly smile spread over his face. "But by far our most productive method of producing matches is our oldest and simplest."

Archie said yesterday that Darius used mystics to match his entire empire. I raised my eyebrows. "As effective as the Persians were?"

He pointed at me. "Tell me who can get pictures of everybody's eyes."

I shrugged. "Drivers license agencies?"

"Their images are not detailed enough to match." He smiled. "Try eye doctors."

"You're in cahoots with the optometrists?"

He chuckled. "That idea was my biggest contribution to the organization, over thirty years ago."

"It's brilliant," I said.

"Thank you. We ended up doubling our membership and our recovery rates."

I could imagine. "What percentage of soul lines do you actually recover?" I asked.

He looked at me. "Do you really need to know this?"

Of course not. "I'd imagine you'd be advertising this figure," I said.

"Seventy-seven percent of all soul lines are recovered within the first three centuries, and ninety-three percent overall."

I took a minute to digest this. "You must have one hell of a large organization, Archie."

He nodded. "Over two million living members, and at a rough guess, one hundred thousand recruiters and soul seekers."

We sat silently for a few minutes while I tried to absorb the sheer size of Soul Identity. The organization probably controlled hundreds of billions of dollars, yet they had found a way to stay in the background of society.

"Okay," I said. "I want to know more about the original overseers. What else were they doing?"

"Putting together our operational guidelines—the ones we still use today. They set up the systems of recruiters and seekers, the depositary, and the delivery organization. They established our annual fees on account balances. And they managed the depositary investments."

The depositary investments, whether or not Archie would admit it, must be the prize his attackers sought.

"Where does the depositary invest?" I asked.

"In those days we financed the Persian wars. Then when Darius stopped fighting, we purchased tax rights for some of the empire's territories."

"And today?" I asked. "You're not still financing wars, are you?"

He stared at me. "That information is not relevant to this discussion."

I decided to veer back into history.

"Empires don't last forever," I said. "What happened when Alexander the Great rolled through Persia and ripped it to shreds?"

"Not a single loss," he said. "By 321 BC we were already established in Persia and Greece, and we boasted over fifty thousand living members. When Alexander arrived in Babylon, he joined us as a member."

"A lucky break for Psychen Euporos."

He shrugged. "Not so lucky. By focusing only on tracking soul identities, our organization has remained appealing to both the conquerors and the conquered."

"Didn't Alexander die in Babylon?"

"He did. Just two years later, after returning from India. A month before he turned thirty-three."

"Good thing he had his soul identity captured."

"Yes," he said, missing my sarcasm. "And we know of at least two recoveries to his line since."

"Why wouldn't you know of them all?"

Archie shook his head. "Except for the overseers, members have always been granted total anonymity, unless they choose to share."

"So somebody shared."

He smiled. "If you were carrying the same identity as Alexander the Great, what would you do?"

I saw his point. You may not admit it if your previous carrier was a loser, but who wouldn't talk about a glamorous past? "What happened once Alexander died?" I asked. "Those must have been turbulent times."

He nodded. "One of his generals preserved his body in honey and hauled it, the depositary, and the overseers to Egypt. Alexander went into a crystal coffin and Psychen Euporos went into the Library of Alexandria. Our depositary fit right in."

"And the organization was back in Egypt, after three hundred years abroad." I thought of something. "I remember learning that the library was one of the wonders of the world. But wasn't it destroyed?"

"It was, but we left a century before. Our executive overseer then was the Christian historian Origen, and he had run into trouble with the Bishop of Alexandria, so he moved us to Palestine in 231 AD. We remained in Caesarea until we moved to Constantinople in 605.

"In 1453 the Ottomans reached Constantinople, and we moved to safer grounds in Pozsony, now known as Bratislava. Then in 1732 we came to America and settled in Sterling." He spread his hands out. "This site has been our home for almost three hundred years."

I wanted to get back to the problems they were facing. I asked him, "Has the organization ever been in the situation you find yourselves now?"

He looked at me for a minute before speaking. "You have to realize that some of these facts are pretty murky. But I will share what I have been told, and what I have pieced together from the archives."

I nodded and waited for him to continue.

"The first overseers in Babylon worked in harmony," he said. "There were no politics for sixty years—when the original overseers were gone and we had recovered five others."

"You had five baby overseers?"

Archie shook his head. "To become a member or an overseer, you must be at least nineteen years old. This is an original rule."

"Is that because your irises change throughout your life?"

"They change through adolescence, but interestingly enough, the soul identity remains the same." He reached up and straightened his bowtie. "I believe the rule was to prevent the organization from being run by guardians of children overseers."

That made sense. "So sixty years in, Psychen Euporos had five recovered overseers and no original ones left. What happens next?"

"Problems," he said. "We recovered no new overseers for the next forty years."

"What happened to the brute force method of mystics scouring the empire?"

"The method failed," he said. "For the next forty years, the only matches made were for non-overseer members."

"That sounds like now," I said. "What caused the gap?"

"Our historians believe that one overseer bribed the match committee to reject any overseer match," he said. "The bad overseer eventually met with a bad accident, and the overseer matches resumed."

My bet was that Soul Identity's overseers had as much corruption running through their ranks as medieval Catholic bishops.

"Your overseers sound like politicians," I said.

"But so much worse." He ran his fingers through his white hair. "The soul line collections compound our problems. Carriers bring grudges forward far into the future. Battles thought to have ended hundreds of years ago can be re-launched after a new recovery opens old wounds."

Archie's voice rose in volume. "Scott, we are down to two overseers. Someone or something is stopping overseer matches. Somehow they are diverting new members and convincing existing members to withdraw their money. We must find them and stop them before it is too late." He got up and went back to the window and stood staring outside, his forehead resting against the glass.

He turned and looked at me. "I am getting old, Scott," he said. "I do not want to pass on and leave only Mr. Feret in charge. We need at least two overseers to function properly."

Archie seemed to be acting like a Supreme Court Justice trying to stay alive until a new administration took over the government. Maybe that explained Brian's bran muffins and skim milk.

"Don't you trust Andre Feret?" I asked.

He stared at me for a minute before answering. "I do not," he said firmly. "We overseers have spent too many centuries making and breaking alliances with each other." Then he looked at the floor. "But I need to be fair. Mr. Feret is not the problem. As an overseer, whether we politically agree or not, he is loyal to the organization, and he is as concerned as I am with this threat against us."

I wondered what Andre Feret thought about running Soul Identity alone. I also wondered what could possibly be driving Soul Identity to put its business online, right in the middle of all this turmoil and uncertainty. "What's the big push to get on the Internet?" I asked. "Don't you have enough going on?"

He came back and sat down on the couch. "I would prefer to avoid an online presence, as it is a distraction, and it will bring us unnecessary scrutiny," he said. "But we must compete to stay solvent."

There was more than one organization like this? "Don't tell me you have competitors," I said.

Archie shrugged. "Every century or so, one group or another tries to take away some of our business. They are a nuisance, really. They create a stir, but they fade away after a few years. It is hard for them to beat our depositary."

I thought about that. The true value of the depositary extended beyond its money: only Soul Identity could connect you to an existing soul line. Competitors could only offer futures.

I thought about how proud Bob was of his soul line's delivery heritage. "That makes sense," I said. "You offer your members a past, which puts your way ahead of anybody else."

"One would think so." He scowled. "WorldWideSouls seems different. They are seven years old now, yet still they grow." He leaned forward. "They do everything online, Scott. They tell our members we are out of date and out of touch. We need to get online before more members withdraw their entire collections and shift to them."

Archie sighed. "At first I ignored WorldWideSouls, but Mr. Feret has since convinced me that they are a real threat and we must have an online presence."

"But you don't trust Andre Feret," I said.

Archie shrugged. "In this case I do. It is in Mr. Feret's interest, just as it is in mine, to preserve Soul Identity and its assets. When it comes to competitors, we overseers have always stood united."

I doubted that was true.

twelve

ARCHIE AND I WRAPPED up at noon, and Val and I went out for sushi. I wanted to know more about the match committee. "Can their decisions be disputed?" I asked her.

She shook her head. "The decisions are final."

"Are they ever made public?"

"No—except for the overseer matches, all decisions are private."

I told her about the second generation of overseers and how one had corrupted the match committee to prevent new overseers from joining.

"But without access to their decisions, we can't know if that's happening now," she said.

"Maybe there's an indirect way to infer their actions," I said. "What kinds of information do you store in your database?"

"We have membership lists, soul line recovery counts, lost soul lists, complaints, and investment balances," she said.

"Lost soul lists? What are they?"

"When a soul line hasn't been recovered for a thousand years, it goes onto our lost soul list, and the finder's fee doubles. We want to recover everybody," she said.

I nodded. "And the complaints?"

"We store member, employee, recruiter, and soul seeker complaints."

I thought about Madame Flora and how she was upset about missing out on my neighbor Berry's commission. "I'm guessing the soul seeker complains are mostly about match committee rejections."

"That's most of them," she said. "Are you thinking of trying to correlate their complaints against periods where no overseers matched?"

I nodded.

"I'm not sure if our sample size is large enough," she said. "We recover overseers only every ten to fifteen years. Finding a correlation is going to be like finding a needle in a haystack."

"Or like finding a matching soul identity." Just a bit of sarcasm from a non-believer.

Val ignored it. "A simple program could do the hard work." She dipped her chopstick into the soy sauce and drew on her napkin. "We could target the times when the gaps between finding overseers were the biggest, then analyze the anomalous complaints." She glanced up. "What would make them anomalous?"

"Making a complaint and then withdrawing it, or making a complaint and then disappearing," I said.

She nodded. A few more scribbles, and she held up the napkin. "Here's what I'll do," she said.

Drops of soy sauce left brown trails down the napkin. "I hope you've got a backup," I said.

Val looked at the napkin. "Oops." She crumpled it up and tapped her temple. "Don't worry, it's all up here."

Val and I walked from the parking garage toward the elevator. "Which overseer is helping you the most?" I asked.

"Andre—I mean Mr. Feret," she said. "He's been just great."

"Not Archie?"

She stopped and turned to face me. She spoke in a harsh whisper. "Mr. Morgan does everything he can to stop us. It's been frustrating trying to get anything done when he's involved."

"He blocks you?"

"No, it's more that he slows us down. He sits in our design sessions and makes silly comments about the way things used to be." She shook her head. "My whole team is frustrated. We've been working around him whenever we can."

"Maybe he doesn't want you online," I said.

She shrugged. "He needs to get with the times. Andre says he's doing what he can to keep him under control, but it's been difficult to say the least."

I couldn't help but feel a twinge of jealousy at Val's first name basis with the mysterious overseer.

I returned to Archie's office. "Do you have time for a couple more questions?" I asked him.

He was just finishing his own lunch. He wiped his mouth with a napkin, then carefully folded his sandwich wrapper and threw it away. "Of course."

I sat down in front of him. "Can you make a match from a photograph?"

"Yes, you can. Many soul seekers scour yearbooks and magazines. The match committee requires reader-certified images and identities, though, before they grant membership."

"What do you do in the case of an injury to the eyes? Will non-certified photographs suffice?"

"Only if there was sufficient proof that the images were truly of the person's eyes."

So maybe my neighbor did have a chance to get in.

"Thanks," I said. "Now can you tell me what the dinner at Ann Blake's is all about?"

He got up and shut his office door. He bent down and whispered in my ear. "A special meeting with George, Sue, Bob, Elizabeth, Val, you, me, and Ann." Then he straightened up and said in a normal voice, "Ann always has a dinner on Thursdays for the visiting members. There could be many people there." He shook his head and negated his last comment.

Archie looked pretty funny doing the espionage thing. "I guess I'll see you there tonight," I said. "It would be good to meet some more members."

I checked the time. Val probably hadn't gotten any results from her correlation program yet. "I'd like to learn how soul identities are read and matched," I said. "Can you set me up with somebody this afternoon?"

"I can." He smiled. "Ann Blake was a recruiter before she moved to the depositary." He picked up his yellow phone. "I will check on her availability," he said.

Brian walked me down the hall to Ann's office. "Are all the bigwigs located here on the third floor?" I asked him.

He nodded. "The depositary chief, the executive overseer, and the three members of the match committee all have offices here on this side. You already know the depositary is on the other side."

"I heard Andre Feret is coming to town next week. Where is his office?"

"The second floor," he said. "Mr. Feret isn't happy about it, though."

"Is the coffee not as good?" I asked.

It took him a second to realize I was kidding. "The coffee is fine, Mr. Waverly," he said. "The second floor is the overseer floor, but since Mr. Feret is the only other overseer, he's alone down there."

Alone enough to plot against Archie? Or alone enough to get on a first name basis with Val?

We had walked around to the front of the building. Brian knocked on a door and opened it. Ann Blake sat behind her desk, wearing a lime green blouse and green scarf. She stared at her yellow computer monitor and typed on her yellow keyboard.

Brian cleared his throat.

"Yes?" She kept her eyes on her screen.

"Mr. Waverly is here to see you, Ms. Blake."

"Just a sec, hon." She clicked her mouse and said, "There—sent."

"Email?" I asked.

"It's the bane of my existence." She extended her hand to me. "Afternoon, Scott."

Again the strength of her handshake surprised me.

She let go of my hand and pointed to two couches in the corner. "Let's sit and chat. Brian, can you rustle up some coffee?"

"I'll ask your assistant to bring it," Brian said.

"Shucks, Brian, it's just some coffee." Ann smiled. "Maybe I should go get it myself?"

Brian held up his hand. "No, no, Ms. Blake. I can do it."

"Get a move on now," Ann called. After he left and shut the door, she looked at me. "That boy's been getting too big for his britches."

We sat down on the couches and talked about the weather until Brian brought the coffee. Then he left and shut the door.

Ann tilted her head to one side. "So what can I do for you?"

I wanted to get my neighbor Berry into the system. But before digging into that, I thought she could expand on the crisis Archie thought Soul Identity was facing.

"Do you know why I'm here?" I asked.

"You're to evaluate the security of our new online system."

I nodded. "Anything else?"

Her eyes crinkled as she smiled at me. "I'm sure there's more. It wouldn't be Archibald if there wasn't a hidden agenda."

I grinned. "Then tell me why I'm really here."

Her smile faded and her eyes went wide. "Because we're less than a month from going broke," she said.

So Archie was telling the truth. I nodded somberly. "But I don't understand how that can be," I said.

"You would think that we'd be safe." She sighed. "We're not like public banks—we have no complex derivatives, and we do no over-leveraging.

We refuse to reduce risk by bundling good and bad assets together. The majority of our investments are safe and conservative."

"Then why are you threatened with insolvency?" I asked.

"Withdrawals," she said. "Too many members are emptying their collections—more than we budgeted for."

"Somehow I thought you operated like a mutual fund," I said. "Paying people off shouldn't hurt you that much."

"There's two things you've gotta understand." She held up her fingers. "One—we're on a gold standard, and two—we lock account values at the end of the year."

"What's the gold standard?" I asked.

"Since way back in the beginning, members' account balances have been measured in gold. We live on commission, so we invest the funds to earn enough to cover our administrative costs."

"That drives you to invest as much as possible."

"You're darn tooting it does—otherwise we don't get any money for ourselves." She pointed at me. "But that leads me to my second point—the annual account settlement."

"I don't get it," I said.

"Let's say you're an average Soul Identity member," she said. "You're in your fifties, married with children in university. You're over-exposed in the stock market, and you carry a depositary balance of three hundred or so ounces of gold."

That much gold was worth over a quarter million bucks. "That's the average account size?" I asked.

"That's right. Remember, it's an average," she said. "Now let's say you got creamed in this latest economic crisis, so to cover your debts, you decide to cash in your depositary account."

I nodded. "Sounds good to me. Gold's gone up since January, hasn't it?"

"Bingo." She sighed. "It's up more than thirty percent. You withdraw your money, and we have to bail out of losing investments to come up with the cash to pay you off."

"So again, why would that drive you to go broke?"

"Ninety percent of our investments are super long term," she said. "We can't touch them for decades. And the rest are down at least fifty percent. Every time a member cashes in their account we're losing over eighty percent."

"But surely this has happened before," I said.

"It has," she said. "We weathered the gold spike and recession combination in 1980. And even though we underestimated our current economy and have gotten caught with our pants down, it's really another factor that's killing us—a competitor is stealing away our members." She held up her hands and let them fall to her lap. "The money's almost gone, Scott."

Now I understood why Archie was panicking, and why he agreed to go online—WorldWideSouls was about to put him out of business.

I nodded. "What can you tell me about WorldWideSouls?"

She sighed. "They've got an appeal that we can't match. Our members are flocking to them, and if we don't get our butts in gear and get ourselves online, we're dead."

I nodded. "I'll keep digging."

"Let me know how I can help," she said.

Time to bring up Berry. "I have a different set of questions," I said. "They're about reading identities. Archie said you used to be a recruiter."

"That's a more pleasant topic." She smiled. "What do you want to know?"

"I think I understand the basics," I said. "You take pictures of the irises, calculate the difference, and that's the identity."

She nodded. "Today it's all computer-driven, but when I was actively reading, it was a mighty tiring process."

"I can imagine," I said. "How long does it take to learn to read identities?"

"Back in my day, it was a four year apprenticeship." She shook her head. "Now kids take a two week course. It's a darn shame."

"Why is that so bad?"

"You can't learn how to treat a match candidate with respect in two weeks. We can't figure out if you're ethical in two weeks. And nobody sure as heck builds any organizational loyalty in two weeks."

So Soul Identity was feeling the same technology growing pains as many other industries, where an old guard mentality persists among the experienced workers. They complain that the newer generation barges in without learning the trade, and as the company saves on labor, it loses on quality, customer service, and employee loyalty.

But technology brought more than cost savings. "The accuracy of the readings must have increased," I said.

She frowned. "How would you measure it? The match committee uses the same computer programs to do their validations."

"Doesn't that make them sort of redundant?"

"You wouldn't know it by talking to them." She paused for a minute. "I supposed they do serve as a check on the readers."

"Meaning nobody can be blatantly forced through."

"Right," she said.

"What's stopping them from submitting somebody else's eyes?"

She pointed at me. "That is exactly why we need to make sure our readers have integrity, and did not get their certification through a two week training program."

I nodded. Ann's comment got me thinking: if the same program read and then validated the identities, we'd have to make sure that the program had just as much integrity as a human reader. Well, not the program, but the programmer behind the code.

There was no need to worry Ann about this now. I needed to do my own digging first. In the meantime I could fulfill the promise I made to Berry by getting him in the system.

"Ann, can you still do readings?"

"Can a colt find his momma in the dark? Of course I can."

I pulled Berry's photograph out of my pocket and handed it to her. "I'd like this guy's identity read and certified."

She put on a pair of glasses and scrutinized the picture. "It'll be tough, but doable. We used to take photographs of the iris and then do our matches from that. This focus is clear and the colors aren't faded. Who is it?"

"Somebody who wants to become a member. He lost an eye a while back, and one of your newer computer-trained readers told him he couldn't join. I was thinking you could do it by hand."

She nodded. "I'll do my best."

"Is a hand reading as accurate as a computer?" I asked.

"It's just as accurate. Friendlier, too, I would imagine."

"There's a bunch of us computer geeks who prefer the technology."

"You want the reading or not, hon?" She smiled. "Would you like to test my accuracy?"

"Sure. How?"

"We can go to the dungeon and have the images read by the computer, and then you'll see."

Anytime somebody wanted to go down where Val worked, I was ready. "Now?"

"It's as good a time as any. And it sure as hell beats doing email all afternoon." She knelt in front of her credenza. "I've got to grab my old reader." She pulled out a dusty steel container that was shaped like a lunch box. "Let's go."

thirteen

JAMES BROUGHT ANN AND me to the basement, and we headed to the dungeon. I rang the bell, and Forty opened the door.

"Is your boss around?" Ann asked him.

He brought us in and knocked on Val's open door. "Yo Val," he said. "Ms. Blake and Scott are here to see you."

Val smiled at me, and I thought I had died and gone to heaven all over again.

Ann was all business. "Val, can you access our identity and match programs?"

"Of course," Val said. "What do you need?"

"I'm going to use this here photograph," Ann held up Berry's picture, "to generate a manual soul identity. I want you to verify my accuracy and show Scott how good I am."

Val winked at me as Ann handed her the photograph. "I'll just scan this in so I can also work from the images." She looked at Ann. "You want me to burn you a larger copy?"

"That would be great, hon. These eyes ain't what they used to be."

"No problem." Val looked at the picture. "Who's the guy?"

Ann pointed at me over her shoulder with her thumb. "Scott's friend wants to join, but he lost an eye."

"Okay." Val turned to me. "This is going to take us at least a half hour."

"And I haven't done email for a while. I'll go get my laptop from the guesthouse. Be back in a bit, ladies." They were busy planning their reading and missed my exit.

I walked back to the guesthouse and ran into George coming out of my bathroom. "Any luck with the shower?" I asked him.

George was wiping his hands on a dirty towel. "You're all set now, Mr. Waverly. The valve stem was rusted and the hot water was blocked. Tomorrow morning you and your friend will be nice and cozy."

"Thanks, George," I said. "Hey, I have a question for you."

"Shoot." He stuffed the dirty towel into his pocket.

"You said Feret stayed here for several weeks?"

He nodded. "His validation took a while."

What could take so long? "Isn't it all computerized these days?"

He scratched his head. "I remember something about him having an eye infection. They had to wait for a clear reading."

"And he stayed here and waited?" I grabbed my laptop from the table.

"Overseers' soul lines are old and rich. If it were me, I'd stick around as long as it took." He grabbed his tools and we left together.

A large sheet of paper lay in front of Ann. Like Archie's depositary images, the paper had two circles on top and one on the bottom. She looked at me over the rims of her glasses. "Val enlarged the images and I cut them out. I need to verify the placements, and then do the reading."

She pulled a magnifying glass and a glass disc out of her steel lunchbox. The disc had hundreds of thin lines radiating from the center. "The trick is to make sure we keep the eyes on the same plane. If we're off, the identity will be wrong."

Ann put Berry's original image on the disc. She peered at it through her magnifying glass. "Gotta get this right," she muttered.

Val glanced over. "I printed some numbered tick marks on the enlarged images, to save you some time. The scanner kept them on the same plane for me."

Ann looked with her magnifying glasses at the large eye images. "So you did. Bless you." She put the glass disc away and got out a bottle of rubber cement. "Now I can glue the images to the reading sheet."

Val smiled. "And I printed onto adhesive paper. You can peel the back off and line up the tick marks."

Ann shook her head. "When I was reading, we didn't have all these new fangled tools. It was pretty damn hard." She peeled the backs and carefully aligned the images with the numbered tick marks. She reached into her steel box pulled out a dark green velvet bag. She withdrew a tripod with three miniature gold telescopes attached.

"That's your reader?" I asked.

"It is." She wiggled the tripod. "I'll line this up with the images and do the reading." She detached a metal loop that hung from the side of it.

Ann placed each tripod leg on 'X' marks printed on the reader sheet. Two of the telescope barrels pointed at the images; the remaining barrel pointed at the empty circle underneath. She threaded the metal loop into the velvet bag and attached the other end of the bag to the third barrel. The bottom dangled a couple inches above the empty circle.

"You wanna see the identity?" Ann asked me. She pointed to the bottom circle.

I looked closely. Sure enough, a faint image projected onto the paper. "How do you record it?" I asked.

"By hand." She reached into her steel lunchbox and pulled out a long wooden carton. "With my trusty colored pencils. It should take me another half hour."

"Cool. I'll do my email." I fired up my laptop and entered the wireless key Val gave me. I browsed to Web mail. I had two messages: one from Dad and one from Val.

I looked at Val. "How'd you get my email address?"

"It wasn't easy," she said. "You're pretty much undetectable."

"I know. So how'd you find it?"

She smiled. "I looked it up in our contracts system."

Clever girl.

"Hey, keep it down while I concentrate," Ann said.

I went back to my email. Val had sent me an online card thanking me for a great night. I returned the favor with my own private note.

I clicked Dad's message. He had forwarded a list of questions from Jane Watson about my airport report, along with her proposed solution for fixing the security hole at the airport exit. I answered the questions and wrote that her plan looked good.

I closed the laptop. "How's the reading coming, Ann?"

"Just finished." She put down her colored pencils and shook her head. "I may be out of practice, but this here image is balls-on accurate."

"I'll print out the system generated identity," Val said, "Then we can compare."

Val came back with the printed reader sheet and laid it down next to Ann's hand-drawn sheet. "Uh oh," she said.

I looked at the two identities. They were different. In fact, they were not even close. "Um, Ann, what were you saying about accuracy?" I asked.

Ann looked at the papers. "No way. My identity is accurate." She used her magnifying glass to look at both sets of eye images. "Our eyes match, so one of us must be wrong."

"Let's both run them again," Val said. "Maybe one of us goofed."

"One of us meaning me?" Ann asked. "I doubt it. But in the interests of accuracy, let's see. Print me some more images, would you?"

"I'll surf while I wait," I said. Again they weren't listening. Time to see what I could learn about Valentina Nikolskaya. I found some postings she made to email distribution lists, a couple papers she co-authored at a previous job, her contributions to her alumni association, and a leftover Web page from a university course seven years before. Nothing earth shattering.

Ann was still coloring her identity, so I searched for Andre Feret. The name was more common than I had imagined. I checked images too, but I didn't find anybody matching the portrait I had seen in the lobby.

"I'm done," Ann said. "Let's see where we are." She held her two reader sheets up in the air. "Just like I said, my two images match."

Val had just returned with her printout. "So do mine."

The three of us looked at each other from across the table. "So why are your two identities different?" I asked.

Ann shrugged. "Maybe I am out of practice. But I can't believe I'm consistently out of practice."

"Could your reader be broken?" Val asked.

Ann picked up the tripod and looked down the barrels. "I don't think so," she said. "There's no moving parts inside—just some prisms, lenses, and mirrors." She held out her hand. "Let me see your computer sheet, hon." She scrutinized it. "Did the computer match to an existing line?"

Val shook her head.

"I wrote a little program last week which also calculated soul identities," I said.

They both looked at me.

"I was trying to figure out what the reader did," I said. "I have the program here on my laptop. Let's run mine and see what happens."

"You're such a geek." Val smiled. "I'll get you the images." She saved them to a USB key. I copied them to my computer and loaded my program. I clicked the delta button, set my slider, and the identity appeared on the screen.

"Here we go." I turned my laptop so they could see.

"Ha! Scott, you are such a darling." Ann held her reader sheet next to the laptop screen. "Mine matches yours perfectly."

The two were identical. I turned to Val. "What's wrong with your program?"

"Nothing." She looked troubled.

Ann looked from Val to me. "What do we do now?"

"Val, could you check who this identity matches?" I saved it to the USB key.

Val loaded it to her screen. She dragged the image onto a match icon, and a window popped up.

"Matching, please be patient," I read. I looked at Val. "How long does it take?"

"The match program turns the identity into a list of shapes with their color, size, rotation, and location," she said. "That takes a few seconds to work out. Then it calculates twenty bit hash values from this list of data."

Hash values distributed large amounts of information into a smaller number of buckets. Instead of trying to match on the trillions of combinations that fifty or so shapes could make, they narrowed down the list to match on a little over one million individual values. "How many identities do you have in your database?" I asked.

"Over fifty million," Val said.

"*Fifty million?* Archie said you have two million active members."

"Did he tell you about his optometrist project?" Ann asked.

"He mentioned it. I didn't realize you were keeping non-matches."

"We only keep the identity, name, location, and time for our soul cycle research," Val said. "If we do find a match, we also keep the original images, and the names of the reader, recruiter, and soul seeker."

I did some mental calculations. It was one heck of a database running here. "Still, this first cut of matching by the hash should filter out all but fifty or so possibles, right?"

"Right. But I said that we calculate hash *values*, not just one value. We calculate three hundred sixty hash values for each soul identity match." She smiled at me. "Can you tell me why?"

"Nope." Then it hit me. "Wait, I do. Because you don't know which way is up, right?"

"*Molodets*," Val said. "That's *good boy* in Russian. Our readers only made sure the eyes lined up, but we don't know the orientation of the images or the identities. So we run through all three hundred sixty hashes. That gives us somewhere around eighteen thousand checks. It takes thirty seconds at most."

"How long have you been using this hash index system?" I asked.

"Ten years now," Ann said. "It was a big project we did right before Y2K, when we upgraded the readers."

"Hey, we have a match," Val said. "And the winner is—" She looked at the screen and put her hand over her mouth.

Ann came behind her and looked. "It can't be." She shook her head. "There has to be a mistake."

I got up and looked. Underneath the identity image it read, "Match found: Soul line #26. Current carrier: Andre Feret."

fourteen

ANN GLARED AT ME. "What kind of trick are you playing on us?"

I held up my hands. "No trick. Honest."

"If somebody even whispers a rumor that two different people match to a single identity, we can lock the doors and go home for good." She held her head in her hands. "Let me think." After a minute she straightened up. "Val, remove that image from the computer. Scott, get that photo and those reader sheets out of the office. Nobody can know about this until tonight, got it? Not your mothers, not your best friends, not your diaries. Not even Mr. Morgan."

Ann walked out of Val's office, slamming the door behind her.

Val stared at her screen. Then she started typing. After a minute she said, "I've removed the images and the log entries from the scanner, the printer, and the match program." She frowned. "What's going on?"

"Not what Ann thinks," I said. "You'd know after twenty-six hundred years if identities were unique or not. I'd say your matching program is either busted or dishonest."

She crossed her arms. "How can you be sure?"

"Let's figure it out." I went to the white board and grabbed a marker. "We know it's spitting out a bad identity for either my guy or for Feret. Our next step should be to run a control against a known identity."

"Do me," she said. "Once with your program, and once with mine."

I wrote 'test Val' on the board, followed by 'test Archie.' "I'm putting Archie there just in case this only happens with overseers," I said.

"I'm sure the match program is fine," she said. "But let's verify Mr. Feret's eyes and make sure his images match."

"Good idea," I said. "How do we get the images?"

"Overseers' records are publicly available."

I wrote 'test Feret' on the boad. "We can also check your database, and make sure Feret is tied to only one identity," I said. I wrote 'check Feret hash' on the board.

"That gives us four things to check," Val said. Then she slapped the desk. "With all this excitement, I forgot to tell you about the correlations I ran this afternoon."

She was checking for abnormal soul seeker complaints to see if the match committee had been compromised. "Did you find anything?" I asked.

"I pulled all the complaints from the long gaps of no overseer matches, but there was nothing abnormal in the rates, the withdrawals, or the resolution times."

I sighed. "That was a dead end. I guess the match committee is off the hook."

Val nodded. "It would've been no fun if it was that easy to solve. Let's get going and do my eyes." She reached into her laptop bag and fished out a yellow reader that looked just like the one Bob had brought to my house. She read her eyes, then flipped open the top and plugged it into her laptop. She copied the images off and passed the reader to me.

I looked at her screen and saw she had her identity showing. "Jeez, you're quick." I entered in the reader's serial number as the password, and images of Val's eyes came up on the screen. I aligned the eyes on each axis, clicked the delta button, and fiddled with the slider. The computed identity came up. I positioned my laptop next to her monitor so we could compare the identities.

"You match," I said. "So now we know that your program isn't totally busted."

She picked up Berry's photo. "Are you sure that this guy isn't really Andre Feret in disguise?"

I shrugged. "I don't know Andre Feret, so I can't say for sure." I pointed at the white board. "But you're jumping to conclusions—we need to test Archie."

She put down the picture. "Humor me for a minute. If we did jump to conclusions, what would they be?"

I shrugged. "With only this much data, we can only make intuitive leaps. I'd probably conclude that your match program only works for girls."

She smiled. "Or persons under thirty."

"Or for redheads."

"Or blue eyes."

I looked at the photograph. "Wrong, Berry's eyes are blue, and he didn't match."

She looked at me. "Berry?"

Oops, I didn't want to tell anybody his name just yet. "Uh, yeah. His name is Berry." Good thing it was his nickname.

"So who is he?" she asked.

I shook my head. "Not yet, Val. I'll tell you once we figure out what's going on."

She gave me a funny look. "Why the secrecy?"

I didn't really want to tell her that I didn't trust her. So I pointed at the ceiling. "I guess I don't know who else might be listening to what we say."

"So?"

She wasn't buying it. I had to try harder—Berry told me he lost his eye in an accident, and now that sounded coincidental. "If somebody has stolen Berry's identity, he could be in danger," I said. "I know it doesn't sound like a good reason, but I think we should play it safe."

She stared at me for a few seconds. "Okay, Mr. Security Geek. This is your area of expertise, not mine." She stood up. "Let's visit Mr. Morgan and read his identity."

I pressed the elevator button, and leaned toward Val. "Ann said we shouldn't tell Archie," I whispered.

Val nodded. "We won't."

James brought us to the third floor. Archie's office door was open, and we walked in. He stood staring out his back window. I cleared my throat to get his attention.

He turned around. "Scott, Val. What can I do for you two?"

"We are testing the new systems, Mr. Morgan, and we need a volunteer," Val said.

"Count me in," he said. "What can I do?"

"We want to read your identity," I said. "Val's showing me the matching program."

Archie nodded. "Other than at the depositary, I have not been read in almost sixty years. How long does it take these days?"

"About five seconds," Val said.

His eyebrows went up. "That is all?"

Val nodded. "That's how long it takes to capture the images. Then we'll use the computers downstairs to calculate the identity. That'll be another thirty seconds." She pulled the reader out of her pocket. "You can stand right there, Mr. Morgan." She read Archie's right eye, then his left.

"Let me know if you need anything else," he said. Archie headed back to his window as we left his office.

Val and I got in the elevator.

James looked at us. "You two ride with me a lot these days," he said.

"We do," I said.

"Would you be interested in joining my frequent traveler program?" he asked. "Make five trips, and we bump you up to first class."

"Most people here take the stairs," Val whispered in my ear.

"They're missing all the fun," I whispered back.

Val smiled at James. "Sign us both up."

James pulled the elevator to a stop somewhere between the first and second floors. "Wonderful!" he cried. He handed us two slips of paper. "Just complete these applications and we can continue."

Val took his pen and filled them out. I looked over her shoulder; the form asked for our favorite destinations. "I like the dungeon," I said.

"And the depositary for me." She handed the sheets back to James.

James put the applications in his pocket. He pulled out two plastic cards and wrote our names in the blanks on the front. "I'll stamp the back each time you ride," he said.

James restarted the elevator, and we dropped to the basement. He stamped our cards, we got out, and we walked down the hallway to the dungeon.

We sat in front of Val's computer. "I'm thinking Archie's eyes will check out fine," I said. "He just used the goggles with me to verify his identity at the depositary."

"Maybe you're right." She plugged the reader into her system, then handed it to me.

I took the reader and went through my manual steps. The identity popped onto my screen, and sure enough, it matched the one on Val's monitor. "Told you," I said. "Archie and you are both fine."

"So where does this leave us?" she asked.

"In the same place as before—we still don't know why my friend's identity matches Feret's."

She pointed at the board. "Let's check Andre's records." She clicked through some menus. "I just printed out his official reader sheet," she said. "I'll be right back with it."

Val walked in a minute later with Feret's reader sheet in her hand. "Here it is," she said. "Let's compare."

I pulled Berry's sheets out of my laptop bag and laid them on the table around Feret's sheet. "The left ones are from your matching program. The right ones are Ann's."

She leaned over the table. "So which ones match?"

Feret's eyes were different than Berry's, but there was no question about it: Feret's official identity matched the one drawn by Ann. To be sure about it, we both calculated Feret's soul identity from his sheet's eye images, and they both matched Feret's official record.

I drummed my fingers on the desk. "We need a photograph of Feret to verify that these eye images are his."

"You're still doubting him?" she asked.

"I don't know what else it could be."

She nodded. "Maybe I can find a photograph in one of our newsletters." She went back to her computer and started searching.

I walked around Val's office while I waited. I saw a tiny hole on the wall opposite her computer. The paint around it looked fresh. "Was there a picture here?" I asked.

She looked over her shoulder. "This used to be a conference room. There was a fire evacuation sign hanging there."

The nail hole seemed a little large. I looked in it, and saw a glint of light reflected from the back. Was somebody watching us? I scrounged the bottom of my laptop bag and pulled out an old toothpick. I pried at the shiny thing, but I wasn't able to dislodge it.

Tomorrow I could come back with a small screwdriver. In the meantime I broke the toothpick in half and jammed the pieces into the hole.

"Okay, I've found several photos of Andre," Val said. "But none of them have clean eye shots. He's either wearing sunglasses or standing in the shadows in all of them."

Could an overseer really be here for ten years without somebody capturing a picture of his eyes?

Val pointed at the white board. "We need to check the database."

I watched as Val opened the database program. "This join table holds current members, their eye images, and the soul line identifier," she said.

"Where's Feret?" I asked.

Val typed on her keyboard. "Right here." She moved her finger over her screen. "And there's just one record for him."

I looked. The soul line identifier field showed 26, the same number that came up for Berry's identity. "Can you see if there's anybody else listed on the soul line identifier?" I asked.

"I sure can... the only 26 is Mr. Feret's record."

"We have to see your hash table, I guess, to look for duplicates."

She pulled up another screen. "This is the matching table, the one with fifty million records. It's got the identities and soul line identifiers."

"Let's search for soul line 26 again."

She ran the search. "Just the one record. No problems here."

I sighed. "I was hoping we could just write this off to a database problem."

"My database doesn't have problems," she said.

"Your database looks fine." I walked over to the white board and erased it. "Our four bright ideas are done and we've come up empty. How about looking at the match program's source code? We can check out what it's doing."

Val printed out a copy of the code. We spread it out on the table and went through it line by line, but we didn't see anything obvious. It looked similar to the code I had written to calculate the bluefish identity.

"The code looks fine," I said. "But are you sure that this is the same stuff running on your system?"

"I can check."

"Check the binaries, just to be sure." I looked at my watch. "I'm going to have to go."

She looked at me. "Don't we have a date tonight?"

I grimaced. "I didn't know contractors needed black uniforms. This is my second day in these clothes. I need to do some shopping. I got kind of tied up yesterday, if you remember."

"I didn't tie you up." She smiled. "I'll verify the program while you do your shopping." She stacked up the source code papers. "See you at eight fifteen, okay?"

"Cool." I got up to go, took a peek into the hall to make sure nobody was there, and gave her a quick kiss. "Are you interested in stopping by my place after Ann's dinner?" I asked.

She kissed me again. "*Konyeshno.* That's *of course.*"

"Wow." I waved goodbye and left.

fifteen

BOB SAT ACROSS FROM Elizabeth at the reception desk. They seemed to be engaged in a serious conversation. "You guys need some time?" I asked.

He stood up. "No sir, we're done. What can I do for you?"

"I'm on day two with this outfit. I need some more clothes."

"There's a mall fifteen minutes from here," Elizabeth said. She gave us the directions, and Bob and I headed out.

"Can you help me understand something?" I asked Bob as we returned from the mall. I sat up front with him. Two pairs of black jeans and shirts lay in the back next to a box of cut roses and a vase that I had picked up at a florist.

"Yes, Mr. Scott?"

"Archie said that tonight's meeting tonight was more than just a dinner."

"Mr. Morgan told me that too," he said.

"He also told me that others will be there. Val, George, and Sue."

"That's right. The whole team."

"Which team is that?"

"Just a second, sir." He pulled the limo onto the road's shoulder and stopped. Then he shut off the engine and the lights. We were in a forest, and it was pretty dark.

"You're getting me spooked," I said.

I could see only his teeth as he smiled at my comment. "Sir, the six of us were hand-picked by Mr. Morgan. We're a secret task force assigned to help him defend Soul Identity."

I thought about this as Bob drove me back to the guest house. It was a risky strategy to rely on the total trustworthiness of all your team members. I wondered if Archie was aware of how Val viewed his stance on technology.

We reached the guesthouse at seven fifteen. I put the box of roses and the vase on the table and went into the bedroom to change.

I decided to ensure there would be no repeats of this morning's cold shower. The water was fine, the pressure was great, and when I was done I wrapped the towel around my waist.

I filled the vase and carried it over to the table, but then almost dropped it when I stubbed my bare toe on a chair leg. Half the water sloshed out of the vase and onto the floor. I used my towel to sop it up, then left it hanging to dry out in the bathroom. I got more water and put the dozen roses in the vase.

My game plan had Val and me returning here after Ann's, sitting down in the gadget room with a glass of wine, and listening to some music on the sound system. The roses would add a touch of class and show what a sensitive guy I was.

I carried the vase to the gadget room door and was careful with my toes. I reached in and switched on the lights.

George and Sue were on the reclining couch, watching the large screen television. Actually, George was watching, and Sue was on his lap facing him with her skirt bunched up around her waist. I had interrupted a very private moment.

Things happened pretty quickly after that. I shoved the vase and roses down to my waist to cover myself up. Water from the vase splashed all over my chest. Sue jumped up, turned away, and buttoned her blouse. George grabbed a couch pillow and put it in his lap, then stood up and turned around and fixed his pants.

I looked at the television screen. "I didn't know you got those kinds of channels here, George."

He grabbed the remote and clicked off the screen.

"I told you we shouldn't use this room when a guest is here," Sue said. She looked at me and smiled. "What pretty roses, Scott."

"Thanks," I said. "I don't know who should be more embarrassed."

"No need to be embarrassed," George said. "We'll be going now." They headed for the door and I stepped out of the way.

Sue stopped in front of me. "I must smell these beautiful roses." She bent down and sniffed.

"That's enough, Sue," George said. "We need to get ready for Ann's party." As he walked by, he winked at me. "Sixty-one years old, and still going strong." He pointed at the roses. "May I?"

I nodded. "I'd say you earned it."

He pulled out a rose and held the stem with his teeth. He started humming a tango, then caught up to Sue, put his arm around her, and danced her out of my quarters and into the hall.

I threw on some clothes and refilled the vase with water. I went back to the gadget room, put the vase on the coffee table, and raised the couch back to its sitting position.

It was ten minutes before eight, and I needed to get ready to intercept the phone call. I opened up the communications center and turned on the radio. I set its scanner to the cell phone frequencies and hurried to get my laptop set up and plugged into the signal.

I planned to use the scanner to grab the call and use the laptop to decrypt and play the message. Cell phone encryption sounds secure, but all it really protects against is direct listening by scanners. Any security geek with half a brain can decrypt and listen in on most mobile conversations.

The scanner locked onto the incoming call right on schedule. My laptop kicked in, and after three seconds I had enough data to decrypt. I clicked record and turned up the volume.

"…make this quick, as I have a meeting. Did Waverly get the present?" The man had a strong French accent: *Deed Wavehrly get zee pwezent?*

"No, sir, not yet." That voice was the same as yesterday.

"Why not?" the French voice demanded.

"Tonight, sir. After his little party, he'll have a big surprise."

"Good." The voice paused. "Make it bigger, he's getting too close."

"Yes, sir. It seems he found the camera."

"Take care of it—now. *Quod sum eris.*"

"I can't wait, sir."

The call was over. I saved the recording in a file and put the laptop in my bag. Then I called my parents.

Dad answered. "How's the work going?"

"Fine. These guys are in some dire straits. They may be bankrupt soon."

"I'm glad they paid us up front," he said.

"Hey, do you still remember your high school Latin?"

"Of course," he said. "*Sola lingua bona est lingua mortua.*"

"What's that mean?"

He chuckled. "*The only good language is a dead language.* You need something translated?"

"*Quod sum eris.*"

"Sometimes you see that carved into gravestones. It means *I am what you will be.* Where did you see it?"

"I overheard it," I said. "Thanks, Dad. I've got to run." I hung up the phone just as Val knocked on the door.

Val had dressed in shorts, sandals, and a halter top. She looked ravishing. "I need to see something on television," she called as she walked into the gadget room.

A second later, she asked, "Are these flowers for me?"

I came in behind her. "Yes, but you've gone and ruined my surprise. They were for later on tonight."

"Oh, Scott, they're beautiful." She gave me a big hug, then held my cheeks in her hands. "You are so sweet." She kissed me and my disappointment evaporated as I returned the kiss.

She broke away. "I've really got to watch this." She turned on the television and stared at the adult television channel. "Is this what you watch?"

"No, no, that wasn't me." I pointed at the screen. "I caught George and Sue on the couch in almost that exact same position just a half hour ago."

She laughed as I described what happened. She counted the eleven roses, and said, "Actually, it's good that George took the twelfth rose. In Russia, living people get odd numbers of flowers. Only dead people get even numbers."

"So George did us a favor after all."

"He may be keeping us alive." She changed the channel. "One of our friends from Maryland is being interviewed today on the financial channel, and I told her I'd watch."

The interviewer came on screen. "Our feature story tonight shows how a family-operated hometown business successfully repelled a takeover bid."

The image cut away to a reporter standing on the side of a highway. "Kent Island, Maryland. It's the home to—"

"Hey, that's my town," I said.

"Shush, I want to hear this."

The reporter continued. "This is Madame Flora's, a fortune telling business located along the busy Route Fifty." The image flashed to the front of the palm reading joint.

Madame Flora spoke on the screen. "They offered me a boatload of money, but I told them to stick it," she said.

"Who offered you the money, ma'am?" the reporter asked.

"WorldWideSouls. They're thugs, either swallowing up us little independents or forcing us out of business. And they're fakes. Not the real thing at all." Madame Flora put her face right into the camera. "I'm talking to you, WorldWideSouls! You're fakes!"

The news show editors switched from the live interview to a previously taped background story on Madame Flora's establishment. We saw pictures of the palm reading room and a small segment on the growing fascination that people had with learning about their future and their past. Then we were live again with the twins, standing on the highway a couple hundred yards east.

"Rose and Marie are Madame Flora's granddaughters," the reporter said.

They both giggled and nodded their heads. "We're really proud of Grandma for standing up to WorldWideSouls," Rose said.

Marie pointed behind her. "This morning they came and put these nasty billboards on both sides of Grandma's business." The camera zoomed out, and we saw the advertisements for WorldWideSouls, reading 'Don't trust your future to an itty bitty local. Go World Wide for the real Truth.' The signs had an unflattering picture of Madame Flora with a big red 'X' marked through her face.

"Grandma fought back, and tomorrow the signs are out of here." Marie grinned. "But the guys who put them up were really cute."

"Hopefully they'll be back to take them down," chimed in Rose. They both waved at the camera as the image faded out on them and in on the news room.

Val shut off the remote. "These guys are terrible."

"WorldWideSouls?" I asked. "Both Archie and Ann mentioned them to me today."

She nodded. "They're tough competitors. Flora may have stopped them this time, but they'll be back. They're ruthless."

So I'd been hearing. "How do you know Madame Flora?" I asked.

"I use her equipment for secure video conferencing with my team here in Sterling."

I shook my head. "No way. I saw that super duper communications device she has. It's just a fax machine."

She laughed. "She showed you her fax machine?"

I thought about that. "Did she pull a fast one on me?"

She laughed even harder. "Flora has her own communications center." She grabbed a rose, broke off the stem, and stuck it behind her ear. She put a mock serious expression on her face. "Believe it or not, this rose is a secret Soul Identity camera." She smiled. "Did you believe that?"

"No, Soul Identity uses only yellow equipment, and that rose is red." I grinned. "See? I'm not as gullible as I look."

She pointed at me. "And what color was the fax machine?"

It was beige. I groaned. "How did I miss that?"

She sat on my lap and draped her arms around my neck. "I'm still pretty impressed." She had a mischievous look on her face. "Was this how George and Sue were sitting when you walked in on them?"

"Almost. Hold on." I shifted her just a little bit to the left and pulled her in closer.

"Like this?" She was rocking her hips ever so gently.

I closed my eyes. "Just like that. Wow."

I felt her lips nibbling my ear. "Was there anything else?" she asked.

"There was. Can you take off—"

The doorbell interrupted us.

I sighed. "Talk about bad timing."

She got up and arranged her clothes. "George and Sue must have thought the same thing," she said.

I opened the door, and Elizabeth smiled at me. "Time to go, Mr. Waverly. We can't keep Mom waiting, you know."

"Okay, we're ready." I grabbed my laptop bag, and the three of us headed out to the limo.

Elizabeth got in front. Val and I climbed in back and found George and Sue sitting on the couch. "Thought we'd catch a ride with you," George said.

Sue and Val looked at each other and burst out laughing.

"What's so funny?" I asked.

Sue held up her rose and pointed at the one still behind Val's ear. "Now we know who shared that cold shower with you, Scott."

Val laughed. "And we know how that twelfth rose was earned."

Elizabeth turned around and smiled. "Look at the two happy couples in the back, Bob," she said.

Bob beamed. "Yes, Elizabeth. And we're another happy couple up front." He leaned over and gave Elizabeth a kiss.

Elizabeth held up her left hand and flashed us a diamond ring. "Bob and I got engaged at lunch today."

Val and Sue examined the ring. I clapped Bob on the shoulder. "Congratulations."

"Thank you, sir. I am very nervous, but very excited." He paused. "We have a big battle coming up, and I don't want to fight alone."

"We'll fight together, Bob darling," Elizabeth said.

"That's so sweet," Sue said.

"When's the big day?" I asked.

"Very soon," Elizabeth said. "But first we have to tell Mom."

"Will that be a problem?" I asked.

Bob shook his head. "I've been practicing telling her all afternoon. I can do this."

Elizabeth patted his arm. "Show them, Bob honey."

Bob cleared his throat a couple of times and took a deep breath. "Ms. Blake, that's a fine outfit you're wearing, ma'am." He looked at Sue. "Can you pretend to be Elizabeth's mother?"

Sue nodded and cleared her throat. "Why, thank you, Bob," she said with an inflated Texas accent. "That's a nice green uniform you're wearing."

Bob smiled. "Thank you, ma'am." He looked at Elizabeth. "I forgot what comes next."

"The weather."

"Oh yeah." Bob looked at Sue. "And isn't the weather tonight just beautiful, ma'am?"

"Yes, Bob, it is." Sue looked at Elizabeth. "It's supposed to rain this evening, so be careful with that line."

Bob cleared his throat. "Ms. Blake, I love your daughter, and she loves me, and we're getting married. Can you give us your blessing?"

Sue smiled. "That was very good, Bob."

Elizabeth giggled. "See, Bob darling, you can do it!"

"I guess I can." Bob grinned at the four of us. "Now we have to hurry." He backed out of the driveway and drove us to Ann Blake's house.

The house was only fifteen minutes away. Elizabeth mentioned that they had lived there ever since her mother had become the depositary chief.

"When was that?" I asked.

"About ten years ago," she said.

George jumped in. "You know, that was right before the millennium. We were in the middle of the dot com boom, and Soul Identity was flush with money." He pointed at Elizabeth. "If I'm not mistaken, your mother got her position partly because of her success as head of investments."

Elizabeth nodded. "She chose some great startups."

"So what happened two years later when the dot com went dot bust?" I asked.

George shrugged. "We take the long view. After almost twenty-six hundred years in the game, we have some tricks up our sleeves."

"Not to mention a large enough pile of money to weather any storm and significantly influence any market," added Sue.

Archie and Ann must not have told them how dangerously close to the financial edge Soul Identity had slid.

"That was also the year we upgraded all our systems—new readers, new communications centers, new computers, and new programs," George said. "Like every other company in the world, we didn't want the millennium bug to bite us."

We got out of the limo, and Elizabeth rang the doorbell.

Ann answered the door and stood there with her hands on her hips. "What a motley crew you drug in here, Bob."

Bob cleared his throat and wiped his palms on his pants. "Ms. Blake, that's a fine outfit you're wearing, ma'am."

"Why, thank you, Bob." Some sprinkles of rain began to fall. "Let's get inside before we all get wet." She opened the door wide.

But Bob wasn't done. "And Ms. Blake, isn't the weather tonight just beautiful, ma'am?"

Elizabeth slumped against Sue.

Ann stared at Bob. "Ducks might call this weather beautiful."

Bob gulped. "Me and your daughter are getting married, ma'am. We are in love with each other, and we're hoping you'll bless us."

Ann stood with her hands on her hips and stared at Bob. Then she turned to Elizabeth and raised her eyebrows just a little bit. Elizabeth nodded. Ann gave a single nod back, and Elizabeth's whole face lit up in a big grin.

We all applauded.

"Come inside." Archie stood in the doorway behind Ann. "We have much work to do tonight." He led us through the foyer and out the back door.

A covered terrace extended across the back of the house and overlooked a manicured lawn bordered with raised flower beds. The rain settled into a slow drizzle, and the water drops on the flowers glistened in the solar garden lights' glow.

I walked over to Bob. "Good thing the terrace is covered," I said. "We need protection from all this beautiful weather."

Bob smiled. "I really messed that up, sir."

"It was fine, and it worked." I clapped him on the back.

Sue and Val passed out flutes of champagne, and Archie raised his high. "To you, Bob and Elizabeth," he said. "We wish you many happy years together."

Val came over and slipped her hand into mine.

"Hey, Bob was talking about a battle," I said to her. "Is this a war you're in?"

She squeezed my hand. "It's a war we both are in."

I squeezed back and smiled. In for a penny, in for a pound.

sixteen

ANN TAPPED A KNIFE against the side of her champagne glass to get our attention. "Tonight's an old fashioned Southern barbeque, so load up your plates and bring 'em on into the dining room."

After we ate, Archie aligned his notepad with the corner of the table. He ran his fingers along the edges, then looked up at us. "It is a sad occasion when we must meet in secrecy to defend our organization." He cleared his throat. "I think everyone has met Scott Waverly."

Everybody nodded.

"You should be aware that Scott is neither a member nor a believer," Archie said. "He is a skeptic who hasn't accepted the transmigration of soul identities through various lives."

"He's not a believer *yet*," Bob said.

I smiled. "That's fair, Bob. I'm not *yet* a believer." I looked at him. "However, I have seen what Soul Identity means to you and others, and I'm ready and willing to help you defend your organization."

Archie looked around the table. "So what have we learned?" he asked.

Val leaned toward me and whispered, "Mr. Morgan assigned each of us areas to investigate."

"Let us start with our competitor," Archie said. "Sue, I asked you to find out what WorldWideSouls is doing to our affiliates."

Sue sighed. "It's not good news from the churches, I'm afraid. The complaint rates are way up. Some churches have even stopped talking to us altogether."

"Why would they do that?" Bob asked. He stroked the bump of the pendant under his shirt. I remembered him telling me yesterday that he attended a weekly service.

Sue leaned forward. "They're going to WorldWideSouls. I just got confirmation this week on eighty of them. I'm still checking on the rest."

I turned to Val. "We just saw WorldWideSouls on the news tonight."

She nodded. "They tried to buy out Madame Flora."

"So now they've started invading our recruiters," Sue said. "What was reported?"

"They tried to intimidate her into selling her palm reading business to them," Val said. "Flora called them a bunch of fakes, and so far she's resisted."

Archie looked at me. "Last week we decided that WorldWideSouls must be getting help from people inside Soul Identity. I asked our team to look into various trends to see if we could find the traitor."

I nodded. "That makes sense."

George motioned to Sue, and she passed us each two sheets of paper. George put on a pair of reading glasses. "Mr. Morgan asked me to track communication trends," he said. "This first sheet contains last year's average monthly volumes for various communications between our offices."

The paper showed tables of data with columns labeled Type, Source, and Destination. The sheet was covered front to back with hundreds of rows of tiny print.

"That's pretty hard to read, so I plotted the connections onto a world map." George held up the second piece of paper. "This makes it easier for everybody to spot the trends."

The paper showed four world maps. With dots and lines between various cities, they looked like flight maps shown in the back of airline magazines. The maps were titled Calls, Intra-office Mail, Emails, and Deliveries. The hub and spoke patterns on each graph were the same: most communications were between Sterling and other offices. Almost no lines connected remote offices directly to each other.

"I see that headquarters is either the originator or recipient of most communications," I said.

George nodded. "That was last year." He frowned. "Now look at this year's data. You'll notice the trend has changed."

Sue passed us two more pages. These maps showed the same traffic load passing through Sterling, but a new hub had appeared. Most of the remote offices were communicating directly with Venice.

"Have you changed your operations to send more work through Venice?" I asked.

"Not officially," Archie said. "Elizabeth, please tell us about member visits."

Elizabeth held up her hand and smiled. Her diamond sparkled as she waved it in front of us. "With all the excitement today, I didn't have a chance to put together a presentation. But I have my notes here." She pulled a piece of paper out of her purse and unfolded it. "Member visits to our headquarters is down twenty percent for the year," she said, "but visits to most of our other offices is stable." She turned the paper over. "Except for Venice, that is. Last year they had three thousand member visits. This year they have that many per month."

"I'll go next, and I'll get right to the point." Ann passed us each a sheet of paper. "Our depositary withdrawals from our Venice branch have skyrocketed this year, with virtually no deposits."

I looked at the paper. It showed the funds coming into and going out of the depositary, broken down by office. Almost a billion dollars had been transferred out of Venice.

"Do other depositaries always bring in more funds than they send out?" I asked.

She handed us another sheet of paper, which contained a table of new depositary funds, along with five, ten, and one hundred year running averages. "Yes, they do," she said. "Historically our members deposit four to five times the amount they withdraw. Every office falls within this range. Every office except Venice."

Val turned to Archie. "Mr. Morgan, last week I told you to stop picking on Andre Feret—that he was a good man trying to help bring Soul Identity into the twenty-first century."

Archie nodded. "I recall you saying that."

Val's cheeks flushed. "Just yesterday I would have attributed the extra communications and extra visits to Andre trying picking up our slack," she said.

"What do you mean slack?" Ann asked.

Val turned to her. "We don't communicate enough. But that's not my point."

"Then let's hurry and get to it," Ann said.

Val nodded. "I've been a big defender of Andre's methods," she said. "But now I'm not so sure." She pointed at me. "I think everybody needs to hear what Scott has to say."

Ann turned to me. "She's right. Show them your mystery man."

I pulled Berry's images and reader sheets out of my laptop bag and laid them on the table.

"Whose identities are these?" Sue asked.

"Somebody who wants to become a member, but he lost an eye and couldn't have a reading done," I said. "We used a photograph to do the reading and matching." I held up the first two sheets. "Ann did these by hand."

Archie took one of the sheets. "Good work, Ann," he said. "It's nice to see somebody remembers how to do things the old way."

I held up the two reader sheets that the computer had generated. "When Val used her computer program to calculate the soul identity, it came up different."

"We ran them again to be sure," Val said, "but we had the same results again—different identities."

"How could that happen?" Archie asked.

"That's what I wanted to know," Ann said.

I pulled the next reader sheet out of the bag. "We calculated the identity using my own program. You can see it matches Ann's hand-run one." I passed it around and everybody took a look at it. "This makes us pretty confident that Ann's reading is accurate, and your computer program isn't."

I glanced around the room. Everybody looked stunned.

"How could something be wrong with our program?" Bob asked. "We've been using it for a long time."

"We're not sure," Val said. "But there's more—when we uploaded Ann's hand-run identity of Scott's friend, it matched on somebody who's alive today," Val said.

"That is impossible," Archie said.

"So you've been telling me, Archie," I said. "But it's true." I paused for a minute before continuing. "It matched Andre Feret."

Everybody started talking at once.

Ann clapped her hands. "Come on y'all," she said, "let Scott finish."

I pulled out the last sheet. "Here's a copy of Feret's reader sheet, where you can see his identity matches what Ann and I calculated." I held it up. "But we couldn't prove that these are really Feret's eyes."

"We searched online, and we came up empty," Val said. "In every picture we have, Andre is either standing in the shade, wearing sunglasses, or closing his eyes."

Archie stood up and paced around the room with his hands clasped behind his back. "I remember it took a long time to verify Mr. Feret's identity," he said.

"Yes, it did, Mr. Morgan," George said. "He stayed with us in the guesthouse while we waited for his eye infection to clear up. Ten years ago."

I pulled Berry's photograph out of my laptop bag and held it up. "And ten years ago, this person who matches Feret's overseer identity lost his eye in a freak accident."

Bob gasped. "Mr. Scott, that's your neighbor!"

I was surprised that Bob recognized Berry. "You're right, Bob. He was pretty upset when you couldn't read his glass eye."

He nodded. "I thought he was going to shoot me."

"Bob, why didn't you just bring us that photograph?" Ann asked. "We could have read it here."

Bob was silent for a minute. "We were taught in class that only living eyes could be read." He hung his head. "I messed up, didn't I?"

"It's not your fault," Ann said. "It's our new approach. We rely too much on these darn computers."

"And it seems they're misbehaving," added George.

"That's not true," Val said. "Each new program is put through comprehensive testing before I deploy it."

"Yes, Val, but only since you got here." George shook his head. "Ten years ago we were scared to death about Y2K. You all remember the predictions of planes dropping out of the sky, power grids failing, and dams bursting. We rushed to get our new systems in place as quickly as possible."

Sue smiled. "We hired contractors for the very first time. You raised quite a stink with that decision, Mr. Morgan."

Archie nodded. "I remember that all too well. But we had no choice. We did not have the skills we needed to upgrade. When a member recommended an offshore outsourcing firm, we were able to get the work done in time for the new millennium."

"You outsourced your computer work?" I asked. That seemed amazing to me.

"We did. SchmidtLabs is a reputable company in India." Archie smiled. "Hans Schmidt and most of his team joined Soul Identity when they started on our work, and they are still active members. We have a thriving office in Hyderabad today, thanks to them."

I turned to Val. "We're both pretty sure that there is some bad code attached to the match program, right?"

"We are. Let me show you what I found." She reached into her bag and pulled out two stacks of paper.

"What's this?" George asked.

Val pointed to the first stack. "The source code of the matching program. Scott and I went through it and we didn't see any problems." She pointed to the second stack. "But then I disassembled the binaries that were running on the system. And I found some extra code lurking in there."

Elizabeth shook her head. "I'm lost."

"We checked the source and it looked good. But the program that's running doesn't come from that source," I said.

Elizabeth still looked confused. "Then where did it come from?"

Val shrugged. "What's more important is what it does."

"I'll bite," I said. "What does it do?"

"Glad you asked. Take a look at the section I circled." Val passed the stack of papers to me.

The decompiled source code wasn't as easy to read as the original, but I could follow it. I ran my finger down the page. "It seems that if one of the identities in this list comes up, there's a simple substitution scheme to change it." I flipped the page. "The list contains thirty-four identities."

"Right, Scott," Val said. "And I checked—Berry's identity is one of the thirty-four."

"You need to bring it up a notch for us non-geeks," Ann said.

"Okay," I said. "Your match program computes the soul identities from the images, but then it changes thirty-four of them to something else. Berry's identity got changed."

Val looked at Ann. "And we only discovered this because you calculated the identity by hand."

"What are the odds of that?" I wondered out loud.

Nobody answered.

"I'm assuming that the other thirty-three identities belong to the other overseers," I said.

Val nodded.

Archie stood up, excited. "Does that mean we've been finding but overlooking more overseers?"

Val shook her head. "I did a quick database check to see if we had added any members who had the changed identities, but I didn't find any." She held up Berry's photograph. "Except for Scott's neighbor, of course."

"I guess we only find an overseer every ten or fifteen years, so it is not surprising." Archie sighed and sat back down. "Still, it is disappointing."

"There's something else. Look at this line." Val showed me the code. "If this specific identity comes up, it gets changed to your neighbor's identity."

"I wonder if that's Feret's real identity, from his real eyes," I said.

"That would be my guess," Val said.

"So our program stops all overseers except Archie from matching, and it appears to make Feret match as an overseer?" Sue asked.

Val nodded. "You've got it."

Ann sighed. "I knew that guy was trouble."

I remembered the phone call I had recorded before Val came over. Maybe somebody here could identify the voices.

"Archie, I have something else." I pulled out my laptop. "I intercepted and recorded a cell call earlier this evening." I clicked on the recording and turned up the volume.

When it was done, Archie asked me to play it again. After the second time through, Elizabeth raised her hand. "That's Mr. Feret. I talk to him almost every week. That's definitely his voice and his accent."

Ann nodded. "Yeah, that was him all right. But who was the other speaker?"

Nobody recognized it.

"It sounds like he tried to disguise his voice," Sue said.

George asked about the recording, and I explained how I used the gadget room scanner to capture and my laptop to decrypt it.

"So what's the big surprise Feret's arranging for you?" Ann asked.

I shrugged. "I guess I'll find out later tonight."

"And where was the camera?" Val asked.

"I've been thinking about that," I said. "It's in your office, where the fire evacuation sign used to be."

She nodded.

"What was Mr. Feret saying at the end?" Bob asked.

"*Quod sum eris.* That means *what I am, you will be,*" Archie said.

Bob looked puzzled. "What is Mr. Feret, that others would want to be?"

"French?" I smiled.

Archie looked around the table. "It would appear that Mr. Feret is not in fact an overseer. What are we going to do about it?"

"Can you kick him out of Soul Identity?" I asked.

"Not without some real proof," he said.

"Then you've got a lot of work to do quickly," I said. "You need a real picture of Feret's eyes, you need to figure out the real story behind the changed computer programs, and you need to get to the bottom of what's really happening in Venice." I frowned. "And you've got to move quickly to protect my neighbor. Whoever is watching Val's camera knows what we know."

Archie had been taking notes. He looked up and nodded. "I like your thinking." He pointed at Val. "I want you and Scott to visit Hans Schmidt and figure out what happened to the matching program. Get to Hyderabad as soon as possible."

"Scott will need a visa, and I'll need mine renewed," Val said. "We can get them from the DC embassy tomorrow."

Archie nodded and turned to George and Sue. "I need you two in Venice," he said. "Take a couple good photographs of Mr. Feret's eyes. Then see what you can dig up about what is happening there."

George and Sue smiled at each other. "Right away, Mr. Morgan," George said.

Archie turned to Bob. "After you drive Scott and Val home to Maryland, bring Berry to Sterling. Try to bring Madame Flora, if she will come."

"How does everybody know Madame Flora?" I asked.

"She is an old friend of ours," Archie said. "I want to hear about her experience with WorldWideSouls." He looked at Bob. "Please ask her to come."

Bob nodded.

Archie turned to Elizabeth. "You can gather more intelligence on WorldWideSouls. Find out who is behind them and what they are doing. Find out why the churches are leaving us and joining with them."

Elizabeth nodded.

"Ann," Archie said, "I need you to find out what kind of people are withdrawing their money in Venice."

Ann nodded.

Archie stood up. "Does anybody have any questions?"

Nobody said anything.

Archie nodded. "Mr. Feret will arrive next Thursday afternoon for the century party on Friday. We will reassemble here next Thursday night. We are adjourned."

seventeen

AS BOB DROVE US back to the guesthouse, George and Sue discussed what they'd need for Venice. Bob looked at me in the mirror. "Mr. Scott, we should leave for Maryland tonight."

I glanced at Val. "It's almost midnight—what's wrong with driving down tomorrow morning?"

"We need to go tonight," Val said. "The embassy only does visas on weekday mornings, and tomorrow is Friday."

So much for my late night gadget room plans. "How long is the flight to India?" I asked.

"Almost twenty-four hours. If we leave tomorrow night, we'll arrive at one o'clock early Sunday morning."

"I hope Soul Identity has a business class travel policy."

George spoke up. "We don't fly business class."

"Oh. That's bad," I said.

He grinned. "First class all the way, baby!"

Well, that was good news. But I was concerned about our timing. "Can we make it back to Sterling by Thursday night?"

Val nodded. "The time zones are on our side coming back. We can leave Hyderabad at two o'clock Thursday morning and arrive in Boston that afternoon. That leaves us with four full days in India."

"How do you know this?" I asked.

"I've flown over there three times in the last two years. SchmidtLabs is helping with the Internet-based programs we're building. This time, though, I'm running the projects. Ten years ago, they designed, built, and delivered the new programs, without any oversight from us." She looked troubled. "And I just took that old code for granted."

I nodded. "Companies taking things for granted is what pays my bills. That's the root of almost all security holes."

Bob drove up the guesthouse driveway. "Let's be ready to leave in ten minutes," he said as we got out.

I pulled George aside. "We need to discuss our communication plan while we're traveling." If we agreed on the encryption codes in person, we'd be able to prevent any eavesdropping.

"I'll generate a one time pad and bring it out before you leave," George said.

We went inside. I grabbed my clothes, toiletries, and the ten leftover roses and headed back to the limo. When I got there I saw Val already loading her bags into the trunk.

George and Sue came out to see us off. George handed a sheet of paper to me. "There are only three copies of this," he said. "I'll give the other one to Mr. Morgan. Each day has its own encryption key."

I looked at the paper; there were seven long strings of letters and numbers. "We use the first key tomorrow?" I asked.

He nodded. "Change keys at midnight Sterling time."

I opened the back door of the limo.

KA-BOOM!

I turned around; an explosion had shaken the guesthouse. The windows had all shattered, and broken glass was strewn around us.

I shoved George and Sue into the back, then yelled at Val and Bob to climb in next to them. I dove in the passenger door and slid over to the driver's seat. "Where's the keys, Bob?" I shouted.

He tossed them to me, and I jammed them in the ignition and got the limo started. I backed out of the driveway. There was another explosion, muffled for us by the limo's windows, and the entire guesthouse blew apart.

I bumped over the curb and across the opposite lawn. "Scott, the tree!" Val screamed, and I swerved just in time. The limo stopped after a three quarter turn, broadsided to where the guesthouse had been.

We stared out the windows at the sight. What remained of the house was in flames, and roofing shingles, bits of wood, and bricks littered the surrounding lawns. I saw some ripped clothing and sheets, backlit by the fire, float down from the sky. A bathroom door had landed on top of a fence post, improbably rocking back and forth. Then a red nightgown landed on one side of the door, causing it to tip and slide to the ground.

In the back of the limo, George had his arm around Sue, her head buried in his chest. Val sat on the front couch and stared at the fire. I reached through the partition, and she grabbed my hand.

"Were any other guests staying with you?" I asked George.

"No, just you two," he said. He reached out and rubbed Sue's back.

Sue sat up straight and glared at me. "It was just by chance that we came outside to say goodbye. Those bastards almost killed us all."

We sat silently for a moment.

"So this was the surprise," I said.

George grunted. "I certainly was surprised."

I looked back at everybody. "Do we show them that they missed? Or should we pretend they got us?"

"How can we pretend? We drove away in the limo," George said.

"They probably didn't stay too close," I said. "It was a huge explosion, and they would have had to be way back. Maybe they don't know who made it out."

"They were after you, so it doesn't help for Sue and me to play dead," George said. "We can buy you some time."

I nodded. "How about if you three go back and start a search for Val and me? We'll hide out here in the back," I said. "Then later we'll have a chance to grab Berry and get him somewhere safe."

Everybody agreed. Bob crawled through the partition to the driver's seat and I crawled to the back. Then Val and I reclined the back couch and climbed behind it.

George raised the seat to hide us from view. "You'll just have to sit tight," he said. "I'll leave the seat back just a bit so you can breathe and watch what's going on."

"Thanks, George," I called. "Remember, get Bob sent home to Maryland as soon as you can."

"You'll be on your way in an hour or two at the most." George flashed us a reassuring smile, and told Bob to drive back.

"Wait a second!" I hollered.

Bob hit the brakes.

"You three need to get your story straight," I said. "Why did you come back to the car? How long were you out there? Who drove? If you don't agree on this, you are going to look pretty silly."

The three practiced their story for the next two minutes. Val and I crouched down and peered out the small gap as Bob drove up the driveway. He, George, and Sue hopped out and ran back toward the guesthouse foundation.

Val shifted. "You think they'll be able to pull it off?"

Sue seemed to be in shock, and judging from his performance at Ann's tonight, Bob didn't do too well under pressure. "It's all up to George," I said.

She wrapped her arms around me. "I'm glad we got out."

I hugged her back. "Me too."

We sat there with our arms around each other. The rescue workers arrived, and we watched them search in the rubble strewn all over the yard. "They must be hoping to find something really grisly that they can share with their friends," I said.

We watched Bob, Sue, and George talk to the police and give their statements. George pointed and gestured; we saw him mime driving backward and swerving. He used his hands to show the explosion. He pointed back to the remains of the house and shrugged his shoulders.

"Looks like they're buying it," I said. "George is pretty good." Then I thought of something. "Hey, let's switch off our cell phones. Just in case somebody is monitoring our location."

Ten minutes later we saw George call Bob and a policeman over, and after a short discussion, Bob walked over to the limo, got in, and drove away.

We stayed behind the back seat until we got off Soul Identity grounds. Bob smiled as we climbed out and stretched. "We did it, sir. The police think you two are toast."

"Good. You had a big day today, dude. Let's split the driving to Maryland," I said.

He nodded. "I'll take the first shift. You and Val can rest."

Which was fine with me. Val and I reclined the rear seat and slept.

I woke at four and switched on the GPS. Bob had driven us halfway down the New Jersey Turnpike already. "Jeez, you've made great timing," I said.

Bob smiled into the rear view mirror. "Yes, sir. It's been smooth sailing so far."

Val sat up and rubbed her eyes. "Is there a rest area coming up?" she asked.

"Another mile, ma'am," Bob said.

"Thanks." She turned to me. "I've been thinking that we need to get Flora somewhere safe. It seems too coincidental that WorldWideSouls just happened to be targeting her."

I nodded. Bob pulled into the rest area, and I called Madame Flora from the pay phone.

One of the twins answered with a groggy "Hello, you've dialed Madame Flora's. Do you have a psychic emergency?"

"I'm sorry for waking you up so early," I said. "But I have a message for you and your grandma."

"Who is this?" the voice demanded.

"I can't say my name, but think about this—I'm the guy who saw your grandma's fax machine on Monday morning."

Dead silence for a few seconds. Then, "Okay, buster. What kind of cookies did I bake?"

I thought for a second. "Chocolate chip. But without the chips." So it was Rose on the phone.

I heard a giggle. "And no salt, either. What can I do for you, Mr.—"

"No names," I interrupted. "Listen, I saw you on television earlier tonight. I think there is about to be a serious problem, and you need to get your grandma out of the house right now."

"Now?" She sounded incredulous. "Right this minute?"

I tried to put some extra urgency into my voice. "Your grandma's life may be in danger. Yours and your sister's, too. Please get out immediately. Let me tell you where to go."

"Hold on," Rose said. "I have to get my sister, so she can help remember." I heard her waking up Marie and giving a quick explanation, and then Marie got on the line. "Go ahead, we're both listening."

"Your grandma wanted me to check on a commission for one of her customers. Drive to that person's house, but don't go in there. Go to the next house south. The back door is open."

"I hope there are beds in there," one of the twins said.

"There are. If you get that far, see if anybody is watching the customer's house. If you can do it without being seen, sneak him out of his house and over with you."

"This is beginning to sound fun," one twin said.

"Not to mention creepy," the other added.

"I'll explain when I get there at seven thirty," I said.

"Great, we'll make breakfast!"

I hung up the phone and shuddered at the thought of a breakfast cooked by girls who baked chocolate chip cookies containing neither chips nor salt.

I walked back and opened the driver's door of the limo. "I'll drive the rest of the way," I said to Bob.

He nodded and slid over.

Val came back and saw both of us sitting up front. "Don't leave me alone in the back," she said. She opened the passenger door. "Bob, scoot to the middle."

He scooted, she got in, and I pulled onto the turnpike.

An hour later I glanced at Bob. He stared straight ahead and stroked his necklace under his shirt. His lips moved in a silent chant.

"You okay?" I asked.

He nodded. "I keep wondering what would have happened if I didn't insist that we leave the guesthouse immediately."

"You'd be picking our pieces up off the lawn." Not that subtle, but it was after four in the morning, and I was still shaken by the explosion.

Bob turned toward me. "Somebody wanted you alive, Mr. Scott. And I was the tool He used to protect you."

"Who are you talking about, Bob?" I asked.

"God, sir. God saved you, and I helped. He must have something important planned for you." Bob's voice rose in volume and rang with certainty.

"I thought Soul Identity members didn't believe in God," I said.

"Of course we believe in God, sir," he sputtered. "Who else could have put our system in motion? It's certainly not random." He paused for a minute. "Not every member believes in God. Just like non-members, we have a mix of different beliefs."

I shook my head. "So how do you mix the two faith systems? Aren't they contradictory?"

Val stirred in her seat. "Scott, it sounds like you think Soul Identity is a religion," she said.

I thought about that. "Isn't it one?"

"No. I did say that we function like an organized religion. But really, we just find the bridges and provide some services to help our members use those bridges."

"Doesn't that require a faith?"

She nodded. "You only have to believe that your soul identity is unique, and that it's going to reappear in somebody else after you die. That's it."

Snowflakes were unique, and so were fingerprints. It wasn't much of a stretch to believe that computed soul identities were also unique. I thought about them reappearing—the organization seemed to have plenty of evidence in their archives, even though most of it was private and inaccessible.

"Maybe you're right," I said. "Barring any great conspiracies, I can believe those two things."

"Did you have to take any great leaps of faith to believe this?" she asked. "Or give up any other beliefs you held?"

I pondered this. "No, I didn't. There's not much difference between that and believing in gravity."

She smiled. "That's why people can join us and still retain their original faith."

"Wait, I didn't follow you," I said. "How is that the reason?"

"If you believe in gravity, you still have room to have faith in God," she said. "And almost everybody's spiritual faith can easily accommodate our two basic beliefs. Think of how many Christians are comfortable believing in evolution."

I thought about what Val had said. Although Soul Identity didn't force any religious beliefs, they certainly got people thinking about religion. "This is interesting," I said. "It's possible that Soul Identity even brings people back to church."

She nodded. "When you start thinking about your soul identity, you start thinking about the meaning of your life, what's important to you, and what you'd like to do in the future. That's when a church can help guide you."

That made sense. At five in the morning, these guys were acting less and less like wackos and more and more like normal, thoughtful people.

A little later Val nudged Bob. "Tell us about your church," she said.

Bob stirred. "We're non-denominational and Christian. We're pretty small, and all of us are Soul Identity members."

"Bob, the previous people in your soul line—where are they now?" I asked.

"They're dead, sir."

"But don't Christians believe that when you die, your soul goes to either heaven or hell?"

"We do, sir."

"So if you're here, and you have the soul identity of somebody who's in heaven or hell, where did that soul go?"

"Some people believe that once in heaven or hell, a soul has the option to come back and be born again," he said.

"If you get bored with eternal life, you can opt to start all over?" I asked.

He nodded. "Others believe that all members of a soul line are different incarnations of a single soul, and they all end up in heaven living together as a family."

That sounded sort of like Christians viewing the Trinity as three forms of a single God, all working together. What do you believe?" I asked.

He shrugged. "Both groups back up their beliefs with Bible texts, and both beliefs appeal to me."

"Will you get married in that church?" Val asked.

"We hope to, ma'am."

"Have you and Elizabeth talked about when?" I asked.

He nodded. "As soon as we can."

eighteen

WE COULD SEE MADAME Flora's place from Route Fifty. The WorldWideSouls billboards looked even more offensive in person than they did on television. I stopped the limo in the breakdown lane. The building was dark.

As I was about to pull back out onto the highway, Val reached over Bob and grabbed my arm. I hit the brakes, and we watched a gray sedan pull into Madame Flora's tiny parking lot.

The predawn light was bright enough for us to watch two figures get out of the car. They walked to the sides of the building and peeked in the windows. Then they disappeared around the back.

I got back on the highway. "Let's hope Madame Flora and the twins made it to my place," I said.

I reached my neighborhood, turned left down a side street, and approached my house from the south. I pulled over about two hundred yards short of the driveway. I turned to Bob. "We're still considered dead, so we'd better not be seen," I said.

"Okay, Mr. Scott. I'll wait here."

We got out, and I pointed out my house to Val. "Berry lives just beyond me."

She nodded. "Watch out," she said. "There's another gray car." It pulled into Berry's driveway. Val and I crossed the street and ducked behind a shed.

Two men got out and walked around Berry's house. When they were on the north side, we ran across my neighbors' backyards. We reached my back door just as they rounded the corner, and froze until they walked out of our sight.

Someone had locked the door. I knocked softly, and it swung open. Berry stood holding his shotgun. He looked ready to use it on us.

"Careful, Berry. It's me. Scott."

"What's going on?" he demanded. "I'm sleeping soundly, minding my own business, and next thing I know there's this terrific hammering on my back door."

"I'll explain in a minute." I looked around. "Where's Madame Flora?"

He pointed over his shoulder. "She and her granddaughters are keeping an eye on the guys from that gray car." He looked at Val. "Who's this?"

"Val works for Soul Identity," I said.

Berry nodded. "Who are these guys casing my house?"

"Let's get everybody together," I said, "and I'll tell you what we know."

Berry bolted the door shut. We walked through my office and headed into the front room. I saw Madame Flora peeking out the window.

"They just got back into their car," she said. "But they're not leaving."

"Hi, Mr. Waverly," one of the twins said. "I'm Rose." She gestured to the room. "Nice place."

"Thanks," I said. "Did you guys have any trouble?"

"No, it all worked out great," Marie said. "I think we really scared Mr. Berringer, though, when we banged on his door."

Rose giggled. "He scared us even more with that shotgun." She peeked out the window. "Are these guys from WorldWideSouls?"

I pointed at the dining table. "Let's sit down."

The six of us sat.

Madame Flora pointed at Berry. "I'm assuming this isn't about his commission," she said.

"Maybe it is," I said. "We ran Berry's identity by using an old photo, and it turns out he's an overseer."

She frowned. "That's good news, isn't it? Get him verified by the match committee, and then he'll be the third. Archibald will be thrilled."

"There's one catch," Val said. "Our computers say that Berry's identity matches Andre Feret's."

Madame Flora stared at Val for a minute. "How can he share the same identity?"

"We're guessing that Feret isn't really who he says he is," I said. "And that car outside Berry's house seems to support that."

Val told Madame Flora about the gray car we saw at her place.

"And how am I involved?" Madame Flora asked.

"Maybe they know you're his recruiter," I said.

Berry shook his head. "Can somebody go through this again, but this time in English?"

I turned to him. "Remember you gave me a photo so I could try to get your soul identity read?" I asked.

Berry nodded.

"We did read it, and it looks like some guy stole your identity."

"What's wrong with his own identity?"

"Apparently yours is special, Berry—one that makes you somebody rich and powerful. He must have wanted it for himself." I remembered something. "Berry, you mentioned you lost your eye in a freak accident. What happened?"

Berry seemed lost in thought for a minute. "It's been ten years now, but I remember it like it was yesterday. I was walking my dog Tubbers around my old neighborhood—"

"I love dogs," Marie said.

"Me too," added Rose. "I wish Grandma had a dog."

"Girls, let Mr. Berringer tell his story," Madame Flora said.

Berry smiled at the girls. "I love dogs too. Anyway, we had turned for home. The next thing I remember, I was lying face down on the ground. Tubbers was licking my ear. My nose was broken, and I had big bruises on the backs of my legs and a long splinter of wood sticking out of my left eye."

"Ouch," Marie said.

"Ouch is right. A neighbor found me and called an ambulance, and the paramedics brought me to the hospital. They patched up everything but my eye."

"Did you call the police?" I asked.

"I did. They asked around the neighborhood for witnesses, but nobody saw anything. They said I was the victim of a hit and run accident."

I heard an edge to his voice. "Do you agree?" I asked.

"I think a car came at me from behind," he said. "I flew through the air and hit the ground. But the funny part is this—I have always been careful on the streets. Maybe it comes from selling wheelchairs to too many unfortunate pedestrians. I always walked against traffic. Always." He stared at me. "If a car came from behind and hit me, it really went out of its way to do so."

Val looked at me, then turned to Berry. "Did you happen to go in for an eye examination before your accident?"

He thought for a minute. "I had just gotten fitted for some reading glasses a few weeks before," he said. "What a waste of money that turned out to be."

So somebody had tried to hurt, or even kill, Berry ten years ago. Chances were they belonged to the same crowd that was staking out his house. We had to get him somewhere safe. I went to the office and called Dad on his cell phone.

"What are you doing in Maryland?" he asked.

"There's been a slight change of plans," I said. "Are you guys on your way down?"

"Yeah, we're on the bridge now," he said. "Ten or fifteen minutes, tops."

I hung up and headed back to the dining room. I caught a whiff of smoke in the air. "Something's burning in the oven," I said.

Marie and Rose bolted for the kitchen.

Madame Flora frowned. "I think they were trying to make sweet rolls."

I raised my eyebrows. "I have flour, but I'm sure I don't have yeast."

"They substitute all the time," she said. "You wouldn't believe what they made me eat these last few weeks."

I looked over at Berry. "Bob is waiting at the end of the street to bring you guys to Sterling."

"Virginia?" Berry asked.

"Massachusetts," Val said. "Our headquarters."

"Why would I want to go there?" he asked.

"It's your way into Soul Identity," I said. "They'll keep you safe while we figure out what to do about those guys watching your house."

Val walked into the front room and peeked out the window. "Now there's two gray cars outside."

I joined Val and saw four men standing in a huddle in the street. I pointed at a yellow VW Beetle in my driveway. "Madame Flora drives a bug?"

"We drive the bug," Marie said. "Grandma drives a Hummer." The twins came over to us, wiping their hands on a towel.

"Breakfast is ready," Rose said.

"We're having juice and coffee," Marie said.

"And we were going to have sweet rolls, before you let them burn."

"Girls," Madame Flora said, with a slight edge in her voice. She went back to the table.

"What kind of juice?" Berry asked.

"It's a mix," Rose said. "There was only a little bit of orange juice, and cup of grape juice, and since there still wasn't enough, we added some lemon juice, sugar, and water."

Berry grimaced. "Coffee sounds good. You have cream?"

Marie shook her head. "No, there was none. We added some hot chocolate mix into the coffee, though. Everybody likes chocolate, right?"

Val bit her lip and looked at the floor. She caught my eye and we both burst out laughing. "I'll take whatever you two are serving," I said.

The front door opened. "Scott, what's with the spooky guys outside of Santa's house?" Mom called.

"We're in here," I said.

"Madame Flora, girls, Berry," Dad said. He looked at Val and stuck out his hand. "I'm Scott's dad." He nodded to Mom. "And this is his mom."

Val smiled. "I'm Val." She shook both their hands.

"So what's going on?" Dad asked as the eight of us sat down around the table.

I got them up to speed, and then Val and I explained our alleged death in the guesthouse explosion. "We're buying time to get Flora and Berry someplace safe," Val said.

"Bob is sitting in a limo just out of sight," I said. "He's ready to take you guys to Sterling." I looked at them. "If you're willing to go."

Berry nodded. "If that's the way to get me into Soul Identity, that's the way I'm going."

Madame Flora laughed. "And of course I'm willing. I wouldn't miss this for the world. But the girls are coming, too."

Berry walked over to the window. "Uh oh," he said. "We're going to have some issues getting out of here."

I joined him and peeked outside. Three gray cars were in front of Berry's house, and I could see another car parked halfway down the street.

"We need a diversion," Berry said.

"But first we need a plan," I said. "And we need to hurry. It won't be long before they wise up and start looking in my windows."

Val pointed out the back window. "They won't be able to follow us on the water."

"Wow, great idea," I said. I turned to my parents. "Could you guys grab some fishing rods and get the boat ready to go?"

"Of course," Mom said.

I called Bob on his cell phone. "Have you seen what's happening outside of Berry's place?" I asked.

"I have, Mr. Scott. I had to back off a bit. That fourth car almost spotted me," he said. "How are you going to get everybody out of your house?"

"We're going to take my boat."

"All the way to Massachusetts?"

I was supposed to be the smart-aleck. "No, Bob, to Baltimore. You can pick them up at the Inner Harbor and drive them the rest of the way."

"Okay," he said. "Let's meet at the dock behind the National Aquarium."

"Fine. But first we need a diversion," I said. "Can you drive up and knock on Berry's door?"

"Why would I do that?" he asked.

"We need to get these guys paying attention to you and not to us as we hop on the boat," I explained.

Bob was silent for a long minute. "Okay," he said. "When do I knock?"

I looked at my watch. "It's eight o'clock now. How about in thirty minutes?"

"Okay." He paused. "Good luck, Mr. Scott," he said.

"You too, Bob. Be careful, okay?"

"Yes, sir."

I hung up and turned to our team. "In a half hour, Bob is going to get the gray guys' attention. That's when we run to the boat."

Dad stood up. "We'd better get out there and get everything ready." He and Mom grabbed a couple of fishing poles and a tackle box. He grinned. "Props."

When they left the house, I turned to Val. "I need to get some clothes. How's Hyderabadi weather in August?"

"As hot as Maryland. It's the monsoon season, so it's almost as humid."

I nodded. "Khakis and polo shirts for me. I'll go pack." I went into my bedroom and threw together some clothes.

Val came in and closed the door. "We've got twenty-six minutes. That's enough time for a shower, right? It was a long night in the limo."

I smiled. "Can I join you?"

"Are you quick enough not to slow me down?"

"Watch me," I said. I tore off my clothes and hurried into the bathroom.

Val came in. "How about a spare toothbrush and razor?" She had left her clothes back on my bed and was now standing in front of me.

"Wow." I shook my head. "I have no idea what you just asked me."

"Bad boy." She smiled. "Extra toothbrush and razor."

"Under the sink."

While she bent over to look, I brushed up against her. "Did you find them?" I asked.

"No," she said. "You sure they're down here?"

"Nope."

She stood up. "So where are they?"

I grinned. "Behind the mirror. But boy, I was wishing they were down there."

She smiled and gave me a lingering kiss which weakened my knees so much that I had to step back to keep from falling over.

I pulled away and stared into her eyes. "There's something about danger that really gets me going," I said.

"Me too," she replied. "I like how naughty you are." She grabbed my spare toothbrush and razor and hopped in the shower.

I handed her the toothpaste and joined her. "Twenty-three minutes," I said. "Let's use the time wisely."

nineteen

I POINTED AT THE clock. "In a little over a minute, Bob's going to create a diversion."

Out the back window I could see that my parents had lowered the boat into the water and maneuvered alongside the dock. They held the boat steady by grabbing the large cleats bolted through the dock.

Rose and Marie peeked out the front windows. "Here comes a dark green limo. That must be Bob," Rose said.

"He's getting out. I see six, no seven, people watching him," Marie said.

"Where's the eighth guy?" I asked.

"He was up the road, waiting in his car...Okay, he just came over. They're all talking to Bob."

Bob walked up to Berry's door and knocked.

"Everybody to the boat," I ordered. "Quickly!"

Madame Flora stepped outside with the twins. The rest of us followed. Half way down the lawn, Madame Flora slipped and caught herself by grabbing onto Rose's arm. "My ankle," she gasped, hopping on one foot.

I looked back. One of the guys in the gray suits was watching us. I smiled and waved.

We almost reached the dock when the guy let out a shout and pointed at us.

We had twenty yards to go. "Time to run," I said.

Dad gunned the boat's engine. The gray guys ran toward us. It was going to be close.

I tossed my bag and laptop to Val and scooped Madame Flora into my arms. I carried her to the boat and eased her onto the deck. Everybody else clambered aboard.

They gray suited guys reached the far end of the dock. "Go!" I hollered, and Dad pushed off from the cleat and shifted in gear. The boat pulled away.

The suits ran down to the end of the dock. Two of them reached under their jackets and pulled out handguns.

"Get down!" I yelled, ducking under the gunwale.

Bam!

I looked up. Berry stood at the back of the boat, his shotgun pointed toward the dock.

"Jeez, Berry, don't kill them," I said.

"I aimed high," he said. "I had to give them some discouragement." He grinned. "See how they run?"

We watched the gray suits scramble off the dock and run back up the lawn. I saw Bob's limo pull away.

"Let's hope they don't have a boat," Val said.

"Where are we headed, anyway?" Dad asked.

I pointed north. "Past the bridge and up the Patapsco. We're meeting Bob behind the National Aquarium."

He nodded. "You all might as well get comfortable. It'll take us over an hour to get there."

Madame Flora and Berry sat on the stern bench. The twins went below to explore. Val and I hung our feet off the sides at the bow.

Val leaned her head against my shoulder. "I could get used to doing this every day," she said.

"Minus the shooting part." I rubbed her back.

"I thought for sure they'd catch us." She shivered. "Especially after Madame Flora slipped."

We watched the waves sparkle in the morning sun. Then I thought that we should call Archie. I got up. "I'm calling Sterling—I'll use Dad's phone."

Archie seemed happy I called. I told him about the gray suited people snooping around, and how they had chased us to the boat.

"Who do you think they are?" I asked.

"Did you get any license plates?"

And I call myself a security guy. "No, dammit, I guess I'm still not thinking straight after last night's bombing." I described Bob's diversion to him. "We're rendezvousing in an hour. Where should Bob deliver Berry, Madame Flora, and the twins?"

"Take them to Ann Blake's house," he said. "I will make arrangements by the time they arrive this afternoon."

"Cool. Now what about Venice? Are George and Sue still going?"

Archie chuckled. "They are already on the plane."

"They had their passports?"

"George had them in his pocket."

I thought about my parents. Their car was left in front of my house. I didn't want the gray suits tracking them down. "Archie, I am afraid I've dragged my parents into danger," I said. "They can't return to my place, nor can they go home."

"Would they be willing to take a vacation for a week?" he asked. "My treat."

"I'll talk to them about it." I hung up and sat back down with Val. "My parents need to disappear for a week. And we need to get to India. Do you know anybody in Baltimore who could help us with the tickets? I don't want to use our credit cards."

She frowned. "There's a large Russian community in Baltimore. Can I use the phone?"

I handed her Dad's cell. I gave her a kiss on the cheek and got up to talk to my parents.

"So who's this Val?" Mom asked when I reached the cockpit.

"Soul Identity's lead programmer," I said.

"Am I supposed to like her?"

I grinned. "That's entirely up to you, Mom. I know I do."

"We can tell," Dad said.

Mom frowned. "Isn't she a Soul Identity wacko?"

"She is. But they're not so wacko to me anymore. They seem to help."

"As long as they don't help get us killed," Dad said. "How are we supposed to get the boat back to your place? Or pick up our car?"

"That's why I came over. Archie is willing to send you guys on a week's vacation. Anywhere you'd like to go. But you have to leave today."

"Why would he do that?" Mom asked.

"To protect us, dear." Dad looked at me. "Your mother and I were thinking about going back and seeing more of Iceland."

"We were?" Mom asked.

"Of course we were," he said. "Remember?"

"If you say so," she said. "I did like it there. All the geysers and hot springs and mountains. Maybe we'll be able to take a horseback ride this time."

I smiled. "I expected more of a struggle."

"We're not stupid, son," Dad said. "Those guys were shooting real bullets." He shook his head. "Get your mess cleaned up quickly. We want to be safe just as much as the next person."

I nodded. "We should have it figured out by next Friday."

"A week in Iceland—at least the weather will be cool," Mom said.

"How do we get the tickets?" Dad asked.

"Val's calling the Russian community for help."

Mom shook her head. "Weren't the Russians our enemies?"

"The wall came down twenty years ago," Dad said. "Get with the program."

Apparently Mom wasn't ready yet. "I remember doing air raid drills in school," she said. "We wore dog tags so our bodies could be identified. We closed the blinds and crouched under our desks and waited for Armageddon. Now I may get a Russian daughter-in-law?"

"Slow down," I said. "I'm not that lucky yet."

"Who's lucky?" Val asked, entering the cockpit.

"Tell you later," I said. "Hey, I remember seeing reports that you Russians waited in line all day long just to buy toilet paper. Is that true?"

"Nobody ever bought toilet paper where I lived," she said. "Even now my parents have a box of newspaper strips in the bathroom." She pointed at me. "Our Soviet television showed Americans carrying guns and shooting at each other. Did that really happen?"

"Today it did," Dad said.

"But not every day," Mom said. "We're good people."

Val smiled. "I know. I've been living here for eleven years, and I've found that we Russians and Americans have an awful lot in common."

"Like what?" Dad asked.

"We both get teary-eyed when we see our flag and hear our national anthem," she said. "We both believe in hard work and innovative thinking, and we both come from socially conservative societies." She smiled at them. "Russian and American people get along better than almost any other two cultures. We won't have any problems."

Val had cast a spell over my parents. They both wore huge smiles.

"Scott, she's a keeper," Dad said.

"Keeper?" Val asked me.

"It's a fishing thing. We keep only the big ones," I said.

She smiled. "Don't throw me back."

Val and I went to the stern. Madame Flora had nodded off in her seat, and Berry looked back toward Kent Island's shores. We sat down next to him.

Berry turned to me. "You said that overseers are powerful."

I nodded.

"How powerful?" he asked.

"They run Soul Identity," Val said. "Like bishops, only you have to be born into an overseer soul line."

"How many are there?"

"Usually we have eight or nine," she said. "But now there are only two."

"And I'm one of the two?"

"It looks like it," I said. "But there's a fake one standing in your place—Andre Feret."

He nodded. "Are the gray suits working for this Feret?"

I shrugged. "Either for him or for one of Soul Identity's competitors—we don't know yet."

He turned back to us, a fierce look on his face. "They probably are the ones who poked my eye out." He tightened his hands on the stock of the shotgun.

"Easy, Berry," I said. "Careful where you're pointing that."

Berry looked down and grimaced. "This has been the second time this week I wanted to kill somebody. Something about Soul Identity really stokes my fire."

"Give me the gun, then, before you burn out of control," I said.

He handed it to me, and I put it in a closet below decks.

We sailed up the Patapsco and into Baltimore's Inner Harbor. The National Aquarium was on the right and Dad angled us toward some tie-ups.

I pointed. "I can see Bob over there."

He nodded. We docked next to the green limo. Val and I jumped off, tied up, and helped everybody climb on shore.

Bob got out of the limo and walked over to Berry. "Mr. Berringer," he said, "I want to tell you how sorry I am about not getting your reading done properly. I should have thought about asking for a photograph of your eyes."

"No harm done, son," Berry said. "I'm sorry for chasing you off with my shotgun. I hear you're going to be driving us north."

"Yes, sir." Bob turned to me. "I got away before the gray cars could follow me."

"That's great," I said. "Did you speak with Archie?"

He nodded. "We'll be heading straight to Ms. Blake's house."

"Did you happen to get any of their license plates?" I asked.

"Of course, Mr. Scott." Bob smiled. "I've already passed them on to Mr. Morgan."

Then Bob handed me two large envelopes. "Mr. Morgan had me stop at the Baltimore depositary. This envelope contains cash for you and Val, and this other one is for your parents."

I took the envelopes. "Thanks. Drive safe, okay?"

The five of them got into the limo and drove away.

Dad turned to me. "We passed a few marinas around Fell's Point. We can dock at one of them."

"Good idea." I opened his envelope and thumbed through the hundred dollar bills. "Here's your present from Soul Identity. There's at least twenty grand here—don't use your credit cards."

Dad took the envelope. "Thanks."

I looked around. "Where did Val go?" I asked.

Mom pointed. Val stood at a pay phone a hundred yards away.

"She must be calling the Russians," I said.

Val waved her arms and called me over. She put her hand over the mouthpiece. "We have taxis coming, and they'll bring the tickets. Where should they pick us up?"

I pointed downstream. "At the first marina by Fell's Point."

Val said something into the phone, listened, and then hung up. "Thirty minutes," she said.

"Good, let's stash the boat."

The marina was happy to rent us a slip for a cash advance of twice the going rates. I turned to my parents. "Get in and get out of your house right away, okay? It won't be long before those gray suited guys track you down."

Mom nudged Dad. "What are we bringing to Iceland, anyway?"

"Passports, warm clothes, boots. We can rent fishing rods."

"The taxis are here," said Val. She waved, and they pulled up.

Two men got out of the taxis. "*Zdrastvuite*," Val said to the closer man. "Valya."

"*Ochen priyatno.* Boris." He nodded at the other driver. "Yuri."

"This is Boris and Yuri, and they're happy to meet us," Val said.

Boris pulled two packets out of his pockets. "Your tickets."

I held out my hand, but he kept the packets out of my reach. "Four first class tickets," he said. "Thirty-nine grand."

I opened my envelope from Archie and pulled out eight packets of bills. "Here's forty. Is the extra grand enough to keep the cabs all day?"

"*Da.*" Boris stuffed the money in his pocket. "Where you want to go?"

I reviewed our plans. Yuri would drive my parents home. They would pick up their clothes and passports, find someplace safe to hang out, and then take the eight p.m. flight from BWI to Iceland.

Meanwhile, Boris would drive Val and me to Val's apartment, then on to the Indian embassy. If all went well, we'd fly out of Dulles by six.

"*Horosho*," Yuri said.

I said goodbye to my parents and we headed our separate ways.

twenty

A FLIGHT ATTENDANT ANNOUNCED we'd be landing in Hyderabad in thirty minutes.

Val's blindfold had risen up off her eyes and sat on her forehead. Her orange earplugs balanced provocatively on her chest and rose and fell with each breath. Her blanket bunched around her waist and exposed her first class airline pajamas.

I reached out and ran my fingers through her hair. She woke up and smiled at me.

"Nice earplugs," I said. "Even nicer location."

She looked down and smiled. "How'd they end up there?" She put the plugs and the blindfold on the armrest. "How long did I sleep?"

"Another hour this time. But no more dozing, we're landing soon."

"I'll get dressed." She retrieved her bag from the console next to her and headed to the lavatory.

The eighteen hours of flying time had left me restless. I couldn't wait to plant my feet on the ground.

Val and I had figured out what we'd do in India. Sunday was time zone adjustment day. Monday we'd work at Hans Schmidt's office and see if we could figure out who sabotaged the match code. Based on what we learned, we'd figure out how to use our time until we left for the airport late Wednesday night.

Val came back to the seat and put her bag away. "Did your parents make it to Iceland?" she asked.

"They did. Mom sent an email twenty minutes ago from their hotel room." I turned my laptop toward her. "Take a look at her geyser and waterfall pictures."

She clicked through them. "I can see why they wanted to go back," she said. She read what Mom had written, and then she smiled and passed the computer back to me.

Mom had told me to say hi to Val, and then she said that I had better grab her, as she thought my luck wasn't going to get any better.

She gave me a quick kiss. "Good advice," she said.

The flight attendant came by and made me stow my laptop.

"Are you excited?" Val asked me.

I nodded. "Of course."

"Have you worked with Indians before?"

"It's the computer field, right? We're loaded with Indians, Chinese, and Eastern Europeans." I stretched my legs out and flexed my toes. "I can't wait until we can walk again."

"Me too," she said. "But we won't be walking much. I emailed Hans Schmidt, and he's sending a driver to pick us up and bring us to the hotel."

"Can't we just rent a car?" I asked.

"You can't drive here."

"I can drive anywhere."

She shook her head. "The rhythms are all wrong for us Westerners. You'll see."

The plane landed, and we were the first two off the jetway. We walked up to the first counter in the immigration room.

The examiner raised his bushy eyebrows as he looked at our forms and swiped our passports through his scanner. "Your first trip to India, sir?" he asked.

I nodded. "Will I like it here?"

He wobbled his head back and forth. "A very good welcome to India."

I wobbled back. "Thank you." I looked over at Val. "Did that head wobble mean yes or no?"

"It meant yes. But it looks silly when you do it."

"I kind of like it." I wobbled again.

"Watch it or you're going to insult people here."

"Good point." We went down some stairs and put our bags through a metal detector. "Now why would they look for weapons after we land?" I asked.

"They're not looking for weapons. They're looking for reasons to tax you."

"Ah." The guard handed me my laptop bag, and I smiled at him. "How are you?" I asked.

The guard wobbled his head. "Very good, sir. Welcome to Hyderabad."

I wobbled back, and Val elbowed me in the ribs.

"Sorry, I couldn't help it," I said.

We passed through customs and into a large hall. Metal barricades lined our path, and hundreds of people stood pressed together on the outside of them. Everybody's eyes followed us as we walked. I caught the eyes of a man leaning on the barricade. I smiled at him, but he just stared. Same with the next guy, and the next.

"Why aren't they smiling back?" I asked.

"They don't know they're supposed to smile," she said. "Russia is the same way. When I first came to America, I thought everybody was laughing at me."

We reached the end of the hall. The sliding doors opened, and we walked outside. We were back on stage behind more metal barricades. All sorts of vehicles filled the road and parking lot behind the hundreds of people jammed tight against the barrier. The air was hot and full of strong, spicy smells.

Val looked around, and then pointed. "Our ride's over there."

I saw a guy holding a sheet of cardboard that read "Valentina Nikolskaya." Val waved, and he and the girl next to him waved back.

"They're smiling," I said.

"Yeah, our guys work with lots of Westerners." Val gave them each a hug. "Scott, I'd like you to meet Bhanu and Sheela, SchmidtLabs employees."

I shook their hands. Bhanu was dark and skinny, maybe five and a half feet tall, wearing a winter coat and ski hat. Sheela was lighter in color, a couple inches shorter, and also wearing a winter coat. "How can you survive in those jackets?" I asked. It was at least eighty degrees outside.

"We're not used to the cold weather." Bhanu shivered. "Don't worry, it will warm up tomorrow."

We crossed the street and dodged the cars, trucks, bikes, and small yellow three-wheeled vehicles. "What are the yellow things called?" I asked.

"Auto taxis," Bhanu said. "One step above a rickshaw."

Two old ladies and a bunch of young kids came up to us with their hands outstretched. "*Bhaiya, bhaiya,*" they wailed.

"What's *bhaiya?*" I asked.

"*Older brother.* They're begging for your money," Sheela said. "Just keep walking."

I opened my wallet. "Can they take US money?" I asked.

Bhanu shook his head. "They can't exchange it."

"We have to give them something," I said. "Look how skinny they are. Can you lend me some money until I get to a bank?"

Bhanu handed me some coins. "These are each five rupees."

"How much are they worth?"

"Eleven cents each."

"Is that enough?"

Bhanu nodded. "Plenty. But they may keep pestering you, though. You're *gora*. That's what we call whites."

When I passed out the coins, a crowd of beggars surrounded me. I looked back. "A little help here?" I asked.

Bhanu and Sheela shooed them away.

"There's not enough money to help all the beggars in India," Sheela said.

We reached the car, a small red hatchback. Val and I squeezed in the back. Bhanu backed up and then shot into a gap in the line of cars exiting the airport parking. "Sheela, give me some money for the parking," he said. "Scott gave all of mine away."

Sheela opened her purse. "Here's two hundred." She looked back at Val. "How long will you be here?"

"We're leaving very late Wednesday night," Val said.

"Then take rest in the morning, and in the afternoon we'll give you a tour of the city." She laughed. "When Hans Schmidt said you were coming, we both told him that he just had to let us take care of you."

"And Sheela didn't take no for an answer," Bhanu said. "Hans Schmidt wanted to hire you a driver, but she told him that we'd do it in our own car."

Val squeezed my hand. "I flew over for Bhanu and Sheela's wedding last year."

"Cool," I said. "Did your parents arrange your marraige?"

They both laughed. "No, Scott," Bhanu said. "We are a love marriage."

The light ahead of us turned red, and Bhanu beeped his horn and cruised through it. "In the daytime you have to stop at those red lights," he said.

"But only if there's a policeman around," Sheela said. "Otherwise you beep and keep going."

I nodded. "So the traffic light color doesn't really matter. It's all in the horn."

Bhanu smiled. "You have just received your first Hyderabadi driving lesson."

We said goodbye to Bhanu and Sheela at the hotel. When we reached the room, Val closed the door and smiled at me. "Let me give you a very personal welcome to India."

I wobbled my head at her, and she started laughing.

"I read the *Kama Sutra* when I was a teenager," I said.

She came close and tugged my shirt out of my pants. "And?" she whispered.

I unbuttoned her jeans and tugged them downward. "There's some positions in there that I've been wanting to try," I said. "What better place than India?"

Her eyes twinkled. "Show me."

twenty-one

IT WAS NOON, AND I was lucid enough to get up. Nine and a half hours of time difference made for some serious jet lag. I heard the water running. I swung out of bed and went into the bathroom.

The shower curtain moved, and Val peeked out. "Ready to see India in the daylight?" she asked.

"Sure." I opened my toiletry bag. "Hey, are Bhanu and Sheela Soul Identity members?"

She stepped out of the shower. "Of course."

"Don't most Hindus already believe in reincarnation?"

"They do."

"I can't imagine that Soul Identity is that popular in India," I said.

"It isn't," she said. "Hindus focus on their current lives' duties, and they don't seem to search for information on their past and future lives. You don't need us if you don't care about the bridges."

That made sense. I laid a row of toothpaste on my toothbrush. "Do you think we knew each other in our past lives?"

"No, I don't." She said this with some certainty.

I pouted at her reflection in the mirror. "Come on, Val. Maybe we were Anthony and Cleopatra. Or Romeo and Juliet."

"I don't think so."

"Why not?"

"I don't believe in reincarnation."

I dropped my toothbrush and stared at her. "You're kidding, right?" She shook her head and smiled.

"Didn't you tell me that you're a believer in Soul Identity?"

"I did, and I am."

"And didn't you tell me that I'd believe soon?"

"I did, and you will."

I crossed my arms. "Didn't you say that you wanted to start your own soul line to create a legacy?"

"I did, and I have."

"And now you're saying that you don't believe in reincarnation?"

"That's right. I don't."

I shook my head. "I'm totally lost. How can you join Soul Identity without believing in reincarnation?"

She shrugged. "Like I said on our drive to Maryland, religion is something that lies on top of the organization. Believing in reincarnation has nothing to do with the repeating identity."

"Bob seems to believe in reincarnation."

She nodded. "That's his church talking. Soul Identity finds a member's connection, but it's the church that defines its significance."

"So what sort of significance do you give to your soul identity?"

She smiled. "I see it as a magical time machine. I can write down my philosophies, or even cook up a totally fictional story about my life. I stick these documents in the depositary, and sooner or later, somebody matching my identity will read them and make a decision on what it means to them."

"And you don't think that somebody is you, wrapped up in a new body?" I asked.

"No. That person will feel a connection to me, and that's the magical part. But I don't believe that person will be me."

I nodded. "I get it—I think. Soul Identity gives you a way to be relevant far out into the future."

Val kissed me. "You do get it."

I kissed her back. "But don't you think it's cool to imagine that we once were Romeo and Juliet?"

She smiled. "Only one night together before dying? If our past was connected, I hope it wasn't in a tragedy."

I sat up front with Bhanu as we toured the city. We visited Golkonda, Charminar, and the Birla Temple. The colors, sounds, and smells overwhelmed my Western eyes, ears, and nose. Ladies in bright yellow, orange, and pink saris walked down the sidewalks and browsed the rows of stores and stalls. Cars, trucks, motorcycles, horse-drawn carts, camels, auto taxis, and water buffalo made their way through the streets in a rhythm that was indiscernible to me. Horns beeped, jackhammers stuttered, and donkeys brayed. The smells of sewage and spices assaulted my nose. India was so different from home.

Bhanu put away his phone. "I just talked to Hans Schmidt. We're going to meet him for dinner at Bawarchi."

"Yay!" Sheela said. "Bawarchi makes the best biryani in Hyderabad."

On the way to the restaurant, I pointed out the window. "I've seen signs in at least four different alphabets."

Bhanu nodded. "Which ones do you recognize?"

"English in the Roman alphabet, though the spelling is appalling. Look at the signs on this one restaurant. Chaines Food. Chinees Restaurent. Chineese Food Inside."

Bhanu smiled. "Indian English. What else?"

"That sign looks Arabic to me. Isn't it read right to left?"

He nodded. "That's Urdu. It uses an Arabic script. The Muslims in India and Pakistan speak it."

"Okay, then this other script has its characters connected by a line across their tops. Lots of square edges and vertical lines."

"That's Hindi. Read it left to right, like English."

"So this curvy script must be Telegu. I like it the best," I said.

"Why's that?" Val asked from the back.

I grinned. "Look at all those curves. It's a boob language. Like that sign over there. Here's what I see—big boob, little pair of boobs, small boob, another pair of boobs."

Sheela giggled. "That sign says clothing store."

"Writing in South India developed on palm leaves," Bhanu said. "They used lots of curves so the leaves wouldn't split along the fibers."

"I'm glad they didn't have papyrus," I said.

We reached Bawarchi and parked along the street.

"Let's sit on the roof," Sheela said. "There's no air conditioning, but it's more real."

We climbed two flights of stairs. "*Hum panj hai*," Bhanu told the waiter. He looked at us. "I said *we are five*. Hans Schmidt should be here in a couple of minutes."

Sheela smiled. "He'll be prompt. There is no India time at SchmidtLabs."

"India time?" I asked.

"Five minutes late here, ten minutes late there. We don't do that at work, no way. Hans Schmidt won't allow it."

The waiter seated us in wrought-iron chairs around a marble topped table. We watched servers carrying platters to the many diners. A plastic canopy overhead protected us from the sun. The satellite radio blaring from the speakers tied to the canopy's support poles almost drowned out the street noises from below.

A man came by and placed five metal cups on the table.

"*Doh mineral water lie yay.*" Sheela told him. She looked at us. "Will two mineral waters be enough?"

"Just for Val and me?"

She shook her head. "For all of us. We don't drink the local water either."

The waiter brought two bottles of water and left them on the table. The packaging on the bottles read "Oxyrich water—with 300% more oxygen."

"That's interesting advertising," I said. "I didn't even know I needed more oxygen in my water."

"I think Oxyrich does this so we remember them." Sheela said.

"Imagine if you guys advertised that way," I said. "Soul Identity—with three hundred percent more chicken soup."

"Chicken soup?" Val asked.

"It's good for the soul." I ducked the napkin Val threw at me.

"Hans Schmidt is here!" Bhanu said. He waved, and a big man waved back.

Hans Schmidt stood six and a half feet tall. He had a large chest and solid looking limbs. His blonde hair hung halfway down his back in a ponytail, and he sported a half-gray goatee. He smiled and walked toward us.

"He's a big guy," I said.

"He's a big teddy bear," Val stood up and gave him a Euro-kiss on each cheek. "Hans Schmidt," she said, "I'd like you to meet Scott Waverly. He's working with us."

My hand disappeared in Hans Schmidt's massive paw as he shook it up and down. "It's good to meet you, Scott Waverly."

"Call me Scott, Hans," I said.

"Call me Hans Schmidt." He smiled. "Hans sounds like the Hindi word for swan." He spread his arms and mimed flying. "I'm more of the ugly duckling than a beautiful swan—I use my full name here."

He looked over at Bhanu and Sheela. "Hi kids. Did you show our guests a good time?"

Bhanu and Sheela both smiled back. I saw a lot of affection between the three. "Yes, Hans Schmidt," Sheela said. "We took them to all the major places."

"How long have you lived here?" I asked him.

"Thirteen years, and I've loved every minute of it." He sat down and beckoned to a waiter. "One jumbo mutton biryani and two Bawarchi special mutton curries." He winked at me. "Bawarchi's mutton biryani is great, but it's even greater when you put extra mutton curry on top." He kissed his fingertips.

The waiter wobbled his head and walked away.

Hans Schmidt turned to Val. "I must say this is a surprise visit," he said. "Are we still on schedule for the Internet rollout? You're not changing anything?"

Val shook her head. "We're not changing. But Scott and I have some questions about the Y2K work that SchmidtLabs did for Soul Identity ten years ago."

"I remember that work," he said. "If it wasn't for the money we banked from that contract, the dot com crash would have put us out of business."

The waiters brought our food. Hans Schmidt filled his plate with steaming rice and chunks of meat. He smothered it with the mutton curry gravy. "This is the food of the gods," he declared.

I followed his lead. I lifted a spoonful of rice and sniffed it. I could smell cinnamon and cloves, and maybe some turmeric and saffron. I tasted it. The rice was perfectly cooked: not too soft, and with just the right amount of chili to offset the other spices. "Wow," I said.

Val poked me. "I thought that word was reserved for me."

I lifted another spoonful. "It was until we came here." I tasted the mutton. "Oh my God, this is perfect."

Hans Schmidt beamed at me, then he turned back to Val. "What do you need to know?" he asked.

"It's about the match program," Val said. "The binaries don't match the source code we have on file. Why not?"

He looked startled. "They ought to match," he said. "We haven't touched that code for ten years."

Val stared at him. "Are you sure, Hans Schmidt? I decompiled the binaries myself, and they were different."

He frowned. "I don't know what you're talking about."

Val tapped the marble tabletop with her fingernails. "Only SchmidtLabs and I can change those binaries. I checked your original submission, and they match the current ones. The binaries came from your lab, ten years ago. They don't match the source you provided. And I want to know why."

Hans Schmidt sat for a moment with his mouth open. "I don't know what to say—I hate the idea of SchmidtLabs looking like we did something tricky," he said.

Bhanu and Sheela whispered back and forth. Bhanu cleared his throat. "Hans Schmidt? May I say something?"

Hans Schmidt nodded.

"Last time Val was here," Bhanu said, "she mentioned that it takes thirty seconds to match an identity. After she left, I got to thinking that there had to be better algorithms for doing this search, so I pulled up the code."

"Why would you do that?" Hans Schmidt leaned forward in his seat.

Bhanu gave him an embarrassed smile. "One of my batch mates works for a competitor to Soul Identity, and he was bragging about some new search they've put in place—one that takes less than ten seconds to do a match."

"Bhanu, you talked about Soul Identity to their competitor?" Hans Schmidt's tone had become harsh.

"No, Hans Schmidt," Bhanu said. "My batch mate was bragging about his new job at WorldWideSouls. I didn't tell him anything about Soul Identity. He only knows I work for SchmidtLabs. He doesn't even know I'm a Soul Identity member."

Hans Schmidt frowned. "I'm listening."

Bhanu cleared his throat. "I pulled up the match code and took a look at the algorithm. I found a couple really inefficient chunks in there."

"What kind of inefficiencies?" I asked.

Bhanu turned to me. "The calculation of the three hundred and sixty hash values is slow," he said. "And breaking up the database query into a set of smaller sub queries would decrease the time of each search to microseconds. With two days to test, I bet I could tune it to match in less than three seconds."

"Did you code up any of your ideas?" Val asked.

Bhanu shook his head. "I tried, Val. I made my changes and checked, but the match still took thirty seconds. I went back to the code to see what I had done wrong, and all my changes were gone."

"Gone?" I asked.

Bhanu nodded. "Like I had never written them. Since it was three in the morning, I thought that maybe I had dreamed the whole thing, so I tried again. This time I made a copy of my changed file."

"And what happened?" Val asked.

"Same thing. The builds made a binary that was just as slow, and my changes were gone," he said. "That's when I called Sheela."

Sheela nodded. "I dug into the build scripts, and found some clever code that modifies the match source program, builds the program binaries, and then covers up its tracks by replacing the source with a hard-coded fake."

"The hard-coding threw away all my changes," Bhanu said.

Hans Schmidt banged his fists on the table, making the metal cups bounce. "And why didn't you tell me about this?"

Some of the other diners looked at us and whispered to each other.

Bhanu hung his head. "We were already running a very tight deadline on the current Internet rollout, and I wanted to get it all together before showing you what we had found."

Hans Schmidt turned to us. "Obviously my staff knows more than I do about this." He looked at Bhanu. "Is there anything else I should know?"

Bhanu shook his head.

Sheela shifted in her seat. "There is something else. In the build script, right where the clever code is, I found a very strange comment."

"What does it say?" Hans Schmidt asked.

"That if anybody has any questions in the future about what this code is doing, please contact Tinless Tiksey."

Hans Schmidt sighed. "That name is a blast from the past. Tinless Tiksey was an interesting man with an even more interesting story." He paused as the waiters cleared our plates and cleaned up the spilled rice.

Val smiled. "Our bellies are full. Tell us the tale of Tinless Tiksey."

He paused for a minute. "Very well," he said. "Once upon a time, Tinless Tiksey was my most valuable employee." He looked at Bhanu and Sheela. "How long have you two have been with SchmidtLabs?"

"Three point one years," Sheela said.

"That's longer than Tinless—he stayed just a bit over two," he said. "Tinless was an amazing programmer. I had just moved to Hyderabad, and I needed a large enough contract to pay our bills."

He laughed. "One day this tiny little man walked into my office and told me a company he knew needed a bunch of Y2K programming done. That man was Tinless. He said that if I hired him, he'd introduce me to the company.

"So I hired Tinless, and we flew to Boston and met with Mr. Morgan. And we ended up building some incredible software for you. Software that is still running today." He smiled. "I even joined Soul Identity and got active in the local office. But that's a bit off subject."

"What happened to Tinless?" Val asked.

"On the day we made our final delivery, he quit." Hans Schmidt sighed. "I tried my best to talk him out of it, but he told me that he had more important things to do with his life than just program."

I smiled. "What could possibly be more important than programming?"

"That's what I asked him," he said. "It turned out Tinless was from northern India, right up in the Himalayas next to Tibet. He was the lama for a local *gompa*."

"What's a *gompa*?" I asked.

"It's a Buddhist temple," Bhanu said. "Sheela and I visited lots of them on our honeymoon." He looked at Hans Schmidt. "Do you know which *gompa*?"

"Let me think." Hans Schmidt scrunched up his forehead. "Lamayuru. Does that sound right?"

Bhanu nodded. "That's in the Ladakh region of Kashmir, a few hours from Leh. We've been there. Nice *gompa*. You're saying their lama is the same Tinless who worked for us?"

Hans Schmidt nodded. "Every year he sends me a post card, reminding me that I promised to visit him. But I've never made it up there."

"Is that a lama as in the Dali Lama?" I asked.

Sheela nodded. "The Dali Lama is the spiritual leader for most Buddhists, but up in the Himalayas, each individual *gompa* has its own lama. He is in charge of the temple and the surrounding town."

Val stared at Hans Schmidt. "Your key programmer on the Soul Identity work was a lama?"

He pursed his lips and nodded.

"And this lama is the same person who introduced you to Soul Identity?"

He nodded again and looked down at the table.

"Who quit the day he delivered this software?"

An almost imperceptible nod.

"Why didn't you tell anybody about this before?" she asked.

He sighed. "What would I have said? That a lama had written our code and then quit? In any case, it all works, doesn't it?"

"Yes, it certainly works," she said. "At least, we assumed it did, until we found this problem in the matching binaries." Val looked at me. "We have to find this lama."

"In Kashmir? This week?" I asked.

She nodded. "We can fly up in the morning and come back on Tuesday."

Bhanu and Sheela whispered back and forth again. "Val, we were just there a few months ago. We will come as your guides," Bhanu said.

"Good idea," said Hans Schmidt. He turned to Val. "I am very sorry about all of this."

Val nodded. "Let's just get it fixed. I need you to deliver your Internet stuff too. Tell me there are no lamas on that project."

He chuckled. "No, no lamas."

"There is something you can help us with," Val said. "We need to use the Hyderabad communications center."

He nodded. "Would you like to go there now?"

"Yes, please." She turned to Bhanu and Sheela. "We'll ride over with Hans Schmidt. Can you book the flights to Kashmir?"

Sheela nodded. "We'll do that at the office," she said.

Val smiled. "Great. We'll meet you there, and then dig into that build script and see what else we can find."

As we all headed down the stairs, Val caught me grinning at her. "What's up?" she asked.

"The way you took charge, questioned Hans Schmidt, and decided on our plan of action," I said. "I like being with such a strong chick."

"Thanks. Though I have my soft spots, too."

I nodded. "The mix is great. I'm a lucky guy." I gave her a quick kiss, and we followed Hans Schmidt out the door.

twenty-two

VAL AND I SAT in the communications center at the Hyderabad Soul Identity office. I entered the third encryption key from George and tuned the radio to the proper frequency. I picked up the microphone. "This is Val and Scott," I said. "Is anybody out there?"

"Hello, Val and Scott. You must be in Hyderabad already," Archie said. "I am sitting here with Bob."

"Hi, Mr. Morgan," Val said. "We made it. How are Berry and Madame Flora?"

We heard Archie chuckle. "They seem to be getting along just fine. Though I heard that Mr. Berringer has requested a full refund on his palm reading sessions."

Val told them what we learned. "We're flying into Kashmir in the morning," she said. "Hopefully we'll find Tinless so he can explain what he did and why."

"I remember meeting with Tinless and Hans Schmidt," Archie said. "It always struck me as peculiar that a Tibetan Buddhist would work with Soul Identity. And now that you say he is a lama, it is rather disturbing."

"Why's that?" I asked. "Your beliefs seem compatible."

"Not really, Scott," he said. "Iris image deltas get in the way of the Buddhists' proofs of rebirth. They base theirs on retained memories and physical characteristics. Instead of science, they rely on a strong and localized faith."

"So Soul Identity doesn't have many Buddhists in its ranks?" I asked.

"We do, but not from the Tibetan region, and definitely no lamas," he said. "They tend to keep themselves apart."

George's voice came over the radio. "This is George and Sue reporting in from Venice. We've made it, and we're here to tell you that Venice is fine, fine, fine!"

"George, have you gotten a photo of Mr. Feret?" Archie asked.

"It's Sunday afternoon here in Venice, Mr. Morgan. We'll get that picture tomorrow, when—"

Sue interrupted. "We've been keeping an eye on the offices and guesthouse," she said. "People are streaming in and out. We scheduled an appointment with Mr. Feret for eleven a.m. tomorrow, and hopefully we'll have that photo ready by your morning."

"Another thing," George said. "We found some old buddies here—guests who stayed with us in Sterling. They told us that something big is about to happen, and they're getting prepared."

"Did they tell you what was going to happen?" I asked.

"They didn't want to share many details," he said.

"Did they say how they're preparing?" I asked.

"No, but we'll keep digging," he said.

"Thank you, George," Archie said. "I want to remind everybody about the urgency of your tasks. Last week we were surprised, but we were lucky. This week we must be prepared."

"I'm assuming Bob passed on the license plates. Do you know who tried to blow us up and shoot us?" I asked.

"We hit a dead end on the plates, Mr. Scott," Bob said.

"We will figure this out soon," Achie said, "and when we do, we will stop them from hurting our organization ever again."

We signed off the radio call.

I looked at Val. "What do you think is going down in Venice?"

She shrugged. "We can search the blogs from SchmidtLabs."

"Great idea," I said. Web logs, known as blogs, had become fascinating, shareable, online diaries for millions of Internet users. They were also treasure troves of information—somebody must have blogged or micro-blogged about the event.

Hans Schmidt joined us as we headed out. "Anything new?" he asked.

Val looked at me and then said, "Not really. We told Mr. Morgan that we're heading north, so he'll know where we are."

Hans Schmidt nodded. "I guess we'll all know more in a couple of days then."

We walked next door to SchmidtLabs. Hans Schmidt flashed his badge, and we went upstairs and over to where Bhanu and Sheela were working.

"We have the tickets," Bhanu said. "Our flight is at three forty tomorrow morning. We have to reach Delhi in time for the six thirty flight to Leh."

"I guess we'll sleep on the plane," I said. "Where can we plug in?"

Sheela led us to a training room. "You can set up here. Our wireless is wide open, so use your VPN to be safe."

VPN, or Virtual Private Network, software would encrypt all network traffic going in and out of our laptops. "SchmidtLabs practices safe computing?" I asked.

Sheela nodded. "And we practice lots of snooping. We're building a network sniffer for one of our clients. If you don't encrypt, you can assume that half of SchmidtLabs will be watching what you're doing."

Sheela left, we got our secure connections up, and I started on my emails. My parents were having a blast in Iceland. They went on horseback to a camp in the interior. I wrote back and told them we arrived safely.

"Look at this blog I found." Val turned her laptop my way.

The blog was titled "Finally in Venice," which sounded like something George would write. The short entry said, "We made it to Venice, and I can't believe that we have only five days left to prepare for the new order. After all the waiting we're finally here!"

I looked up at Val. "New order? Is that a Soul Identity term?"

She shook her head. "It sounds spooky."

I continued reading. "We went to the depositary yesterday and emptied our accounts. We are so lucky to be part of this. Only five more days!"

We searched other blogs, but all we found were links to the same entry.

"We should check out the WorldWideSouls site." I said.

"Let me try," Val said. After a few minutes of typing she looked up and smiled. "I had to hack into the members-only section, but look at this." She pointed at her screen. "They have a major event coming up Saturday afternoon in Venice."

So WorldWideSouls was also heading to Venice.

"Main speaker, Fred Antere," I read on Val's screen. "Paving the way for the launch of the new order. Mandatory attendance for all level 3 and up members."

Bhanu popped his head into the room. "We have to be at the airport in three hours, but Sheela and I need to get to our flat and bring some warmer clothes. Do you want a ride to your hotel?"

"I need to get the build scripts printed out before we go," I said.

Bhanu held up a stack of papers. "I've got them right here."

We decided to stay checked in at the Hyderabad hotel. That way if any of the gray guys had latched onto our trail, they could waste their time staking us out. We left our laptops locked in the in-room safe and packed an overnight bag.

When Bhanu and Sheela drove up, we saw they were dressed in ski jackets, hats, and gloves.

I looked at Val. "Our khakis and polos may not be enough for the Himalayas."

Val nodded. "We'll have to buy stuff there."

The plane landed in Leh, and we climbed down the stairs and walked over to the bus. The air was dry and crisp at eleven thousand feet, and the snow-covered mountains surrounding us were jagged and forbidding.

Bhanu and Sheela pulled on their gloves and hats and gave each other a kiss.

"Are you two remembering your honeymoon?" I asked.

"It's nice to be back here already." Sheela pointed. "Lamayuru is way up high in those mountains."

The bus creaked to a stop at the terminal. Val and I filled out the Foreign Visitor Registration forms that the military guards handed us, and Sheela bought a road map from the tourist bureau.

"Let's get a car," Bhanu said. We walked outside, and he headed over to the taxi dispatcher. After a few minutes they shook hands, and Bhanu led us to a white Toyota Qualis.

The driver got out and smiled. "*Julay,*" he said.

"*Julay,*" Bhanu said. He looked at us. "That one word means hello, goodbye, and you're welcome. It probably means some other things too. When in doubt, just say *julay.*"

"It sounds like aloha," I said. I smiled at the driver. "Do you speak English?"

"A little." He gave a little bow. "I am Tenzin."

"We need to get to Lamayuru as soon as possible," I said.

"We first need some warmer clothes," Val said. "Where's the closest store?"

Tenzin thought for a minute. "Now is getting to be eight o'clock. Leh stores opening at eleven."

"How far is Lamayuru?" I asked.

"Four hours. By twelve we reach if leaving now."

"Do you have heat in your Qualis?" Val asked.

Tenzin nodded.

I pointed at our sandals and short sleeves. "Will we survive in these?" Tenzin shook his head. "You will be too cold. Maybe we find blankets at a village along the way."

I nodded. "Let's go to Lamayuru."

Bhanu and Sheela climbed in the back, Val and I got in the middle, and Tenzin hopped up front and started the engine.

Bhanu and Sheela fell asleep. Tenzin drove east out of town, and Val and I fought motion sickness as we read through the build scripts.

I showed her one of the pages. "Here's the comment from Tinless that Sheela told us about," I said.

"What's it doing?" She traced her finger down the page. "Okay. If the file is the match program, they overwrite it here."

"Where's the overwrite file?" I asked.

Val examined the code. "It uses some compressed source contained in this file here." She waved one of the pages from the stack I gave her.

I tapped my finger on the page. "That one comment Sheela showed us is the only comment in all the scripts."

"Maybe Tinless was hoping somebody would see it," she said.

"We'll know soon enough." I folded the page and put it in my pocket. Then I looked out the window. I had to crane my head to see the tops of the snow covered mountains. Underneath the snowline was a lot of dirt and sand. There were very few trees.

I looked down. The road clung to the side of a mountain, about one third the way up. A river flowed in the valley below us. I could see a small cluster of houses a mile or so ahead. "Tenzin, can we stop at that town?" I asked.

"Yes, sir. You will be eating breakfast there."

I shook Bhanu and Sheela awake.

Bhanu looked out the window. "We're more than halfway there," he said. "I remember this place. It's called Khaltse. We cross the river here and head up into the mountains."

Tenzin stopped in the center of town. I pointed to a six foot wooden cylinder mounted vertically inside a gazebo. "What's that?" I asked.

Sheela answered, "That's a prayer wheel. Somebody will come by and spin it pretty soon."

A man walked by our car. "*Julay*," he said to Tenzin.

Tenzin smiled at him and they conversed for a moment in Ladakhi. Then the man entered the gazebo, grabbed a handle on the prayer wheel, and walked clockwise around the tiny room. When he finished his loop he gave the wheel a spin and headed off.

"All day long that wheel gets spun." Sheela nodded at an old lady sitting in the sun. "She has her own personal prayer wheel in her hand."

I watched her spin her wheel with one hand, finger her rosary with the other, and move her lips in prayer. "She's pretty coordinated," I said.

"She should be," Bhanu said. "She does it all day long."

"What's the prayer she's saying?" I asked Tenzin.

"*Om, manni padmi ho.* One time, one bead. One hundred eight beads in rosary. She saying one hundred eight rosaries every day."

I gestured at the gazebo. "Every town has a prayer wheel?" I asked him.

"Every neighborhood," Tenzin said. "Our way of life in Ladakh." He pointed to a shack next to the gazebo. "We getting food here."

"What do they serve?" I asked.

"Only two Ladakhi dishes. *Momo*, which are dumplings. You get them steamed, fried, or half fried. Fried is best. Also *thukpa*, which is noodle vegetable soup." He motioned us toward the door. "You please eat. I finding something warm for you to wear."

The four of us sat at a small table and drank the *thukpa* right out of our bowls. I picked up a *momo* with my fingers. "All the food has the same bland taste," I said.

Bhanu snorted. "The guide books rave about Ladakhi food, but it's got no spice at all."

Tenzin came in carrying two shawls. "Yak wool. Very warm. After you eat, talk to store owner." He pointed out the door at a building across the street.

Val and I put on the shawls, and they did take the edge off the bitter cold.

We paid the bill, walked across the street, and negotiated for the shawls. Then we got in the car and continued to Lamayuru.

"We almost arriving," Tenzin said after another hour of driving. He pointed. "Lamayuru *gompa* there."

We looked up. The town was ahead of us, and a set of large buildings were nestled on the hill above.

When we reached the town, Tenzin parked next to a prayer wheel. He pointed to a small path. "Up that hill is *gompa*. Lama living there."

We walked up the hill. After fifty yards, I held up my hand. "The oxygen is too thin," I said, panting. "I have to catch my breath."

We rested and admired the view of the mountains around us. After a few minutes we continued the rest of the way up. We followed a path that led us between two buildings. We climbed another set of stairs and stood in a large courtyard in the middle of the *gompa*.

A monk in a red robe came up to us and showed us a receipt book. Bhanu spoke with him. "Scott and Val must pay a suggested donation amount," he said. "It's fifty rupees each." He pulled out a hundred rupee note, and the monk detached two tickets.

"Thank you for your donation to our building and restoration fund," I read. I looked up and smiled at the monk. "Glad we could help."

"*Tok jye shye.*" The monk bowed.

"What did he say?" I asked Bhanu.

"I think *thank you.*"

I turned to the monk. "*Julay.* We are looking for Lama Tinless Tiksey."

The monk said something to Bhanu, and Bhanu replied. The monk launched into a long speech, and Bhanu nodded his head.

"The lama is not receiving visitors today," Bhanu said. "He wants us to come back next week."

The monk walked away.

"Get him back here," I said.

Bhanu called out, but the monk kept walking. He reached a door on the far side of the courtyard, and he used a key on a chain around his neck to unlock it.

"Excuse me!" I hollered.

The monk had just opened the door. He paused and looked at me.

"I have a personal invitation from the lama," I called.

The monk shook his head and walked through. He closed the door behind him.

Bhanu shouted something. "I translated it into Hindi," he said to me.

We stared at the door. It opened a minute later, and the monk came out. He walked up to Bhanu and said something.

Bhanu turned to me. "He wants the invitation."

I handed the code sheet with the comment to the monk.

The monk bowed, took the paper, and walked back through the door. He closed it behind him.

I looked around the courtyard. "We paid our fifty rupees. Why not see the temple while we wait?"

"That would be nice," Sheela said. "We have to leave our shoes here." She and Bhanu bent down and unlaced their boots.

Val and I slipped off our sandals and stood barefoot on the cold paving stones. "I hope there's carpeting," I said.

Sheela smiled. "I'm sure it has a mat."

We stepped through a door and into a large room. Low benches and tables sat in rows on our left. Tall glass-fronted cabinets stood along the right wall.

I walked up to the cabinets. "Look at all these old books," I said.

Another monk came out of the shadows in front of us. "Our *gompa* is very lucky to have three complete sets of Buddha's writings," he said. "Each set is one hundred and eight books. These books are hand written and are hundreds of years old."

I looked at the monk. He stood five feet tall and wore a red robe. He was barefoot, but the cold didn't seem to bother him. "It doesn't look like anybody reads them," I said. "They're covered in dust."

"These days we use digital files and the Web, which make sharing information more efficient. There's not much need to go back to the original books." He sighed. "That is a shame, because these books are illustrated with beautiful pictures, delicately drawn in rich colors."

"You can learn a lot when you look back in time," I said. I ran my finger down some carvings on the cabinet door. "Things you wouldn't understand from just seeing the words on a computer screen."

"Exactly," he said. "Welcome to our *gompa*. Please let me know if you have any questions."

We walked to the far end of the room. In front of us we found an open area. On our left we saw a grand scene painted on the wall; lots of people and dragons and trees, but I couldn't make out the story. I looked at the wall on the right. Somebody had painted images of Buddha in three columns of nine. Dust-covered gold Buddha statues filled a cabinet next to the wall.

We walked toward the open area. "Whoa," I said.

Val stood next to me. "Incredible."

The room ended with a long wooden railing. We stood on a balcony that overlooked a huge hall dominated by an enormous statue of a seated Buddha. The floor of the hall was at least thirty feet below us, and the sky-lit ceiling was another fifteen feet up. We looked directly into the Buddha's large face.

Bhanu stood next to me. He pointed to a stairway barely visible in the corner. "Want to go down?" he asked.

We headed down the stairs and walked clockwise around the statue. Bowls of fruit lay on tables. Various coins and notes were scattered around. I looked into one of the bowls and saw more coins and jewelry lying under the fruit.

The little monk had followed us down the stairs. "It's considered auspicious to leave a gift of the smallest note in your wallet," he said to me.

"How auspicious?" I asked.

He nodded at the bowl. "Give it a try."

I opened my wallet. I had spent my last rupee notes on the shawls; all I had were hundred dollar bills. "Can you break a hundred?" I asked him.

"That's not auspicious," Val said. "That's cheap."

I sighed and took out a hundred dollar bill. "This had better be super auspicious." I dropped it in the bowl and looked at the monk. "Am I supposed to make a wish?" I asked.

The monk smiled. "I already know what you want."

I raised my eyebrows. "Can you read my mind?"

He shook his head. "No, but I can read my ten year old code." He held up the sheet of paper I gave to the other monk in the courtyard. "It's about time somebody found this. I was beginning to think you guys would never come."

twenty-three

WE SAT ON THE carpeted floor in Tinless Tiksey's private quarters and sipped tea from ancient golden bowls. Tinless gave Val and me wool socks to wear, and for the first time all day I felt warm.

I set my bowl down on the floor. "Tinless, I'm really struggling to believe your story," I said.

"It seems rather fantastic, doesn't it?"

"It does. You said that a young man forced you to do the Soul Identity work."

He nodded.

"But you went to SchmidtLabs in Hyderabad, and then you flew to Boston with Hans Schmidt," I said. "That doesn't sound forced."

"It might be that I need to some more details to my story." He stood up and clasped his hands behind his back.

"Start at the beginning again," I suggested. "You were here in Lamayuru, and a new monk had just joined your *gompa*."

Tinless nodded. "Yes, a very interesting monk. A young Western monk. That was twelve or thirteen years ago."

"Why would a foreigner join your *gompa*?"

Tinless shrugged. "He had recently lost his grandfather and his parents. He claimed to be seeking out a path through life, and he had chosen Buddhism as the way. He told me that he came to Ladakh to find peace."

"And you welcomed him in," I said.

"Of course we did. He was devoted, friendly, and interested in learning our traditions. He helped me finish my reorganization of the monastery finances, we put the lama incarnation genealogy online, and together we digitized and published the *gompa's* manuscripts and artwork."

Bhanu held up his hand. "Lama Tinless, can you tell us the monk's name?" he asked.

"Fred Antere," Tinless said. "But here in the *gompa* we all called him Red Tree."

Fred Antere was speaking at WorldWideSouls on Saturday. I looked at Val and put a finger to my lips. Might as well be careful.

She gave me a nod. "Why Red Tree?" she asked Tinless.

He smiled. "In his monk robes, he looked like a tall red tree. But he named himself. Now that I think about it, it's really just words made from the letters in his name. A piece of him, but not all of him." He sighed. "Which, we found out later, was all we ever had."

Tinless stuck his head out the door of his quarters, then pulled it back in and turned to me. "I fell in love with Red Tree. We all did."

I raised my eyebrows.

"Not that kind of love," he said. "But Red Tree was special to all of us here at the *gompa*."

"Now you said it went bad. What really happened?" Sheela asked.

Tinless walked to the window. He used his thumbnail to scrape away some frost, then peered outside.

What was he looking for?

We waited for him to continue. After a couple of minutes he faced us. "Six months after he arrived, Red Tree came to me. We sat right where you sit and drank tea from these bowls." Tinless sighed. "And then he ripped my world apart."

"What did he do?" I asked.

He looked at me. "Red Tree had collected a set of compromising photographs of most of the monks in the *gompa*. Including me."

"Compromising?" Val asked.

Tinless sat down on the mats and crossed his legs. He arranged his red robe to cover his knees. "Life in the *gompa* is lonely. Over the centuries, we've learned to handle this through various diversions. We don't expect the outside world to understand, or condone, what we do." He shook his head. "But exposing our activities to others would destroy our *gompa*."

I didn't know, nor did I want to know, what kinds of compromising activities the monks in the Lamayuru *gompa* engaged in.

"He blackmailed you." I said.

Tinless nodded.

"And that's how you ended up at SchmidtLabs."

"Yes, and you know the rest of the story. Red Tree knew about the work at Soul Identity. I helped Hans Schmidt get it." He sighed. "And I inserted the matching code change, and the build override, when Red Tree told me to."

"So who wrote the bad code?" I asked.

He shrugged. "I assume Red Tree did the coding—it wasn't me."

"Do you know what the code did?"

Tinless looked down. "I do. The lamas of Soul Identity—"

"We call them overseers," Bhanu said.

Tinless nodded. "Sorry, I had forgotten," he said. "No true overseers at Soul Identity will be found as long as that bad code is active."

"That would be like somebody eliminating the lamas in this *gompa* and installing their own." I said.

He sighed. "Yes, it would. Though it would be much harder to do that to us."

"Why's that?" I asked.

He stood up and opened the window. "Let me show you something outside."

Val and I came stood. The cold wind stole the warmth I had just restored.

Tinless hung out his arm and pointed down. "You see the *stupas* below us?"

I looked out at the stone structures that we had seen dotted over the countryside. "That's what they're called?" I asked. Some of them were mortar-coated and painted white; others had deteriorated into loose piles of rocks. Each *stupa* stood between five and fifteen feet tall.

He nodded. "Do you know why we build them?"

I shook my head.

"After we lamas are reborn, we recognize our *stupas* and gain memories from our previous life. It's our way to connect our lives together," he said. "They are the bridges between our past, present, and future."

"Soul Identity has bridges too," Val said.

He nodded again. "But our bridges trigger memories, and yours do not. Ours are mystical and harder to prove, and yours are scientific. Yours leave no doubt as to a matching identity, but they do not tell you what it means to be connected."

"We store memories in our depositary, to pass on to future carriers," Val said.

"But then you rely on others to lay faith on top of your science." Tinless shook his head. "I feel sorry for Soul Identity members. They are convinced in the bridges, but they have no tools to benefit from them."

"Is that why you helped to sabotage the matching program?" I asked.

"I only helped so Red Tree wouldn't destroy our *gompa*," he said. "What we did was wrong, and I am sorry." He closed the window after taking another quick peek below.

We sat back down. Tinless poured more tea.

Bhanu cleared his throat. "What happened to Red Tree?"

"He came to Hyderabad, and stayed in my apartment while I spent the days at SchmidtLabs. We installed software that allowed him to program from the apartment. I know Hans Schmidt thinks I'm a genius, but Red Tree did most of the work."

Tinless frowned. "Each night in the apartment I listened to Red Tree rail against Soul Identity. When we completed the matching code, he became unbearable, and spoke of nothing other than his plans to destroy your organization."

It was a bit surreal, sitting on a floor high in the Himalayas, sipping tea out of golden cups, and learning from a Buddhist monk how he was blackmailed by a scheming, revenge-filled teenager.

"He shared all his plans?" I asked.

"Yes, but I'm sure you know them too." Tenzin wore a sad smile.

"We know," I said. "The names are mostly anagrams. Red Tree is Fred Antere, and Fred Antere is Andre Feret. He was trying to become the only overseer." I didn't mention the WorldWideSouls connection.

Tinless nodded. "I think that sums it up. Now please excuse me for a moment. I have something that may help you stop him."

After he left, I asked the others, "Do you think he's telling the truth?"

Sheela nodded. "I think so. Though there seems to be more than what he's shared."

"We just have to ask the right questions," Bhanu said.

"Guilt seems to work," Val said. "We got our best answers when we told him how much he's hurting Soul Identity."

Tinless returned with a photograph. "Red Tree removed all pictures of himself before we left for Hyderabad, but later a tourist sent me this in a thank you note." He passed it to me.

Two white middle aged ladies in shorts and baseball caps stood with Tinless and a tall, slender young man draped in a red robe. In the background a young child was spinning the *gompa's* prayer wheel.

I looked at Val. "Is it Andre Feret?"

"That's him." She sighed. "So what else, Tinless? We've got a real mess on our hands now. Have you told us everything?"

"What else can I tell you?" Tinless looked distressed. "When Red Tree flew to Massachusetts for his own matching, I did my best to block the deployment of the new software." He shook his head. "I convinced Hans Schmidt that we needed a few extra weeks of testing, but it wasn't long enough."

I remembered George telling me that Feret had to stay several weeks in the guesthouse. "He outlasted you," I said. "Feret claimed he had an eye infection. He must have been waiting for the program to get in place before he went to the match committee."

Tinless nodded. "He was, and then he called me up and warned me that if I played any more games, he would release the photos and destroy the *gompa* anyway. So I resigned from SchmidtLabs and returned to Lamayuru." He turned to Val. "I am sorry for the pain I have caused your organization."

"Me too, Tinless." She stared directly into his eyes. "Why didn't you find a better way to warn us?"

Tinless looked at the floor. "I did put the comment in the code, and you eventually did find it. I send postcards to Hans Schmidt every year, asking him to come up here to visit." He met Val's gaze. "Red Tree has two monks stationed here. They watch me constantly. My phone lines are not private, I have no access to email, and I cannot make a trip without them knowing."

Sheela frowned. "Tinless, what's going to happen now? Surely those monks know we're here."

Tinless nodded. "They know. I must hope that as you save your organization, our *gompa* will be spared."

We stood up and slipped on our shoes and sandals. Val and I kept the socks.

"We'll do our best," I said. "We need that picture, though."

Tinless handed me the photo. "I have something else that may help," he said. "Follow me."

He led us back to the base of the giant Buddha statue. He reached into one of the bowls of fruit and pulled out a ring. "After Red Tree left Hyderabad, I found this ring stuck in a crack in the floor under his bed," he said.

The ring looked ancient. Tiny fingers of gold held a seven-sided crystal in place. Small carvings of lions and elephants surrounded the band.

"Was it his?" I asked.

"He said this ring would make him rich. When he called me from Sterling, I lied and told him I couldn't find it." He gave a thin smile.

"Those two monks have torn my apartment apart many times searching for it."

"Sometimes the best hiding places are in plain sight," I said. I put the ring in my pocket. "Thank you, Tinless."

When we reached Leh, Tenzin looked at me in the mirror. "Sir, you already having hotel?"

"No," I said. "Where do you suggest we stay?"

"I finding something for you." In a few minutes, we pulled up to a small building. "Hotel belonging to my cousin."

We said goodbye to Tenzin and checked in. Then we climbed the quarter mile up to the center of town, stopping every fifty yards to catch our breath.

I pulled my shawl tight around me. "Let's find food before we all freeze," I said.

Leh's main street was empty of cars and people. We walked inside the "Holiday Restaurant." Three people were talking to a bartender. "Are you open?" I asked.

The bartender smiled. "*Julay*! We are open!"

We sat in a booth and waited. Soon we stopped shivering, and I motioned to the bartender. "Can we order some food?"

He shook his head. "No food."

I looked at Bhanu. "Maybe you should try in Hindi."

Bhanu called out a question, and the bartender answered. They went back and forth a few times, and then Bhanu turned to us. "They're not serving food tonight."

I looked at the others. "You want to get a drink, and find food somewhere else?"

Bhanu shook his head. "They're not serving drinks either."

"So why are they open?" Val asked.

Bhanu asked the waiter, then said, "He said they're open for visiting, but not for business."

We got up and left. "*Julay*!" the bartender called, oblivious to our dirty looks.

We stood in the street. "There," Sheela said. She pointed up. "On the second floor—Tibetan Food. See it?"

We climbed the building's stairs. Instead of a door, a curtain hung across the entry to the restaurant. Bhanu drew it aside, and we walked into a small dining hall.

A man came out of the back kitchen, wiping his hands. *"Julay!"*

"Are you open and serving food?" I asked.

He nodded his head and led us to a table. "I bring you menu." He came back a minute later with a menu. "The cook only has vegetarian dishes. No meat tonight. Very sorry, sir."

"It's okay," I said. "Can you bring us four bowls of *thukpa*?"

"No *thukpa* tonight, sir."

"So what do you have?"

"We have fried *momos*, sir," he said. "Nothing else."

I sighed. "Okay, bring them on."

"How many would you like, sir?"

I looked at Bhanu. "How many can you eat?"

"Momos?" He pulled a face. "Not very many."

"Twelve *momos*," I told the waiter.

He shook his head. "We only have eight. I bring them all."

"Char chai lie yay," Sheela told him. She smiled at me. "Every restaurant in India has tea."

Val stretched and pulled her shawl tight around her. "So what did you think of the trip?" she asked me.

"It was a bit spooky finding young Feret's picture up there," I said.

She shuddered. "I used to like Andre—a lot. I can't believe he blackmailed a bunch of lonely Buddhist monks."

"I hope Lama Tinless doesn't get in trouble with Mr. Feret's monks," Sheela said.

The waiter brought the *momos*, and we devoured them.

"They're not so bad when you're really hungry," Bhanu said.

We walked back to our hotel and climbed the stairs to our rooms. I figured out how to ignite the gas heater while Val arranged the bed, and we quickly undressed and got under the covers.

Val snuggled into my arms. "Did those *momos* give you any energy?"

Hmm. "Can it even be done at these elevations?"

"People live here, Scott. I'm sure it's possible."

"Not many people, though. Maybe the locals have problems."

She kissed me, and that warmed me up all over. "We're both scientists," she said. "Let's do some research."

twenty-four

I WOKE UP AT four with a headache that felt like needles lancing my eyes and jabbing into the depths of my brain. I sat up and held my head in my hands and winced at the pain.

I squinted and tried to focus on the heater's dancing flames. My mouth was dry, and I reached over Val to grab the water bottle.

"Save some for me," Val murmured. She sat up and took a few swallows. "What's happening to the heater?" she asked.

I looked at the now sputtering flame. It flickered out, and the room went dark.

I heard Val set the bottle down. "Are we out of fuel?" she asked.

I got up and rocked the tank. It felt at least half full. "There's plenty left," I said. "I'll try to light it again."

I pressed the gas button and heard the hiss of propane. I punched the igniter and saw its spark. But no ignition. Even after five or six tries.

"Try a match," Val suggested.

I grabbed one from the table and struck it on the box side. The match flared brightly for a second but went out right after. Same results with the next match. And the next.

"I guess we'll sleep without heat," I said. I lay down, but my head still pounded, and I sat back up. I found myself panting. "I can't seem to catch my breath," I said.

"Me either. I guess we're not high altitude people. We need more oxygen."

"Like that match." I lay there and tried to think. "Wait—the match didn't light because there's no oxygen. The heater used it all up." I struggled to think. "We need to get oxygen right now." I tried to stand, but my legs buckled, and I fell to the floor. I crawled to the window.

"It's stuck," Val said. We both pushed, but couldn't open it.

"The door," I said. I crawled over to it, fumbled with the latch, and pushed it open. Fresh, cold air lashed our bodies, and we stood up and sucked it in. Our headaches quickly faded.

I went back to the table and struck a match. It flared up and continued to burn brightly. I ignited the heater and examined the window.

"I left it open a crack," Val said. "I'm sure of it."

I nodded. "But now it's jammed shut." I got up close to the window and peered directly upward. I saw a wooden wedge stuck in the frame.

I showed Val the wedge. "Who would do that?" she asked.

I shrugged. "Let's check on Bhanu and Sheela." I headed for the door.

"You might want to put these on first." Val tossed me my boxers.

I slipped them on and went into the hall. Bhanu and Sheela were staying across from us; I knocked on the door, but got no answer.

"Where could they be?" Val asked. She had thrown on my t-shirt.

"I don't know. They're not answering." I rattled the handle again.

"Kick in the door," she said. "Hurry!"

I backed up and planted the sole of my foot against the wooden door. I tested my footing, and then drew back and gave the door a solid kick.

A panel broke free. I pushed it out of the way, reached in, and unlocked the deadbolt.

"Bhanu? Sheela? Are you there?" Val called.

A snore from the bed. Bhanu and Sheela were sound asleep, arms wrapped around each other.

"Their heater is fine," Val whispered. She pointed to the dancing blue flames.

I saw a shadow move outside the window, so I grabbed Val's arm. "Get down," I hissed.

We dropped to the floor. I peeked around the bottom of the bed, and could see the top of a ladder moving along the bottom of the window frame.

"What's out there?" Val whispered.

"Somebody climbing a ladder," I whispered back.

A couple seconds later I saw the head, then the red-robed torso of the monk who collected our donations in Lamayuru.

"It's that first monk we saw at the *gompa*," I hissed.

The monk reached into the room and undid the latch holding the window open. He pushed the window closed, cupped his hands on the glass, and peered inside while I kept still. Then he reached into his robe, pulled out a wooden wedge, and jammed it high in the seam between the window frame and the window. He tapped on it with his fist.

"He just sealed the room," I whispered. "They're really trying to kill us."

The monk climbed down, and a few seconds later the ladder slid away. We ran to the window and watched the monk shove the ladder into the back of a small van. The van drove down the hill and made a left on the road toward Lamayuru.

We shook Bhanu and Sheela awake and told them what happened. Their eyes grew wide when I showed them the wedge in their window frame.

"Let's leave before they come back." Sheela said.

"There's nowhere to go." Val said. "This town is closed until morning."

We decided to get up and pack. Then we sat in the lobby and waited for the staff to come to work. We took turns dozing and keeping watch.

The hotel staff arrived at six. Bhanu and Sheela went to the dining room while Val and I settled the bill.

Bhanu grinned at us when we came to the table. "Guess what they're serving for breakfast," he said.

"Eggs and toast?" I asked.

"Nope. *Momos*."

"Great."

We spent a few minutes in silence, watching the glaciers out the window after we took off from Leh. Then Val grabbed my hand. "It's good to be with you—alive," she said.

I squeezed back. "Tinless said something that seemed to hit you pretty hard," I said.

She was silent for a minute. Then she sighed and turned away from the window. "He said that we have the knowledge, but we don't help our members figure out what it all means."

I frowned. "Isn't that the way the system was designed?"

She nodded. "And for me, it's good this way. But what if somebody came along and offered a mix of the science and religion all wrapped up in a single, neat package?"

"You're thinking of that blog we found about WorldWideSouls, aren't you?" I asked.

"I am."

I thought about what she said. "So that's how Feret is building WorldWideSouls—he's telling people what to do with their bridges."

"Yes, and that would be fine if he wasn't a fake," she said. "Scott, Andre is very powerful and very charismatic. It's easy to get yourself sucked into following him. No wonder WorldWideSouls is growing."

Something was bothering me. "He sucked you in too, didn't he?"

She turned back to the window for a minute. Then she faced me. "He did, but I don't want to talk about it now."

I had to respect her privacy. So I changed the subject.

"Maybe Bob can help us a bit more," I said.

She raised her eyebrows.

"Last week he told me that he needed more than belief," I said. "He needed the meaning behind it. I'm guessing that his church has already been approached by WorldWideSouls. Bob should be able to find out more about what they're up to."

She nodded. "Good idea. What will we do?"

I sighed. "Figure out what Feret is planning before it's too late."

We flew through New Dehli. Eventually we landed in Hyderabad. Bhanu drove us to the front of the Soul Identity building.

I checked the time: three p.m. in Hyderabad and five thirty a.m. in Sterling. "We have a radio check in a half hour."

"Good, we've got time to eat," Val said. "That airplane bag of spicy nuts didn't hold me very long." She turned to Bhanu. "Where can we find some *momos*?"

He laughed. "Nowhere, if we're lucky. How about a chicken tikka pizza?"

"That sounds great," I said.

Back in the communications room I entered the fifth encryption code. Bob, Archie, George, and Sue were all waiting on the air.

"Did you find Tinless Tiksey?" Archie asked.

Tinless was in danger from Feret's monks, so we needed to protect him as long as possible.

"We found him," I said. "But he claimed to know nothing."

"Did you pressure him?" Archie asked.

We were in no rush to share what we learned. I glanced at Val and hoped she agreed. "We did," I said, "but he wasn't sharing."

Time to change the subject. "George and Sue, did you get a picture of Feret's eyes?" I asked.

"No, but we have quite the adventure to share," George said. "Picture this—after our Monday meeting with Mr. Feret, we sneak into his office closet when he leaves the building."

"We were hoping to get the photo when he came back," Sue said.

"We sit there for a long time," George said. "A couple hours at least. Finally Mr. Feret returns, but again we miss our photo opportunity."

"The batteries had died. George had forgotten to turn off the camera," Sue said.

"Anyway," George said, "Mr. Feret works at his desk, and I'm thinking that we're stuck all afternoon. We try to get comfortable—I move some boxes and end up spilling some old paperwork. The papers go everywhere."

"And what did you find?" Val asked.

"Nothing at all," he said.

Val looked at me and sighed.

"But get this," George said. "Next thing we know, Brian walks into the office."

"Archie's Brian?" I asked.

"The one and only," he said. "Our coffee joke man."

"What did they talk about?" Val asked.

"We don't know," George said. "Their voices are muffled. But they talk for over a half hour, then Brian and Mr. Feret leave together."

"George told me this yesterday," Archie said. "This morning I checked with our travel team—Brian booked a personal trip to Venice for a long weekend. He flew back to Boston last night."

"So you'll see him in a couple of hours," I said.

"I will," Archie said. "Though I do not plan to say anything to him about this matter."

That seemed wise. No need to tip our hand.

"Did you find out anything about WorldWideSouls?" I asked.

We could hear Archie sigh over the radio. "No, Scott. Nothing new."

Time to get Bob to dig in for us, like Val and I had discussed. "Bob," I said, "I'm sorry for bringing this up over the radio, but we could really use your help."

"Anything, sir," he replied. "What can I do for you?"

"You told me about this group in Baltimore that you belong to."

A long pause. "What about it?" he asked.

"Were they approached by WorldWideSouls?"

A longer pause. "Yes."

"Did they join WorldWideSouls?"

"I think so."

This was like pulling teeth. "Bob, these are the bad guys," I said. "They're trying to hurt Soul Identity."

"I know, sir." Bob's voice was full of fear.

"Can you help us find out what's going on?" I asked. "It means you'll have to get to Baltimore quickly."

We could hear Archie talking softly to Bob in the background.

"Okay, I'll do it," Bob finally said. "I'd like to take Elizabeth so it won't look suspicious. We can talk to them about our wedding plans."

"We need you to find out why everybody's going to Venice, and what's supposed to happen there," I said.

"We'll leave this evening," he said.

"Hey, one more thing," George said. "I talked to my old buddy again. He's saying that Soul Identity is corrupt and is in need of brand new leadership. He says that I'd understand it all in a couple days."

"On Saturday in Venice?" I asked.

"No, he hints it'll all make sense by Friday. In Sterling." George paused for a moment, then said, "Mr. Morgan, do we stay in Venice, or do we return to Sterling?"

"I think you and Sue should stay in Venice." Archie's voice sounded urgent. "You must find out as much as you can."

"Yes, sir," George said.

"We've got one more day in Hyderabad," I said. "We'll dig into the actual code to see if there's anything we're missing."

We shut down the equipment and left the building. Bhanu and Sheela were sleeping in their car.

Val rapped on the windshield. "You want us to take a cab back to the hotel?" she asked.

Bhanu rubbed his eyes. "No, we'll drop you off," he said. "But let's start late tomorrow."

"We'll meet you in the office at noon," Val said.

twenty-five

WE PACKED UP BY nine a.m. "Ready for some pearl shopping?" Val asked me.

Val wanted another string of pearls, she said, because they were one of the most popular items Soul Identity members left in the depositary for their future carriers. Her own collection was growing, all of them obtained from this city.

I had read a brochure in the hotel that claimed Hyderabad was for pearls what Antwerp was for diamonds: the world's crossroads. Ninety percent of all pearls sold passed through this Indian city for piercing and stringing.

"I'm ready," I said. "How are we getting there?"

"Auto taxi."

I had watched the three-wheeled yellow cages with at least seven or eight people crammed into them zip around the city. "Are you crazy?" I asked. "I don't want to share with so many others."

She laughed. "We can get our own—just you, me, and the driver."

That sounded better.

Thirty minutes later, I shouted, "I think I prefer the spoiled American way of traveling."

"Why's that?" she asked.

I gestured. "This is loud, hot, and stinky."

She laughed.

Five minutes later we pulled up to a small shop. The driver pointed. "Sir, ma'am, one stop first on way to pearls."

"We don't have much time," Val said.

"Just see," he said. "Good things inside."

"Why did we stop here?" I asked him.

The driver pointed. "That man my wife's older brother. Every auto customer I must bring here first."

Two minutes later we climbed back in the auto taxi. I pointed at the driver. "Your wife's brother sells light switches," I said.

"Light switches, yes. You like, sir?"

"Just take us to RMR," Val said. She smiled at me. "What would you call that, coercive marketing?"

"Maybe I could use that in my own business."

She shook her head. "It doesn't seem that effective. There was only one other customer, and he wasn't buying either."

RMR Pearls was a little bigger than the light switch shop. We stepped over sandals scattered around the steps. A guard saluted us and opened the door.

It was dark inside. Somebody barked an order, and a boy ran to switch on the lights. The shopkeeper stood beaming in front of us. "Welcome back, my favorite customer!" he said to Val.

"Thanks, Shiv," she said. "I'd like to buy another pearl necklace."

Shiv wobbled his head at us. "You have come to the right place. Please have a seat."

We sat down and watched as a boy laid a white towel on top of the glass cabinet. "Can you show me some jet black pearls?" Val asked.

"Of course." Shiv motioned, and the boy ran into the back room. He returned with a bulging plastic shopping bag. Shiv put the bag at his feet and spread out the wrinkles from the towel. "Jet black ones are South Sea pearls." He pulled out a bunch of strands tied together at one end. "These are eight millimeter. They are perfect for you." He splayed the strands onto the towel.

Val looked. "You have anything bigger?"

Shiv pulled out another bunch. "These ones are ten millimeter. They are perfect for you."

"I thought the last ones were perfect," I said.

Shiv looked at me and smiled. "My friend, all pearls are perfect."

"Ah." I looked at the towel. These pearls were huge, round, and almost perfect. "Wow."

Val smiled. "There's that word again."

"They're gorgeous." I held up the end of a strand. "But how do you know they're real?"

"Every American customer asks this question," Shiv said. He snapped his fingers, and the boy opened another drawer and withdrew a knife, a cigarette lighter, and two small white pearl necklaces. "Let me show you."

"He loves doing this," Val said. Her eyes sparkled. "This is my fourth show."

Shiv grabbed the strand of pearls I was playing with. He pulled hard at the end and separated the strand from the bunch. "Pearls are eighty-six percent calcium, two percent organic compounds, and twelve percent water," he said.

He held up the strand. "A real pearl is grown by the oyster. You find natural ridges on it. You can feel them like this." He rubbed one of the pearls against his teeth, then handed me the strand.

I rubbed the pearl against my teeth, and it was rougher than I expected. "What's a fake pearl feel like?" I asked.

Shiv handed me one of the white necklaces. These slipped against my teeth with no friction at all. "Yeah, that is different." I said.

"Now some fake pearls do feel real," Val said.

Shiv nodded. "Some fake pearls have real nacre. That is the deposits made on top of the seed put in the oysters," he said. "Cheap pearl shops use big seeds." He snapped his fingers, and the boy handed over the other white necklace and the knife. "Feel these pearls."

I did. They felt real.

"Real pearls, bad quality," he said. He took the knife and scraped the blade against one of the pearls. The top layer flaked off and revealed a white plastic bead inside. "Cheap pearls." He handed the necklace to me.

I looked at the ruined pearl. "And yours are different?"

"Watch." He took the strand of black pearls and pulled one off. He shaved it down to its middle. "You see we have no seed."

Shiv snapped again, and the boy handed him the cigarette lighter. Shiv took the cheap pearls from me and used a pair of tweezers to hold one over the flame. Within five seconds the pearl bubbled and melted. He pulled a black pearl off the strand and held it to the flame. The shine disappeared under a layer of soot, but it didn't melt.

"You've ruined it," I said.

Shiv rubbed the pearl with his fingers. The soot came off, and the pearl looked like it did before. He handed it to me, and it was cool to the touch.

"You've got to get some pearls," I told Val.

She smiled at Shiv. "Another converted customer."

Val chose a stunning strand of South Sea jet black pearls. A small man took the strand and clasp, sat in the corner, and got to work turning it into a necklace.

Another customer walked into the store and sat by the door. He wore gray slacks, a white shirt, and a gray tie.

Val kicked me on my leg. She pointed with her chin at the other customer. "That guy was in the light switch store."

The man was looking into the case in front of him, but every few seconds his glance darted our way.

I got up and stood over him. "Can I help you?" I asked.

The man handed me his card without saying a word. I read it out loud. "V.R.A.S. Reddy, Security, WorldWideSouls."

He pointed to his chest. "Myself V.R.A.S. Reddy. And you are Mr. Scott Waverly?"

I nodded.

"I am here to protect you and Valentina Nikolskaya. Please call me Reddy."

"Who told you to protect us?"

"My supervisor, sir. Soul Identity has outsourced its security to WorldWideSouls."

Things must be going downhill in Sterling. Had Feret made his move already?

"We don't want your protection," I said.

"But it is my duty."

I glared at him. "Do your duty somewhere else."

Reddy blanched under my stare and backed out of the store. I saw him pull a phone out of his pocket.

Val joined me at the door and we watched Reddy talk on the phone. She sighed. "So the gray guys caught up to us."

"They did. And now we know they're WorldWideSouls. Let's get out of here."

Shiv called us over and handed Val the completed necklace. She put it around her neck.

"It's gorgeous." I said. I pulled out my wallet and paid him with some more of Archie's cash.

Shiv beamed. "Thank you, my best customers! This is an auspicious day. You buy my best pearls. Please come again!"

We got into our waiting auto taxi. V.R.A.S. Reddy waved to us and got into his own auto, and we all headed to the office.

When we reached SchmidtLabs, we noticed the security guards in front of Soul Identity were dressed in gray outfits matching Reddy's.

"Looks like WorldWideSouls is also protecting the premises," I said.

Val shook her head. "Protecting is an interesting word. Remember it was the gray guys who shot at us in Maryland."

We walked inside, and Bhanu came up to us. "Why is our competitor now guarding Soul Identity?"

"Don't you have a buddy who works for them?" I asked.

He nodded. "I talked to him this morning. He doesn't know anything."

"Like us," Sheela said as she walked over. "What is happening to Soul Identity?"

"We don't really know," Val said.

Bhanu shook his head. "You must know something. Andre Feret is Fred Antere. We learned in Leh that he changed the match program. That means he's a fake. And I did some Internet searching. Antere is connected to WorldWideSouls."

"You're right," Val said. "But we don't know why Feret is bringing WorldWideSouls into Soul Identity."

I was glad she didn't mention the pending activities in Venice on Saturday. Or George's early warning about Friday.

Bhanu opened his mouth to say something, but then he stopped. "You'll tell us if Sheela and I are in any danger?"

I shrugged. "I doubt you are." I told him about V.R.A.S. Reddy at the pearl store and how he'd been assigned to us. "He's right outside," I said. "You can see for yourself."

Bhanu and Sheela both looked, and Reddy waved.

"Did anybody follow you to work this morning?" I asked them.

They shook their heads.

"So you're probably okay. But keep an eye out," I said.

We walked to our conference room, and Bhanu and Sheela left.

"Let's find a scanner," Val said.

I grabbed young Feret's Lamayuru photo, and we headed for the door.

twenty-six

"JUST LIKE TINLESS SAID." Val turned her laptop screen my way.

Red Tree, also known as Fred Antere and Andre Feret, was definitely not an overseer. His real eyes produced the same soul identity that we had found in the sabotaged matching program. Berry was the true overseer, and Feret had stolen his identity.

Now that we had proven this, we had to stop him before Soul Identity went under.

"We've got to figure out Feret's plans." I pushed my laptop to her. "Show me how you hacked the WorldWideSouls Web site."

She started typing. "The dummies that put this site together didn't protect their upload section. My script makes me an administrator when you go to this URL." She pointed to my screen. "We're in, and we didn't even need a buffer overflow to get there."

"Nice job." I pulled my laptop back. "My turn to drive."

Within ten minutes I had uncovered a list of users, and I logged in using Fred Antere's account.

"What can he do that an administrator can't?" Val asked.

"Let's see." I brought up the Web page source and scanned it. "There." I pointed at the screen at a hidden button, right next to the WorldWideSouls logo. I clicked on it, and a menu showing email, chat, calendar, and files popped up.

"Careful, Scott," Val warned. "Don't get caught."

"I'll be quick," I said. I clicked on the calendar and went to last Monday's schedule. I saw George and Sue's eleven o'clock meeting with Feret.

Feret was flying from Venice later today, arriving in Boston on Wednesday night. And on Friday he was flying out to Venice at six p.m.

"Click on Saturday," Val said.

Feret was booked from noon to two at a "New Order Planning Session," and from three to five at a "New Order Presentation." Both sessions were to be held at the Venetian Soul Identity amphitheatre.

"This dude seems pretty confident in mixing the two groups together by Saturday," I said.

"He's already done it," Val said. "Look at the guards outside."

"Hiring them on as outsourced security guards is one thing," I said. "But using the Soul Identity facilities for a WorldWideSouls meeting seems rather presumptive."

I went back to the menu and clicked on the files link. The list started with one called "New Order: Raison d'Etre." That sounded promising: I clicked on the link and a download progress bar started chugging away.

Then a chat dialog popped up. It was Brian, wanting to talk to Feret. He had typed something in Latin: *Qui audit adipiscitur.*

Val did a Web translation. "It means *he who dares wins*," she said.

I opened the logs and looked for a saved chat session. Last time Brian had chatted with him, Feret answered *Aut vincere aut mori.*

"That means *either to conquer or to die*," Val said.

"It sounds pretty serious," I said as I pasted it into the chat window. I typed *What news?*

Brian wrote back immediately. *1st phase now complete. 90 offices guarded by WWS.*

I thought Feret would act pretty arrogant with Brian. *Why are you behind schedule?*

Events beyond my control, came back after a minute.

And? I glanced at Val. "Maybe he'll tell us something."

After a moment the reply came. *AB and AM got in the way. He fought the outsourcing order: said you had no authority, and she backed him up. I gave him an extra dose, but that blew four hours.*

AM and AB must be Archibald Morgan and Ann Blake. And it seemed that Brian was lacing Archie's coffee.

Val typed on her keyboard for a minute. "Let's feed him some Latin," she suggested. "How about this? *Aut viam inveniam aut faciam.* It means *either find a way or make one.*"

I typed it in. Then I wrote *Anything else?*

Brian wrote back after a minute. *S/V still in Hyd. We are following them. I will get them for sure this time—no more misses, I promise.*

So it was Brian who blew up the guesthouse and tried to suffocate us. I needed to put a stop to that. *Not yet. We must know what else they learned.*

OK. I will ask B what he hears. He returns from Balt tonight. Can't wait to get past this stage and start running the dep for you, boss.

Val's mouth dropped open. "Bob is working for them!"

Maybe he was; maybe he wasn't. "Careful—they could know it's us, and they're just stirring up shit," I said.

She frowned. "How can we know for sure?"

"I'll give Brian an order and see if he executes." *Email V and confirm the demo for Friday. End their investigation before they discover anything else. Right away.*

Time to sign off before we blew it. I scanned through the log and looked for how these two usually ended their chats.

I typed *Quod sum eris*. "That's the same thing he said on that phone call," I told Val.

I verified my download had completed and I logged off. Then I turned to Val. "Can you remove this chat log from both accounts?"

"Sure." She typed for a few minutes. "All gone," she said. "And the email from Brian just arrived—he's asking if I'm still doing the demo on Friday. Mr. Feret wants to know."

So it was Brian on the other end, and not somebody playing us. "Don't answer the email," I said. "We don't want Brian forwarding your reply to Feret."

She nodded.

"Are you still logged in?" I asked.

"I am."

"Can you see if Bob and Elizabeth are on the membership list?"

She pulled it up. "Do you know Bob's last name?" she asked.

I thought back to Kent Island when he first delivered me the reader. "I know it begins with an O."

She typed for another minute. "They have three Bob and Robert O's," she said. "One of them was added yesterday, along with an Elizabeth Blake."

I sighed. "Dammit."

"Why would they do this?"

"Maybe they think they're doing the right thing," I said. "But we can't let them know that we found them out."

She looked troubled. "So we don't tell Mr. Morgan?"

"We don't tell anybody until we get back and see what's really going on," I said. "Now let's find out why Feret thinks you need a new order."

Twenty minutes later I scrolled back to the top of the New Order: Raison d'Etre document. It was a copy of Feret's speech that he was giving in Venice on Saturday.

The first part discussed his goals: Feret stated that he wanted to take over the Soul Identity leadership and redistribute all the assets according to a new order.

The speech went on to describe the motives. It was presented as something Feret called his testimony, and it tied in to what we learned from Tinless: apparently his grandfather was a very rich man who didn't pass any money on to his son. His father had spent like crazy, expecting to inherit a fortune when the old man died.

"Are inheritance problems common in Soul Identity?" I asked Val.

She sighed. "Every now and then we have problems with surprised families."

Grandpa Feret died and left all his money to his soul line. Feret's father went berserk and killed his wife and then himself. Their only child, seventeen old Fred Antere, who we knew as Andre Feret, was left to fend for himself.

"This stuff happens?" I asked. "Good grief."

Val nodded. "Fortunately it's rare—most people preserve only a portion of their wealth for their future carriers and save the rest for family."

"Maybe we'd be fine today if Gramps had been a little more careful with his notes," I said. Feret wrote how he had found a stash of Soul Identity papers in his grandfather's office thirteen years ago. Those papers had driven his urge for revenge.

Feret conveniently forgot to mention his stint at Lamayuru, his blackmailing of the *gompa*, and the match program adjustments he had to make to become an overseer. He did describe his first trip to Sterling, where he discovered his destiny. This, he claimed, was to fix Soul Identity and institute his new order.

Feret's speech then described how WorldWideSouls members would benefit. He claimed that only the enlightened members would gain from the new order, while everybody else would suffer all sorts of calamities.

Val turned to me. "He's using their need to feel special to reel people in."

"That's a pretty common theme in fundamentalist religions, isn't it?" I asked. "They call their members Chosen, Remnant, Martyrs, or Enlightened. Everybody likes thinking they're on the inside track."

In the last part of the speech, Feret had outlined a creed for the new order members to recite: answers to why the bridges were there, what they meant, what a member's duties were to the organization, how they should act, and what their reward would be.

Feret's game appeared to be about sucking the money out of Soul Identity and into his church of WorldWideSouls. And it seemed to be working.

Bob, for example, wanted somebody to tell him what to do with his impressive soul line. He had told me during the drive to Sterling that he still sought meaning.

Feret was dishing up plenty of meaning in his creed.

I closed the file, and we both sat back and pondered what we had read.

Then Val stood up. "Scott, we must stop Andre—he's going to ruin everything!"

I nodded. "We will, Val."

Whether Feret's quest for revenge was justified or not, I couldn't let one jerk screw up this organization for so many people.

It was now early evening. I did a quick email check. My parents were having quite a time in Iceland. One of the three major volcanoes had a minor eruption under its icecap, and the ensuing hot lava melted the ice and caused a *jokulhlaup*, which is what Icelanders call a glacier outburst flood. It wiped out the roads, but the Internet connection was strong.

"Aren't they scared?" Val asked when I showed her some spectacular pictures of rising steam and ash.

"They're having a blast," I said. I looked at my watch. "Our flight's at two this morning. Let's get Bhanu and Sheela to take us to Bawarchi for another dose of biryani before we go to the airport."

twenty-seven

THE PLANE SCREAMED OVER the bay and dropped toward the water. Just when it looked like we were going to get wet, the runway appeared beneath us. Another Logan landing.

Val stretched her arms over her head. "Is it still Thursday?"

I grinned. "Yes, and we've still got another ten hours to go before it's over."

She sighed. "We've been running around for a week now. Did you think this Soul Identity work would be this fun?"

That was an interesting question; a little over a week ago I planned to spend a few weeks in Boston, alone in a hotel room, sacrificing my valuable fishing time in order to make Soul Identity's application safer while I helped my neighbor become a member.

"Almost getting us bombed and suffocated?" I smiled. "I wouldn't trade it for anything."

We got off the plane and went through immigration and customs. Rose and Marie picked us up and brought us to Ann Blake's house.

We stood in the foyer with the girls, Berry, and Madame Flora.

"How was India?" Berry asked.

"Very hot," Val said.

"And very cold," I countered.

Val looked at me. "Very informative," she said.

I smiled. "And very mysterious."

"You guys sound like Grandma when she's reading palms," Marie said.

"Only then she adds, 'that's all for today—come back next week for more information,'" Rose said.

"Girls, you're giving away all my secrets," Madame Flora said.

The twins rolled their eyes. "Goodness, Grandma, everybody here knows the game," Rose said.

The girls showed us to our room and then drove us over to the Soul Identity offices.

"Mr. Morgan told everybody that you both survived the blast and would be back at work soon," Marie said. She unrolled the window and gave our names to the guard. The gates opened and we were through. "We'll just drop you off." She pulled around to the front of the building.

A man in a gray suit sat at Elizabeth's desk. Val and I walked right by, and he frowned and reached for his phone as we passed him. Val badged us in, and we headed to the elevators and pressed the down button.

James peered at us from his stool. "Welcome back, frequent travelers," he said as he punched our cards. "On your next ride you two are going first class."

Val smiled. "We can't wait, James."

Forty stood inside the doors to the dungeon. "Jeez, Val, when Mr. Morgan told us you survived the explosion, the whole dungeon cheered."

"That's so sweet, Forty." Val gave him quick hug and kissed his cheek.

Forty's face went red, and he mumbled, "We're all glad you're safe." He smiled at me. "You too, dude."

In Val's office, I looked at the tiny hole in the wall. The toothpick I had placed there was gone. I peered inside, and I could see the lens.

"I wonder if there are others," Val whispered.

"We should expect that whatever we do here, we'll be watched and listened to rather closely." I looked up at the ceiling. "If anybody is listening, please tell Mr. Feret that we'd like to see him this afternoon," I said.

"You think he'll meet with us?" she asked.

I shrugged. "I hope so. In the meantime, I'll do my email."

I reached into my laptop bag and found a penny. "Do you have any tape?" I asked.

"On the desk."

I taped the penny over the camera hole, and I faced my laptop screen toward it, hoping that was the only camera along the wall.

I brought up my email and clicked on the latest message from my parents. Its subject was "More fun in Iceland." As it came up, I tapped Val on the shoulder.

She leaned over and read with me. My parents had hitched a ride from some NATO soldiers working on opening the washed out roads. They spent the afternoon back at the Blue Lagoon hot springs.

We looked at the pictures together, and I was about to close the email when Val grabbed my arm and pointed at the bottom.

After the "Love, Mom and Dad," there was a postscript. Dad had written, "Wanted to let you know that we overheard two marooned travelers in the steam room. They were pissed they were going to miss the birth of the new order of Soul Identity on Friday, and they were calling to see if there was a way they could reach Venice by Saturday."

Val opened her mouth to say something, but I put my finger up to her lips. I opened a text window on my laptop.

Talk here, I typed. *Birth on Friday—that matches what George said.*

She nodded. *What could that be?*

I thought about it for a minute. *They like blowing things up. Maybe they will destroy the existing leadership in one big blast.*

She shook her head. *That won't help Feret gain legitimacy.*

I opened his speech and pointed to the goals in the first section. Feret wrote that he had "taken over the Soul Identity leadership and will be redistributing all the assets according to a new order." I went back to our text window. *My parents heard birth. Feret says take over. Neither tells us how.*

We needed to figure this out today. Before Friday.

We'll have to get rid of Bob and Elizabeth tonight, I typed. *Send them home early or something. Maybe even feed them some disinformation.*

She went over to her desk, opened the bottom drawer, and pulled out a small yellow cloth pouch. She brought the pouch back to the table and sat back down.

What's that? I typed.

A bug for Bob. She opened the pouch behind her laptop screen. She pulled out a tiny microphone and a small gold transmitter.

How do we get it on him?

Tonight, at the meeting.

Can we test it first?

She shook her head. *Someone might hear.*

Sounds like a plan. I smiled. *Hey, this chatting over computers is fun. It almost feels like we're in the same room.*

Val erased what we had typed. "You're crazy." She put the microphone and transmitter back in the yellow pouch, and put the pouch in her laptop bag.

I pulled the laptop back in front of me. *I think Feret is going to kill Archie and Ann.*

She sat back in her chair for a minute. Then she leaned forward and typed, *That would definitely change the leadership and cause a rebirth.*

We may be targets too. Don't forget the guesthouse and hotel.

She frowned. *Andre seems well prepared and hard to beat: it seems like we're just reacting to his moves. We need some leverage.*

We have a few tricks up our sleeves, I typed. *Berry, our knowledge of Bob and Brian, our proof that Feret screwed up the match program. But it's all just defense if we can't project where he's going next.*

Brian stuck his head in the doorway. "Welcome back, Val. Hello, Scott," he said.

I closed my laptop cover. "Hey Brian, what's up?"

He put an ominous expression on his face. "Mr. Feret would like to meet with both of you," he said. "Right away."

I looked at Val. "I guess the walls do have ears."

We packed our laptops and took them with us. Then we followed Brian to the elevator.

Val and I handed James our cards, and he said, "You two are riding first class." He squinted at Brian. "Where is your frequent traveler card, young man?"

Brian stared at James. "Just bring us to the second floor," he snarled. "Now."

"Would you like a card?" I asked. "James bumps you to first class after just five trips."

Brian shifted his gaze between me and James. "What kind of moron has frequent traveler plans for elevators?"

"Suit yourself," James said. He hopped down from his stool and opened a panel right behind him. "Sir, you're going to have to shift a little bit to your right," he said to Brian. He pointed to the front of the elevator. "How about standing right there?"

Brian shifted and glared at James, who smiled back and drew a curtain across the elevator, leaving Val and me in our own compartment in the back.

I bit my lip to keep from laughing. James entered our section. "Let me get your seats," he said. He pulled a recessed lever, and a velvet-covered bench folded down from the back wall.

Val and I sat, and James went back to the other side of the curtain. Val was shaking with suppressed giggles.

James poked his head through. "Where are my first class passengers going today?" he asked.

I pointed at the curtain. "You'll have to ask the man riding in cattle class."

"Yes, sir." James disappeared, and we heard him speak to Brian. "Where to today, sir?"

"We have an important meeting with Mr. Feret."

"Who, sir?"

"Mr. Feret." Brian's voice had grown sharp.

"Never heard of him."

"Second floor! Now move it, you idiot!"

"Just a minute, sir."

The curtains moved, and James poked his head through again. "Sorry for the delay, folks. We have an unruly passenger in the front. We'll be leaving in just a second." He disappeared again.

We heard the doors open, a thud, and a loud "Ouch!" from Brian. Another thud, and we heard James say, "Stay off my train until you learn your manners!"

The doors closed, and James popped his head through the curtain. "Some people should stick to the stairs." He pulled the curtain all the way open. "We'll have you on the second floor in two shakes of a lamb's tail."

The elevator went up, and James opened the doors. Brian was standing outside, panting from having apparently run up the stairs. He glared at James, hands on his hips.

James smiled. "Second floor! All first class passengers please disembark!"

We stood up and got off the elevator.

"How was your trip?" I asked.

"My trip was fine," Val said. "A luxury ride."

"I was asking Brian."

Brian opened his mouth. Then he closed it and walked off down the hall to the right. "Follow me," he said over his shoulder.

Brian knocked on a door that was directly below Archie's office.

"Enter!" a voice called, the same voice I had heard on the recorded call. It had a strong French accent, and it sounded like *entair*.

Brian opened the door, and Val and I stood face to face with Andre Feret.

twenty-eight

FERET HADN'T CHANGED MUCH from his picture with the tourists in Lamayuru eleven years ago, although he had traded in the red robes for a suit and added a splash of gray at his temples.

He shook my hand. "Mr. Waverly, welcome to Soul Identity." He offered a slight bow to Val. "Good afternoon, Valentina. Please come in and have a seat." He closed the door on Brian.

Feret crossed his legs and folded his hands over his knee. "Let's get down to business, shall we?" he said.

I nodded. "Where do you want to start, Andre? Or do you prefer Fred?"

Feret gave a broad smile, showing perfect teeth. "Either name will do, I suppose," he said. "You seem to have made some good progress in your investigations."

"Not enough, though," I said. "We still don't know what you're up to."

He laughed. "I very much enjoy your American straightforwardness." He stood up and walked behind his chair and put a solemn look on this face. "I am trying with all my might to save this place."

"Save it from what?" I asked.

"From ruin," he said. "Soul Identity is an uncaring organization that is disconnected with its members and unable to move ahead with the times. Its members are voting their displeasure by withdrawing their deposits."

"Some may say that as an overseer, you are part of that problem," I said.

"That is an interesting hypothesis, but it is not so," he said. "For the last ten years, I have worked very hard at changing this organization, but I have been stymied at each and every step." He pointed at Val. "If you don't believe me, ask your friend Valentina—she knows."

I turned to Val, and she nodded at me.

Feret gave Val a short bow. "Everybody knows I moved to Venice as a sign of my unhappiness with the way Archibald was running Soul Identity."

"There's a big gap between getting upset at the management and starting a competitor," I said.

He cocked his head to one side. "A competitor, you say?"

"WorldWideSouls," Val said.

Feret smiled. "WorldWideSouls? Our security guards? They're not a competitor."

"Then why are you addressing them in Venice on Saturday?" she asked.

Feret's eyes narrowed. "I see some members have been talking out of place. No matter, all will be resolved shortly," he said. "I am giving a speech to WorldWideSouls. Nothing more."

"Why not just tell me the truth?" she asked.

Feret glared at Val. "Ms. Nikolskaya," he said in clipped tones, "I will not discuss the private business of the Soul Identity overseers."

"I'm having a hard time believing that it's overseer business to talk about a new order." I said.

He raised both his hands. "I need you to stop asking questions and listen to what I have to say."

The three of us shared a moment of silence as we glared at each other.

Feret smiled. "Thank you. As I mentioned earlier, you two have been very productive and innovative in your investigations. I appreciate all you have been doing for us, and I am looking forward to working with you more in the future. You have a lot of potential for growth at Soul Identity."

Why would he be praising us?

"But," he continued, "I am working hard at ramping up our new security team and assessing our current security posture. I have no time to worry about your investigations, and I fear that you two will be getting in the way of my efforts."

That's why—he was sidelining us.

A sly smile crept over his face. "At this time," he said, "I wish you to inform you that you both are suspended for a period of one week. No more investigations, no more work on the new system. You will immediately turn over your badges and all company equipment to me for the duration of this suspension." He looked at each of us. "Do you have any questions?"

"Why a week?" I asked. "Won't you have everything wrapped up by Saturday?"

Feret smiled. "I plan to. But I will not return to Sterling right away." He walked over to his desk and sat down. He picked up his handset and spoke into it. "Please come up. I need Mr. Waverly and Ms. Nikolskaya escorted off the premises."

He hung up the phone and looked at me. "We have approximately ninety seconds before my guards will remove you from my office. Then I will see you two next Thursday afternoon at," he looked at his watch, "shall we say four p.m.?"

Val had opened her laptop bag and was using the chair to shield her motions. I saw her pull out the yellow pouch.

To buy her some time, I got up and started walking toward him. "Why can't you tell us your plans?" I asked loudly. "What's the master stroke you're delivering tomorrow?"

Feret rolled back in his chair until he was up against his credenza. "Mr. Waverly, I find your behavior threatening. Please sit down, or I will ask my guards to shoot you."

Val was probably done. "Don't worry," I said. "I've got no reason to hurt you." I returned to my seat.

Feret rolled back to his desk. "Ms. Nikolskaya, I must confiscate your laptop bag along with its contents."

Val slid the yellow pouch and the photo of young Feret over to me. "I have some personal items in here," she said. "May I take them with me?"

He allowed a brief smile to escape his lips. "Of course you may," he said. "Please do it here on my desk, though. I would hate the thought of you leaving with any of our organization's property."

Val opened her laptop bag and extracted her passport, a lipstick tube, and a pair of sunglasses. While this was going on I was able to slip the yellow pouch and photo of Feret into my bag.

Feret made a show out of going through Val's items, even opening and twisting the lipstick tube. Then he handed them to Val. "Everything looks in order," he said.

He looked at me.

"Don't even think about looking in my bag," I said.

The door opened. Two gray suited men came in. Feret pointed at us. "Please remove them from our premises," he said. "I have suspended them."

We stood up and walked to the door. I looked over my shoulder and caught Feret smiling. "See you soon," I said.

"But not too soon, Mr. Waverly." His lips curled into something between a smile and a sneer.

"This is *causus belli*," I said. Pathetic, but *an occasion of war* was the only Latin phrase that came to mind.

"*Dulce bellum inexpertis.*" He smiled. "Since your Latin is clumsy, allow me to translate—*War is sweet to those without experience.*"

One of the gray suited guys prodded me in my back. I walked through the door and caught up with Val.

We took the stairs down to the lobby. The guard at Elizabeth's desk smiled as we walked past him.

"Can you call us a cab?" I asked the guy in the rear. "I forgot my cell phone today."

He shook his head. "I need to get you off our property as soon as possible. There's a gas station a mile or so on the right. They have a pay phone."

I nodded. The other gray suit left, and the three of us walked outside and headed up the driveway toward the gates.

"Don't you have a golf cart we could ride in?" I asked the guard.

"That would be nice," he said.

"Seems like you've done this before," I said.

He nodded. "You two make number five and six today. But you're the first ones he's suspended, and the other four had vehicles. Where's yours?"

"We just flew in." I stuck out my hand. "My name's Scott."

He looked around and then shook my hand. "John," he said.

"Hold on a sec, I've gotta tie my shoe," I said.

John nodded. He pulled a pack of cigarettes out of his pocket and lit one.

"John, there's no smoking on Soul Identity grounds," Val said. "You should know that."

"The rules have changed, ma'am. You're not the first to ask me that. As of today we can smoke on the grounds, but not in the buildings."

"Who's changing the rules?" I asked.

John shrugged. "I assume it was Mr. Feret. That's what he did last time."

I threw a glance at Val. "You knew him before?" I asked.

"Of course. I was there when he became the boss at WorldWideSouls." He smiled. "This team is in for a rude awakening."

"He runs a tight ship?" I asked.

John snorted. "In WorldWideSouls the boss is king."

"You're not a member, are you?" I asked.

He shook his head. "Just a hired hand."

"Me too," I said. "Be careful, okay? They're suspending even us contractors."

He frowned. "What kind of work do you do?"

"Security, just like you," I said. "They brought me up here from Maryland a bit over a week ago." I pointed at Val. "She arrived a day before me."

John's eyes narrowed. "How come I haven't seen you around?"

"Special assignment," I said in a low voice. "Out of the country." I pointed at our clothes. "We've been out of uniform and under cover."

He raised his eyebrows.

"We left on Thursday, right after the blast," I said.

John stubbed out his cigarette. "I heard about the blast."

I nodded. "And this is how they say thanks."

"You must've pissed somebody off," he said. "What'd you do?"

"We, ah," I looked at Val, and then leaned close and whispered, "We got too close for these guys to handle."

John's eyes widened and he checked out Val's figure. "I'd trade a suspension for her," he whispered back.

I nodded and winked.

We reached the gate, and John pulled out a business card. "Since you're fellow security officers—call if you need something." He wrote his cell phone number on the bottom of the card.

Val turned on her smile. "Thanks, John."

He smiled back. "Doing my job, ma'am."

We reached the gate and shook John's hand. Then we started walking down the road. When we reached the end of the Soul Identity property, Val turned into the woods and beckoned me to follow. I started to stay something, but she put her finger to her lips.

We walked another hundred yards and entered a small clearing. Val grabbed a little stick and wrote in the dirt, "Bugs."

She kicked off her shoes, slipped out of her blouse and slacks, and stood in her bra and panties. I stripped down to my boxers.

We started with her shoes. They were clean, and we moved to her pants. Nothing. But when we got to her blouse, Val found a tiny microphone glued to her collar. She pulled it off and set it down on a rock.

We found another one under my shirt collar. Val brought her lips to my ear. "We have to find the transmitter."

We didn't see it in my bag. "Maybe it was in yours," I said.

"Andre wouldn't have taken it back. It has to be in yours."

"Let me check in your bra."

She stifled a giggle and pointed to my boxers. "Careful, your own transmitter is peeking out."

I fixed myself. Then I rechecked my bag's outside pockets and found the transmitter hiding under the stubs of my boarding passes. It looked identical to the one in Val's yellow pouch.

I cupped my hand to her ear. "You think that's all the bugs?" I whispered.

Val nodded.

"How do you deactivate it?"

"On the bottom." She switched it off.

I thought for a minute. "We should use these bugs to our advantage," I said.

"Like make a fake recording?"

I nodded.

We got dressed and replanted the bugs. Val turned the transmitter back on. "How far until we reach a pay phone?" I asked in what I hoped was a normal voice.

"Less than a mile," she said. "Let's hurry up."

We reached the gas station just as a familiar green limousine pulled up.

Before Bob could get out, I pulled Val close and whispered, "Maybe we can get Bob to spill the beans."

Bob came over with a big smile on his face. "Hello, Val, hello, Scott. Elizabeth and I just got word that you had some trouble with Mr. Feret, so we came to give you a ride back to Ms. Blake's house."

"How sweet," Val said.

So now Bob was calling me Scott.

"Thanks, Bob," I said. "Who told you what happened?"

He stared at me for a second. "One of my delivery buddies called and told me you and Val were escorted off the grounds."

I needed to give Bob more credit. He could think on his feet.

Val flashed him a smile. "How was your trip to Baltimore?"

"It was great, Val," he said. "I showed Elizabeth my apartment, my delivery van, and my church." He opened the rear door. "Come on inside."

We climbed in. The partition was down, and Elizabeth looked back at us. "What a terrible thing that man did to you," she said. "Wait until I tell my mother. She can help you get your suspension lifted."

I shot a glance at Val. "I'm not so sure we should go back, Elizabeth. It's getting pretty scary in there." I paused for a second. "Anyway, why is some guy in a gray suit sitting at your desk?"

Elizabeth looked at Bob and then back at me. "He's just a substitute. I decided to take the next couple days off," she said. "I needed a break after our trip to Baltimore. I'll be back to work on Monday."

"I could use some vacation time too." I leaned my head back on the cushions. "Though I do owe Archie a report on what we learned since our last radio conversation."

Elizabeth frowned at Bob, and Bob shook his head at her. "We'll bring you to Ms. Blake's where you two can rest a little bit," he said. "Tonight at the meeting you can tell us what you learned."

"Scott, you don't owe them anything. They suspended your contract." Val looked at Bob and Elizabeth. "Soul Identity didn't protect us when we needed it the most."

Bob and Elizabeth exchanged covert smiles.

I sighed. "What can you expect from this organization, anyway? They seem to be in it just for the money."

Bob eyed me in the rear view mirror. "Does it seem that Soul Identity is just about the money?"

"To me it does," I said. "Everybody talks about dollars and statistics instead of faith and convictions." I shook my head. "I've been wondering if anybody here really knows what it means to have a soul line."

He cocked his head to one side. "But you don't believe in soul lines, do you?"

I needed to be careful here. "How can I possibly believe when the only exposure I've had has been with a bunch of hypocrites?" I upped my volume a notch. "Even Archie is happy that I'm not a believer. What does that say about his leadership?"

Val reached over and took my hand. "I hope I haven't been a hypocrite to you."

"No, Val, you haven't been a hypocrite," I said. "You've been a victim of this system, just like Bob."

We sat silently for a minute. Then Val looked at Bob. "I do feel like a victim—I left my job and joined Soul Identity because I wanted to pay back the organization that helped me build the bridge to my soul line. But nobody even acknowledged my sacrifice."

The limo was still idling in the parking lot of the gas station. Bob pulled a pamphlet out of his shirt pocket. It had been folded and refolded many times, leaving the creases worn and dirty. He held the pamphlet for a second then extended it toward us. "Scott, Val, I want to you read this little pamphlet," he said. "It has changed my and Elizabeth's lives."

I took the pamphlet. "IT MEANS MORE THAN THEY ARE TELLING YOU" was written across the cover. The Soul Identity logo at the bottom had been modified: the top of the triangle was crumbled, and the eyes looked old and tired.

I opened the pamphlet. It started, "To Soul Identity members who deserve the whole story."

I looked up. "Where did you get this, Bob?"

"In Baltimore," he said. "Our church has a stack in their foyer. It really hit home for me." He shifted into gear and pulled onto the road.

I read out loud, "When you joined Soul Identity, you made the most important decision of your current life. You chose to listen to your past, and you undertook the responsibility to guide your future."

"So far so good," I said.

Bob nodded. "Keep reading."

"But if you're an intelligent and enlightened member, you need more," I read. "Your heart burns to know why your soul line exists. And once you know that answer, you need the truth about what you must do."

"The truth?" Val asked.

"Just keep reading," Bob said. "It explains everything."

"You are not alone in your need," I read. "Soul Identity has been hiding the truth from you. The truth you need to be complete. Without this truth, your soul line will die."

"Why would they hide the truth from us?" I asked.

"They're afraid," Bob said.

I continued reading. "Is Soul Identity afraid of what would happen if we discovered the truth? They should be! They focus on your money, and not on your soul. And because of this, your soul is in peril. Shame on them."

Val shifted on the couch. "I want to hear this truth."

"You will, Val. Scott, keep reading," Bob said.

I looked at him. "Does this describe you?"

"It describes how I was, Scott," he said. "I now realize that I was enslaved by Soul Identity. They fed me scraps when I needed a feast. Once I learned the truth, I was able to throw off the chains that bound me." He smiled at Elizabeth. "We are both charter members of the new order of Soul Identity."

"The new order?" I asked. "George and Sue heard people talking about the new order in Venice. And we saw it on the Internet. Is this that same one?"

He smiled. "Yes, Scott. The new order will right the wrongs brought on by the leadership at Soul Identity, and leave us with an organization where only deserving members are rewarded."

I held up the pamphlet. "And that's explained in here?"

"It's all there," he said.

"Then I'll keep reading." I held the pamphlet so Val could also see, and we read through the next section together.

When we were done, I looked at Bob and Elizabeth. "That was interesting."

"What did you think?" Elizabeth asked.

I raised my eyebrows. "It's a lot to absorb at one sitting." The pamphlet said soul lines only existed for people who believed in the truths that WorldWideSouls taught, the truths they claimed Soul Identity hid from its members. If you didn't believe the truths, it was over: your soul line would die with you and never return. "Only those who believe get to the next level, right?" I asked.

Bob nodded.

The pamphlet went on to explain that those with long soul lines were heirs of refined souls. They were ready to hold high offices in the new order. Anyone at level three or above was eligible to be a leader in WorldWideSouls.

This must be what attracted Bob to the new order. I looked at him. "You must be very valuable to WorldWideSouls. Where are you, level eight?"

"You remember!" he said. "Yes, they were thrilled when I joined. In fact, I'll be flying to Venice tomorrow night to be at the opening ceremonies on Saturday." He glanced at Elizabeth. "You're coming too, by the way. Mr. Feret just approved it."

Elizabeth giggled. "Oh, Bob darling, this is wonderful!" She reached out and stroked his hair. "My big, strong, powerful man."

"Now, now, Elizabeth, we must act with dignity." He stared in the mirror at me and Val. "So what do you say?" he asked. "Will you believe the truth?"

I looked at the final section. It was entitled "The Secret Truths."

"Hold on—we need to read them," I said.

Val pointed at the first. "Truth one: you have a very special soul," she read. "You are alive today because this is either your first life, or because you accepted the truths in each of your past lives." She looked up. "That's pretty straightforward."

Bob and Elizabeth nodded.

I read the next. "Truth two: your duty is to learn and accept the truths. There is no other way." I frowned. "I'm not thrilled with this one."

Bob nodded. "It was hard for me too, Scott. But there is only one way. All other paths will destroy your soul."

Val cleared her throat. "Truth three: if you do accept the truths, you will be reborn, refined, and rewarded in your next life." She looked at Elizabeth. "I like the rewards part."

"Me too," Elizabeth said.

I turned the page. "Truth four: your purpose in this life is two-fold: to bring the message of the truths to others, and to help your leaders weed out the unbelievers." I glanced up front. "How do you weed them out, Bob?"

He looked at me in the mirror. "That's not covered in this pamphlet, Scott. It's only available to level three and up members."

Special knowledge for special people like Bob.

"And here's truth five," Val said. "Your soul's destiny is in your control. The truths give you the power to direct the outcome of your future lives."

Elizabeth smiled. "I like the last truth. Bob's pastor said you can even choose who your parents, siblings, and spouse will be in your next life."

"Amazing," I said.

Elizabeth nodded. "Isn't it? I wanted us to get eternally married right then and there, but Bob says we need to save up for it."

Bob cleared his throat. "Elizabeth, let's keep our private lives just between believers, okay?"

She smiled back. "You're right, Bob darling."

As we pulled into the driveway, I said to Bob, "When we were driving to Maryland last week, you told Val and me that it didn't matter what you believed, because you'd find out the truth when you reached heaven."

He frowned. "I did say that, and I know now that I was wrong. I have grown so much over the past two days."

I nodded. "It must feel good to find what you've been searching for."

"I feel at peace," he said.

I had heard this before. I raised my eyebrows. "Do you know you told me the same thing last week?"

Bob paused for a minute. "You are right, Scott. The evil ones medicated me with half truths." He turned around in his seat and stared at me with wide eyes. "They almost succeeded in stealing my soul away from me. Could you imagine how happy they would have been to destroy a level eight, refined soul? But I was able to fight them off and find the true path."

He reached over the partition and grabbed our hands. "Elizabeth and I want you and Val to be part of the new order," he said. "Won't you accept these truths with us?"

I sighed. "I'd love to, Bob, but I think today is not the day. We just flew in from India—we need some rest before we make any eternal decisions."

Bob gave me a sad smile. *"Cras credemus, hodie nihil."*

Even Bob was speaking Latin. "What's that mean?" I asked.

"Tomorrow we believe, but not today." He gripped our hands tightly. "Be careful, my friends. Don't take too long to decide. Soon it will be too late."

Val and I both promised to ponder on the truths.

I held up the pamphlet. "I'd like to review this."

Bob hesitated before he answered. "Sure. But just for tonight. I'll need it back tomorrow before my century party."

We waved goodbye to Bob and Elizabeth and walked up to the house. "Don't forget that we're still bugged," I whispered.

Val nodded. "I remember."

twenty-nine

WE WERE BUG-FREE for the meeting, but not trouble-free.

Archie interrupted me about twenty minutes into the discussion. "Could you repeat that, Scott?" he asked. "I am afraid I have misunderstood what you mean."

"Sure—I said we can't win this fight," I replied.

He frowned. "So I understood your meaning perfectly. But why do you think we cannot win?"

I was in a bit of a tight spot here, because only Val and I knew the script to our ruse. We were the only ones who knew that Bob and Elizabeth had joined WorldWideSouls, and just before the meeting we staged a conversation between ourselves, for the benefit of our bugs and their listeners. We discussed how we'd try to convince Archie's group to join with WorldWideSouls. Now we sat in the meeting, in front of Bob and Elizabeth, acting out the rest of that script.

Even though I knew we were doing the right thing, I still felt like a jerk. Archie had brought me in to fight—not to tell him to quit.

Ann banged her fist on the table. "Can't win? You'd better explain yourself right now, buster."

I took a deep breath. "Here's the thing," I said. "You hired me to figure out who was trying to destroy Soul Identity. And now we know— it's Andre Feret and his WorldWideSouls organization."

"Right," Archie said. "Now we stop them."

"Wrong—we can't stop them," I repeated. "We can't even slow them down. They're pulling our strings and watching us dance. And if we keep fighting, they're going to completely destroy Soul Identity."

"But if we don't fight, they're still going to destroy Soul Identity. What in tarnation is the difference?" Ann asked.

Val turned to me as we had planned. "Are you saying that WorldWideSouls won't destroy Soul Identity if we work with them?" she asked.

Now to see if we could build credibility for Bob.

"Bob, what do you think?" I asked. "You and Elizabeth went down to Baltimore to find out more about them. Are they trying to drive us out of business?"

He shook his head. "WorldWideSouls wants to cleanse Soul Identity and focus it back on its fundamentals. Not destroy it."

"What does cleanse mean, Bob?" Archie's face was flushed.

Bob stared at Archie. "They want to remove any leader who hides the truth from our members," he said.

"I didn't know we had any hidden truths," Ann said. "Son, what truths are you talking about?"

Bob opened his mouth. I held my breath, but Elizabeth cut him off. "We're not sure, Mom. The pastor didn't say." She squeezed Bob's arm. "Isn't that right, Bob sweetie?"

Bob smiled at her. "That's right, Elizabeth." He shot a brief glance at Val and me.

"Archie, I think WorldWideSouls will crush us in a head-on fight," I said. "But if we work with them, we have a chance of survival."

"Why do you think they'll crush us?" Val asked.

I had been waiting for her to ask me that question.

"They've been ahead of us every step of the way," I said. "Val and I are alive because we were lucky when they blew up the guesthouse. Berry and Madame Flora too—they got off Kent Island just in time. We've survived each stage through luck, and now I think we've run out of it."

"Why's that?" Ann asked.

I sighed. "Like I already said. They booted Val and me out today. You have nobody on the inside of the systems any more. Feret controls the new security, and his altered match program is still in effect."

"So what do you suggest?" Ann asked.

"That we negotiate with WorldWideSouls and see what they want," I said.

Nobody was smiling, and I couldn't really blame then. I wouldn't like the plan either.

"I will never, ever give in to these people." Archie was shouting. "I will never, ever negotiate with WorldWideSouls."

I crossed my arms. "Then everything in which you believe will die."

"Hold on a second," Val said. She turned to me. "That's it? You want to quit? Just give up?"

"No," I said. "I want to survive. We need to live to fight another day." It was time for my dramatic pause. "Unless…" I let my voice trail off.

"Unless what?" Val asked after a few seconds of silence.

I shook my head. "Forget it. It's too risky."

"I would like to hear what you were about to suggest, Scott," Archie said.

I shook my head again. "It was just a dumb idea."

Ann cut in. "Damn it, son, spit it out already."

"Okay—we could infiltrate." I looked at Bob. "We could find out what Feret and WorldWideSouls are up to. We may even feed them some disinformation. And maybe, just maybe, we'd start to get the upper hand on these guys."

"Infiltrate?" Madame Flora asked.

I nodded. "Bob and Elizabeth could pretend to join WorldWideSouls. They have already established a relationship in Baltimore, and WorldWideSouls would welcome two insiders."

As expected, Bob acted surprised at the suggestion. I just hoped he was smart enough to play along.

"Would it be dangerous?" he asked. "I'd do anything for Soul Identity, but I'd hate to put Elizabeth at risk."

"Speak for yourself, Bob darling," Elizabeth said. "I'm in, Scott—just tell me what to do."

Bob and Elizabeth reacted better than I expected.

"If you and Bob were to join WorldWideSouls, you might be able to find out what Feret has planned for tomorrow," I said. "You may even get them to send you to Venice." I shook my head. "But it's risky, and it's a long shot."

"But it is the best idea we have." Archie gave me a stern look. "A lot better than negotiating with those people." He turned to Bob and Elizabeth. "Are you two willing to take on this dangerous assignment?"

Elizabeth nodded at Bob.

Bob cleared his throat. "Yes, Mr. Morgan, we'd be happy to do it for you."

"Thank you, Bob," Archie said. "I knew I could count on you."

Now to get them going. I stood up. "They need to start right away," I said. "It's already late, and they must try to find out what WorldWideSouls is attempting to do tomorrow."

"Scott is right, Bob," Archie said. "Talk to Mr. Feret tonight if you can."

The two stood up. Elizabeth gave her mother a hug, and they walked toward the door.

Now I had to get them going. I stood up and said, "Bob, I left some papers in the limo. Let me come with you and get them before you take off."

On the way to the limo, I snuck Val's yellow pouch and a small tube of glue out of my pocket. "What do you think of my idea?" I asked Bob.

He grinned. "You were brilliant, Scott. You solved my biggest problem. Now I don't need to explain my attendance at WorldWideSouls events, or my meetings with Mr. Feret."

"Yeah, well, don't forget about Val and me. We're sacrificing here to get you two out." I tried to sound worried. "Let me find those papers." I climbed in the back and pretended to search. When Bob and Elizabeth climbed in, I reached through the partition and held out my hand. "Good luck, you two."

While Bob shook my hand, I dropped the transmitter down behind the driver's seat and stuck the bug to the back of his headrest. This was close enough to keep them on the air for the rest of the evening.

Bob and Elizabeth drove off, and I hurried back to the meeting. I saw Val typing on my laptop while the rest of the team sat silently.

Val nodded at me.

I cleared my throat. "I just bugged Bob and Elizabeth," I said, "and Val is accessing Soul Identity security to listen in on what they're saying."

"You bugged my daughter?" Ann asked.

"I did, and it will all make sense shortly." I looked at Val. "Turn up the volume."

We heard Bob and Elizabeth laughing. Elizabeth spoke first. "Bob darling, you were so strong in that meeting. I am so proud of you."

"This is sick," Ann said.

Then Bob answered, "I'm doing it for us, my love." He laughed. "This worked out better than we could have hoped for. Now nobody will question why we're spending our time with WorldWideSouls."

"You are so smart, Bob darling. WorldWideSouls is lucky to get you."

There was silence for a minute. Then Bob said, "I'm going to call Mr. Feret right now and tell him the good news."

We waited for a minute. Then we heard, "Hello, Mr. Feret. This is Bob... No, there's no problem. You'll never guess what happened, sir, at the meeting tonight."

A pause, and then Bob said, "No, they don't know anything new. Your plan is working. I told them they should give up, but Mr. Morgan didn't agree." He laughed. "So I suggested that they make us spies!"

I nudged Val. "He just stole my lines. The nerve of him!"

After a couple of yes sirs, Bob said, "We'll be at the reception hall in ten minutes, sir. See you then."

"What did he say?" Elizabeth asked.

"Great job to both of us," Bob said. "And that we need to make final preparations for tomorrow."

"Bob darling," we heard Elizabeth say, "don't you feel weird using your century party as the place where it will happen?"

"Not at all. It is a privilege and an honor for Mr. Feret to start the new order at my party."

"Will it be dangerous?" We could hear the fear in Elizabeth's voice. "I don't know what I'd do if something happened to you, Bob my love."

"Now, now, Elizabeth. Remember Mr. Feret told both of us that we must be ready to risk it all for the truths."

We heard Elizabeth sigh. "Yes, and we know the price of curing Soul Identity is very high. Do you think we could get eternally married tomorrow morning? Just in case?"

There was dead silence on the end as we looked at each other around the table.

"Did we lose them?" Berry asked.

"I think Bob's trying to field a curve ball," I said.

Finally Bob answered. "Ah, Elizabeth, I've been meaning to tell you something. We can't afford an eternal marriage."

"Why not, Bob darling? Mr. Feret paid you a big signing bonus when we joined WorldWideSouls. How much does it cost, anyway?"

"Fifty thousand. Mr. Feret only gave me twenty-five." Bob's voice was glum. "Not nearly enough. We'll have to wait until after Venice, when we'll have the other two hundred."

Silence for a minute, and we all looked at each other. Then Elizabeth's voice came on strong. "Bob darling, you are a very powerful level eight member. You will be a centuriat tomorrow, their prized possession. WorldWideSouls owes you this. Get on that phone again and tell Mr. Feret to grant us an eternal marriage first thing tomorrow morning."

"But I—"

"No buts about it. Do it now." Her voice went from sharp to sweet. "Bob my love, show me how powerful and important you really are."

A long pause. "Hello, Mr. Feret, it's Bob again...No, everything is fine. Hey, Elizabeth wanted me to ask you if we could be eternally married tomorrow morning. With all the danger that we'll be going through, she thought it was a good idea."

Another pause. Then Bob said, "That's what I told her, sir. But she's rather insistent. You know how they care about these kinds of things."

Bob paused again. Then we heard him laugh. "You will? Thank you, sir. That's really good news. Yes, I'll tell her. Thank you again, sir."

"Is he going to do it?" Elizabeth asked.

"I was just about to tell him that he had to do it, or I'd quit," Bob said. "But he saved himself by agreeing to do it at eight tomorrow morning, after the planning breakfast."

"Oh, Bob darling, you are the best," Elizabeth said.

Val turned down the volume on the computer. "I think everybody has heard enough," she said. "I'm recording the rest."

Silence in the room.

"How did you know?" Ann finally asked.

Val answered. "We hacked the WorldWideSouls Web site and found their names in the membership lists."

Ann shook her head. "Why would they do it?"

"It's not just them," I said. "Archie, we also found Brian in the lists— and you may want to go easy on the coffee and bran muffins. We think he's sedating you."

Archie's face fell. "After his trip to Venice I was expecting to learn of Brian's betrayal, but it still hurts to find out I have been played the fool."

"We're both fools." Ann's voice was sharp. "My own daughter and her brand new fiancé tried to trick us."

"Mr. Feret must be stopped," Archie said. "Before he destroys us."

I held up my hands. "Before we get into how we stop them, do we know why members and employees are switching sides?"

Madame Flora cleared her throat. "They want more."

"More what?" Ann asked.

"More meaning," Madame Flora said.

Archie threw up his hands. "Soul Identity is all about meaning—how can you say otherwise?"

The old Gypsy lady shrugged. "You focus so much on the bridges and the technical proofs that you've forgotten that people just want to it all to mean something. Andre Feret has come up with a great story, and he uses it to make people feel valuable, important, and relevant. Of course he's attracting your members."

Archie clenched his hands into fists. "As long as I have been the executive overseer, I have drawn the line between business and spirituality. It always has worked in the past, and it always will work in the future."

She stared at him. "You know I have never agreed with you on this, Archibald."

It seemed like Archie and Madame Flora were having an old, well-worn argument with each other.

Berry wiped his palms on his lap. "I know I'm just a guest, but I'd like to say something."

Archie nodded. "Please, Mr. Berringer, you are steps away from being sworn in as an overseer. I would very much like to hear your perspective."

"Thanks," Berry said. "From what I see, you have a successful financial gig going on."

Archie smiled.

"But," Berry continued, "Soul Identity doesn't seem to have a soul."

"Of course we have a soul," Archie said loudly. "How dare you say that?"

Ann put her hand on Archie's arm. "I'd like to hear the man out, Archibald." Her voice was gentle, soothing.

Archie slumped back in his chair. "Fine." He stared at Berry. "Continue educating us, Mr. Berringer."

Berry didn't falter. "You know my story—I almost didn't make it in because everybody seemed so caught up in following their rules that they forgot about why people needed you in the first place."

"Go on," Archie said.

Berry stayed silent for a moment. "I didn't want to join because of your science," he said. "I wanted in because you offered me something worth living for."

"That is good, is it not?" Archie asked.

Berry nodded. "It's great. But once I came here, you focused only on the science and the business. You talked about membership counts instead of the members, and depositary totals instead of the depositary contents." He paused. "Mr. Morgan, I've been here almost a week now. We've had, what, seven sessions together?"

Archie nodded.

"In those seven meetings, you've never once asked me what it meant for me to become a member."

"Of course I did not ask you this," Archie said. "You joined for your own reasons, and I respect that privacy."

Berry sighed. "But what if I want more, like Flora says? Will you send me to a church for that deeper meaning?"

"That is the idea," Archie said.

I jumped in. "But if that church is after your throat—like WorldWideSouls is—then you'll be screwed."

A long moment of silence.

Archie let out a big sigh. "Scott, you are not even a believer. How can you possibly have an opinion on this?"

I pulled Bob's pamphlet out of my pocket and held it in the air. "I read this WorldWideSouls pamphlet. Bob said two things—it changed his life, and it convinced him that Soul Identity needs to be cleansed."

I read them the first few paragraphs, and there was silence around the table again.

"These guys are fighting dirty," Ann said.

"But it's effective," Val said. "Everybody loves a conspiracy. If they think you're exploiting them, they'll get angry enough to leave."

"Angry enough to mutiny," I said. "That's what Feret's planning, isn't he? We know he's paying your employees to join WorldWideSouls. He ordered Brian to blow up the guesthouse. He's plotting to hurt us at the party tomorrow. He's sucking the money out of the depositary. Feret won't stop until he wins it all."

"Why would Mr. Feret do this?" Archie asked. "Is it for his personal gain?"

"It's revenge," Val said. She shared what we learned about Feret's past from the speech we found online. "Soul Identity destroyed his family, and now he's out to destroy us."

"But he won't," I said. "Ignore my talk about quitting. That was so Bob could go and share that with Feret." I grabbed Val's hands under the table and took a deep breath. "For the past two weeks, I've been flip-flopping on whether you guys ran a freaky cult or a sophisticated con job. But I get it now—the promise of Soul Identity is that it can let us focus on spiritual matters without having a religion rammed down our throats."

I looked at Archie. "The Soul Identity bridges carry us across the most important chasms in our lives. I'm now a believer, and I believe we can win, and we must win, this fight. An independent Soul Identity is too important to too many people to be destroyed."

Val squeezed my hands hard, then let go and wiped the tears from her eyes. Somebody started clapping, and everybody joined in.

"That's the spirit, son," Ann said. "Now where do we start?"

"First we fill in the gaps." I pulled out the ring Tinless had given me. "Does anybody know what this is?"

Madame Flora held out her hand, and I passed it to her. We waited while she examined it. "Where did you get this?"

"In India," I said. "Do you know anything about it?"

"I do." She looked at Archie. "Scott may have stumbled across something very precious, Archibald."

"That ring?" Archie asked.

Madame Flora shook her head. "It's not just any ring." She unzipped her purse and pulled out a tiny flashlight. "Somebody turn off the lights."

I flipped the switch, and in the dark, Madame Flora held the ring over the table and aimed the flashlight's beam onto the crystal. The soul identity logo was projected onto the table. "This is one of the original overseer rings," she said.

I turned the lights on.

"Those rings are gone!" Archie said. He stared at me. "Where did you get this, Scott?"

I told him what Tinless had said: how Feret had lost it, and how Tinless had hidden it for ten years. "He said Feret believed this was his secret weapon." I looked around. "What does an overseer ring do?"

"That ring is ancient," Archie said. "Each original overseer of Psychen Euporos was given one by Darius." He held out his hand. "May I?"

Madame Flora gave it to him.

He looked at the mounting. "There are seven sides to the crystal, and each side of the mounting has five fingers. That's thirty-five fingers."

"One for each overseer," I said.

"Correct." Archie looked at Ann. "Does the depositary still know how to verify an overseer ring?"

Ann snorted. "Of course we do. Though I never actually saw one before." She held out her hand, and Archie passed the ring to her.

"Why would you need to verify it?" Val asked.

Ann looked up. "You know that every soul line collection is private, and it can only be opened by the current holder."

Val nodded. "Of course."

Ann smiled. "What you may not know is that there is a special case where an overseer may also open any soul line collection."

I raised my eyebrows. "Special case?"

"The only one." She held up the ring. "All they have to do is present their overseer ring to the depositary."

"Then they can open anybody's collection?" I asked.

"Anybody's," she said. "However, that rule has been moot for the last century, as all the rings were gone."

"And now Mr. Morgan can peek into everybody's collection. How can that help us?" Val asked.

Nobody answered.

"I think we need to nail down Feret's next move." I looked around the table. "We know from the pamphlet that he wants to install himself as the only overseer, and we know from our online chat that he plans to make Brian the head of the depositary. We know that tomorrow is his chance to cleanse the organization."

They all looked at me as I paused.

"My guess is that he's going to somehow try to kill Archie and Ann at Bob's century party," I said.

"Do you know how?" Val asked.

I shrugged. "In some very public and dramatic way." I turned to Archie. "Can you walk us through the agenda for the ceremony?"

Archie nodded. "The overseers, depositary chief, and the centuriat march down the aisle and sit on the dais. The overseers and centuriat make speeches, each overseer toasts the centuriat, and we all march out."

"Sounds like a graduation," Val said.

Archie smiled. "It is a graduation of sorts. Bob will be one of two serving centuriati in our employ." He scratched his head. "It is more like a tenure ceremony for university professors. Centuriati can never be dismissed for any reason."

"Hold it right there, partner," I said. "Bob will have a free ride for the rest of his life?"

Archie nodded. "He and his future carriers. And I cannot understand why he would give it all up to join WorldWideSouls."

"He's not going to give it up," I pointed out. "The century party is tomorrow. Nothing's going to happen until after he graduates. And after tomorrow, Bob will be a delivery person for as long as he wants, no matter what he does."

Archie nodded.

"That would make him pretty valuable to Feret," I said.

His eyes widened.

"Who came up with this centuriat idea, anyway?" I asked.

"The rule has been around for more than a thousand years," Archie said.

"So get rid of it." Berry said.

Archie frowned. "We cannot. It is inviolable."

"Come again?" Berry asked.

"Once upon a time our executive overseers could write inviolable rules. This particular rule dictates century parties on the hundred year anniversary, and grants eternal tenure to all centuriati. Inviolable rules cannot be changed."

Ann cleared her throat. "Actually, that's not entirely true."

Archie stared at her. "Of course it is. I reviewed the rule this morning as part of my preparations."

She shook her head. "The 'cannot be changed' is wrong."

"You cannot change any executive overseer's inviolable rule," Archie said. "To do so would tear apart the very fabric of our organization."

Ann held up the ring. "It took an overseer ring to enact an inviolable rule. And it takes an overseer ring to change it."

"That explains an even better reason why that ring's so valuable," I said.

I looked around the table again. Everybody had their eyes on me. "So we have a working hypothesis," I said. "Feret will try to kill Ann and Archie tomorrow and become the executive overseer. He's planning to make Brian his depositary chief, and he'll to turn this organization into his own private Venice-based bank account."

Everybody nodded.

"How are we going to stop him?" Val asked.

I thought for a minute. "We do have a few arrows in our quiver," I said. "We know about Bob, Elizabeth, and Brian when they think we don't.

We have proof that Berry's the real overseer. We have a ring which gets Archie into the depositary and lets him override some rules." I pointed at Val. "And we can hack into both WorldWideSouls and Soul Identity."

"We're using those arrows to try and stop a tank," Ann said.

I shrugged. "It's what we've got. But I like your analogy. Feret's tank must be disabled with just four arrows."

"Then we'd damn well better shoot straight." Ann looked around the room. "You heard the man. Let's put together a plan for how we're gonna save our organization."

And in the next four hours, we did.

thirty

VAL LOOKED UP FROM my laptop. "It's almost ten," she said. "They should be back from their depositary trip."

We had wrapped up the meeting shortly after midnight. Val and I had been tag-team programming since early morning while Ann, Archie, and Berry went to depositary and match committee. We had planned for everybody to meet at ten to fine-tune our plan based on what we all learned.

She sighed. "Mr. Morgan is acting awfully stressed out—do you think he can he keep it together?"

"He has to last for two more days, and for half of that, he and Ann will be playing dead." I smiled. "Hopefully the forced rest will do him good."

"Let's hope so." She leaned back. "I'm all done. Your Dad's now a level four WorldWideSouls member, and he's registered to be in Venice on Saturday."

"Did you hijack somebody's soul line?"

"No, I faked a brand new identity." She pointed to the screen and I saw Dad's eyes in close-up. "That photo of him in Iceland produced the cleanest image."

"Great," I said. "I still need to finish the match program fixes and write the injector—my turn on the laptop."

She slid it over my way. "Don't forget to email your parents," she said.

We decided late last night to fly my folks to Venice to help us turn Feret's meeting around.

"They're always clamoring to do something cool," I said. "And how could they say no to getting whisked off to Europe in a private jet?" I sent the email, then banged out the rest of my code. "When should the injector kick in?" I asked.

"As late as possible," Val said. "We don't want any matches failing until after the meeting in Venice starts."

I nodded. "The de-wormed matching program will go live at three fifteen p.m. Venice time. After that, we'll block all fake matches."

"*Molodets.*" She pointed at the clock. "It's now ten—let's see how everybody made out."

The six of us arrived in the dining room at the same time.

Archie set a thick folder in front of him and gave us a weary smile. "The ring worked like a charm, and the depositary procedures were just as Ann said."

"Show them what you found, Mr. Morgan," Berry said.

Archie opened the folder. "I took the liberty to peek into Brian's soul line collection."

"It's probably chock full of corny coffee jokes," I said.

Archie shook his head. "No coffee jokes, I'm sorry if that disappoints you." His eyes were twinkling.

He seemed awfully perky. "Did you skip your coffee this morning?" I asked.

"I fed it to my plants, and I feel great." He looked around the table at each of us, then smiled. "Last night we started fighting back," he said. "By tomorrow evening, Soul Identity will be safe again."

"And improved, I hope," Berry said.

"Yes, Mr. Berringer, improved. For you shall become an overseer, and together we shall recover our soul."

"Now we're talking." Ann wore a big smile.

He nodded to Ann. Then he pulled a sheet of paper out of the folder and passed it to me. The front side showed two medicines, some measurements, and long medical descriptions.

"He was putting the first in my coffee and the second in the muffins," Archie said.

"No wonder you were depressed," I said. "Listlessness, inattentiveness, mild paranoia, clinical depression," I read aloud.

He nodded. "I always knew that little bastard was trying to kill me. But turn to the most important side."

The back contained one short phrase: "Century party toast: palytoxin."

Archie turned to Ann. "That is neither a brand of champagne nor is it a type of bread. That is how they wish to kill us this afternoon."

"Well, now we know," Ann said. "Let's get ourselves an antidote."

Val was typing on my laptop. "I'm afraid not," she said. "Palytoxin is a fast acting vasoconstrictor." She read for a minute and then looked up. "Your only antidote is an immediate injection of papervine directly into your heart. And then you'd still probably die."

Ann looked at Archie. "Suddenly this doesn't sound so fun."

I leaned over and read Val's screen. Palytoxin—formula $C_{129}H_{223}N_3O_{54}$—was derived from a soft coral. "It causes unconsciousness in seconds, and death in minutes," I read.

"Great," Ann said. "Just great."

I read further down the page. It told how the Hawaiians ground up the coral and dipped their spear tips in it. I kept clicking. I read that palytoxin was stable in lower alcohols, and that the lethal dose for humans is less than five micrograms.

We had to adjust our plan. "Does anybody know of a drug that appears to kill you but doesn't?" I asked.

Madame Flora smiled. "You're thinking about putting Archibald and Ann into a medically induced coma?"

I nodded. "So everybody thinks they're dead."

"Hold on now," Ann said. "You want to drug us into a coma?"

Madame Flora looked at me. "Thiopental, or sodium pentothal, could work."

"Isn't that truth serum?" Val asked.

"In the right dosage—but it's also an anesthetic that knocks you out quickly." Madame Flora turned to Ann. "It has no side effects."

Val was typing on the laptop again. "Except death," she said. "It says here that many Pearl Harbor victims died after being treated for shock with overdoses of sodium pentothal."

"Well, there is that," Madame Flora said. "We've come a long way medically since nineteen forty-one." She smiled. "If you'd like, we can do a dry run."

"I'm sure my future son-in-law would love to be a guinea pig," Ann said.

I liked that idea. It would be good for Bob to help our cause, even if it were unknowingly.

"I can call him," I said. "He's trying to recruit me and Val, anyway."

Ann nodded. "Then when he rings my doorbell, we'll nab him." She looked at Val. "How long does it take to wear off?"

Madame Flora answered. "Five to ten minutes," she said, "unless you keep up the dosage. It's also an amnesiac, so he won't remember being drugged."

Maybe we could take advantage of the truth serum and figure out what else Bob knew.

Ann turned to Archie. "It ain't what we wanted, but we've got to fool Feret."

Archie nodded. "We must do it. We need Mr. Feret, and all of WorldWideSouls, convinced that they have cut the head off Soul Identity."

Ann pointed at the clock. "We're running out of time to get in front of the match committee."

Archie and Ann were going to use Berry's old photograph and the computer-generated reader sheets to make Berry a member while the sabotaged match program still showed him with a non-overseer identity. Then, with any luck, the fixed matching program would automatically declare him, not Feret, the overseer.

"Good luck," I said.

"Piece of cake," Ann said. "I'll wrap those committee members right around my pinky."

Madame Flora cleared her throat. "While you're busy wrapping, I'll work up three doses of thiopental."

Now why did Madame Flora know so much about thiopental?

The six of us met again after lunch.

"The match committee made Berry an official Soul Identity member," Ann said.

"And you did wrap them around your little finger." Berry pulled a plastic card out of his pocket. "The image is a picture of my good eye's iris."

I took the card and looked at it. "How does it work?" I asked.

"Whenever I need to have my identity read, they verify my right eye and call the depositary. My soul identity is now on file with them."

"Nobody else can use the card?" I asked.

He shook his head. "Their right eye won't match mine."

"We've been using these cards for years," Ann said. "Members who lose an eye after joining Soul Identity still need a way to identify themselves."

I nodded. "What do you do for people who lose both eyes?"

"We give them cards with their fingerprints on them." Archie smiled. "To anticipate your next question, we have never had an eyeless, fingerless member. Our security is sufficient on these cards."

The card was definitely convenient, but not secure.

I held it up. "All I'd have to do to become an overseer would be to keep this card and replace the image on front with a picture of my own right eye."

Archie's brows furrowed, and then he sighed. "You would have to poke out your other eye to really look authentic, but you're right, Scott." He shook his head. "Maybe it's secure because we have less than a hundred cards out there. Our delivery people get to know the one-eyed card carriers."

That made sense. "Your system works for its size." I handed the card back to Berry. "Did you guys get the rest of your work done?"

"Archie revoked the centuriat rule, effective tomorrow morning," Ann said.

"The depositary will keep it quiet until then." Archie smiled. "And lastly, we had a chat with Mr. Feret."

"Did he take the bait?" Val asked.

"Hook, line, and sinker," Ann said. "Archibald told Andre to shape up, because he was going to start using the ring on Monday to write some new rules."

Archie frowned. "Mr. Feret could not take his eyes off that ring. It seems that we dodged a major bullet when he lost it in India ten years ago."

Madame Flora passed Archie a box. "Here's the fake ring—the jeweler did a nice job with it. Wear it to the party."

Archie slipped the real ring off his finger and exchanged it for the one in the box. "I wonder if we will even need this," he said.

Madame Flora placed three plastic sandwich bags on the table. "I have three sets of thiopental ready to go."

"How does it work?" Ann asked.

Madame Flora slid a bag to Ann. "We stick a needle in your arm, and then we'll use a remote control to knock you out during the toast."

Ann opened the bag and pulled out a white plastic container the size of a matchbox. Plastic tubing connected the box to a needle.

"That box holds a pump that sends the serum into your blood stream," Madame Flora said.

Ann glanced at me. "Is the guinea pig coming?"

I nodded. "At two thirty. He's driving me and Val to the party."

She smiled. "We'll have to hurry to be ready."

Bob arrived on time, and I opened the door for him. "Before we go," I said, "Archie and Ann want a quick update on what you learned from the WorldWideSouls guys last night."

Bob looked at his watch. "We need to hurry," he said. "I can't be late to my own century party." He looked past me. "Is Val ready?"

I nodded. "Come on in, we're all in the dining room."

"We'd better make this quick," he said as he followed me in and sat at the table.

Ann smiled at him. "How are you Bob?"

He smiled back. "Fine, Ms. Blake. And yourself?"

Ann frowned. "I barely saw Elizabeth last night."

Bob shifted in his seat. "I guess you can catch up at the century party." He looked at his watch again. "We really need to leave."

"Bob, were you able to meet with Mr. Feret?" Archie asked.

Bob shook his head. "No, Mr. Morgan. He hasn't been available. I'm afraid that I will have to fly to Venice to meet him."

As Bob was answering Archie, Madame Flora crept up behind him. I put my hand on his shoulder. "Hold still, Bob, just for a second. You have something on your neck."

Bob sat still, and I smacked him on the back of his neck. His hand flew up, and Madame Flora poked him with the needle. Within ten seconds, Bob's eyes glazed over, and he slumped forward in his chair.

I caught his head and lowered it to the table.

Madame Flora had her fingers on Bob's neck. "His pulse is steady, but he's not breathing." She motioned to me. "Straighten his neck before he suffocates."

I repositioned Bob's head.

Ann threw Archie a nervous glance. "He looks dead all right," she said.

Madame Flora looked at her watch. "He'll be fully recovered in five minutes," she said. "Now's the time to ask him questions."

"Are you sure he won't remember anything?" Ann asked.

"Positive," Madame Flora said. "I've done this a few times."

I raised my eyebrows. "At your palm reading place?"

"Of course." She looked at our shocked expressions. "What, did you really think I could tell somebody about their past without their help?"

Berry shook his head. "I'm never getting my palm read again."

Madame Flora smiled and checked her watch. "He should be just about ready."

Bob moaned and opened his eyes.

Madame Flora nodded at Ann. "Ask him something."

"Bob, do you know who I am?" Ann asked.

He answered like he had a mouth full of cotton balls. "Of course, Ms. Blake—you're Elizabeth's mother."

Ann nodded. "Did you get married this morning?"

"Yes, Elizabeth and I celebrated an eternal marriage."

Ann frowned. "Why wasn't I invited?"

He shrugged. "Mr. Feret said there will be a necessary separation between you and Elizabeth, ma'am, and there was no sense on you attending on your last day."

Ann looked at Madame Flora and spoke through her teeth. "If you overdose the son of a bitch now, you'll save me from strangling him later."

Archie reached out and patted Ann's shoulder. "He is a simple man caught up in a complicated world." He turned to Bob. "Why did you join WorldWideSouls?"

Bob swallowed. "Mr. Morgan, I don't want to disappoint you, because you have done so much for me. But I need more than you can offer. I need help understanding what it all means."

He licked his lips. "You surround yourself with smart people, and nobody ever asks me what I think. But WorldWideSouls listens to me, Mr. Morgan. They seem interested. And they know how special I am."

Archie sighed. "What can we do to get you back?"

Bob smiled. "I don't know, sir. Why not join WorldWideSouls yourself?"

Archie frowned.

I tapped Bob on the shoulder. "We really need some information about your party. What's going to happen to Mr. Morgan and Ms. Blake this afternoon?"

Bob turned to look at me. "When?"

"At your century party." I stared at him. "Are they in danger?"

Bob shook his head. "I don't think so, Mr. Scott. Mr. Feret says that they won't be talking to me and Elizabeth after the party. I think they'll be too mad at us."

"Mad at what?" I asked. "Feret's new order?"

Bob nodded.

Maybe he was just not getting it. "Do you ever hear people talking about things you don't understand?" I asked.

He nodded. "That happens to me all the time."

"Did it happen with anything about your party?"

"Let's see." He closed his eyes. "Brian told Mr. Feret that my toast would be the best ever, but I know there's no toast being served. Just cookies afterward."

Archie sighed and turned away.

"He's about to come out of it," Madame Flora said. "I need to make some suggestions to him so he won't remember any of this."

While she murmured in Bob's ear, I walked over to Archie and Ann. "Are you two ready to do this?" I asked.

"Just make sure you kill us before we're poisoned," Ann said.

I nodded. "Don't let that champagne touch your lips."

"Bob's coming out in thirty seconds," Madame Flora called.

Val frowned. "Will he be able to drive?"

Madame Flora shrugged. "If not, you guys can. I suggested to him that he had fallen down, bumped his head, and is still a bit woozy."

Then the old Gypsy lady opened her eyes wide. "Oh, he needs a bump!" she exclaimed. She took off her shoe and, holding it with both hands, swung it hard. The heel hit the back of Bob's head with a solid thunk.

I winced. "Did you have to do that?"

"Without a bump he wouldn't believe he fell." She checked his eyes. "Okay, he's with us again," she said.

I bent over him. "Bob, are you okay?"

"Wh-what happened?"

"You just banged your head."

Bob reached up. "How did it happen?"

"Maybe all this spying is stressing you out and causing you to faint." I helped him stand up. "But we have to go—you're taking us to your century party."

Bob sat back down. "My head really hurts, and I'm dizzy," he said.

"It is a big bump you have there." I glared at Madame Flora. "Maybe somebody has some medicine?"

Ann opened her bag and pulled out a bottle of baby aspirin. "Take these, son." She shook out a handful of pills.

Bob chewed and swallowed. He tried to stand up, and Val and I each grabbed an arm and helped him to his feet.

"Maybe I should drive, Bob, and let you rest on the way over," I said. He nodded.

We walked out to the limo and loaded Bob into the back. He fell over onto his side.

I looked at Madame Flora. "Will we be able to wake him up?"

"He'll be totally fine in ten minutes." She handed Val a tiny remote control. "This button starts both pumps. Just press it when it's time."

Val nodded and hopped in the limo. I started the engine and headed for Soul Identity.

thirty-one

I STOPPED SHORT OF the main gate. Val shook Bob awake and made him get out and stretch.

"How's your headache?" I asked him.

"I think I'm okay." He reached up and rubbed his head. "I must have fallen pretty hard."

I looked in his eyes, and it seemed he was having a hard time focusing. "You sure you can drive?" I asked.

He nodded. "Elizabeth must be wondering where I am."

Val and I hopped into the back and Bob drove up to the gate and rolled down the window.

The gray-suited guard smiled. "Hey Bob—ready for your party?"

Bob smiled back. "I am. Are you coming?"

"Nah—somebody's gotta watch the gate." The guard leaned on window. "Hey, who are these guys?" he asked, pointing at Val and me.

"My guests," Bob said.

"Do they have badges?"

Bob shook his head. "They were suspended yesterday."

I cringed. Now why did Bob have to say that?

"Suspended?" The guard stood up. "They can't come in here."

Bob turned around in his seat at looked at me. "I don't have time to drive you back to Ms. Blake's house."

And we didn't have time to come up with another plan—Val had the remote, and Archie and Ann were dead if she wasn't there to trigger the thiopental.

"We really want to celebrate with you," I told Bob. "You're a level eight member—you must have clout."

He stared at me for a moment. Then he turned back to the window. "These two are my honored guests," he told the guard. "Let them in."

The guard reached down and rested his hand on his pistol. "I'm afraid I can't do that," he said.

"Yes you can," Bob said. "Would you like me to call Mr. Feret to sort this out?"

The guard narrowed his eyes. "Don't try me, Bob. I'm just following orders."

"We have to get in there," Val hissed in my ear.

I pulled John's business card out of my wallet and called his cell phone. "Hey, we're guests for Bob's centuriat party, but we're stuck at the gate. Can you help us get in?" I asked.

"Be right there," he said.

Five minutes later, Bob and the gate guard were still glaring at each other. I saw John walking up to the gate, and I got out of the limo and approached him.

"What's the problem, Scott?" he asked after we shook hands.

"We want to attend Bob's century party, but your buddy here," I pointed at the gate guard, "won't let us through."

John looked at the guard. "That true?" he asked.

The guard nodded. "The boss said nobody but badges are allowed in today."

John scratched his head. "The party's outside—how about we give them grounds-only passes?"

"You gonna vouch for them?"

John nodded. "They'll behave." He looked at me. "Won't you?"

"Of course," I said.

The gate guard looked back and forth between me and John for a minute, then finally nodded. "Lemme get some temporary badges," he said. He headed into the gate house.

I smiled at John. "Glad you were here today," I said.

"Glad I could help." He waved and walked back toward the building.

Bob parked in the circular driveway of the main building. A large white tent was set up on the lawn. "Mr. Feret moved the party outdoors for security reasons," he said.

Good for us. Even better for Archie and Ann.

"It's a great day to be outside," I said. "Bob, you must be pretty proud of reaching your century mark."

He smiled. "I sure am, Scott. Do you know that there's only one other centuriat working for Soul Identity?"

"I heard that somewhere. Who is it?" I asked.

"James the elevator man. He had his party over twenty years ago." He smiled. "Now it's my turn. And in a few years, I'll be the only one."

That explained why James still lurked in the elevators. We climbed out of the car. "Where do we go, Bob?" Val asked.

He pointed to the tent. "I reserved seats in the second row for you."

We wished him luck and headed over to the tent. We stood in the back and watched the preparations. Two men ran audio visual cables and tested the system. Others aligned the hundred or so chairs.

"Do you think our plan is too risky?" Val asked me.

Of course I did. "It doesn't really matter—if Archie and Ann don't show up for the centuriat party, Feret will claim victory and take over Soul Identity anyway. And even if we could stop him, this is the only way to get the WorldWideSouls members back in the fold."

She sighed. "I guess you're right. But it's awfully scary."

I waved to Archie and Ann when they came in, and they walked over to us.

"You ready for the big show?" I asked.

"Damn right we are." Ann turned to Val. "Just be careful with that remote, honey. Don't go pressing it too early." She paused. "Or too late."

Archie patted under his arm. "The boxes are taped here, and the needles are in our veins." He held up his left hand. "I am wearing the fake ring."

"We've got to get moving," Ann said. They hustled out the back.

I pointed to the front. "People are coming in," I said. We went to our seats. I pulled out my camera and Berry's cell phone.

The seats filled up, and the buzz from the crowd dropped off when a cameraman stood on the stage and turned on his video light. He nodded to the sound guy in the center of the tent, and the opening notes of Clark's *Trumpet Voluntary* blasted out.

We looked back and watched Archie walk down the center aisle. Feret followed Archie looking straight ahead. Ann came last. She gave Val and me a tight smile as she passed.

The song ended. Archie, Feret, and Ann sat on the dais. The sound man pressed another button, and Elgar's *Pomp and Circumstance* floated over us.

Archie, Ann, and Feret stood up. The cameraman repositioned for a clear shot down the aisle.

I looked back and saw Bob standing next to Elizabeth. She gave him a kiss on the cheek, and he gulped and marched toward the front. He climbed the stairs onto the dais and walked to his center seat.

Everybody up front sat down as the music faded.

Feret walked to the podium. He grabbed the gold microphone in his hand and smiled. "The overseers of Soul Identity welcome you to our twelfth centuriat ceremony. Robert Osborne is the eighth carrier of a special soul line that has labored in the service of our organization for exactly one hundred years. This is a most solemn occasion for Mr. Osborne."

Feret continued. "The length of his soul line shows how faithful Mr. Osborne has been, and how worthy he is of this honor."

"That sounds like the pamphlet," I whispered.

Val nodded. "But why is he talking about that now?"

I pointed at the cameraman. "Maybe he's planning to show the film tomorrow in Venice."

Feret was still speaking. "And just as today is the first day of Mr. Osborne's new career," he said, "it is also the first day of a new order for Soul Identity." He paused with a smirk on his face.

"Uh oh," I said.

Feret stood motionless. People in the crowd began whispering to each other. Brian wore his own smirk as he watched from the front row.

Ann leaned over and said something to Archie, but Archie put his finger to his lips and pointed at Feret.

Feret readjusted his microphone. "Let me repeat that. Today marks a turning point for both Mr. Osborne's career and Soul Identity itself. We are embarking on a new order. Tomorrow we will unveil this new order for all to see. A newly cleaned house. One that rewards only deserving members such as Mr. Osborne. Where the truths are not hidden by vicious leaders focused only on your money." He banged the podium with his fist. "It is your destiny!"

"He's counting his chickens," I said.

"We can't let them hatch." Val said.

Feret bowed to Archie with a mocking flourish and sat down.

Archie smiled and adjusted the microphone. "Mr. Feret called this our twelfth centuriat ceremony. I call it Bob's century party. His dedication and commitment to Soul Identity are worth celebrating."

Archie glanced back at Feret. "This party is all about Bob. This is his celebration, his major event. Tomorrow we can talk about Soul Identity's business. Tomorrow we can discuss new orders. But today we shall put that aside, for today belongs to Bob. We salute you, Bob. We salute your dedication, and we salute your commitment."

Bob came forward and shook Archie's hand. Archie went to his seat while Bob unfolded a sheet of paper. "Hello everybody," he said nervously. He looked down at the paper and swallowed. "My soul line predecessors and I have served this organization for exactly one hundred years. The entire century of service we have provided has been devoted to our delivery group."

Bob took a deep breath. "Mr. Feret's words resonated in my heart," he said. "I am looking forward to his new order, one where I can help right the wrongs of the past."

"What's with these guys?" I asked. "Can't they wait one stinking day?"

"Maybe Feret wants to show that he's a prophet," Val said. "Get your camera ready."

Bob was wrapping up his speech. "I promise that as a centuriat," he said, "I will work to release the chains that bind our minds to our enslavers. I will fight to make our truths available to all. And I will work to convert new believers." He looked at the crowd. "Thanks for attending my ceremony." He headed back to his seat.

"There goes Brian," Val said.

I pointed my camera at Brian and started recording. He popped open a bottle of champagne and poured four glasses.

Val squinted. "He dropped a tablet into each of the middle two glasses. That must've been the palytoxin."

"I saw. Hopefully my camera did too," I said. "Is your remote ready?"

"It is."

Brian carried the tray of glasses onto the stage. The four participants stood up. Bob took the glass on the right. Feret reached for the glass on the right, but Brian gave his head a tiny shake, and Feret took the glass on the left.

Ann took one of the glasses and threw me a nervous glance. Brian smirked at her and walked toward Archie with the remaining glass.

"Don't forget me!" a voice shouted from the back of the tent. I looked back and watched James march down the aisle. He pointed at Brian on the stage. "Ahoy there, you rude boy, give me a glass of the bubbly. I'm a centuriat too. I'm part of this toast."

Brian shook his head and gave the remaining glass to Archie.

James clambered onto the stage and headed to Archie. "I can share with Mr. Morgan."

Feret jumped up and intercepted him. "You can have my glass." He handed it to James.

Archie smiled. "That was nice of you, Mr. Feret." He held out his glass. "Here, you are giving the toast. Take my glass, and I'll share with James."

Feret eyed the glass and shook his head. "Nonsense, Mr. Morgan. You are the executive overseer. You deserve your own glass. Brian can pour another one for me."

Archie gave him a sad smile.

Brian poured another glass of champagne. He brought it to Feret, who now stood at the podium.

"You ready with that remote?" I asked Val.

She nodded.

"*Consuetudo pro lege servatur.*" Feret held up his glass. "That means *custom is held as the law.* Our custom is to drink a toast to the new centuriat."

Feret turned around and looked for a minute at Archie, and then at Ann. He turned back to the audience, his glass still raised. "The custom here has also been to hide the truth from the members. But I say to you today, *consuetudo est altera lex,* which mean *custom is another law.* It is not our law anymore. Custom is the law of the past. The new order is about to begin, and it's time for new leadership."

Feret turned to Bob and saluted him with the glass. "I call upon our present and future souls to stop all who may oppose the new order. Let us drink to the futures of our newest centuriat and his beloved organization, and may all who drink be cleansed of their mistakes."

Everybody raised their glasses in the air. Just as Archie's and Ann's reached their lips, Val thumbed the remote.

"You still filming?" she asked.

"Of course. When will they—"

Archie fell first, crumpling to the floor. Ann followed a second later. A gasp went up from the audience, and Elizabeth shrieked from the back.

Val and I rushed up to the stage. I dialed Madame Flora's number and shouted into it. "Send an ambulance to the Soul Identity front lawn—two people have collapsed!"

Val pushed Brian out of the way and reached Ann's body. She straightened Ann's neck and put her fingers to her throat. "No pulse, and no breathing!" she yelled. "What about Mr. Morgan?"

I knelt next to Archie. Bob was already there, his eyes wide in shock. "Is Mr. Morgan dead?" he asked.

I checked Archie's neck. "None here either," I yelled back to Val. I looked at Bob. "It looks like it."

Bob grabbed his knees and crumpled his body into a ball. He started rocking back and forth, moaning.

Elizabeth rushed up to Ann. "Mommy!" she cried. "Mommy, wake up!" She shook Ann's shoulders.

Brian and Feret stood at the stairs to the dais and kept the rest of the audience back.

I dialed John the security guard's cell number. "John, it's Scott again. There's been a terrible accident here in the tent. Two people have collapsed."

"Oh my God," he said.

"I called an ambulance," I said. "Let it through the gates, okay?"

"No problem," he said. "It's just coming up now." I could hear the sirens through the phone.

I hung up and checked my camera. It was still filming. I held it down low and pointed it at Brian and Feret, still blocking the stairs.

Val walked over to James and helped him sit down. "What happened?" he shouted.

Those closest to them quieted down and listened to her response.

Val raised her hands in a helpless gesture. "They both just collapsed." She looked at Feret with tears in her eyes. "What have you done?" she yelled.

Feret put his chin up. "I have spoken the truth," he said in a ringing voice. "Mr. Morgan and Ms. Blake have paid the ultimate price for their treachery. This signifies the start of the new order."

Sirens punctuated Feret's speech, and an ambulance backed up to the side of the tent. Rose and Marie, almost unrecognizable in their wigs and orange uniforms, dragged a stretcher out of the back. They placed Ann on it and hauled her out. They came back with another stretcher and loaded Archie.

"I want to come with you!" Elizabeth screamed.

The twins looked at each other, and Marie pulled a hypodermic needle out of her pocket. She popped off the plastic top and jabbed it into Elizabeth's arm.

"Ouch!" Elizabeth rubbed her arm. She wore a dazed expression.

"That was a sedative to calm you down," Rose said. "I'm sorry, but there's no room in the ambulance."

Elizabeth nodded, and the twins climbed into the back and slammed the doors. The ambulance roared off, sirens blaring.

I held the camera at my waist and swung it back toward Feret and Brian. They wore little smiles as they walked over to Bob and Elizabeth.

Feret turned to me. "We'll take care of these two, Mr. Waverly. Take Ms. Nikolskaya and kindly get off my property."

I nodded. "Bob, give me your keys," I said.

Bob only moaned.

I reached down and pulled the limo keys out of Bob's pocket. Val and I walked out of the tent.

I shut off the camera. "Let's hope we have a good recording."

"Let's hope Mr. Morgan and Ann are okay," Val said.

I nodded. "Let's find them and get to Venice." We got into the limo and drove out of the gate.

thirty-two

DAD POINTED AT A smoking crater. "That's the volcano right there." He leaned his forehead against the airplane window. "You can see why they canceled the flights in and out of Iceland."

My parents sat with Val and me around a small table.

Rose and Marie came by. "How's the flight?" Marie asked.

Mom looked around. "Do rich people always fly in such style?"

Rose giggled. "We wouldn't know—it's our first time too."

The twins moved on to talk with Berry, Madame Flora, Ann, and Archie at the table behind us.

"You made me a WorldWideSouls member?" Dad asked Val.

She nodded. "Level four. You have three predecessors in your illustrious soul line."

"Is that good?" Mom asked.

"Apparently so," I said. "WorldWideSouls invited only members at level three and above to Venice."

He nodded. "What are we going to do in the meeting?"

"We need to trap Feret with your questions." I said.

"Why us?" Mom asked.

"Because Feret won't recognize you," I said.

She frowned. "What are we supposed to wear in Venice?"

"George and Sue have arranged everything," I said.

"At least we're rescued from the hot springs, and the same old conversations with the same old people," Dad said. "How long will we be in Venice?"

"Maybe five or six hours," I said. "Then we fly home."

"Or we die." Ann stood in the aisle. "You ought to try it, it's quite exhilarating."

Archie came up next to her. "Now, Ann, just because we are considered dead does not mean you have to be so morbid." His eyes twinkled. "Besides, we shall be returning to life soon."

"What was it like?" Mom asked.

"The last thing I remember is putting that glass to my lips and thinking that Val had better press that darn button." Ann rubbed her shoulder. "Next thing I knew we were flying to Iceland."

I grinned. "So you don't remember all the confessions you made as you were waking up?"

"I've got no confessions to make, darling. Go bark up some other tree." Ann smiled. "But I would like to see the movie you took. Can you play it for us?"

I nodded. "It's on my notebook. Just a sec."

Val closed the shades. We clustered around the screen as the video began to play.

I hit pause when Brian poured the champagne. "Watch his hand," I said. "He's about to drop the poison into the two middle glasses."

I advanced the video a frame at a time, and we watched two tiny white pills plop into the champagne.

"That sneaky little bastard," Archie said with a snarl.

"He's not done yet," I said. We saw Brian climb onto the stage and pass out the drinks. "Watch him guide Feret."

Brian shook his head, and Feret shifted to take the left glass.

The camera jerked around as James came down the aisle. "Here's James almost spoiling the whole surprise," I said.

"My goodness, how old is he?" Dad asked.

"A bit older than me," Archie said. "James is a fixture at Soul Identity."

We saw James climb on stage and ask for a glass.

"He doesn't seem to like Brian very much, does he?" Mom asked.

"They're not the best of friends," Val said. "You should have seen them in the elevator together."

We watched Feret give James his glass. I smiled. "Here's where we see Archie's genius."

Archie frowned. "Genius?"

I paused the video. "You don't remember?" I asked.

Archie shook his head.

"Must be the thiopental," Madame Flora said. "It is an amnesiac, after all. Show us, Scott."

I hit play. Archie offered his poisoned glass to Feret and Feret refused it.

Archie smiled. "That was brilliant of me."

We listened to Feret's toast.

"Boy, he's arrogant," Dad said. "This guy's due for a fall."

"That's the idea," I said. "Have we seen enough?"

"Not by a long shot. I want to watch my collapse," Ann said. "How often do you get to see your own death?"

"I was hoping to skip that part." Archie said. "But then again, why not?"

We watched Archie's and Ann's fake sips and their immediate collapse. "Notice how Feret is not surprised in the least," I said.

"Let me see that again," Ann said.

I rewound and replayed the collapse.

"That's why my shoulder hurts," she said. "I banged it right there on the chair."

"Archie, watch what happens next," I said.

Archie peered at the screen. "Who is that bending over me?" he asked.

"Feret," I said. "He's only there for a second." I advanced the movie frame by frame, and we watched Feret slip the fake overseer ring off Archie's finger.

Archie looked down at his hand. "I did not even realize it was gone."

I resumed the video. We watched Elizabeth's and Bob's anguish.

Archie turned to Ann. "Their shock and grief seem genuine."

Ann nodded, but she didn't say anything.

Then the twins made their entrance.

"I like our wigs," Rose said.

"But we can lose the uniforms—they're freaky looking," Marie said.

We saw Marie inject Elizabeth. Then Feret acting nasty with me and Val as the video ended.

George and Sue stood waving outside of customs at Venice's Marco Polo airport. I introduced them to Berry and my parents.

"Is everything ready?" Archie asked.

"Of course," George said. "Now I need you all to climb aboard the water taxi—we're going to the staging area."

"Staging area?" Val asked.

Sue sighed. "George has been tagging everything with a nickname, and it's driving me crazy. The staging area is the house we rented."

"Which just so happens to back up to the Soul Identity amphitheatre. Right behind the stage." George beamed. "Get it? Our staging area."

"I can see how it could wear you down, Sue," I said.

George was undeterred. "Even better than that, our staging area has its own concealed entrance," he said.

Sue rolled her eyes. "He means it has a boat garage."

"Which we need, since two of our company are supposed to be on ice in the Sterling morgue," George said.

Ann shuddered. "Don't remind me."

It was almost two in the afternoon, and the new order planning session was winding down. We had been eavesdropping for the last hour from George's staging area.

I cleared my throat. "Is everybody ready?"

"We are," Dad said. He and Mom wore semi-formal outfits.

"Tell me what you're going to do," I said.

He smiled. "We're taking the water taxi out and walking back to Soul Identity so I can register."

"Then we're going to walk around San Marco," Mom said. "I want to see the Basilica, the Doge's Palace, and the Clock Tower."

"We'll join the meeting by three." Dad looked at Val. "My eyes will scan?"

She nodded. "But be there by three."

I turned to Archie and Ann. "Are you two ready for your resurrection?"

They both nodded.

I turned to Berry. "How's the speech?"

"As good as it's going to get," he said.

"Val?" I asked.

"I've been able to penetrate the audio video control for the amphitheatre," she said. "We've been watching the proceedings, but we'll be able to switch to our own feed whenever you're ready."

"And I poked into the WorldWideSouls scheduling system and added a two thirty meeting in Feret's office for Feret and Brian," I said.

"I would think that they see enough of each other," Archie said.

"We need them both around when Val and I shatter their world," I said.

"Maybe they will give up when you show them what we know." Archie looked hopeful.

I shrugged. "Stranger things could happen, I suppose. But I doubt it—they're in this all the way."

He nodded. "Mr. Feret would say *ad vitam aut culpam.*"

Dad smiled.

Archie stood up and cleared his throat. "I wanted to say thank you to everybody for their dedication to our organization." He put his hand on Berry's shoulder. "And I want you to know that when we prevail, Soul Identity will change for the better. Mr. Berringer, Ms. Blake, and I have agreed that the reforms will start tonight."

As everybody left, I turned to Val. "Ready to see the bad guys?"

She shuddered. "Are we going to be safe?"

"Of course," I said. "And if we're not, George will be listening."

She nodded. "We still have half an hour."

"Then we'll have time for a slight detour," I said. "I want to see the Ponte delle Tette."

As we crossed the Grand Canal, Val asked, "So what's so cool about the Ponte delle Tette?"

I smiled. "I read a story about it on the Net this morning."

She held my arm as we walked. "Tell it to me."

"First of all, Ponte delle Tette translates to Bridge of Boobs."

"Boobs?"

"It's the closest match."

She shook her head. "Go on."

"It was the early fifteen hundreds, and the city senate was in an uproar about the growing number of homosexuals who had moved in."

She smiled. "Venice was a happening place back then."

"It seems so. The conservative senators wrote some tough laws against anybody caught engaging in homosexual behavior. Several citizens were hanged."

"Oh my."

"After a couple of years, the senate realized that they were losing the battle. They established a new committee to determine the causes of homosexuality and issue a report and recommendations on what could be done to eradicate it."

"They had committees back then?"

I smiled. "Now get this—the report said homosexuality was increasing because Venice's young men didn't have enough opportunity to enjoy the city's ladies. They needed more exposure."

We stopped walking, and I pointed. "That's the Ponte delle Tette over there. It leads to Carampane, Venice's sixteenth century red light district. The prostitutes lived in these buildings overlooking this canal. This bridge was the way in."

She turned to me. "Exactly what kind of exposure did the report recommend?"

I smiled. "They asked the ladies of Carampane to appear topless in these windows and entice the young men to enjoy the fruits of good old heterosexual behavior. Five hundred years later, it's still known as the Bridge of Boobs."

"So did the law work?"

I shrugged. "The Web page didn't say. I don't even know if the story is true, but we had a good walk, saw some of Venice, and talked about boobs. What more could I ask for?"

She led me to the middle of the bridge and gave me a long kiss.

I pulled back after a couple of minutes. "Wait a minute, this isn't the bridge of kisses."

"You're right," she said. "Come back here." She grabbed my hands and placed them under her blouse. "Kiss me again."

thirty-three

BRIAN GLARED AT VAL and me. "You're not welcome here." He tried to close Feret's office door, but I kicked out and bounced it open.

"I think you want to hear what we have to say." I pushed him out of the way.

Feret looked up from his desk and sighed. "What are you two doing in Venice? We have so much to do, and no time to worry about your suspensions. You're trespassing."

"Guilty as charged." I stared at him. "Guilty like you."

He put down his pen. "Of what, might I ask?"

"Murder," I said.

"You've got to be kidding," Brian said. "Mr. Morgan and Ms. Blake were our dear friends, and we are totally devastated by their passing."

"Save the theatrics, Brian," I said. "Your boss here just told your new order planning team that Archie and Ann's deaths were the direct result of their refusal to share the truths with Soul Identity members."

"Do you dispute my statement?" Feret asked.

"Not at all," I said. "You're deadly accurate. I just want to understand what 'direct result' means."

He stared at me for a moment before answering. "Mr. Morgan and Ms. Blake paid the ultimate price for their refusal to support our new order."

"And who charged that price?" I asked.

Feret shrugged. "They either died of shock when they realized they were wrong, or a higher power took their lives."

"Maybe it was two little white pills in their champagne glasses," I said.

Feret waved his hand as if brushing away a fly. "Mere conjecture on your part."

"Your video shows Brian correcting your choice of glasses," Val said. "It looks premeditated."

Feret shrugged. "It is an interesting theory."

"Is it true?" I asked.

He stared at me. "Does it really matter? As you told your friends at Ms. Blake's house, I hold all the cards."

"You do," I said. "But can you tell the real cards from the jokers?"

He smiled. "All right, I'll show you what I've got. I'm holding the executive overseer and depositary chief positions, a delivery man who can never be fired, an overseer ring, and several thousands of loyal and even fanatical members."

Brian smirked. "Sounds like a royal flush to me."

"Are you sure about the ring?" I asked. "I'm guessing you swiped it from Archie's finger when he collapsed."

Feret reached into his pocket and pulled out the ring. "Where do you get your strange ideas? Mr. Morgan himself gave this to me on Friday morning."

I nodded at Brian. "Did your coffee boy and new depositary chief verify it for you?"

Brian rolled his eyes and spoke in a bored voice. "Seven sided crystal, each side having five prongs—of course it's real."

"And what does it project?" Val asked.

Brian shrugged. "The Soul Identity logo."

"That's right, Brian." I paused. "But does it?"

"Duh," Brian said. "Mr. Morgan showed us just yesterday morning."

"Right," I said. "When he gave you the ring."

Brian looked at Feret. "May I see the ring, sir?"

Feret handed it to him, and Brian pulled the shades almost shut. "Watch and learn." A small shaft of light entered the room. He held the ring in the light and focused the image on the wall.

"There's the projection," Val said. "That's not our logo."

The projection showed some letters: s-d-o-o."

I smiled. "It's upside down."

Brian flipped the ring over.

"How appropriate," I said.

"I didn't think the old man had it in him," Feret said. He turned to me as Brian opened the shades. "I'll admit I was devastated when I lost the ring ten years ago, but now I'm happy to say that my plans no longer rely on it."

"Can you afford somebody else having it?" I asked.

"I'm the only overseer—the ring's useless to others."

"Good point," I said. "Let's see what other bum cards you're holding. You said your delivery man cannot be fired—who is that?"

"It's Bob, you ignorant man," Brian said. "Don't you remember the century party yesterday? What you don't know is how long he's been helping us."

Val raised her eyebrows. "I think we all know that Bob is a centuriat, Brian. And we heard him declare for the new order. But why do you say that he can't be fired?"

"Because that's an inviolable rule!" Brian shouted. "You may not know this, but Soul Identity's inviolable rules cannot be broken."

"Really?" I asked. "How did the rule get enacted?"

"It takes an overseer ring to make an inviolable rule..." Brian's voice trailed off.

"And it takes an overseer ring to reverse it." I looked at Feret. "Did you ever wonder why Archie was carrying the ring yesterday? That rule is gone."

Feret glared at Brian. "Inviolable rules can be overturned?"

Brian hung his head. "All the overseer rings were gone."

"So you didn't bother telling me?" Feret's eyes narrowed.

Time to sink the weasel who twice tried to kill us.

"Don't be so hard on your coffee boy," I said to Feret. "After all, you already know his limitations."

Brian growled and started toward me, but he stopped when Feret held up his hand.

"What limitations?" Feret asked.

I ticked them off on my fingers. "You've been waiting a few years now for him to get rid of Archie. He missed us when he blew up the guesthouse. He took orders from us over a chat session, thinking we were you." I looked at Brian. "You didn't know about that, did you?"

"That's quite enough," Feret said.

"I'm not done," I said, holding up my hand. "Coffee boy does have one success—the palytoxin." I nodded at Brian. "That was good, although it's too bad we taped you dropping the tablets into the glasses."

Feret turned to Brian. "How does he know about the palytoxin?" he asked in a calm but deadly tone.

Brian shook his head. "He must be guessing, sir. Those papers were kept safely in my—"

"Soul line collection," I finished for him. "The other really nice feature of the overseer ring." I smiled at Brian. "One more limitation to add to the list."

"I learned a cool Latin quote on the flight over here," Val said. "*Adde parvum parvo magnus acervus erit.* It's from Ovid."

"What's it mean?" I asked.

"*Add a little to a little and there will be a great heap,*" Feret said. "I couldn't agree more."

"Final limitation, Brian," I said. "Your coffee jokes suck."

"I've had enough of this." Brian jumped on me before I could get out of my chair, and I struggled to push him off. He went limp and I shoved him as hard as I could.

Brian fell backward onto the floor.

I wiped my face and looked at blood on my fingers. "You cut me, you little prick."

Val shook her head and pointed, and I looked down at Brian. His wide eyes stared at the ceiling. He gave a gurgle, coughed up a mouthful of blood, and started shaking. He groaned, and the sound stuck in his throat for a long time before it faded away. Then he was still, his eyes unblinking.

Val and I turned to Feret when he cleared his throat. He held a small pistol in his left hand.

"Did you just shoot your coffee boy?" I asked.

Feret nodded. "*Ad vitam aut culpam.*"

I shot a glance at Val. She sat frozen, staring at Brian's body.

Feret looked at his pistol. "Brian wasn't totally useless. A seventeen caliber bullet coated in palytoxin is rather effective." He tossed a handkerchief to me. "I am sorry about the little mess."

I wiped off my face and fingers. "Aren't you just digging yourself a deeper hole?"

"On the contrary, I'm filling in the holes." Feret smiled. "Here is what I see. You two came to my office with proof that Brian poisoned Mr. Morgan and Ms. Blake. Together we confronted him, but he attacked you and Ms. Nikolskaya. I grabbed his gun and stopped him." He stared at me. "The only question remaining is whether you two survived his attack."

I cursed myself for not anticipating this kind of problem. We were only going to waltz in here and give Feret a false sense of success—not get ourselves shot while doing so.

I frowned. "I don't think Brian was able to kill us."

"Why not?" He aimed the pistol at me.

"Because if he had, I wouldn't be able to stop the evidence from reaching the people investigating the deaths of Archie and Ann." I was having a hard time keeping my voice steady with the pistol trained on me.

Feret wagged the pistol back and forth. "What evidence would they have?"

"Nothing direct, but quite a bit of circumstantial evidence that may make your life messy." I stared at him. "Your video, for one, with your speech that predicts their demise, along with you changing glasses and refusing to drink from Archie's."

"I believe I could beat that video," he said.

"You could if that was the only evidence that the investigators looked at," I said. "But if they read your own story of revenge that you saved on your system, or went through your chat logs with Brian where you plotted my and Val's deaths, they might think they had a shot of getting you convicted."

"Or maybe they'd be interested in the match program," Val said. "Tinless Tiksey has gotten over his scare of your threat to destroy his *gompa*, and would be only too happy to explain how you blackmailed him ten years ago."

Feret shrugged. "Given their despicable activities, it will be child's play to portray the lama as non-credible."

"It's moot, anyway," I said. "Your match program, along with your overseer status, disappears in twenty minutes."

That got his attention. He stared at me with his mouth open, then finally asked, "You would leave Soul Identity with no overseers?"

"No, that would be bad." I smiled. "Arthur Berringer is more than willing to become executive overseer and fill the gap. Yesterday the match committee issued him a special card that works even without the eye you had poked out." I shook my head. "No, Andre, I'm positive that Brian was unable to shoot us. His boss would have lost everything."

Feret pursed his lips and stared at me for a minute. Then he nodded. "You are right, Mr. Waverly. A happy ending for both of us would be much better."

Whew. But I couldn't see any way this could end with both of us being happy.

"What do you have in mind?" I asked.

Feret smiled and put the pistol in his suit pocket. "Why not join me?"

"And be your coffee boy? No, but thanks anyway."

"You both could become my partners."

"Partners?" Val asked.

"Limited minority partners," he said. "I've contributed most of the effort, after all."

"Partners won't work," I said.

"Why not?" Feret's eyes narrowed.

I was afraid he was going to reach into his pocket and pull out the gun, but I plowed ahead anyway. "I learned a couple of Latin phrases this morning, hoping that I'd get to use them. Here's one—*nihil curo de ista tua stulta superstitione.*"

Feret laughed. "I'm not interested in my crazy cult either."

I cocked my head to one side. "What do you mean?"

Feret walked around the desk and sat on its edge. "You said you have read my online papers?"

"Just your Raison d'Etre."

"So you know that I am one hundred percent consumed with destroying Soul Identity." He sneered. "But nobody knows how difficult these last ten years have been, working with these silly people who believe there is meaning in their soul lines. These people disgust me. They are pathetic." He spat these words out.

"I'm missing something," I said. "Haven't you established a Soul Identity alternative?"

"I have. And a very successful alternative it is."

"If these people disgust you, why are you helping them?"

"Helping them?" He smirked at me. "Helping them?" He started laughing. "I'm not helping them, Mr. Waverly. I'm using them. All that money coming out of Soul Identity—where do you think it goes?"

"You tell me," I said.

His eyes were wild now. "The money all goes to me!" he shouted. "All of it. I give them false statements showing how much they've saved up for their future lives, and they are thrilled. Meanwhile I'm getting rich—very rich."

I shook my head. "You're doing all this because your father died?"

Feret jumped up, but then seemed to regain control. He sat back down. "Do not mention my father again," he said in a very soft voice. "He was a saint, and Soul Identity killed both him and my mother."

We had to stay alive and get Feret over to the meeting. I stared at the floor. "I'm sorry," I said. "That was insensitive of me."

Feret nodded. "Do not do it again," he said. He walked behind his desk. "Now I must give my speech to our big meeting of fools. They're waiting for me to tell them how wonderful they are, when in reality I wish they would hurry up and die."

"That's pretty sad," Val said.

"It's practical." He pulled some note cards out of his drawer and put them in his jacket pocket. Then he sat back on the edge of the desk. "Mr. Waverly, I assume you are also practical. You can see the big picture. Bob told me how you advised Mr. Morgan and Ms. Blake to stop fighting during your meeting." He shook his head. "They didn't listen, but now that I've killed them, it doesn't really matter."

"I suppose I am a practical kind of guy," I said. "Where are you going with this?"

"We can find a way to work together." He looked at Val. "Did you tell him how much money your organization manages?"

She shook her head.

"No?" Feret smiled. "Over two trillion dollars. That's twelve zeroes—and it could be ours. What would it take to make you break your word, forget what happened, and lose the evidence you have? A billion dollars? Two billion? A hundred billion?"

"I see your point," I said. "Everybody and everything has a price." I looked at Val, but she glared back at me.

"I'd rather die than cheat our members," she said. "They trust us. How dare you destroy that trust?"

Feret reached into his pocket and pulled out the pistol. "I am very sorry to hear you say that. I was rather hoping that you'd see it my way."

Now why did he have to test my 'everything has a price' theory so quickly? I jumped up and hollered, "Wait!"

Feret looked at me.

"On second thought, some things are priceless," I said. "If you shoot Val, there's no amount of money that will keep me from finding a way to destroy you." I pointed at him. "Put that gun away. Go to your meeting. Let me talk to Val, and we can figure this out when you return."

Feret shifted the pistol to me. "Nice try. What will prevent you from walking out of here?"

My mind raced through various scenarios, but it came up blank. I wasn't planning on hanging out for him to return. So I sighed. "I don't know," I said.

He gave me a thin smile. "Good answer," he said. "I still admire your forthrightness." He jerked the pistol toward Val. "Take off Brian's clothes."

Val crossed her arms. "I'm not touching him."

Feret's voice went soft and quiet. "Do it. Now."

Val started to undress Brian.

"You too," he said to me.

"Me too what?" I asked.

"Put your clothes with Brian's. Then help her."

I nodded, and started undressing. "Everything?"

"Everything." Feret walked to the closet and looked inside.

After a minute we stood naked next to Brian's body. Val covered herself as best as she could with her hands.

Feret bundled up our clothes and grunted as he heaved them out the window. We heard them splash into the canal below.

"Get in the closet," he said. "Bring the body with you."

We dragged Brian into the closet.

Feret stood at the door, pointing the pistol at us. "This should hold you until I return from the meeting."

"Then why'd you take our clothes?" I asked.

He smiled. "If you do manage to escape, I don't want you interrupting me."

It was hard to argue with that logic.

Feret started to close the door, but then he paused. "Now that I'm thinking about it, you two can help fill in for Brian right after my meeting." He sighed. "He and I had planned a cleansing event during my speech, but now he's not around to help me clean up the bodies."

"Cleansing event?" I asked.

He stared at me for a full minute. "You saw the first one yesterday, Mr. Waverly, with our previous executive overseer and depositary chief."

Val gasped. "You're going to kill your members?" she cried.

"A few of them, Ms. Nikolskaya," he said. "Just enough to leave some fear in the survivors."

"You can't do that!" she cried.

"Of course I can," he said. Then he laughed. "And what fun—now that Brian is gone, the deaths will be truly random. Even I don't know which bottle of champagne he poisoned."

One last sinister smile, and Feret pushed the door shut. The closet went dark. I felt for a knob, but the interior of the door was smooth metal.

We heard the lock turn and the door handle click as Feret tested it. Something heavy slid across the floor outside. "I'm barricading the door with my desk," he said. "Don't bother trying to get out."

As soon as we heard the office door slam shut, Val grabbed my arm. "Scott, your parents will be in the audience," she said.

I was thinking the same thing. "We have to get out of here and warn them," I said.

I threw myself against the door, but it didn't budge. We felt around the walls and floor, trying to avoid Brian's body, which was now leaking fluids. But we found nothing to use to pry the door open.

After a few minutes more of searching we slumped against the door. "Now what?" Val asked.

"George and Sue should have heard everything until our clothes and the transmitter went out the window," I said.

"They better get here fast."

We stood silently for a couple of minutes and held hands. Then Val gave a nervous laugh.

"What's wrong?" I asked.

"I was thinking about how we'll look when they come to rescue us."

"They've already seen me naked," I said. I pulled her close again and stroked her back and thought about how it took Feret almost shooting her for me to realize that she was priceless.

We held each other and waited for our rescue.

After what seemed like hours but was maybe only fifteen minutes, we heard the desk scraping along the floor and somebody calling, "Scott, Val? Yoo-hoo!"

I banged on the door. "George, we're in here."

"It's locked and there's no key," we heard him say.

"It's just a door knob. Break it off," Sue said.

"Great idea, my love. With what?"

Silence for a minute. Then Sue said, "Don't use that, George. It will—
" We heard a crash. "Shatter. Here, try this instead."

Another thump, and then another. The door shook.

"Now wiggle that piece right there," Sue said.

"Got it," George said. The door swung open and we stood squinting in the light.

"Pee yew!" George held his nose. "What is that smell?"

"You don't want to know," I said.

"Careful where you walk. Here, we brought you some clothes," Sue said. "No underwear, socks, or shoes, but enough to get you guys mobile." She held out a bag.

As we dressed, I said to George, "Obviously the bugs and transmitter worked. Did you record it all?"

He grinned. "Every word, from the Bridge of Boobs to the big splash."

Oops.

George looked in the closet and whistled. "He really did kill Brian, didn't he?"

"What a monster," Sue said. "We'll have to clean this up later."

"Let's get to your staging area," I said. "Before Feret poisons somebody—like my parents."

thirty-four

AFTER I WARNED MY parents about the champagne, the rest of us listened to Feret's speech from the staging area.

I turned to Archie and Ann. "Are you two ready to be resurrected?" They nodded.

Sue stood up. "I'll take you to the stage entrance. Mr. Berringer, come along."

The four of them left the room.

I watched Val and George working on the video controls. "You ready to interrupt the broadcast?" I asked them.

Val nodded.

I turned back to listen to the speech.

Feret had strayed a bit. "And the proof lies in the death of the traitorous Soul Identity leaders," he was saying. "These leaders refused to divulge the eternal truths, and so they were cleansed from the organization."

Feret paused and leaned close to the microphone. "As of yesterday afternoon, I am the undisputed executive overseer of Soul Identity."

We had to do this now, before Feret started his deadly toast. I keyed my microphone. "Dad, you're on."

I turned to watch the monitor showing the video display of the audience. Dad stood up from his seat in the hallway. "Excuse me!" he shouted.

Feret stopped talking. "Yes?" he asked.

"I'm sorry for interrupting," Dad called. "But how do we know that Mr. Morgan and Ms. Blake are dead?"

"I just told you," Feret said, in the same soft voice he used when he pointed his pistol at Val and me.

"I've been checking the news, but I can't find anything," Dad said.

The audience started whispering to each other. Feret raised his hand, and they quieted down.

"Who are you, sir?" he asked.

Dad smiled. "My name is Mr. Waverly."

Feret seemed rattled, but only for a second. "It's nice to meet you, Mr. Waverly," he said. "We should chat later, for I may have something that belongs to you." He scanned the audience. "Mr. Waverly wants to see proof that the head has been cut off the Soul Identity leadership. I am sorry that he does not trust me, but I understand the need for everybody to be absolutely sure.

"We have a video, taken yesterday at Soul Identity headquarters," he said. He signaled to the sound desk, and a projection screen came down at the back of the stage.

I smiled at Val. "The movie sets up the grand entrance."

She nodded.

Feret looked at the screen as the video came on. It started with Feret's toast. We listened to him say *let us drink to the cleansing of our past mistakes*, and then we saw Archie and Ann collapse. The video played until the ambulance drove away.

"That's amazing," George said to me. "It looks like they really died."

"It was enough to fool Feret." I keyed the microphone. "Dad, say thanks."

Dad was still standing as the lights came back on. "Thank you, Mr. Feret," he called. "They look pretty dead to me."

"We will talk later, Mr. Waverly." Feret spread his arms wide. "I predicted their deaths three weeks ago," he roared. "A power greater than us, the power of the eternal truths, has silenced them once and for all." He bowed his head and spoke softly. "I am but a humble messenger sent by the source of those truths."

The projector screen went up as Feret spoke. The audience gasped and started to stand up.

"They're alive!" Dad shouted.

Feret turned around and looked at the back of the stage. Archie and Ann stood shaking their heads at him. They walked to the center of and faced Feret.

Archie turned on his microphone. "As Mark Twain once telegraphed to London, 'the reports of my death are greatly exaggerated'."

Ann switched on her own mike. "Mark Twain also said this, Mr. Feret. 'Prophecy is a good line of business, but it is full of risks.'" She pointed at Feret. "You, sir, are a fraud."

Feret stood frozen.

I motioned to Val. "Roll the video."

She overrode the controls and brought the screen back down. Ann said, "Y'all need to watch that movie from another angle."

The audience watched my recording. Val stepped frame by frame through Brian dropping the pills into the champagne glasses while Archie explained. He showed Brian directing Feret to an un-poisoned glass, and Feret refusing to take Archie's glass for the toast.

The video stopped. The audience sat still.

"Mom!" Elizabeth came running down the aisle. Ann moved to the side of the podium, and they embraced.

Feret screamed at the audience. "Do not believe what you are seeing! They are fakes!"

Archie smiled. He walked over to the podium and held up a set of Soul Identity verification goggles from the depositary.

"Zoom in on its display so everybody can watch," I told George.

"Got it." He maneuvered the joystick. Val hit a button and the image appeared on the projection screen.

Archie put on the goggles. The display flashed, and thirty seconds later it showed "Archibald Morgan, executive overseer."

Archie held the goggles up to Feret. "Care to try them on, Mr. Feret?"

Feret brushed the goggles aside and crowded Archie away from the podium. He turned to the audience. "These people have lied to you. They have tricked you. They have withheld the truths from you. WorldWideSouls members, you must trust me." He held up his hands. "Trust me because I am the only one who cares about you."

I signaled Val, and she flipped a switch.

"Hello, Andre, can you hear me?" I said into the microphone. There was some feedback, and George adjusted the volume.

"Who is it?" Feret asked.

"It's Scott Waverly. Remember me?"

Feret nodded. "I do. You are also a fake, and a liar." He looked at the audience. "Ignore this voice!" he shouted.

I walked over to Val and turned up the volume. "LISTEN FOR JUST ONE MINUTE," I said, and my voice reverberated through the hall.

Feret stopped.

I turned down the volume and continued. "I want the audience to hear a conversation you and I had thirty minutes ago." I nodded at Val.

Feret's recorded voice came through the speakers. I turned up the volume, and it flooded the room.

We watched the audience respond to Feret's comments. Many shook their heads when they heard him say *these people disgust me. They are pathetic.* When he mentioned that *the money all goes to me. All of it,* they started murmuring. Their restlessness grew when he said *I just wish they would hurry up and die.*

Val stopped the tape after he offered to make us partners. By this point, the crowd was buzzing like an angry wasp nest. Many people were standing on their chairs.

Feret banged his hands on the podium and leaned forward to speak. But as he opened his mouth, my Dad hollered out, "You're a cheat!"

Several others in the audience joined in with loud boos. Whatever he tried to say was lost in the noise.

Feret glared at Archie, then he darted out the side entrance on the stage.

Some people in the audience chased after him, but Archie moved to the podium and held up his hands. "Let the poor man go," he said. "He has been through enough already."

The audience took a few minutes to quiet down. In the meantime, Berry walked onto the stage. He and Ann stepped forward and stood next to Archie.

Archie cleared his throat. "Good afternoon, ladies and gentlemen of WorldWideSouls, and members of Soul Identity. Many of you must be both surprised and unhappy to discover Ms. Blake and me alive and well."

He looked around the room. "And many of you right now must be awfully confused," he said.

Quite a few heads nodded at that.

Archie gave a sad smile. "I am truly sorry. Just the fact that you are here means that we, your Soul Identity leaders, failed you."

He put his elbows on the podium. "It would be easy for me to stand here and blame everything on Mr. Feret," he said. "I could tell you how he tricked and misled and used you for his own selfish purposes."

Another pause. We watched many in the audience nod their heads.

"But that is only half of the story," Archie said. "Here is what I believe—if we had run Soul Identity properly, Andre Feret would never have been able to pull you away. If we had met your needs, you would have thought he was crazy. You would have told him to get lost."

He watched the crowd for a minute. "This is what pains me the most," he said quietly as the room went silent. "If we had met the needs of his family twelve years ago, Andre Feret would neither have thought about nor resorted to revenge."

He sighed. "I have spent too much of my life trying to make sure we ran our organization as a business. But as a good friend pointed out, it is time to return the soul to Soul Identity. We need to bring it back. We must bring it back." His voice rose in volume. "We will bring it back."

Dad started applauding, and many others joined in.

Archie waited for the applause to die down. "I want you to meet somebody very important to Soul Identity," he said. "Ladies and gentlemen, this is Arthur Berringer, a true, honest to goodness overseer."

I looked at Val. "Our job here is finished. You think we should head down there and bask in the glow of success?"

Val pointed to her clothes. "Dressed like this?"

I grinned. "I like your no-bra look, and I'm fine with going commando."

As we entered the connecting hallway, Val grabbed my arm and pointed ahead. "Somebody's in trouble," she said.

We ran barefooted as fast as we could, but slid to a stop when we saw who it was: Bob sat on Feret's chest and punched him again and again with both his fists.

Blood and mucus covered Feret's face. Each punch from Bob snapped his head one way and then the other.

I tackled Bob, and we tumbled to the floor.

"I was supposed to help him escape if anything went wrong, but I couldn't do it." Tears streamed down Bob's face. He wrenched free from my grip and kicked Feret in the ribs.

Val grabbed his shoulder. "That's enough!" she yelled.

Feret let out a groan and lifted his head, only to let it fall with a thud.

"He's still alive, Ms. Val. I need to stop him!"

I stood up. "You have stopped him, Bob. He's going nowhere."

Bob's eyes grew wide. "Then I need to finish him off, Mr. Scott."

I thought how Feret had ordered Brian to kill Val and me—twice. And how my parents could have been killed during his "cleansing."

But then I shook my head. "I want to kill him too—but it's wrong," I said.

Bob's eyes darted between me and Val. Then he took a deep breath and turned his back on Feret.

I put my hand on Bob's shoulder as the three of us walked toward the stage. "Even if you had killed him," I said, "another Feret would pop up in a few years."

He looked at me. "You think so?"

"They always do," I said. We reached the side door, and I stopped and faced him. "The only way to stop a Feret is to show people they don't need a Feret. Give them exposure to something better."

He stared at me.

I smiled. "Let's get in there and watch Archie and Berry do just that."

Val opened the door, and Bob went inside. Val put her hand on my chest and smiled. "Exposure to something better? Didn't I just hear that an hour ago?"

"The lesson's straight from the Bridge of Boobs." I gazed past her shoulder. "Uh oh."

Madame Flora stood over Feret. Her back was to us.

"What is she doing?" I asked.

Val shrugged, and then gasped. The old lady pulled a revolver out of her purse, bent down, and wrapped Feret's right hand around it.

Val and I ran back down the hallway.

Madame Flora glanced at us when we reached her. "You stopped Bob," she said, "and now I have to finish the job myself." She cocked the hammer and moved Feret's finger to the trigger.

Val dug her fingernails into my arm.

"Wait!" I said.

Madame Flora spoke through gritted teeth. "Go. Away. Now."

I shook my head. "He's got a pistol in his jacket, and he has already used it to kill Brian. No sense wasting your own revolver."

Madame Flora smiled. "Good boy." She switched her revolver for Feret's pistol. "Now run along," she said.

"Don't shoot!" Val said.

Madame Flora sighed. "Now what?"

I wondered if Val was going to make her stop.

"Andre is left handed," she said.

"Thanks," Madame Flora said. "Now scram."

I grabbed Val's hand, and we walked back toward George's staging area. We flinched when we heard the pistol pop, but neither of us turned around.

Val pointed. "We're going the wrong way."

I squeezed her hand. "We're not," I said. "Let's go home."

epilogue

THE WORLDWIDESOULS MEMBERS WARMED to Berry by the end of his speech. Most of them returned to Soul Identity within a month.

Berry and Madame Flora moved to Sterling to work with Archie and Ann on reviving the organization's soul. Deposits were up, memberships were up, and every church had come back. Soul Identity had dodged the insolvency bullet.

They also recovered most of the money Feret had taken. Ann was able to trace down its sources from the records Berry found in his soul line collection. Apparently Feret had trusted Soul Identity security after all.

James the elevator man finally retired. He had misunderstood his duties as a centuriat, and thought he was stuck at work. When he discovered Archie revoked the rule, he packed his bags and took a train to Florida.

The twins ran Madame Flora's palm reading joint on the weekends and after school. One Sunday I got them to don their wigs and ambulance costumes and sneak a rifle past Jane Watson at the airport.

Val sat next to me on the dock, on one of those Indian summer afternoons when the Maryland air felt clear and crisp, and the bay water remained warm and inviting. She wore a blue bikini, the same shade as her eyes.

"You look ravishing," I said.

She smiled, and that got me just as weak and dizzy as it did the first day we met.

She put down her fishing rod. "Want to take a swim?" she asked.

We held hands as we jumped, and then we swam under the dock. Val wrapped her arms and legs around me and gave me a kiss. "I like it here," she said.

I untied her top and it floated up in the water. "Even when I do this?"

"Especially when you do that."

We heard footsteps on the dock above us.

"Figures," I said. I swam out while Val retied her top, and I saw Bob above us.

We climbed out of the water and grabbed our towels. Bob stood in his green uniform and silver sunglasses and smiled at us.

"It's been a while," I said to him.

"It has indeed, Mr. Scott. How are you, Ms. Val?"

Val smiled. "Fine, Bob. How's Elizabeth?"

"She's just great." Bob handed me a package. "This is addressed to both of you."

"You need a signature?" I asked.

"We trust you."

As I tore open the package, I asked him, "so you're back at Soul Identity, making deliveries like old times?"

Bob nodded. "Yes, Mr. Scott. I'm back in the business."

I read the letter and handed it to Val. Then I grinned and said, "And so are we."

Soul Intent

by

Dennis Batchelder

is coming soon!

Turn the page for a preview of *Soul Intent.* ...

prologue

ARCHIBALD MORGAN WITHDREW HIS hand from the prisoner's clammy grasp and wiped it on the sleeve of his brown robe. "The deposit is complete," he said.

The prisoner, a large man in a larger baggy uniform, licked his lips and spoke in a whisper. "Everything left was accepted? My gold and my papers?"

"All of it." Morgan dipped his hand into his pocket and pulled out a flimsy sheet of paper. "Your depositary receipt."

The prisoner took the paper and used his finger to caress the listed items. "Sleep well, my little darlings." He handed the receipt back to Morgan. "Please destroy it. If the guards discovered it after they…" His voice trailed off.

"We would not want that to happen." Morgan secreted the paper inside his robe. "Good luck, sir."

"I believe my luck has, how do you Americans put it? Run out." The man frowned. "Keep everything safe." His voice rose in volume. "For soon I shall return and gaze upon my own marble monument in Berlin."

The white-helmeted guard banged his stick on the door. The sound bounced off the stark walls. "Enough already with that monument crap. Keep your noise down, Nazi."

The prisoner bowed his head to the guard, then glanced at Morgan. "Since the verdict two weeks ago, they have become unbearably rude," he whispered.

As the guard let Morgan out of the cell, the prisoner called out, "I won't forget this, Archibald Morgan. Upon my return, I shall find and reward you for your good work."

The Soul Identity overseer shuddered at the thought. He shuffled as fast as he dared out of Nuremberg Prison's Cellblock C and almost tripped on his robe. He climbed the two flights of stairs, nodded at the soldier behind the desk, and escaped into the brisk October evening.

As far as Morgan was concerned, Reichsmarschall Hermann Goering's promises had fallen upon deaf ears. The Nazi general should rot in hell and never return.

He paused after he crossed the *platz* and stepped onto the sidewalk. Spotlights mounted on the Palais du Justice walls cast an array of sinister shadows in front of him. He had done his despicable duty. He alone had understood that the journey to a better world required distasteful compromises. Maybe someday Flora would also understand…

He shook his head. Enough. The journalists he had met in the Grand Hotel's bar were giving four-to-one odds that the eleven condemned Nazis would hang before sunrise. He had finished the deposit just in time. His work was finally over—he could flee this war-torn country and return to his own battles in Sterling.

one

"THEY EXPLOIT PEOPLE WHO believe in reincarnation," Lester the reporter said. He glanced up at me, pen poised over his pad. "Did I get that right?"

"I didn't say that, Lester." If I squinted just right, the white streaks of scalp poking through his greasy comb-over hairdo looked like a bunch of tiny bananas. "You're putting words in my mouth," I said.

Val sat next to me with her arms crossed, and her smile looked decidedly more forced than it did ten minutes ago, when this interview started.

The reporter gave me an oily smile. "I'm sorry, Mr. Waverly. Maybe you could repeat what you said."

"Soul Identity assists people who like the concepts behind reincarnation," I said. This was my fourth rendition.

He wrote that down again. "Got it. Exploits people who like the concepts behind reincarnation."

"I said assists. Not exploits." I pointed at him. "You put all kinds of words in my mouth last year, and it's not going to happen again. Either get it right, or get out."

He flashed that used-car salesman's smile again. "Assists. That's what I said."

Val uncrossed her arms and rubbed her palms on her tanned legs, just below her white shorts. "Let's just show him how it works, Scott."

"You think that's wise?" I asked.

She shrugged. "We've got only twenty minutes until your picnic, and Lester seems tireless in his search for dirt." She smiled at him. "No offense."

He smiled back, showing off a gap between his front teeth. "None taken, Ms. Nikolskaya."

"Do you have a reader?" I asked her.

"I always have a reader." She dug into her purse and pulled out a yellow device about half the size of a matchbox car. It had a tiny lens on one end and a big button on its side.

"What's that?" Lester asked.

"A camera," I said. "Let Val take your picture, and we'll use it to explain how everything works."

Lester licked his palm and used it to smooth his hair. He sat up straight, sucked in his gut, and attempted to pull tight the gap where his belly hair poked through. Then he smiled at Val. "Ready when you are."

She looked at him steadily. "I'm taking a picture of your eyes, Lester. It's not a portrait." She brought the reader to six inches in front of his right eye and clicked the button.

"My eyes?"

"Keep still." Val held the reader in front of his left eye and clicked again. "Okay, I'm done." She tossed me the reader. "Work your magic."

I beckoned to Lester. "Come with me to uncover your soul." I followed that with the opening notes of Beethoven's Fifth. *Da-da-da-dum.*

The three of us walked out of my living room and into the office.

Lester headed for the windows. "You waste this scenery on your workplace?" He gestured at the panoramic view of the Chesapeake Bay. "Why not make this your living room?"

"Because this way we get to enjoy the view all day long." I flipped open the top of the reader, exposed its USB port, and plugged it into my laptop. "Now watch carefully."

I clicked on my latest Soul Identity icon. Images of two brown eyes appeared on opposite sides of the screen.

Lester stood next to me. "Those are my eyes?" he asked.

I nodded. "Watch."

The eye images cut away all but the two brown irises and pupils, then sprouted grid lines on their outside edges. The right iris rotated clockwise until it aligned with the left.

"You've improved your program," Val said. She stood behind my chair, her arms on my shoulders.

I leaned my head back and looked up at her upside-down face. Her red hair caught the sunlight. "One hundred percent automated," I said.

She smiled, which upside-down looked like a frown.

"Is this some kind of way to steal my identity?" Lester asked.

I straightened up. "So far it's just your eyes. It's not yet your soul identity."

The two irises moved toward each other, but instead of colliding, the left overlapped the right. The screen filled with an enlarged view of the resulting single image.

"Now it'll calculate the differences between your two irises," I said.

A few dozen arcs, whorls, lines, and starbursts glowed on the screen, and the overlapped irises faded to a very light brown. The computer beeped.

I pointed at the screen. "And there you have it. That's your soul identity."

"Is it like a fingerprint?" Lester asked.

"If you mean, is it unique, then yes, it's the only one just like it in the whole wide world."

"At least for now," Val said. "But after you die, that identity will come back in somebody else's eyes."

He turned to her. "What does that mean?"

She smiled. "Soul identities repeat. Before you were born, another person carried your identity in their eyes. And after you die, somebody else will get it."

He narrowed his eyes. "Can you prove this?"

She sighed. "It's a matter of faith, not proof."

He smiled and pulled out his pad. "So Soul Identity is tricking people into thinking they're reincarnated."

"Hold on a second," Val said. "It's faith, but there's some science behind it. We've read over fifty million sets of eyes, and we've never found two living people sharing the same soul identity."

He shrugged. "So?"

I spun in my chair to face him. "Lester, you're missing the point. These guys have been tracking soul identities for almost twenty-six hundred years. They have examples of identities repeating eight, ten, and even twelve times over the centuries. If you like reincarnation, you'll love Soul Identity."

"I still don't get it. What's there to love?" he asked.

"What they offer you," I said. "Are you married?"

He shook his head.

"Any kids?"

"Nope."

"So what happens to your wealth when you die?"

He shrugged. "I don't care. I'll be dead."

"But if you knew you were coming back in the future, wouldn't you want to give yourself a head start in your next life?" I asked. "Soul Identity can hold onto your money and memories until you reclaim them."

He scratched his head. "You're saying I could give my future life an unfair advantage? I could've used a leg up this time around."

"Check with the folks at Soul Identity," I said. "Maybe your previous soul carrier left you something."

"I can do that?"

He looked like somebody just told him he might have won the lottery. But I didn't want to raise his hopes, or his greed level, too high; if he found nothing in his soul line collection, he'd pen a nasty piece about us.

So I smiled and said, "Of course you can. The chances of having a recorded past are slim, but you can at least plan for a bright future."

Lester scratched his chin, and after a minute he nodded his head. "I'll do that."

Val handed him a card as she let him out the front door. "Give Madame Flora a call," she said. "She'll get you started."

As I straightened up the office for the party, I thought about how easy it was to seduce Lester with Soul Identity's promise.

Like everybody in the world, Lester's identity in his eyes will remain unique as long as he is alive, and then after he dies, somebody else will be born with it. That new person and Lester will share a *soul line*, and they each will take their turn being the *carrier* of the line. Soul Identity's first job is to keep these identities and soul lines connected—they maintain the bridges between Lester's past and future carriers.

Their second job is to be the world's largest bank. Once they calculate Lester's identity, they check to see if any previous carriers have left him any money, memories, and lessons in his *soul line collection*, stored in Soul Identity's *depositary*. Soul Identity invests the money on his soul line's behalf. They've been doing this for almost twenty-six hundred years. They have several million soul lines, and they're managing over two trillion dollars' worth of investments.

Over the past year, I've noticed quite a range in the way Soul Identity members think about their soul lines. Some become deeply religious: they attribute a grand plan to God, and they bask in the glory of how special they are. Others treat it as their proof of immortality. Neither of these approaches sits well with me. I prefer the way Val sees it—she hopes to pass on her memories and lessons to others who'd feel they were significant. This makes her relevant far into the future.

I sighed. I didn't think Lester was searching for relevancy. He probably was just gold digging.

two

MY PARENTS ARRIVED FIVE minutes after Lester bolted in search of his destiny. They wore shorts, our company polo shirts, and sandals. Dad carried a stack of red folders, and Mom wheeled a large cooler up to the front door.

She poked her head inside. "Yoo-hoo! You guys decent?"

"Of course we are," I said. I pulled the door open. "Come on in."

"Are the girls here?" she asked.

"Not yet," Val said. She reached for the handle on the cooler. "Let me take this to the kitchen."

Dad followed Mom inside. He dropped the red folders on his desk. He went to the refrigerator and helped himself to a beer. Then the two of us headed out back.

"You got any bait?" he asked.

"It's all ready," I said. We walked out to the end of the dock, and I chopped a couple bloodworms in half. We baited, cast out, set the rods into their holders, and parked ourselves on the bench.

"Bluefish are running, I read online this morning," he said.

I grunted.

He drained his beer, then turned to me. "Something bugging you?"

I nodded. "Lester the reporter just left. He was back digging up dirt on Soul Identity."

"What'd he want, an anniversary story?"

"I can't believe it's been a year already."

Dad smiled. "His exposé was yellow journalism at its worst."

Last summer our tiny security company contracted with Soul Identity, and we helped them unravel an insider attack. It took us a little more than a week to help save the organization. It took me a little less than a week to fall for Valentina Nikolskaya, the gorgeous redhead in charge of Soul Identity's software development efforts.

At the time I had thought Soul Identity was some kind of wacky, New Age cult. But they're not. They don't force any religious accoutrements on top of their identification and depositary. They let people focus on spiritual questions without having to cater to any one group's thoughts on what the Almighty or the Everlasting is all about. Instead of acting like another religion, they foster personal spiritual thinking.

At least now they do. Some time in the last decade they stopped paying attention to personal growth, and they left themselves open to a nasty insider attack. It came from someone they thought was a leader: Andre Feret. He started his own religion called WorldWideSouls, and he conned many Soul Identity members into transferring their deposits to his new church. Val and I helped to catch and expose him as a fraud. Now Feret rots at the bottom of a Venetian canal, WorldWideSouls languishes at a fraction of its former size, and Soul Identity flourishes as a place where spiritual thinking is encouraged.

Lester the reporter got involved because my parents, Val, and I were shot at by some of Feret's WorldWideSouls people. We escaped on my boat, but while we were out of town in India, Iceland, and Italy, Lester ran wild with speculations on a mob invasion of Kent Island. His exaggerated tales of mayhem brought in more work for our security consulting firm, but it also made my number one client nervous about our notoriety.

"If he writes more dirt, Archie's gonna be pissed," I said. Archibald Mogan was Soul Identity's octogenarian executive overseer.

My cell phone rang, and I glanced at the caller ID. "Speak of the devil," I said as I thumbed the answer button. "Archie, we were just talking about you."

"Scott, I require your immediate services," Archie said. "Can you come to Sterling right away?"

I threw the call on speakerphone so Dad could hear. "We're in the middle of our company picnic, and then Val and I were going to celebrate our first year together with a trip to Aruba. What's the emergency?"

"Our depositary has been robbed!" Archie's voice shrieked out of the phone.

Soul Identity's huge investment pool made its depositary quite a target. It explained why they preferred anonymity over notoriety.

"The whole depositary?" I asked, glancing over at Dad.

Heavy breathing over the phone.

"Archie?" I asked.

"I may have overstated the problem," he said.

I looked at Dad, and he shrugged. We waited until Archie continued.

"During the Nuremberg trials in 1946, I helped a Nazi general establish his soul line collection. Today I happened to look inside that account, and the items I helped him deposit are missing."

"Does the account have a current carrier?" I asked.

"It does not."

"Has anybody opened the collection since 1946?"

"The depositary has no records of any activity."

I scratched my head. "So you're telling me that a soul line collection was broken into sometime in the last sixty-four years, and you want me to solve it?"

"That is correct. Find out who broke in and how they did it, and then make sure they cannot do it again," he said.

I glanced at Dad as I spoke into the phone. "You do realize how cold the trail could be?"

A big sigh over the speaker. "Of course I do. But you must realize how important this is. Please come to Sterling, Scott. I need your help."

I figured Val and I could always leave for Aruba from Boston. "We'll fly up in the morning." I disconnected and turned to Dad. "Soul Identity took Nazi money?"

"You'd better not tell Lester," he said.

Val came down the dock. "Have you seen the girls?" she asked.

I cupped my hands around my eyes to reduce the glare bouncing off the water, and I tracked the closest boat heading south from the Bay Bridge. "That looks like them coming now."

"You let them use your boat?" Dad asked.

"They needed to get their diving credentials re-certified," I said. "They've been taking it out all week."

"Let's hope they sail better than they cook," he said. He got up and lowered the boatlift into the water.

While Dad readied the lift, I told Val about Archie's call. "He's acting kind of strange," I said. "I told him we'd fly up tomorrow. We can leave for Aruba from there."

She nodded. "I'd love to meet with my team before our launch."

I smiled. "Then I'll book us a room at the guest house."

Rose and Marie waved to us and brought the boat close to the dock. Rose sat in the cockpit, and Marie stood at the bow, a coil of rope in her hands. The twins wore huge sunglasses and tiny bikinis. They each sported an official company baseball hat, and they had their long dark hair pulled back into ponytails through the hats' fasteners.

"That's quite the summer uniform," Dad said. "I'm thinking we should distribute a company calendar featuring the twins. It would be great advertising for the business."

Rose and Marie worked part-time with us, mostly on weekend assignments, as this was the only time that fit around their freshman-year university schedule. Their exotic Gypsy beauty, happy laughter, and earnest acting made them perfect for their assignments.

Rose steered the boat into the slip, and Dad raised the boatlift.

Marie jumped onto the dock. "Sorry we're late, Scott," she said. "We had to drive Grandma to the airport this morning."

"She's taking a vacation?" I asked.

She shook her head. "Mr. Morgan asked her to come up to Sterling. Some problem with an old account from the forties that they both worked on."

Madame Flora, the twins' grandmother, operated a palm reading joint here on Kent Island. She recruited Soul Identity members, and earned a commission when they matched existing soul lines. My parents and I met her and the twins last year as we started our Soul Identity work.

Madame Flora's involvement in Archie's current predicament didn't surprise me. The old Gypsy lady's entanglements with the organization appeared to run deep.

"Your grandmother's been working with Archie for a long time," I said.

Rose hopped onto the deck. "She told us she first met Mr. Morgan in Germany, right after World War II," she said.

"It's amazing how everybody's so connected," Val said to me.

"What did you girls make for the picnic?" Dad asked.

"Pasta salad," Rose said. "Only Marie forgot to peel the onions before she chopped them up."

"I was pulling out the little bits of onion paper all morning, bawling my eyes out," Marie said.

"And I soaked the pasta all night long, but it never did get soft," Rose said. "Good thing salad's supposed to be crunchy."

I looked down at the dock, biting my lip and trying not to laugh. Then Rose poked Marie, and the two burst out in giggles.

"What's the joke?" I asked.

"We know you guys never trust our cooking," Marie said. "We didn't really make a pasta salad. We ordered pizza."

And our fourth annual company picnic was a success. Rose and Marie whipped us all at badminton, Dad and I held court at the barbeque, and Mom and Val cooked up a storm. We sat out under a large maple and told stories about the adventures we had over the past year. When we were all full, Dad got us arranged into a semicircle and handed us each a red folder.

"Why so formal?" I asked.

"It's our annual report," Mom said. "Your father worked on it most of the night."

I flipped open the folder to the first page. "You're gonna walk us through it?"

"Of course," Dad said. "Look at the graph. Our business grew by seventeen hundred percent this year."

"In just one year?" I asked. "What was the difference?"

"Your Soul Identity work made up half the increase," Mom said. "But my testing business has more than tripled in size."

This year Mom and the twins established a girls-only penetration testing service. The three went out on the weekends to various banks and government facilities. They used low-tech hacking to break in, then they held seminars on making security improvements. Every now and then they'd invite Val, Dad, and me to join them on their escapades. Mom had made friends with a bunch of commercial insurance underwriters, and those guys fiercely promoted her services.

I flipped the page. "How about our costs, Dad?"

"That's even better news," he said. "Our profits are way up. Even after tripling our bonuses, paying taxes, and buying new equipment, our five person company has a little over a million dollars in cash reserves."

Smiles all around.

Val raised her hand. "Have you thought about donating to charity? It's a great way to give something back to the community."

I shrugged. "Honestly, no." I wasn't that thrilled with the idea, either. I looked around the circle. "What do you guys think?"

"It sounds like a good idea," Mom said, and everybody nodded.

"If we do this, it has to be a charity that actually uses the money wisely," I said. "Not some group that eats it up in administrative costs."

"You could give us each fifty grand, and we could each choose where to donate it," Dad said.

Everybody nodded again.

"I know Grandma gives money to help the Roma in Croatia," Marie said. "That's where she grew up."

"Those Gypsies don't waste a dime," Rose said. "We spent the summer after our junior year over there, helping them build a community center."

"Rose and I will donate our portions to Grandma's fund," Marie said.

Rose nodded.

"I can support that," Mom said. She nudged Dad with her elbow. "So can you."

"It appears I can too," Dad said.

I looked at Val, and she nodded. "Let's make it unanimous," I said. I turned to the girls. "Find out from your Grandma where we should send the check."

"And see if you can get them to write us a press release," Dad said. "A quarter of a million should buy us some good will."

About the Author

Dennis Batchelder is a computer security architect. He lives with his family in Bellevue, Washington, and spends his off-hours working on the next Soul Identity novel.

Visit Dennis on the Web at **dennisbatchelder.com.**

OKANAGAN REGIONAL LIBRARY

3 3132 03415 2399